ELIZABETH R
AN
UNCOMMON
WOMAN

ISBN 9798644277445

ELIZABETH RAFFALD.

1733 – 1781
Innovator, Entrepreneur, Philanthropist and Author
Known for
The Experienced English Housekeeper – 1st published 1769
Reprinted in a further 12 editions
Also
The Manchester & Salford Directory 1772, 1773 & 1781

Elizabeth Raffald

An Uncommon Woman - the story of a remarkable life, the life and times of an 18th century entrepreneur

Elizabeth Raffald lived in Manchester in the second half of the 18th century. I was born 200 years later and for most of my life I had been unaware that such an inspirational woman had lived all those years ago in my city. Her skills and achievements have been almost totally forgotten by most people in the area.

From humble beginnings she began work at the age of 15, entering domestic service in Yorkshire, and later becoming housekeeper at Arley Hall in Cheshire. At the age of 30 she married the head gardener and went into business, running numerous enterprises before she died at the age of 48. **All** of her many achievements date from that short 18 year period.

The full list of her achievements reads like this:-

She compiled and produced Manchester's FIRST ever **Trade Directory** in 1772, and reissued it in improved form in 1773 and 1781

She wrote a definitive cook book of over 800 original recipes in 1769, called **The Experienced English Housekeeper** (a century before Mrs. Beeton). The first edition sold 800 copies by advance subscription at 5 shillings each (equal to £25 today) or 6s after publication

The second edition ran to 400 copies with nearly 100 extra recipes added. The book was reprinted 13 times with a further 23 pirate editions, including one for America

She sold the copyright to her book for £1400 cash (£150,000 today)

Her book has the first printed recipes for 'Bride Cake', rich fruit cake with double icing, Picallilli and crumpets.
She innovated the idea of double icing a celebration cake, with almond icing under royal icing.

It is most likely that her recipe for sweet patties was the basis for the modern Eccles cake.

She had a recipe for stock cubes, called Portable Soup.

She invented an intricate flummery (a type of blancmange) dish called Solomon's Temple

In 1763 she began with a catering business in Fennel Street

From there she set up a Register Office, an early recruitment agency for servants

In 1766 she moved to a shop in Manchester's market place where she also ran a cookery school for daughters of ladies

She supervised many public and private dinner parties, and was renowned for her delicate and artistic table decorations and desserts. She provided catering for the Bull's Head, the chief inn on the Market place in Manchester

She co-wrote a book on midwifery with Charles White, the surgeon responsible for St Mary's hospital and MR.I

She financed Harrop's Mercury, only the 2nd ever newspaper in Manchester and co-founded Prescott's Journal, Salford's first newspaper.

She went on to run The King's Head, a coaching inn on Chapel St, Salford where she and her husband arranged regular Society entertainments and hired out carriages, including mourning coaches

She catered for the officer's mess in Manchester, based in the inn and the race course at nearby Kersal Moor

She spoke French and attracted many foreign travellers to stay at the inn

She gave daily donations of food and clothes to the poor

She gave birth to 9 children, only 3 of who lived to grow up

I have produced other books about Elizabeth Raffald, all available on Amazon as eBooks and paperbacks-

- The Experienced English Housekeeper of Manchester – a short illustrated biography
- The Experienced English Housekeeper by Elizabeth Raffald – her cookbook reprinted in paperback. Also available as a hardback reproduction of the original 1769 issue but including the additional recipes added to the second edition, together with an introduction giving background information about the book and Elizabeth.
- The 1772, 1773 & 1781 Directories of Manchester & Salford by Elizabeth Raffald – combined in one volume for the first time
- The Complete Elizabeth Raffald – a compilation of all her works – cookbook and directories plus introductions to each section including extracts from all research sources

To publicise her further, I have tried to tell her story in this fictional diary, written, I hope, in a style that I think sounds like her, bringing out her character. I have included in it some of her recipes and words from her own cookbook and directories, and many original references from newspaper articles and advertisements of the time, taken from Harrop's Manchester Mercury. If you would like to know more please contact me via my website,
www.suzeapple.co.uk
or at the website
www.elizabethraffaldsociety.org

An Uncommon Woman,

The Life and Times of Elizabeth Raffald

1763

Married Life Begins

1763 March 3rd Wedding Day

Today I begin a new life as a married woman, and so it is fitting that I start a new volume of my diary. My previous one is as Miss Whitaker and now I will make a fresh start in a new station as a wife, something I had not expected to be my lot. This is the last time I will be alone in my sitting room here at Arley Hall, for by this evening my new husband John Raffald will be sitting here with me.

John to be my husband! How fortunate was I to win this prize? Such a comely man, knowledgeable too, he could have had his pick of the maids here at Arley. They were all daily a-twitter about him, and they didn't know him in his younger days in Yorkshire as I did. I will need to be watchful that he does not think of wandering once we are wed, though how I will bear married life, I cannot imagine.

My whole life is to change with just this one act, and I am not thinking just of my marriage bed but of finding a new place to live. The rules of the house will not allow us to stay on as housekeeper and head gardener and so by marrying we are also leaving the only work we have ever known.

I am accustomed to the ways of living in a grand house, having a wonderful mistress in Lady Betty, and straight dealings from Sir Peter, but now we will need to make a new way. I have loved living at Arley Hall, even with all the dreadful dirt of the rebuilding. I know Lady Betty is sorry to lose me but there is a rule and so we must abide by it. And I confess I am keen to try my hand in the new business that John is certain will make our fortune. We are to go to Manchester where anything is possible. It is an exciting place of new opportunities and John believes that he can make his brother's business better than it ever was. For myself I will be vigilant to find an opportunity.

I have lost sleep, wondering if it is right to do this, so much to risk. At first we must throw ourselves on the mercy of John's brothers, men I have never met, although I have heard much about them. One thing is certain, that we must leave this beautiful place and find our way in the very heart of Manchester. I have heard it is exceedingly dirty and it always rains, making the streets and the houses dirty with the constant mud. I shall be constantly cleaning.

Chin up, Elizabeth. This will not do to be so gloomy. Your father did not raise a coward. Never let it be said that you shirked from a challenge. It is time to show these Lancastrians what some Yorkshire grit looks like. Oh, I can hear my father's voice as clearly as if he stood here now. How I wish he was. I could ask his advice, and yet I know what he would say. 'Take an opportunity and turn it into a prize, never walk the other way and live to regret inaction.' If only he could have been here today. I am sure I would feel stronger with him at my side.

Now I must take a deep breath and step positively towards my future; a future with the chance of a family of my own, a chance to pass on my father's excellent teaching. As he gave it to me so I will pass it to my children, God willing. And there are fine houses in Manchester. Such a big city as that must have its men of importance from whose families I hope to find a market for my cooking, for until babies come I must earn my keep, and I am hopeful of finding other business opportunities there. I am not afraid of hard work.

Lady Betty has promised me a good letter of recommendation though I know she is reluctant to let me go, as Sir Peter is to let John go. My good friend Ann Worsley, while waiting on Lady Betty, heard them have terrible words last week. Sir Peter was angry at losing his fifth gardener in twelve years and he wants to separate his gardeners from the house servants. He told Lady Betty she must be sure the next housekeeper is a sour female past the age of dalliance. Lady Betty, a lady of some spirit, had replied that he must also ensure the gardeners saved their efforts for out of doors and not try to charm her maids.

I am sad to cause them discord but we must take our opportunity. I must set these worries aside, and hope Lady Betty does not hold against me for leaving her. I know Ann won't be too pleased to take on my duties again, but she does enjoy having everyone answer to her, so she may get over that tolerably soon. At least we do not have to leave here directly. That would surely break my heart to go so abruptly. Sir Peter has ordered that we must stay until they have found our replacements. I live in dread of the day that we must abandon the fine standards we have here to move in with John's brother James.

For now I will remember what my dear mama told me every morning. 'Hold your head up high and face the day with determination. Either you get the better of it, or it gets the better of you.'

Oh I wish she could be here, and father too. I had never thought to be getting married at nearly thirty years of age. I had never expected such a prospect, not after my only offer seven years ago. I know I am plain looking and plain speaking, and had thought my one chance had gone years ago. But I should not be dwelling on that on my true wedding day.

I must leave my reminiscences here and now prepare myself for church, to stand next to Mr. Raffald, soon to be Mrs. Raffald. Oh my! Will I like it, I wonder? Still, the deed once begun must be done. I shall like it. I am determined to do so. Farewell Miss Whitaker. Only my sister Mary will carry that name from today.

1763 March 4ᵗʰ Wedding day memories

At last a few minutes to gather my thoughts! All the maids are finally about their tasks preparing the house for the guests this weekend, and I have written my thank you letter to the Reverend Burroughs for conducting a beautiful ceremony yesterday. He gave it a serious dignity and I will ever be grateful to Lady Betty for arranging for us to have the offices of the county's perpetual curate, a very senior member of the clergy. We were very honoured. And so I will endeavour to set down a few remembrances of the day so that they are not forgot. God willing, if I am not too old, I may have a daughter who will one day want to know how her dear mama and papa's wedding day went and I will have some details in perfect memory.

Mr. Raffald, now my husband (oh, how strange it is to think my name is now Mrs. Raffald), had sent me a beautiful posy of carnations to carry, before he himself set off for the church with William Widders as his witness. The flowers are truly beautiful and typical of his ways that he sent them for me to carry on my wedding day. They are in front of me now in a little jug of water. Of course I will dry them and press them in a few days, but for now I like to look at them and my heart swells just to see them. The flowers are a mix of the Raffald family carnation specialties, each one a painting of Nature's bounty and the scent is heavenly, surely one of God's greatest creations.

Ann was kind enough to lend me a necklace, given to her by Lady Betty, for my wedding. She said they were not true gems but I felt very grand with the beautiful blue stones sparkling in the morning sunlight. John said they made my eyes sparkle but seeing him so handsome may have helped. It's not often I have seen him so smart, always in his gardening clothes, but he cleans up very well. I felt my legs trembling as I stood beside him in front of the vicar, repeating my vows before God, sure that I would faint any moment, but as I looked in his eyes at the moment of our vows I knew my heart was true to him and would stay so forever. For better or worse we are bound together for life.

When we came out of the church arm in arm we were welcomed by the farm hands and garden labourers making a guard of honour with their hoes and rakes crossed in the air above us and a few of the countrywomen behind them ready to throw rice over us. I swear that Martha Taylor threw hers straight at me for I had to stop after some got in my eye. I could see her smirking but it turned to a frown as John bent tenderly over me to get it out. I held my head up then and turned to stare her right back as we walked hand in hand from the church.

She had thought to snare John when she and John were the only senior staff working together during the rebuilding of the Hall. While I was at Aston Park with the family she was housekeeper there for a year and a half. Well it was plain who Sir Peter regarded as his housekeeper when I came back with them in sixty-one, but Martha had never forgiven me for taking her place and for taking John off her, as she sees it.

All I will say is that quality will out, and Lady Betty would never have allowed Martha's cooking to go in front of the guests. It would bring shame on the whole household, it is so poor. Good enough to feed a few labourers that is all. John always said it was a sufferance to eat at her table.

As for taking him, I never chased him, he made his own mind up. I could have got along on my own just as well but now we are a married couple and life will change in so many ways. We have not yet made the most significant change yet as we have not yet slept as man and wife. I will not be subject to the smirks and giggles of the lower ranks and we must abide by the rules of the house that servants will not fraternise within these walls, of that I am determined. I am ever grateful for the good that Lady Betty and Sir Peter do for us, and I will not repay that kindness by breaking their rules. Our time will come soon enough.

1763 April 8th first receipt as Mrs. Raffald

Today was a momentous day for me, the first time I had need to write my new name to sign the monthly household receipt for Mr. Harper, the House Steward. If felt so queer for I am not yet accustomed to think of myself as a married woman. Poor John gives me such wretched looks when we meet at meal times and every spare moment he tries to snatch a kiss with me. It is difficult even in my own sitting room as one or other of the maids will find an excuse to knock on my door. I know some of them are doing it for mischief but they will soon grow tired of that game when I find them some of the worst tasks to do. They may giggle now but they will be sorry later when they have the most dirty work to do. While I am here at Arley Hall I am housekeeper first and wife second. It will not be for much longer now and then we will have the rest of our lives to be together and I will find out if I have chosen wisely.

Still, my bed is made now, and today I was present when Lady Betty appointed a new woman, a Mrs. Bromley, to take over my place. She seems competent enough and I will soon be able to test it out for she is to begin next week as my assistant while I show her what is required. She will sleep with the other maids until I have left, when she will take over the privilege of the sitting room but until then it is still my room. I suppose I must for courtesy's sake invite her to take tea in there with me, as there will be some matters we will need to discuss privately, away from the ears of silly young maids.

I feel ill-prepared to satisfy myself in only two weeks that she understands what is expected of her here in such a grand house, for I believe she was housekeeper for a much smaller establishment, just one gentleman. Only two weeks to impart my fifteen years of experience. It cannot be sufficient but it will have to be and I must detach myself from this establishment and prepare for my own. My future is set and an exciting world awaits me, with John, a world of opportunities for John and me to make our fortune and have a family to carry on our name and business. That must be my focus from now on.

1763 April 23rd final receipt for Arley Hall

Today I have signed my final receipt for Mr. Harper for the provisions at Arley and I could weep for the end of an old way of life, the only life I have known as an adult. Since I was fifteen years old I have belonged in service to one great family or another, and I have indeed served some great families, the Warburtons chief among them. I must be lunatic to give up this way of life, my comfortable quarters, the servants I manage and the friendship of Lady Betty. It is becoming real to me now that in a few days John and I will leave this beautiful house to go to Heaven knows what.

However, John has convinced me that we can make a future in Manchester and I have set down a few plans for dishes that I could sell which may keep me in a little business. I believe that I could supply cold entertainments and French fancies for the tables of these up and coming merchants that I hear are flooding the town. Will they like my food in Manchester I wonder? The town sounds such a frightening place, so large, and I am more accustomed to small villages and country life. It is exciting to think of such a grand adventure but now it has come to the moment I have butterflies in my stomach constantly. Each time I think of moving I feel a little sickly. Everything I do is for the final time of doing someone else's bidding.

In a few days we will be in our new quarters, our very own where we may truly be man and wife with no-one to give us rules. Oh my! What will that be like? I must be sure to find a way to keep up with my diary for I know how easily skills are lost when not practiced. I am thankful to my dear papa for sending me a regular supply of paper, keen that his daughters practice their writing. Dear as John is he cannot be the recipient of many of my thoughts for he does not think in the same way and cannot comprehend many of my concerns. Writing in my journal helps me to put my thoughts in order and is a safe place to put some which are best unspoken. I have continued my practice since I was a girl and I suspect I may be more glad of it as a married woman and, God willing, as a mother!

I a mother! It is hard to believe that I will be subject to the trials of motherhood. That is a part of marriage that I do not especially desire but without it a woman is not fulfilling her purpose in a marriage. I have seen from the families I have served what a worry children can be. So many babies and children do not live for long, there are so many dangers in this world. Even carrying a child in the womb brings untold dangers for mother and baby, and so many women die in childbirth of Puerperal Fever, Heaven protect me I do not suffer from that.

For now I will enjoy my remaining days at Arley Hall. John is kept busy making sure the gardens are ready for the summer, that his successor will have no reason to think poorly of him. I have worked my fingers to the bone going over every part of the house and even lending a hand with the dusting and polishing to be sure the house does me credit. The store room is stocked with every conceivable thing for the next month to give Mrs. Bromley, my successor, a good start. I know she cannot wait for me to leave now. I have shown her all the duties and special touches that make life easy for the family but I have my suspicions that she thinks I am fussing over much. I feel so disloyal for leaving Lady Betty to her, most likely inferior, services but she was the best of the choices available. It was better her than that Martha Taylor be taken on again. Then I would have had to seriously reconsider getting married for I could not have left the family to her second rate work. She is one part of Arley I will be glad to leave behind and I will make sure that John and I are most loving as we walk through the village on our way to Manchester.

1763 May 7th Manchester

It has been nearly one week now since we took our leave from dear Arley and I do not have the heart to write much tonight. I only hope that pouring out my sadness onto the page will help me to resolve it, for tomorrow I must set to with my new duties. We are squashed into a back room needed by James and his family and it was here that we truly became man and wife. Not what I would have wished but it could not be helped and I am hopeful that we will soon have the lease of a useful house on Fennel Street behind the market place. It has good, dry, cellars and is much better placed for doing business, being near the market, than James' house on the other side of the river where he has his nursery garden.

For now I will distract myself with memories of that last day at Arley Hall. When I woke that morning I was still the housekeeper at Arley Hall but very quickly Mrs. Bromley disabused me of that notion. She brought two of the housemaids and a footman to change around my sitting room, now her sitting room of course. My few belongings were already packed so I quickly left and went down to the servants' hall to meet with John. Mrs. Hutchin, the cook, had kindly prepared us some pies to take with us for the journey to Manchester, and the gardeners, laundrymaids, dairymaids and coachmen were gathered to take their leave of us.

Just as we were on the point of leaving the kitchen the two

housemaids ran in to say their goodbyes. Young Hannah Bushell shed a few tears and I confess she very nearly disarmed me. She is a good girl and I would have taken her with us if I could, she has been well trained by me. I was very gratified by her due regard and stood with John to take all the good wishes before they were all hurried away to their tasks by Mrs. Bromley.

Then it was just he and I, and we thought we must finally go when Lady Betty and Sir Peter came into the room with Mr. Harper to give us their good wishes too. I could see that she was sad to see me leave, of course, but she kept her composure, great lady that she is, and we bade each other a dignified farewell. Sir Peter was likewise affected and his reluctance to part with John was plain. He swore that he would lose no more gardeners to pretty house servants and he had already ordered plans to be drawn for a cottage away from the house for future gardeners to live in, John being the fifth such gardener to leave in the previous twelve years through marriage to a house servant. Sir Peter was in the worst mood I had ever seen him in my three years of service and, as the cause of his temper, I was most glad when we could finally leave. Quickly we said our final goodbyes, as Mrs. Bromley stood disapprovingly in the background, her face set in a look that could have curdled milk. Sir Peter will have no worries of that woman tempting any of his staff, of that I am sure.

We left the house for the final time and I confess my knees gave way a little. If it had not been for John's strong arm I am sure I should have fallen in a disgraceful heap in the yard. I am so glad I did not do that in front of Mrs. Bromley. We had thought to walk through Arley village on our way to the Chester road but as we passed through the yard William Widders was there with his wagon all cosy with a good blanket and a promise to take us all the way into Altrincham from where we might pick up the stage coach or manage the walk into Manchester, an easy half day from there.

It was with a heavy heart that we bade goodbye to William in the market place there. Our last connection with Arley Hall was gone and I felt cast adrift, just John and I, absolutely alone. Now it would test us to see if we really could make something of the opportunities in Manchester. Up to now it has been quite trying, adapting to the fast pace of life in the town.

1763 May 20th
Oh my! What a lot of changes I have seen since I last wrote in here.

So much in Manchester is different, disappointing and overwhelming that I doubt now that I did the right thing in marrying John, and I feel lost. Taking leave of Lady Betty, was a very sorrowful occasion and I miss dreadfully her help and knowledge.

But, I will not get maudlin, I have too much to occupy me, not least my new husband. I will confess it was a shock at first, his physical demands were overtiring at times but it is a thrill to know I have this power to drive him wild for me. It is not a good thing to have him so close at hand every day, however. I could wish his market stall a few furlongs hence from here. His brothers are too forgiving of him, allowing him to leave the stall each time his passion rises. I hope I know what my duty is as his wife but I must teach him how much more profitable I can be occupied by the selling of my confectionery.

I soon found out there is ready market on hand from my own front door for the sweet confections I can make and it brings in a good sum already. I have noticed how his head is turned by the prospect of extra income and he cares not whether it comes from his own labours or mine, which of course, under law, now belongs to him, as do I. I must cure him however of throwing my good money into the cockpit at the bottom of Market Stead Lane, so near the stall. That too I could wish many miles distant. I know my old master, Sir Peter, encouraged the men to join him at cockfights but he had the good sense to keep the men ruled by him in their gambling. Now Mr. Raffald has no such rein on him and I fear for our money if it continues. I must strive to keep safe some money for our future, for I am sure that as he works so keenly at it, we must surely have a large family before long.

Thankfully word is already spreading that my Vermicelli soup is the best around. I'm sure that Lady Betty would vouch that it was the best she ever tasted. She often commented on the superior taste. It is not difficult but I wish cooks would pay attention to first laying the meat in the bottom of the pan with a good lump of butter with herbs and roots cut small, then setting it over a slow fire. It will draw all the virtue out of the roots or herbs and turn it to a good gravy, giving the soup a very different flavour from putting water in at the first. I had better set down my receipt here so that it is not forgot.

To make a Rich Vermicelli Soup.

INTO a large Tossing-Pan put four Ounces of Butter, cut a Knuckle of Veal, and a Scrag of Mutton into small Pieces, about the Size of Walnuts; slice in the Meat of a Shank of Ham, with three or four Blades of Mace, two or three Carrots, two Parsnips, two large Onions, with a Clove stuck in at each End, cut in four or five Heads of Celery washed clean, a Bunch of sweet Herbs, eight or ten Morels, and an Anchovy; cover the Pan close up, and set it over a Slow Fire, without any Water, till the Gravy is drawn out of the Meat, then pour the Gravy out into a Pot or Bason, let the Meat brown in the same Pan, and take Care it don't burn, then pour in four Quarts of Water, let it boil gently till it is wasted to three Pints, then strain it, and put the other Gravy to it, set it on the Fire, add to it two Ounces of Vermicelli, cut the nicest Part of a Head of Celery, Chyan Pepper and Salt, to your Taste, and let it boil for four Minutes; if not a good Colour, put in a little Browning, lay a small French Roll in the Soup Dish, pour in the Soup upon it, and lay some of the Vermicelli over it.

1763 May 30th catering

I have decided that I must apply myself to the work of getting some orders from the fine houses around King Street and St Ann's Square for it is there that the gentry are chiefly resident and they are the ones who I think will appreciate my fine menu of dishes. Lady Betty has recommended me to her relatives, such as live in this town or nearabouts, for she has often heard them complain of the lack of a good cook here. They, I am certain, will be glad of food with the finesse that I can bring. The best of the nobility is of course Sir Thomas Egerton, Knight of the Shire, but he is often in London, spending much less time at his country residence here. Lady Assheton is next in prominence but she lives very quietly. And of course Manchester is plentiful in very reverend gentlemen of the church. Most of the wardens of Christ Church in Manchester are so excessively fond of their food. I daresay I shall find no end of custom from them. For though they plead poverty, they are not so poor, not like many of the hardworking weavers hereabouts.

As well as the gentlemen of the clergy there are any number of families of consequence who have not the servants or the skills to provide them with the correct way of presenting dinners as they should be served. I could offer to train their servants; most of the girls here come with very little idea of what is required of them. Their manners are simple but often coarse, their ability to understand dulled by not having been taught the correct way a good house is run. I could teach them that very usefully. First, however, I must reach their households, in the most genteel way, of course. I do not wish to give a coarse impression. I will offer my sincerest wishes to be of service to them, indicating my qualifications in knowing the best of service, as evidenced by my character letter from Sir Peter himself. Understanding the pressure they face in balancing economy with elegance, I shall emphasize my skills in both.

I must not rest on my laurels and wait for their enquiries. I know myself on whose say-so help is procured. I will not approach the housekeepers for they will only be envious of my cooking skills. I would certainly never have allowed anyone else in my kitchen that was not under my direction, except perhaps a man-cook. They are often superior in their abilities. I will address myself to the butlers and house stewards with whom the decision will rest. They must despair at the quality of food they are forced to serve to their masters for it is they who bear the brunt of the complaints they make, they who must feel the shame at a poor offering. If they say a certain service is required then the cook must abide by it, and surely they will be glad of being the instrument of bringing pleasure to the families they serve; pleasure which invariably spills over into greater rewards for the servants responsible, especially from the visiting guests who must dread calling on some of their acquaintance in such a primitive place.

So now I must think how best to approach them. I must phrase it very carefully to avoid giving offence or appearing too conceited about my skills. I will assure them that my service is discreet and of the highest quality. The mention of the noble families I have served must impress upon them the significance of my qualifications. I must not appear to teach them their duty but will emphasize my desire to assist them to raise the standards of their households, and the 'rewards' that will follow. These men are, in the main, intelligent men, certainly astute, for that is an essential quality for a house manager. I will not need to say more than that. Perhaps I will add a mention of some of my finer dishes to give them an idea of what they may expect, and of course, I must be sure to send an example of my food with the letters. A message sent straight to the stomach can speak louder than one to the mind. I could easily have some sweet patties made up first thing in the morning. They have such a sweet smell that they quickly bring customers to my door and the recipe is so simple, though the puff pastry takes a little work which I can do the night before. I will write out the receipt here so I do not forget.

> ### *Sweet* Patties
>
> *The Meat of a boiled Calf's foot, two large Apples and one Ounce of candied Orange, chopped very small. Grate half a Nutmeg, mix them with the Yolk of an Egg, a Spoonful of French Brandy, and a Quarter of a Pound of Currants, clean washed and dried, a good puff Paste rolled in different Shapes, some round, some square and three-cornered, with a little of the Meat on them, lay a Lid on and turn up the Edges to keep in the Juices, then either bake or fry them.*

My work now must be to accumulate the names of such households that may benefit so, rain or sun, tomorrow I will traverse the town making my enquiries. First call must be to the Collegiate Church, of course, to say a prayer and whilst there I can also make a list of the names of the prominent families who worship there. I think perhaps Warden Peploe may be persuaded to help me, especially if I take him a little sweetmeat. From what I have seen of him he is an affable, jolly man, gracious and polite and remarkable for his ease among the congregation, regardless of their rank or circumstance. I have great hope that he will aid me in my endeavours to bring better things to the people of this town. Lady Betty's letters will not be sufficient on their own to raise me a business so I must set to and apply myself.

John made the suggestion that I take a stall alongside theirs but, quite apart from all the dirt, I refuse to lower myself to stand on the street, even in the marketplace, to sell my dishes. That may do for James's wife who probably knows nothing else but I will not lower myself. I am used to better and I am determined that my family will have better too. I can sense that anything is possible in this town. The streets may be foul but there is money to be made here and I intend to stake my claim to a share of it.

1763 June 5th John's family

John is now happily settled on the stalls here with his brothers James and George. Between helping out in James's large nursery garden in Salford and chatting to all the women in the market he seems happier than he ever was at Arley. Of course his brother George is never here. He has trouble enough in Stockport with his inn, Ye Blew Stoops, a rather coarse kind of place. His wife Mary comes often but her husband, like mine, takes his marital duty very seriously and she is often with child. This week she told me that even though she had miscarried only three months ago she fears she is with child again. Of course, I do not think it will be long before I am the same.

John is so very keen for us to have a family to carry on his business. I always knew, of course, that he would not be lacking in that respect. He had given me sufficient hints about his interest, but it is quite a different thing when he is free of all restraints and able to indulge his whims whenever they take him. Only yesterday he had taken advantage of Mary's arrival at the stall to come home on the pretext of getting some food. It gave me such a shock when he came upon me as I was bending over the oven to check some pies. I vow I screamed fit to wake the dead and nearly dropped my baking on the floor when I felt my skirts lifted from behind. How I shall blush when I next face Mary. She is no fool when it comes to judging what men have in their minds and she will know exactly why John had an urgent need to come home.

This desire only seems to inflict John and George, however, their other brother James is cut from a different cloth altogether. He and his wife, also called Mary, have only one child, a son on whom they dote, but James himself is a quiet, serious man, given to a lot of superstitions and doubts. They were very kind to us when we first arrived here and would have had us live with them but their house is so dreary and he and John do not get on as well as he and George. It is a pity for I think some of the seriousness would do well to rub off on John, although I could not bear the same melancholy. I cannot abide James's company above an hour and always come away with an itch to shake him by the shoulders to make him see the good that he has a doting wife, although her disposition of timidity only encourages his anxiety. He has one of the best gardens in Salford, reaching from his house on Greengate all the way back as far as King Street, and from Gravel Lane to the workhouse. If only he would be more pleasant and not constantly suspect his men of stealing from him. I am sure they would not think of it if he was a little more pleasant to them. If I have learnt one thing from my years of running great households it is that a little sugar now and then can sweeten the surliest of natures.

Of course I never had much of a problem that way when I had the duty of choosing my maids. I always made it clear what their duties were and as long as they kept their side of the contract I would look out for their welfare. I never had a maid under me that had to go out of town after catching the master's eye. None of that in my household, thank you. Everyone to their place, then there would be no need for poor mites in the workhouse. If only every housekeeper would take such care, the world might be a better place. I believe that if men only had the burden of pushing out new life it would be a different thing altogether.

I got off onto another subject entirely than the one I intended to write today. I merely wanted to record that I had more customers today for my calf's head pies, despite John's efforts yesterday, and it seems my reputation is spreading already. This business may be easier than I had thought.

1763 June 23rd business beginnings

I am slowly learning my way around the business in this town of Manchester and I am finding that business is exactly what the town is made for. It does not have the culture that I remember from my days in York but it has the respectable beginnings of such. There is a theatre and an assembly and enough churches to satisfy the most fervent worshippers of every denomination, but it is the business that is the beating heart, and we have moved to the centre of it here on Fennel-street. The daily thoroughfare of people that pass our front door is only bettered by the gathering in the nearby market place. Anyone with a little sense may turn a profit if he is careful not to be hoodwinked by unscrupulous elements that always find the gullible. I have been too long in watchful service to others to be fooled now I am working for myself. Fortunately John manages the market stalls very well and I am happy that I can make my own money from my labours, keeping some direction over my housekeeping.

It is so easy to obtain all the ingredients I need for my dishes from the number and variety of markets here in the town. There is not in Manchester a general market. Markets here are scattered all over the town under the control of the Lord of the Manor, Sir Oswald Mosley, Bart. I now know that the cattle market is in Smithfield, on Shude-hill every Wednesday. Every Tuesday, Thursday and Saturday fish and lobster from the Yorkshire coast and coldwater fish from the Ribble are brought to the Fish market in a handsome stone building nearby in the Market Place. Meat is also sold the same days with any leftovers from Saturday sold on Turner Street on a Monday, not that the meat is much fit for anything but the flavouring of a vermicelli soup. The butcher's market is held under the Manor Court Room on Brown-street. The Market Place itself yields more vegetables and small fruit than I have ever seen before in my life. On a Saturday the streets around are thronged with farmers and country people who flock to town with their agricultural produce. The market stretches from Smithy Door near the church of St Mary, St Denys and St Michael, all the way though to the market cross and the Exchange. It surrounds the stocks and pillory in the middle in case there is a spectacle to be viewed, which there is most days. It's quite vulgar how much pleasure the people get from the suffering of another. Many of the miscreants are just too poor to afford to live a decent life. If I hear of any deserving poor I always make sure to send a little food their way.

Between my own Fennel-street and the church lies an excellent apple market with so many varieties that they are a wonder to behold. The Methodist Chapel on High Street is the place to go for meal and flour. I make regular visits to there for the oatmeal, some of the best quality I have ever seen. Downstairs from the chapel is where cheeses are sold but I will not go into that vile smelling cellar. I insist that John must go for our cheese for it is he who consumes the biggest portion and he must have the smelliest stinking cheese that he can find.

He knows he must bring me some of his most scented blooms on the day he brings home the cheese for I will not admit bad smells in my kitchen when I am cooking dishes for my public dinners. What would the customers think of me? Of course there is the corn market here on our doorstep on Fennel-street, which is very useful. I believe this area was formerly known as Barley Cross but already I have noticed that things quickly change and adapt here in Manchester. The people of the town have a peculiar knack of noticing what thrives, and making more of that, capitalising on the smallest idea. There is even a regular shoe market on Withy Grove and I declare I will have need of a visit there very soon.

These streets are very bad for walking in with their badly set cobbles, cart ruts and mud, where rain and effluence carves rivers down the sloping streets. A walk up Market Stead Lane from the Market Place to Daub Holes is like a hurdle race. Even with pattens on my feet my shoes are regularly saturated before I return home. The only day I do not go far is a Tuesday when all the cotton manufacturers come from the country all around Manchester to do business at the Exchange. The town becomes so full it is impossible to walk around with any dignity. The people on the market stalls love the extra purses to buy their wares, however they are crafty and inflate their prices for these out of town visitors. I too do a flourishing trade, especially for my portable soup and made dishes but I only ask the same price as I ask every day of the week.

No, Tuesday is definitely not the day for ordinary folk to shop in Manchester, Saturday is a much better day and I can buy what I need to keep me till the following Saturday. I have also found it makes for a certain extra economy when I shop only once in a week. With so much abundance available all the time it is too tempting to spend more than one's budget. Once weekly is an unaccustomed luxury when I have always been used to a monthly account at Arley Hall.

1763 July 15th

My letters seeking work have succeeded so well I can scarce believe it, there really is a great need for good cooks hereabouts. Several more favourable replies arrived today, so many in fact that I will need to find me some good kitchen maids straight away, for there is more work than I can manage alone. I would ask John to send me his brother's girls from Stockport but they follow their father in moods and can be a handful to manage, according to Mary their mother. It could be a fast way to begin a family feud if I had need to chastise them, as I surely would. No, I must cast about me here to find some willing help. I will apply to my neighbour, Mrs. Withnall, who seems a good sort of woman. As a midwife to many of the babies born here, I feel she will be best placed to guide me in this.

I must act soon for the dinner requested by Mr. Briarly's man will need at least one week's preparation from three of such as myself and it is only three weeks hence. I will apply to Mrs. Clowes for a supply of sugar for the gold and silver globes. I may be able to negotiate a good price with her for some double refined for I know she always has a stock on hand for her confectioneries. The veal will need to be got Tuesday next to be ready in time. I would send John for it but he does not have the sense of picking a good animal, he is easily distracted by the seller's chatter. If only it was seeds that I needed, I would have the best bargain in town regardless, but in food he only has the skill of eating it.

1763 August 11th

Manchester is such a busy place and business is very promising but I do not like it as much as my beloved York. If only I could persuade Mr. Raffald to move us, but he is needed here by James. I am grateful that we are so close to a wonderful church, the church of St Mary's, St Denys and St George, although I confess I find St Ann's is pretty too. Not that I have much time for the church, I am finding my time taken up in making a business. John's brother George is still too occupied with his inn at Stockport and cannot much be spared for the family stall in Manchester. I would say Mr. George Raffald would wear himself out with the travelling back and forth from the family land in Stockport to the market place in Manchester but since I have met him I can say there is no worry of that. I've never met a man so sure to look after his own interests. My dear John works so diligently in the family business and I will make sure that his brothers appreciate him. Most of the people here are of good hearted character, used to hard work but there are hard times among the wealth I see growing around us. There is money to be made here in Manchester, and I will have our share for me and our family. Without money this is a dreadful place to live.

1763 August 26th meeting a business rival

Today I met an interesting woman, a Mrs. Blomeley. She is a near neighbour but thankfully not too near. She lives with her son James on Smithy Door, near the Market-place, where they have a business selling confectionaries. I feel she might be a bit overbearing at close quarters for she wants nothing more than a willing audience. She was very complimentary to me and wished me courteous felicitations upon my recent marriage, but then proceeded to give me more advice than I might want, even on such matters as to how I should be preparing my pie pans, as if I needed that.

She is a woman much like me, however, so I cannot fault her for trying to help me. She has been in this town longer than I and she has made a profitable business from her cooking ability so I must learn what I can of her. She had, I suppose, only come to look me over at close quarters. From what she has said to me I've no reason to feel we are in direct competition however. She has a good trade in dishes of the stout, local fare so beloved by the poorer classes here, where I have the skill in finer things. I will look to provide high quality dishes and confectionaries.

Certainly she does not have the knowledge of many of the French dishes which I consider to be essential for a good dinner. I made sure to tell her about my commission for a club dinner that I had already secured at Mr. Priestnall's house next month. It was enough to stop her giving me any more advice but I hope there is business for both of us here and that we will become friends to each other rather than rivals. She certainly seemed glad of some advice I gave her with respect to making pies.

1763 September 5th

I have had such an excellent idea and John assures me I am just the woman to do it. I read today in the Manchester Mercury and Harrop Advertiser newspaper that a person of enterprise has set up an office in London to provide the residents of that city with an office where people may find servants, and for servants to find places. Families in search of servants can obtain a person who they know comes with good characters for no-one can register without a letter from their last employer. I can see that this may be a problem for some servants to obtain suitable letters but I could draft a form of letter that can be easily completed by even the most reluctant employer. Some of the letters I saw in my time as a housekeeper were more use for lighting fires than recommending a person. I had scraps of dirty paper, pages torn from ledgers, and in one memorable case, on wrapping paper from a skein of rough wool. In that instance I followed my instincts to hire the young person despite the poor recommendation and she became, under my guidance, a very capable and presentable kitchen maid. She was a good girl at heart but without the polish I gave her she may never have found a place.

Yes, I think I must do it and set up my own register office here in Manchester for never was a town in more need of some organisation than this one, and who better than I to find the right calibre of servants needed for this rough and ready town? If I do not strive to improve things but only complain how bad they are then I am no better than anyone else. My dear papa always told me that if I ever want something to improve I must set myself into action to achieve it.

1763 September 24th
Well, I cannot believe I ever trusted that fiend Blomeley! I was so naïve to take her into my confidence and show her some of my methods. Only today I received word from Mr. Priestnall that he would not be asking me to make the food for his club's dinner on Saturday fortnight. When I pressed the messenger for a reason it came out that he had accepted an offer from that woman which had been more favourable than mine for the same menu. Ha! I wish them joy of each other and hope his friends and he are as disappointed as they surely will be. It is all very well making it sound good but with food it is the presentation that improves the taste and I can tell from her appearance that Mrs. Blomeley does not have my eye for detail, my fastidiousness for appearance and quality. Well, when Mr. Priestnall does come to me next month, as he surely will, his price will be a little higher, as I will know that my competition has lost him and he will be my customer and ever grateful.

1763 Oct 10th
    Today was a black day in my life, and I am not sure which way to look for comfort. First, when I woke this morning I found such a mess in the bed, more than I have ever seen before. When I stood up to move, more mess came away from me and I was in utter torment of how best to clean myself up. Poor John, he was in such shock, but he went straight to his brother's house to bring his wife Mary to help me. She was here in no time but for all her dithering I was better without her. After I had listened to her wailing for a full hour, I thought she would be better going to get help and I sent her to find me a woman who knows about women's problems. She went straight to Mrs. Withnall who is called to every woman in need in this area. Mrs. W soon put me right and told me it was due to a miscarriage. My first try at becoming a mother and I have instantly failed. She helped me to get cleaned up and made me lie still on a pile of rags till the worst of the flow eased. She said I must stay there for a full day, but I could not afford to lose that much baking time. As soon as I felt safe to move I made Mary help me to a chair by the fire so I could watch the cooking while she set up some pies

for baking.

Word was quickly out that Mrs. Raffald was in need of help and there was soon a queue of lively urchins hoping for some work. I picked the best looking girls and a couple of the boys, promising the rest a chance the next day. I thought they showed signs of some intelligence but I was proved wrong. I managed to get the order ready for the Reverend Mr. Eccleston and sent the boys with instructions to deliver it faithfully or no payment but they were never seen again. I am sure I will know them when I see them again and woe betide them for this mischief.

I only found out when word came from the Reverend Mr. Eccleston's, asking when the dishes would be ready, long after the time they should have got them. Then two of the girls returned, they had got lost, but by then the food was ruined. So I am left out of pocket and out of humour. It is bad enough that I was laid up to begin with, but for my efforts to be wasted is too much. I am sorely tempted to report them to the Constable but it does make me wonder if they were dishonest or just starved. I will try first to make them earn their food, and if that does not work it shall be the law and severe punishment.

I had to send Mary back with more food but she was only a little more useful. I was fair ashamed to send out some of the work she produced but they were better than none at all. She used far too much sugar and has left me with very little for tomorrow's dishes. I will have to send to Mrs. Clowes to beg her to sell me some of her stock, as she always has plenty in her store for her sweet-making. Mary can be more use to me in finding the boys who ran away with my food, and John will give them his justice, to turn them from wrongdoing again, for I am determined to teach them that it will not profit them in the end.

I began so well but there are so many problems in this business that I never thought to encounter. I am used to using the best of ingredients and having useful people to work for me. Starting from the beginning in such a rough place is testing my mettle, but I will not be beaten. I have thought I may be better looking for a housekeeping post here in town, for there are several good houses in dire need of quality servants. Today was a day when I wished I had never left dear Arley where I had everything I needed and a position of respect. It pains me to think of what fresh trials tomorrow may bring, and I am not sure right now if I have the heart to face another day like today.

Perhaps I could persuade my own sister Mary to come and stay with me for a while. I know she will treasure a chance for us to be close again and I will confess her sugar work is more skilled than mine, though I would not like to admit it to her. She can be insufferable if she is seen to be right. I do hope she considers coming to help me for I am sorely in need of good help just now. I will write to her directly then I will sleep easier knowing I have taken a positive step towards making tomorrow better than today.

1763, October 22nd Mary arrives, setting up the Register Office

My dear sister Mary came straightaway in reply to my plea for help. She is a kind, quiet woman and her arrival was typical of her. She arrived at my door straight off the Leeds coach, with two young boys. I knew nothing of it until I answered the door and saw them standing there. I was never so surprised and I confess I had a little weep, it was so good to see her again.

I hurried them inside to get warm by the fire and asked who her companions were. I was overjoyed when she introduced them as our nephews, William and Joshua Middlewood, sent by our sister Jane to work for us. William was the eldest, a fine young boy of eleven and Joshua, only seven years old, huddled behind his brother seeming a little shy. I gave them all some warm broth to help them recover from the dreadful journey over the moors.

Mary was so happy to be with me, and delighted that she could spend her days making sweetmeats and confectioneries, her favourite work. She had been helping Papa in the schoolroom but she did not enjoy that as well as cooking, much preferring a spoon in her hand to a pen. When Jane had heard she was going she had sent her boys, to be useful for their Aunt Elizabeth, there being very little chance for them in Howden. As they sat eating the broth their eyes widened as I told them what their arrival meant to me. I can now undertake a new business venture that I had been considering, one that will need me to take some of my attention from cooking.

Now I will have Mary's help I have no qualms in opening a Register Office for servants. I have been approached so often to find a servant or recommend one for a place that I think I must now put it on a proper footing. A Register Office is what they have in London and so we shall have one here in Manchester. I am surprised that no-one has thought of it before, but perhaps no-one else has my unique qualifications. I sent the boys out to have a look around town and Mary to settle herself in while I set to planning an advertisement to place in the Manchester Mercury newspaper

I was keen to make it clear that I am doing this at the request of people of quality. I will not have it said that I am presumptuous or pushy. First I will make it clear that I am only doing this at the request of people of quality. I can say 'By particular Desire of many Ladies and Gentlemen in this Town and Neighbourhood'. Then must come my name in large type, E RAFFALD, for I am becoming well known in some of the best circles, and where I can be found in smaller type, as it is important that the people looking for work know where to find me.

Next must be the name of the service, A Public REGISTER OFFICE, in big capitals so it catches the eye. Underneath that I can write a short description of the service it provides, for many people will not have heard of such a thing before. I can say that it is to supply Families with Servants of all Ranks, or perhaps Denominations will sound better. I must keep in mind the class of employers I am trying to reach.

Then, to reach the other side of the bargain, I must add that I will also provide Servants with Places, for if I do not reach them I will have to go door to door to find them myself. The few who have already approached me discreetly to find a better situation will not make a business for me, so I needs must have many more to make it worth my while.

Next I think it is important to specify clearly the terms of business, that for One shilling any Person may be supplied with a Servant of Character, for any Place, or their money returned. There is such a demand for good servants in this town of Manchester that if I have not suited someone in a month they must be too pernicketty. For servants looking for Places, they may stand in the books two months and have the chance of what Places are on the List, or may be offered in that time, again for one shilling. Allowing a two month period for the shilling will be generous enough. If they have not been suited in that time they must pay me again to stay on the register.

Now I must think how to show that I will only have the best servants on my register. I will include some words on my experience that will show I am not some upstart but a woman of substantial Qualifications for this Business, which may not have fallen the way of many others of my current acquaintance. I have had Direction of all kinds of Servants, in Noblemen's and Gentlemen's families. That has a good sound to it, I will definitely include that and just to show I am still well connected I can include the information that I have also now Corresponded with most of such Families as there are in this Neighbourhood. That must give any servants the assurance that I am the one to find them a better station. My office will be the one to apply to for quality appointments.

I must specify that No Servant will be entered in the Books without a Character, which must be signed by the Master or Mistress of Credit that they have served. I will allow of no exceptions. I know what is looked for and I have already prepared my Printed Character forms which every Person will be required to get signed, on their first Application for a Place. I hope Mr. Harrop will have the proof copies available for me to scrutinize before my advertisement is placed.

Of course then I must finish with a few words of the most cordial thanks for the business I am currently in, so that people will know my range of Confectionery, Hot French Dinners and Cold Entertainments, a most pleasing business which I think exhibits many of my best skills. It will not hurt to push a little more trade that way, especially now I have my sister Mary coming to join me. We will need more trade to keep us both.

1763 Nov 7th

Finally I received the package from Mr. Harrop of a sheaf of printed characters, ready to be given out to customers of my new register office. These will help make it simple to obtain relevant details from some masters, guiding them in what details to include for a good reference. It is no use writing that Joseph makes very good ale if it does not specify how industrious Joseph may be in applying his skills of economy, or whether he is honest and can be trusted not to drink more than his allotted portion of the ale.

I will have these papers ready to give to those who come to me to procure a position without a letter from their previous master. Although, they have cost me several shillings so perhaps I should claim back some of the costs from those who will benefit from them. For all I know I could give them out then the person may take it and find themselves a position elsewhere and not through my agency. No, these papers are worth a halfpenny of anyone's money. If they do not have the resources for a halfpenny then they are not worth the bother of my efforts, for a shilling is all I ask for the work I may need to undertake on their behalf to find them a good place.

If only I had received these papers yesterday when a most presentable girl had to be turned away for lack of a character letter. If I had been in possession of these papers then I might have been able to save her some trouble and gain what I think would be a respectable asset for my business. Still, I did not have time to ponder on her situation for we were exceedingly busy with the country people come into town on account of the dirt fair on Chapel-street. So many horses, cattle and other beasts were driven past my door, it was a wonder they did not break the bridge over the River Irwell. It was good for my business, however, lots of my portable soup lozenges were sold to grateful hands, as well as any number of Hottentot Pyes. William and Joshua proved themselves more than able at carrying out the errands I set them. They are a credit to their mother and I shall write and tell her so. Mary and I were quite run off our feet but it was just recompense when I sat to count up the takings tonight. It is always a good feeling when hard work produces a tidy profit.

1763 Nov 15th

I like to keep abreast of the news from abroad, in particular from America, which looks promising to be a place of opportunity, greater even than here in Manchester, perhaps in a few years when it has settled down. A person with knowledge of plants and growing conditions, together with a person who knows how they should be cooked and presented may do very well in that new nation. It is a place of great enterprise and possibilities, I can foresee that an experienced businesswoman may do well there. Manchester may yet be just a stepping stone in our careers. Mr. Harrop's Mercury today carried a very hopeful article which I have decided to paste here for future inspiration.

> "New York Oct 11. The present Disturbance amongst the Indians, with whom, as a Body corporate, we are intimately connected, gives us great Uneasiness; we yet foresee these Troubles will be of short duration; for as the late Peace has left us in Possession of the whole Northern Continent, by removing the French as a Military Government, it is hoped as we have taken away the primary Cause, the Effect therefore, an established Maxim in Mechanics, must naturally cease; and the several Tribes of Indians will soon

> be obliged to return to Trade and Alliance with the English. This desirable Event once Effected, we shall soon see another face of Affairs in America; New Branches of Trade will be struck out, the Advantages of which, even the most sanguine among us, cannot enumerate. In the mean Time our Northern Governments, with a laudable Coalition, are now intent on such Measures as cannot fail to produce the most happy Consequences. A scheme is now actually on Foot, for extending the Trade of these Provinces to the most remote Indian Nations, situated on the Banks of the Great Lakes Ontario and Superior, by Means of Shipping, and a Chain of Forts and Settlements on the most important and critical Passes; very proper to protect our Traders, promote Commerce, and render the future incursions of the Savages, or French Policy, fruitless."

This all sounds very promising for a busy, fruitful future for business people such as John and me.

1763 Nov 22

I am so beside myself with agitation today as my first ever newspaper advertisement appeared in Mr. Harrop's excellent newspaper, the Manchester Mercury and Harrop's Advertiser. I think I got the tone just right, it does look very well.

> By particular Desire of many Ladies and Gentlemen in this Town and Neighbourhood
> E. RAFFALD
> At her house in *Fennel-street* has open'd
> A Public Register Office
> For supplying Families with Servants of all Denominations and Servants with Places on the following Terms, viz.
>
> That any Person may be supply'd with a Servant of Character, for any Place, in their Time, for One Shilling, or the Money return'd.
>
> That any Servant may stand in the Books Two Months, and have the Chance of what Places are on the List, or may offer in that Time, for One Shilling.
>
> No Servant will be entered in the Books without a Character, which must be sign's by the Master or Mistress of Credit they have served, --- and for this Purpose she has printed Characters, which every Person will be required to get signed, on their first application for a Place.

> As *Mrs Raffald* has many Years had the Direction of all Sorts of Servants in Noblemen's and Gentlemen's Families, and has a Correspondence in most of such Families in this Neighbourhood, she presumes to hope she has many Qualifications for this Business, which may not have fallen in the way of any other.
>
> She returns her most cordial Thanks for the great Encouragement this Town has been pleased to give her Business of supplying Cold Entertainments, Hot French Dinners, Confectionaries, &c. and still continues to serve her Friends with every thing in that way in the genteelest Taste, and on the easiest Terms.
>
> N.B. Letters from the Country, post paid, will be duly answered.

Mr. Harrop has suggested a few improvements which I may consider for my next advertisement. He advised me that it will take more than one view before people will consider it a regular business and has suggested it is placed for six weeks at least, which I think will be a terrible expence but I would not wish customers to be decided against me, thinking it is some ill thought out enterprise. I am determined it will serve the best families in town, and I hope the mention of my Qualifications will give that due impression.

I would have liked to mention one or two of my connections, just to make clear how noble are some of the families I have served, but that would have been too vulgar for words. One must always be discreet when dealing with the gentry. I will just ensure that when people call in to see me I have the letters lying open on my desk with my character from Lady Betty uppermost.

1763 Dec 3rd

I was disappointed to note that Mr. Priestnall did not send word for me to provide the food for his club's monthly dinner. Perhaps he was too ashamed to approach me after his bad behaviour last month, preferring Mrs. Blomeley over me, or perhaps his friends have deserted him after what must have been a shabbier dinner than any of mine. I did hear it was a rather debauched affair and it could even be that the quantity of wine and spirits they take removes the need for food to taste well. It's of no matter to me now. I have no wish to build my reputation with base, drunken customers. It is no loss to me, in fact it is a gift. She may take the lower elements and I will concentrate on higher society. That will suit me perfectly. I am thankful our paths do not cross often, and as I am at the market before eight I will never meet her, for she does not trouble herself to rise before then, whereas I have done three hours work by that time.

1763 December 20th

Today I had need to amend my advertisement for I am getting so many enquiries coming into my little Register Office. My reputation is spreading and more than one person said to me that only Mrs. Raffald's office would procure a servant for a place of quality. For that I am humbly gratified, for I have always said that I know my trade, having worked it since I was fifteen years old. I am having so many enquiries from families requiring servants that I added these words, 'Women Servants are Wanted for several good places. Several men Servants, Well Recommended, Want Places.' That should bring me some more business.

1764

1764 January 10th

I knew I was right to start my register office for servants but some of the applicants leave a lot to be desired. How some of them have the nerve to turn up at my office I do not know. Some think they can present me with their shilling and that is enough, but their clothing and appearance would never be acceptable to a respectable housekeeper or house steward. I have taken their shilling, of course, for after all business is business, but if they have not taken my advice to be cleaner and smarter then they will never find a place of any respectability and I will certainly never recommend them to anyone of quality. I have already had one that quibbled over paying another shilling to stand longer on the books but I told him if he would smarten up his manner when he spoke with his next possible master that he was more likely to get a place. I have been luckier with some, however. One young girl came to me the very day that Lady Assheton had sent word for a scullery maid so that was the fastest two shillings I ever made.

For some it has been difficult to produce a character from their last employer, and not always their own fault. There are several wicked masters in this town who think the maid's duties extend to their own beds. I've had three young maids this week, in floods of tears, looking for a new position because they did not want to risk disgrace. I gave them the idea of appealing to their local vicar to speak for them instead, or even the housekeeper they worked under, but in some cases I am ashamed to say the housekeepers were not much better, happy to act as little more than procurers for their masters' pleasure.

I know it is difficult for many young girls in this town who have only known labour in the family weaving business, gathering cotton threads from under their father's loom, or helping their mothers with spinning, so there is no-one who can speak for them. It is fortunate I have been able to give these three girls a chance to work in my own kitchen and two I found diligent and clean, quick to learn although, sadly, totally illiterate. At least that means they can be trusted to deliver my notes to Mr. Harrop without needing to gossip about them. Not that there is anything to gossip about but in my experience the lower classes love nothing better than to gossip about their betters. The third one I had to dismiss for stealing from me. If it had been for her own family I would not have minded so much but she was taking my sugar and selling it in the town. I know people around here are dreadfully poor but I will not have dishonesty around me. She can think herself lucky she is not suffering her punishment from the Boroughreeve. It could have meant a whipping in the stocks, or even transportation.

1764 Feb 1st

I have thought myself that I am in need of more tools for my kitchen. At least a new salamander and two or three hair sieves. It really is too much of a struggle to make in a timely fashion all the foods required now. It is just impossible when I have a dinner to provide for. I am now very glad that Mr. Priestnall never came back to me for it gave me the time to take on a much better occasion.

A most elegant member of the best society has been recommended to my work and has commissioned me for a regular dinner for the surgeons and directors of the Infirmary. They have formed a committee with the intention of setting up an establishment for the confinement of Lunatics. It is a very important endeavour and I am honoured to be part of such an auspicious enterprise.

This town is such a surprising place, I vow every time I turn a corner something else is new. Businesses change from one to another as new ideas change how things are done. Sometimes I feel faint with the speed and could wish myself back in the country, though not for long. I wonder how I ever lived that way. It feels now as though I was sleeping through the days. Now I am so busy I long for a little more sleep, but the money I make is more than I ever expected to see in my lifetime and I would not have it any other way. With my cooking and my Register Office I feel I am in the centre of the world. Every day I see new ways of increasing our fortunes which is just as well because unfortunately there is a need for more to be spent on new dishes and pans to satisfy the demand for high quality dishes here in Manchester. More dishes will allow me to do more cooking, and then I will be able to take on more girls to help. There is certainly enough work already and I plan to make sure it only gets better for me and John. I just know that my receipt for Salmon the Newcastle way will be a big success here. I will write it out here that I can be sure to have it written out.

To pickle Salmon *the Newcastle Way.*

TAKE a Salmon about twelve Pounds, gut it, then cut off the Head, and cut it across in what Pieces you please, but don't split it; scrape the Blood from the Bone, and wash it well out, then tie it a-cross each Way, as you do Sturgeon, set on your Fish-pan with two quarts of Water, and three of strong Beer, half a Pound of Bay Salt, and one Pound of common Salt, when it boils scum it well, then put in as much Fish as your Liquor will cover, and when it is enough take it carefully out, lest you strip off the Skin, and lay it on Earthen Dishes; when you have done all your Fish, let it stand till the next Day, put it into Pots, add to the Liquor three Quarts of strong beer Allegar, half an Ounce of Mace, the same of Cloves and black Pepper, one Ounce of Long Pepper, two Ounces of white Ginger, sliced, boil them well together half an Hour, then pour it boiling hot upon your Fish, when cold cover it well with strong brown Paper. This will keep a whole Year.

1764 March 12th a ghost story

I am most vexed today, having received a letter from my oldest sister Jane. It seems that Papa is having trouble with an old cottage they have in Wadworth. Since he and mother went to live with Jane they have tried to rent out this house but no tenants will stay above a month. They all complain that it is haunted and flee in terror. I am confident that it is all utter nonsense. It is more likely to be a clever ruse to save paying the rent for Jane says that none of them has ever seen this supposed spirit. It always happens on the night of the full moon and was worse on All Souls' night.

Jane is asking for my help but I do not see what I can do from here in Manchester. She has asked that I go with her to sit in the house overnight so we can confront the ghost but I do not understand why she does not consult the local clergy, although if it is still Reverend Maddox he would be more full of spirit than any ghost. He was always over partial to his gin and would sleep through anything. Jane could have asked one of our sisters who live closer. It does not make sense for me to pay for travel across the country when Emma and Sarah only live a few miles away and could easily attend with her. She must ask them first, I will write and tell her so.

1764 March 20th

Jane has written to me again asking for help with the ghost. Her husband can ill afford for her to go but Emma is in London with the family she works for and Sarah cannot be spared from her position caring for a frail old lady who needs her night and day. There is nothing else for it, it must be either me or Mary, and dear Mary could not confront even a gentle spirit, her nature is far too tender. At least I can confidently leave her to keep my business going while I make the journey. I must grasp the nettle and book myself on the coach to Doncaster for the next full moon. Joshua can run down to Mr. Sheepley at the White Lion on Deansgate and secure me a ticket for the prior Saturday.

I will write to Jane that she must arrange to meet me from the coach and we can go together to the cottage. Once I have had chance to look around I will know better if anyone has been making mischief for I pride myself that I am a good judge of character. I daresay there will also be some cleaning we can do while we wait for this so-called apparition. Jane was never the most diligent in domestic service, more interested in ribbons and dresses. It did not work out for her when she married however, marrying a flax farmer and having a family all of boys.

1764 April 12th

Oh! My heart, my heart! I felt it was like to give way on me, it was beating so fast. Never was I more thankful that I had brought

John's little flask of brandy than last night. I hadn't truly believed I would see a spirit and if they do exist only my father's or my mother's would be the one I would want to meet. Jane and I sat together in the darkened bedroom reading out bible passages, only one candle between us to cast a little light but I swear that made the waiting worse, watching the dancing shadows and fancying each one to be the beginnings of an apparition.

What a fright it was when the noise began! At first I tried to believe it was the wind down the chimney, as the air had become markedly colder, but Jane had been a-twitter from the start. She screamed when she felt a draught and fainted clean away.

It was then I saw the outline of a young maid, a kind of shadow made form, and she was shaking a parchment at me. My blood ran cold and I too felt close to fainting but I held fast to Jane with one arm and gripped my Bible even tighter with my other hand. I knew I needed to summon all my courage to take care of whatever might happen next. I confess I had taken John's advice and had resorted to a modicum of Dutch courage beforehand, so I opened my Bible at the marked page, though I could hardly read the words in the dark. The candle was wavering madly and I was too frightened to take my eyes off the grey shape in front of me. I don't truly remember what happened next, but I do know I called out as much of the abjuration as I could.

'Who art thou, what wantest thou, speak, spirit, speak and I will listen.'

I fear my courage may have then deserted me for the next thing I remember was a feeling of peace coming into the room. The air felt warmer and I felt that the spirit had released its grip on the house. I said a prayer of thanks to God for his mercies and recited Psalm 23 as I turned to help Jane regain her composure. She and I shed a few tears together then finished the night singing our favourite hymns till dawn came. However certain I was that the spirit had gone, I was glad to leave there in the morning.

1764 May 4th progress and pregnancy

I heard tell today in the Market Place of two men from Leigh who have designed a marvelous invention to increase the work of the spinners, that is to say, to make the same effort produce more thread. It is called a Spinning Jenny, an affectionate name for an engine, and it will be of the most use to the weavers, who I have heard complain about the shortage of good yarn since Mr. Kay of

Bury invented the Flying Shuttle thirty years since. It has taken long enough for these clever men to come up with an improvement.

It is another Mr. Kay, of Leigh, who although is no relation to the previous inventor, is similarly skilled in mechanical work. He was commissioned by his neighbour Thomas Highs to construct a spinning engine to his design.

This other man, Thomas Highs, I have never heard of before but the tale is that he is a veritable Leonardo Da Vinci in his inventions. I will listen out for that man's name in the future, for surely he will become famous if he is so clever. I am certain he must venture to Manchester before long for it is surely the beating heart of all the business around.

There are men here who could buy and sell better than any. I have seen them as I pass by the Bull's Head in the Market Place and I would give anything to hear what is being said in the meeting rooms there, all our town business is decided there and I would find it fascinating. If I offered to provide some food for their meetings it would put my skills in front of some important men. I will approach the landlord there and offer my services. Manchester is a cradle of progress and I am determined to progress with it.

1764 June 13th

I am glad to be at last sitting down for today has been a hard busy day, and just when I was not feeling my best. I felt very sickly this morning and did not wish to take a purgative. I knew I did not have time to be forever squatting so I battled through it. Roasting up the meat was making me worse so I had Mary to take over that while I worked on the puff paste until the feeling passed. I hope it does not happen tomorrow, I cannot afford the time to be ill.

I did have some good news that brightened me up, from my old friend Ann Worsley. I had not expected to hear anymore from Arley Hall though it is often in my thoughts. Ann writes that Sir Peter has arranged for a new cottage to be built away from the Hall in order that the next gardener does not mix as freely with the housemaids. I knew Sir Peter was not well pleased when I took John from him but he must be very angry to pay for a new home for the next one. I feel certain that whoever is employed he will not be tempted by the new housekeeper. She has a face that will curdle milk, and a manner to match. I surmise it was those qualities alone that procured her the job after me, for I did not see much evidence of her cooking skills while I was there.

Ann does not say how she is doing but I can tell from what she says of Lady Betty that she is not well pleased with her. I will not feel any guilt however, we were only acting under their own rules. If they had built that house when John and I were there perhaps we would have stayed, though I could not now go back to that way of life, even if John would. I sometimes think he misses being in charge of the men and respected by Sir Peter for his skills. There is not the same regard here but I have so much more. It is harder work, that is true, but there is profit and progress and it is exciting to be where that is happening everyday. Manchester is the place for me now and where we can become masters instead of forever servants.

1764 July 6th Pregnant again

Today has been a day of very mixed feelings, from the joy this morning at Mrs. Withnall's pronouncement that I am once again pregnant to the fear of how it may end. It was also the day of the Rev Assheton's funeral so I called into church to pay my respects to him and offered up a fervent prayer of my own that this time I will produce a live child. This time I will take Mrs. W's advice on how best to effect a good outcome. I will take whatever advice I can get for I am determined to prove to John that I am not too old to produce a son for him. Of course I also took to the funeral some of the reverend's favourite cheesecakes, to give to his colleagues. Either they will put me in good favour with their Master for my own cause, or at the very least remind them of my name and business.

On another sad note I was distressed to hear some drastic news from my dear friend Ann Worsley that Sir Peter has cut back on servant numbers at Arley Hall. All the dairymaids have gone, and the laundry maids. He has decided they would no longer run these offices and many of the grooms' boys have gone, for they no longer keep a full stable. Ann does not say in so many words the reason why she thinks it has happened but she does not have to. I believe I can read between the lines that it is the Taylors who have wormed their way into Sir Peter's employ. They are not the best money managers I have seen, especially Mrs. Taylor who, according to Ann has the purse strings in a tight grip and for a housekeeper goes above and beyond her station. For all she says about the need to keep spending in check, very little is coming to table but much is being spent.

Ann has her suspicions but as Mrs. Taylor has charge of the

female servants and her husband, as butler, has overall control, no-one is in a position to criticise, least of all Ann, who is feeling her age dreadfully and is not sure how much longer she can carry on working. She has a brother over Knutsford way that she will need to apply to, and he must for duty's sake take her in. I will reply to her letter tonight with a little encouragement.

1764 Aug 16th Register office insult

I am beside myself with temper tonight, having had a very irksome visit from that woman, Mrs. Blomely today, more irksome than usual. In fact, I am still uncertain how I shall respond to her sly accusations. She called to my house on the pretext of introducing her pupils to 'the most excellent Mrs. Raffald's', but then took great delight in regaling me with an account of the play she saw enacted at the theatre last evening.

She had been much taken by a short scene from Mr Joseph Reed's play, The Register Office, a scurrilous tale that has been playing in London for several years. The play puts all register offices under the same cloud of suspicion. Just because there are some disreputable offices in the capital, he should not be allowed to slander honest, respectable people.

In this Manchester version, as Mrs. B delighted in telling me, the main character was tellingly named Marjorie Moorpout, played by her great friend Mrs. Love. She acted as a housekeeper from Yorkshire seeking work at a Register Office, one known for procuring people for a different kind of service. It was a decided slight upon me, that's for certain. I am the only Yorkshirewoman around who runs a register office. Mrs B was determined to put me at a disadvantage, repeatedly mentioning the Yorkshire housekeeper and denying it could be me that was meant but saying how terrible an insult it was all the same.

She was unable to keep the smirk off her face and I vow I was just about to lose my composure when my sister Mary stepped in to thank her for her concern, but desired her to mention no more and to desist from spreading evil gossip. Mary has such a better temper than I for she knows how I get fired up when I am riled. I thank God for her intervention for in another minute more I am sure a pan would have left my fingers towards the woman's head. Now I saw Mrs. B's motive in coming to see me. It was no doubt she who suggested to Mrs. Love to add the little detail to the original script. I imagine they had a fine laugh over it.

Now I must find out how I can prevent the slander from being repeated. I shall go to Mr. Harrop's directly he opens his office to ask his advice. He will know to whom I can apply for justice. I am outraged that they can so easily blacken a respectable woman's character. It must not be allowed, although John says I am being too serious, that anyone who knows me will know if does not refer to me. He says I could never be perceived in such lewd terms, but I have a reputation to protect and I will allow nothing to damage it. A good reputation, once lost, can never be recovered. Mud that is slung is very difficult to remove.

I must act immediately to put this right and Mrs. Love must be made to issue me with an apology. I do not wish any of the gentry hereabouts to get the wrong idea about my service, or any servants to think they are applying to me for anything other than a decent position with good families. My goodness, I doubt I shall sleep tonight, my temper is up and I am ready to fight. Someone will suffer for this. Oh, how I wish it were that woman. I would give anything to be able to wipe that smirk from her face for I know she did take the gossip into the market place. I had more than one commiserate with me afterwards, and they were not ones who may have seen it at the theatre. John has no idea how serious this matter is, but he will find out when he tries his usual moves tonight that he is dining on cold shoulder and not juicy rump. Laugh it off, indeed that I cannot.

1764 Aug 25th

The news in the Mercury, of advice from the colonies, has caused me to change my mind about the possibilities there. The most dreadful barbarism goes on there and I cannot imagine how those settlers can cope with the dangers. In Williamsburgh, Virginia, the incursions by the Indian natives are frequent and bloody. I will include the article here so I may keep the memory of what happens, though it does not make for very pleasant reading.

> A Letter from Carlisle says, that the Enemy in these parts being closely pursued, killed their Prisoners, on the flight, to the Number of six or seven, then scattered as usual, and made their escape. Advices from all Parts are truly distressing, the Indians killing and captivating daily. About eight Days past upwards of 40 Persons

were killed in the Pastures, on the Frontiers of Augusta Country. The Indians came on Friday last, above seven miles from me and took one Man's Wife and four Children. Next morning about Sun-rise, four Families going to a Fort with Horses laden, the Indians way-layed them, and killed and captivated 21, whose names were Lloyd and his Family, Clouper, Jones, Thomas, etc. This morning about two o'clock, I was informed, that about Sun-set Yesterday, six Families were cut off near the Narrow Passage. Two Companies of Men are gone after the enemy, to retake the captives if possible, of which there is as yet no Account.

From Fort Cumberland we are informed, that a large Body of Indians fell on a Party of white People working in a Field near Fort Dinwiddie, in Augusta Country, Virginia, where they killed fifteen, and wounded and took sixteen more; they then attacked the Fort, and fired six Hours successfully on it, but could not prevail.

It all sounds dreadful, just dreadful, I will say a prayer for the poor settlers who live under such threats of attacks, imprisonment and who knows what treatment at the hands of the savages. Please God our brave soldiers will prevail.

1764 Sept 21st

I am most disappointed with our justice system. It appears that there is no-one I can apply to for justice because I have been offended. Mr. Harrop has advised me that because the play has been authorised by the London censors it is perfectly admissible to reproduce any scene from it. It is most unfair but if the law would not allow me an answer then I made sure that the actors would.

Thankfully Mr. Love, the theatre manager, saw sense when I spoke to him and explained the predicament. He agreed that the original play did not specify a 'Yorkshire housekeeper' looking for work. That point I am certain was adjusted for this locality, and must be aimed at me, for in little over a year I have become very well known here. I am the only Yorkshirewoman who runs a register office so it cannot be taken any other way. He said it had been his wife's suggestion, as I knew it must be, and he has agreed to tell his wife not to repeat her performance.

I fear the damage has been done, however. I have already had to endure several lewd persons asking for special services. They got a special service from me, for sure. Their ears were burning as they were driven from my establishment with clear instructions never to return without a civil tongue in their heads and respect for a decent business, such as I have.

It is clearly not enough to wait for the fuss to die down, as John suggested, I must take steps to inform the world that I, Elizabeth Raffald, am not running a bawdy house but a respectable service where decent people obtain genuine employment in good families. I will apply myself to devise a way of achieving that purpose.

1764 Oct 10th

At last I have thought of a means to quell the spiteful rumours still circulating about my register office. My first thought was to take a front page advertisement in the Mercury, but Mr. Harrop has advised against it. He said it may look like too much protesting and I was forced to concede he may be right. I have decided to act like a lady and insert a simple rebuttal in my usual advertisement, but in such words that it is not seen as a reply to the insult, rather that I have risen above it. It will be meaningful but not obvious. I shall simply announce my stock of brawn, etc, and add a sentence or two.

'As several of Mrs. Raffald's friends in the Country have mistook the Terms and Design of her REGISTER OFFICE. She begs leave to inform them that she supplies Families with Servants, for any Place, for One Shilling for each; and Servants with Places for One Shilling each.'

In that way I have an advertisement for the Office and the Brawn and anyone who reads it will know clearly the terms of my office with nothing to be misunderstood. Servants may obtain good places and families gain honest servants. It makes it simple, clear and dignified, no stooping to the level of the gossip or harridan. I am a respectable woman and I will stay that way to my dying day despite what mischief anyone may try to make for me.

1764 Dec babies

Today I must not stay long at my writing for I have my sewing to progress. I have tried to find the time for it but work keeps me so busy I have scarce had a moment. I do so want to do justice to the fine cotton lawn my eldest sister Sarah sent for my first baby's christening robe, for now Mrs. Withnall assures me that I have passed the most dangerous time, I feel more confident that I will have a baby to dress in it.

This baby will have the finest gown I can produce. My sister Mary is working on a bonnet, which must be a difficult thing for her to do, making clothes for my baby when she is never likely to have one of her own. She is very dear to me and I know she will love my baby as her own. She assures me she has quite reconciled herself to the idea that it was not in God's plan for her to marry and have her own family, but that she is quite content to enjoy the children of her sisters and she loves them all as her own.

Our dear sister Jane sent the instructions that she used for the gown for her first child, William, and I am sure that I can do whatever Jane can. All I need is another hour or two in each day. Business is so overwhelmingly busy that I am unable to follow Mrs. Withnall's advice to rest whenever I can. That might be good advice to society ladies but a working woman such as myself has no time for such niceties, and certainly not a woman such as myself, who is building up a business and reputation.

Having babies is nature's way and I am not the only busy woman that has ever given birth so I must trust in God's love and pray that I am worthy to be so blessed. I am sure this baby is a big healthy boy for he is forever moving inside my belly, and always pushing at my side as though he would come out that way, so impatient is he to be born and join his daddy in business.

Mrs. Withnall comforts me that his strength bodes well for an easy birth passage. Her job will be to hold him back so he does not damage me on his way into the world. It sounds most frightening but it is God's will and my duty as a woman so I must face it with courage as many women have before me. And then I must add the duties of a mother to my already long list of jobs; cooking, servants' register office, school instructor and wife, a woman's work is truly never done.

1765

1765 Jan 18th Sarah born

Praise be, I was delivered of a healthy baby two days ago, although not the strong, healthy boy I was certain it was. We have a girl, a beautiful little thing and I have decided to name her for my eldest sister, Sarah. God willing my little mite will grow as strong and healthy as her namesake, although without some good

Yorkshire air in her lungs she may not. This Manchester air can often be foul with the fumes from the constant coal fires they have here. I will write to Sarah and see if she might take her for a time once she is weaned from me. It would be good for both of them.

For now I must be content that I have gone through this pregnancy without any affliction. When I had a bleeding twice last year I feared I would never give John a son and heir. At least with this child I have shown I am capable and God willing a son will come next. John is proud enough to show off his manliness, that he can father a child but, oh, the agonies I suffered. I hope he is not in too much of a hurry to begin his son, I confess I believed I would be ripped apart at times, the pains were so great. Heaven knows what I was screaming but I will never forget Mrs. W's words. 'Less noise, Mrs. Raffald, and more pushing when I tell you and we may get this baby out soon.'

I have heard women cry in childbirth and always believed it was their delicacy that made them unable to bear the pain, but I have never considered myself delicate and that pain was from deep within me, from parts of me that I did not know felt pain. My nether regions are sore even with the poultice my sister Mary prepared under advice from Mrs. Withnall.

I was never so glad that Mary is living with us. She is managing to keep most of the business going, for I cannot perform any cooking from my bed. She has promised that tomorrow she will bring me some sugar to work so that I may at least help her by refining some sugar. I only wish I could make up some pyes because my pastry is surely superior to hers, she does not have the light touch that is necessary. However, Mrs. W has quite dictated terms to me to rest, so until she allows it I must content myself to stay still, however much I am concerned for my business.

I must keep my temper with Mary until I am fit to go back to my kitchen for without her I might lose my customers to unscrupulous practices, of which that Blomeley woman is mistress. I hear she is planning to visit me very soon so I must paint on a smile and bear it with fortitude. Mary must cover up any details of customers when she is about, and forbid the kitchen maids to tell her anything, anything at all. I will not allow that woman to spoil this time. I have been blessed and I think some measure of my success must be given to the midwifery practices here which are quite progressive.

Other births I have attended have observed the traditions of enclosing the mother in dark rooms kept stuffy to keep out draughts from mother and baby. Extra cloths are draped at the windows, the fire is kept banked and as many friends and attendants as can fit in the room are allowed. I have never wanted a crowd at a time when my nether regions are exposed and I have often thought that keeping out good fresh air would be more likely to produce a fever than to prevent one, but that was in Yorkshire where the air was more wholesome than it is here, and it is not my place to contradict experienced physicians.

I have always thought it a bad practice to feed the mother with strong liquor too. Whatever the reason, no good ever came from strong drink. I count myself fortunate that Mrs. Withnall, has worked with the man-midwife, Doctor Charles White, a very knowledgeable man in Manchester, who has led the field in making great improvements in the lying-in practices for new mothers.

Mrs. Withnall attended me excellently and through all the pains she reassured me that it was all going well. Only afterwards did she confess that if I had not held back when she told me to, I would have been ruptured badly by the baby pushing her way out. I am glad she was strong, I had a dread of needing those forceps designed by Doctor Smellie. Mrs. W was telling me stories of several women she knew who had succumbed to inflammation of the womb when they were applied too suddenly or forcibly.

Only last year John Armstrong lost his wife to puerperal fever after they were used for their third child. Poor woman, she suffered for twenty days before the disease released her to a painful death. Mrs. Withnall says there are many who cling to the old ways who also suffer with the fever, so I consider myself fortunate indeed to have found a good woman to trust with my life. When I get the chance I will write to Doctor White to commend him for his actions, radical but of great usefulness.

1765 Mar 12th

I read today a most interesting article in a pamphlet given to me by Mr. Harrop. It had originated from the colonies in America and was protesting against the current Sugar tax and a proposed Stamp tax. I do not see why they should not be subject to taxes as we all are, though I wish they would remove them altogether. Sugar is such an expence and is useful in so many dishes, especially decorative confectionaries

The new tax proposes that all printed materials in the colonies must be produced only on stamped paper, from London, which carries an embossed revenue stamp. This includes legal documents, of course, but also magazines, newspapers, even playing cards, and the tax must be paid in our own British currency not in colonial paper money. The pamphlet explained that the tax is to fund our troops still stationed there to protect the colonies after our victory in the French and Indian War, which has been called the Seven Years War though I do think that England is likely to always be at war with France.

Mr. Harrop reports that the colonies have rebuffed the idea that there are any foreign enemies in their country and that they are quite capable of protecting themselves. How ungrateful! They have the nerve to suggest, apparently, that Britain is asking them to support British soldiers who no longer have a role to play now that the war is over. Who is to say there will not be another one?

It appears that the colonies are most incensed that they have no say over the taxation because it is being imposed upon them by a government in which they have no representation. 'No taxation without representation' is their cry. They should try being poor, or a woman, and they still would have no representation. Who pleads for us? We all have to pay these taxes whether we like to or not.

I do fear this bodes ill for those who have taken their chances in the colonies. As soon as one threat is vanquished another is appearing. I do not see how this can end well, for surely, if they persist in rebelling the army will be put to good use to maintain order. Britain was not afraid to rout a pretender to the throne in '45, so I doubt they will shy away from a fight with a few renegades, if that's what it comes to. I dearly hope not.

1765 May 25th idea for a school

Mr. Green the writing master called to me today for some roast larks for his tea and he told me all about the building work going on at Daub holes, where they are constructing the Lunatic Asylum alongside the Manchester Infirmary. He looked quite frail, poor man; it seems some of his customers are not paying him as promptly as he needs. I took a little pity on him and gave him an extra lark. I do believe mine are superior to most as my recipes are my own devising.

To roast Larks.

> *PUT a Dozen of Larks on a Skewer, tie it to the Spit at both Ends, dredge and baste them, let them roast ten Minutes, take the Crumbs of a Half-penny Loaf, with a Piece of Butter the Size of a Walnut, put it in a Tossing Pan, and shake it over a gentle Fire till they are a light brown, lay them betwixt your Birds, and pour over them a little melted Butter.*

Mr. Green is such a kind gentleman, so polite and well spoken that it is a pleasure to deal with him. He would be an excellent addition to any school and I will keep him in mind for mine. It has become plain to me that I must next establish a school, for this town is in dire need of good education for its daughters. I shall certainly offer him the opportunity to be the writing master for me.

At the moment that prospect seems unlikely while I struggle to keep up with my duties as a mother. I swear that baby is always attached to me. A lusty baby, it seems, needs more nourishment than a small baby, however adverse that seems. If she does not give me some respite soon I feel I may be queuing up to be the first patient of that lunatic asylum.

1765 July 1st

I heard today that Mrs. Blomely's school is not doing well, poor woman. The last few girls that were enrolled have not even reached her low standards. Of course it's all dependant upon the teaching and I'm sure that if I put myself to it I would make an infinitely better job of it. I must say my dinners are keeping me very busy most days and I think it is time I looked for bigger premises. It is becoming intolerable in this small room to be producing so many dishes with only two kitchen maids to help.

My sister Mary has been a boon to me but business is doing so well that I need bigger premises to allow for more girls to work for me, and somewhere with room to accommodate a school. Now, then I would show that woman how it is done.

1765 Aug 3rd pregnant with Emma

I am certain now that I have begun with another baby. It has been a long time since my last bleed and the wave of sickness that overcame me this morning was unmistakable. Please God this will be a brother for Sarah. John is keen for a son to teach his business to, but if I do my part then he must do his.

He is becoming less and less interested in helping James and George on the market stall and more interested in meeting up with some flash kinds at the cock pit behind the Marketplace. If he thinks he will make his fortune there I must have words with him to make it clear what I expect from him.

He is already quite free with taking such of our income that has come from my endeavours but if he will not listen to my advice he is going to find that there will be a drop in my business takings. I will not allow good money to go after bad, and I know him to be a man of intelligence so perhaps he will listen to me if I put it to him in clear terms.

I will remind him of our intentions when we began to dream of a better life outside service to others. Our dream was to have part of the wealth that we heard of others making from their own labour. I must bring him back to good man I know he is.

1765 Oct 15th America

The Mercury today carried a most disturbing report from the American colonies. Virginia seems a most lawless state from the proclamation they have issued. It was reported that the Virginia people have issued Resolves to stand against British taxation.

> Resolved, That the first Adventurers and Settlers of this his majesty's colony and Dominion of Virginia brought with them, and transmitted to their Posterity, and all other his Majesty's subjects since inhabiting in this his Majesty's said Colony, all the Liberties, privileges, Franchises, and Immunities that have at any Time been held, enjoyed, and possessed, by the People of Great Britain.
>
> Resolved, That by the two royal Charters, granted by King James the First, the Colonists aforesaid are declared entitled to all Liberties, Privileges, and Immunities of Denizens and natural Subjects, to all Intents and Purposes, as if they had been abiding and born within the Realm of England.
>
> Resolved, That the Taxation of the People by themselves, or by Persons chosen by themselves to represent them, who could only know what Taxes the

People are able to bear, or the easiest method of raising them, and must themselves be affected by every Tax laid on the People, is the only Security against a burdensome Taxation, and the distinguishing characteristick of British Freedom, without which the ancient Constitution cannot exist.

Resolved, That his majesty's liege people of this his most ancient and loyal Colony have without interruption enjoyed the inestimable Right of being governed by such Laws, respecting their internal Polity and Taxation, as are derived from their own Consent, with the Approbation of their Sovereign, or his Substitute; and that the same hath never been forfeited or yielded up, but hath been constantly recognized by the King and People of Great Britain.

1765 Nov 5th reports of the Boston Massacre
Oh my, the news from America gets ever worse. The Mercury today contained reports of riots over the taxation without representation.

A mob, in Boston, were violent in their dismissal of a British Stamp distributor, Andrew Oliver. The man was hanged in effigy on August 14, 1765 "from a giant elm tree at the crossing of Essex and Orange Streets in the city's South End. All day the crowd toured merchants on Orange Street to have their goods symbolically stamped under the elm tree, which later became known as the "Liberty Tree". The crowd then cut down the effigy of Andrew Oliver, and took it in a funeral procession to the Town House where the legislature met. From there, they went to Mr. Oliver's office—which they tore down and symbolically stamped the timbers. Next, they took the effigy to Oliver's home at the foot of Fort Hill, where they beheaded it and then burned it—along with Mr. Oliver's stable house and coach and chaise. The mob then looted and destroyed the contents of his house. Mr. Oliver asked to be relieved of his duties the next day. This resignation, however, was not enough. He was forced to be paraded through the streets and to publicly resign under the Liberty Tree. This seems to have been just the beginning, more violence and threats of aggressive acts spread throughout the colonies, with some organised groups of resistance, made of members of the middle and upper classes of society who have formed the

> foundation for these groups and called themselves the Sons of
> Liberty. They have burned effigies of royal officials, forced
> Stamp Act collectors to resign, and made businessmen and
> judges to go about without using the proper stamps
> demanded by Parliament

It is dreadful how lawless those colonies have become and I do
not doubt that British forces will be raised enough to squash this
rebellion. They cannot say there is nothing for the soldiery to do
now.

1765 Dec 7th

These days I have more immediate concerns than the troubles
abroad. There can be no doubt now that I am carrying my next
child. God willing this child will be our son, a brother for our little
Sarah.

Mrs. Withnall predicts another three or four months to the birth
so I was barely five months from one to another. I never expected to
catch again so soon but Mrs. Withnall says that once the pathway is
eased, the passage of more becomes easier. I am grateful to be
blessed with babies but it is tremendous hard on a woman trying to
keep a business going as well as having babies.

I must get myself some more help before I become too big to
work near the fire. It will cut into my profits but it is better to keep
business running well so that my customers, who are becoming
more numerous every week, do not lose faith with Mrs. Raffald's
ability to keep them supplied with high quality dishes.

1766

1766 Jan 10th

I had the most interesting conversation with Mr. Harrop when I
called to his office this week. I needed to correct the wording on my
last advertisement. The type he used may have been overused, for
the word Newcastle had turned out most peculiar. It could have
been Newcase which could mean something altogether different.

He believes that we could come to some agreement on the
printing of a book of cookery. I could not believe that there was a
market enough for another book, although I have always thought
that some are very badly worded, particularly those written by men

cooks. They are so accustomed to working in fine houses, with a full range of servants and equipment that they have no understanding of the trials of a smaller household. I understand the needs of the middling household, these new families who thrive in Manchester, and my customers are frequently asking me for details of my receipts, so I do believe I could be the person to do it.

Mr. Harrop assured me of the public appetite for printed matter now that more people are able to read for themselves. The flimsy chap books that he prints are not enough to keep him in business and he was seeking a substantial book to print. He seeks a continuous supply of works and is keen to be seen as the source of books of knowledge that this new audience now demands. The business is there for him if he can but find the authors to produce the work for print. He said that with my reputation for food, well known to be of the highest quality, and skill with the written word we would find a ready market, not just in Manchester, but in the whole country.

I do believe that the knowledge I have to impart could be said better than some of the volumes that are already in print. Some of them are written in words of such high style or glossed over with hard names that it would be impossible to understand them if the reader has no education in such matters.

In my time as a housekeeper I saw several books of instruction, all written by men cooks with omissions of practice that would be necessary for a woman. As all but the best houses must have a woman cook and the housekeeper will always be a woman, it stands to reason that it is a woman who needs to understand the instructions. I am such a person to write those instructions. I understand what is difficult for a woman to do, and how much heat it is possible to stand without fainting away. I can also write instruction that any may understand.

I will confess I had already thought of the possibility of such a thing before, but time is money and I am already busy with the work I have. I have one child only just twelve months old and another soon to join us, God willing, so I do not think I can manage it at present but it is a thing to think of for the future.

1766 Feb 4th

The American question becomes ever more vexed. Reports today in the Mercury tell of the latest progress in the matter of the colonies refusal to honour the Stamp tax. After a meeting of the

Stamp Act Congress of the American Colonies in New York October last, they issued a Declaration of Rights and Grievances, claiming Parliament didn't have the right to impose the tax because it didn't include representation from the colonies.

Here in Britain, our Prime Minister, Rockingham, and his secretary Edmund Burke, organized London merchants to start a committee of correspondence to support repeal of the Stamp Act by urging merchants throughout the country to contact their local representatives in Parliament. When Parliament reconvened on January 14, 1766, the Rockingham ministry formally proposed repeal. The House of Commons has now heard testimony from witnesses, one being Benjamin Franklin, a representative from the colony of Pennsylvania. He responded to the question about how the colonists would react if the Act was not repealed and answered:

"A total loss of the respect and affection the people of America bear to this country, and of all the commerce that depends on that respect and affection."

I do hope it is settled amicably on both sides for men can become so entrenched in their views if not moderated by common sense.

1766 Mar 8th giving birth

Oh me, that is one experience that is better behind me than in front. I have another daughter, praise be. She is a healthy baby who looks for all the world like her uncle George, John's brother. I thought this time I was prepared for the agony but the pain continued for a day and a night, finally ending as dawn on the second day brought a little light to us. Mrs. Withnall would tell me nothing while I suffered and only after I had slept did she tell me how lucky I was to deliver safely.

I had thought a second birth would be easier, everyone told me it would be, but it was not so for me. Little Emma, as we have named her, had twisted herself round and round so tight that every time she tried to come out the cord held her fast by the neck. It took all Mrs. W's skill as a midwife to deliver her still alive and keep me from expiring due to loss of blood.

Of course her worry was intensified due to the experience she has of the undernourished local women that are hereabouts. They have never had to survive tough Yorkshire winters with winds that can cut you through. I think I was given extra helpings of Yorkshire grit as all my life I seem to have been the toughest of all my sisters.

It was always me on whose shoulders the responsibility would rest even though I was only a middle child. It was always me who my mother would ask to take charge. I often think I should have been born the son that my dear papa always wanted. He and I were kindred spirits in our family and I pray that I may be blessed enough to provide John with a son who we will call Joshua for my father. Luckily it is John's father's name too so I will get no argument from him.

Heavens, what am I saying, another baby? Please God I get more time to recover from this one than I did from the first one, although from what Mrs. W said, I am badly torn and will need a long time to recover fully before John comes to call on me again. He will not be happy about that but it cannot be helped.

Maybe I can persuade him to take an extra nip or two of spirits of an evening. That should send him off to sleep. And he always falls asleep easily after a good dish of Sweetbreads-a-la-daub, especially with a little enriching in the gravy to make him drowsy. It is a receipt I can be sure will satisfy him. He may find he is eating very well indeed for the next few months.

Sweet-Breads *a-la-daub.*

TAKE three of the largest and finest Sweet-breads you can get, put them in a Sauce Pan of boiling Water for five Minutes, then take them out, and when they are cold lard them with a Row down the Middle, with very little Pieces of Bacon, then a Row on each Side with Lemon Peel cut the Size of Wheat Straw; then a Row on each Side of Pickled Cucumbers, cut very fine, put them in a Tossing Pan, with good Veal Gravy, a little Juice of Lemon, a Spoonful of Browning, stew them gently a Quarter of an Hour; a little before they are ready thicken them with Flour and Butter, dish them up and pour the Gravy over, lay round them Bunches of boiled Celery, or Oyster Patties: garnish with stewed Spinach, green coloured Parsley, stick a Bunch of Barberries in the Middle of each Sweet-bread. It is a pretty Corner Dish for either Dinner or Supper.

1766 April 21ˢᵗ

Oh I did enjoy church today. It was the first day I truly felt recovered enough to walk there. My two babies were dressed in clean white dresses and little Sarah looked ever so pretty. Young

Emma was quiet for I made sure to feed her before the service and I had on a new dress that was made for me by Mistress Miller, such a good needlewoman. She was happy to take a good price in exchange for a supply of confectioneries, to eke out her own cooking. She would rather sit with needle and thread and has no skills with dainties, whereas I am just the opposite. Each to their talent and the world turns a little more easily, it seems.

The Reverend Doctor Peploe gave a rousing speech to raise funds for the Manchester Infirmary, and he was excellent in his oratory on the need for support. We are fortunate to have excellent physicians in the town and they have such great plans for improvements. Every church and chapel in the neighbourhood was taking part in the fundraising on the same day. I added my small token of support to the collection and saw that the collection plates were overflowing by the time they carried it back to the altar.

The infirmary is going from strength to strength now it has added the lunatic asylum to its services and soon it will be taking in the first patients. Much credit must go to Mr. Charles White, a most superior surgeon and knowledgeable man midwife. This progress is all thanks to him, with the support of Mr. Bancroft.

1766 May 2nd

Praise be, Parliament has seen sense to settle the American question and withdraw the Stamp tax, given the Royal seal by King George. Perhaps now the American colonies can settle to becoming a safe place for settlers to trade and prosper, although I am still not sure I see my future there.

So much of the news that comes from there suggests a very hostile environment and Parliament are still not allowing the Colonies to govern as they would like. Parliament has declared it will act for the colonies with an Act called the Declaratory Act. This says Parliament's authority is the same in America as it is in Britain and it can pass laws that are binding on the American colonies. Mr. Harrop says this is not likely to be accepted and there will be yet more disagreements to come as any edicts will be opposed by the colonists.

1766 June 14th

Today was a momentous day for the poor demented of this town. I heard it from the Widow Dalton who got it from Mr. Ainsworth who was passing through Daub Holes as it happened.

The first patients have been admitted to our town's proud new lunatic asylum. All credit to Doctor Charles White, foremost among surgeons, for his influence on the modernisation of medical practices. This town will rival any in England and be at the forefront of any innovations.

Dear Ann Worsley has written to me with an invite to call at Arley Hall, when I am able. I had written to her about my idea for a book of cookery instruction and Ann is certain Lady Betty would bestow her patronage on it if I were to ask. She wrote that Lady Betty will be most pleased to receive me as soon as I can go, so I must set about making my arrangements. It is a good opportunity that I must not miss and it gives me hunger yet another venture. It I can but keep John away from me for long enough to complete one thing without getting with another baby I might yet make us our fortune.

1766 July 7th Visit to Arley Hall

Oh, what an exciting day I've had today! I took a carriage! Me, as if I was a fine lady. What airs, what graces I felt as I stepped into the carriage in front of everyone. Of course, I needed to set off early so there weren't as many as I would have liked but still, for those that were there it must have made a great impression on them, especially those of weaker minds. This may not have been my first time in a carriage, but it was the first time in a private carriage that was hired just for my use and paid for with money from my business. Now that is what I call success, and after only a few years away. I am certain it will be noticed in Arley.

John was a little curious as to where the money had come from but I told a little lie and said it was an advance from Mr. Harrop for the book he wishes me to write. He wholeheartedly approved Ann's suggestion that I reclaim my connection with Lady Betty. He said it would give my book a much better standing. John knows it is important to the success of the book but he didn't approve of my trip. He said I was getting above myself to presume on visiting, but how else was I to ask Lady Betty for her patronage? He does not understand that it is not the thing to do in a letter. Once I explained the money that could be made from my endeavour, John was quite content.

I intended to flatter her and persuade her how highly I value her advice, and ask her agreement to some changes I wish to make to certain of her recipes. She was so kind as to furnish me with some of her own family recipes and I must not take that honour lightly. It was also an important opportunity for me to have another look at the housekeeper's receipt book there. It is a very useful book of dishes suitable for important occasions, to which I had added a few of my own.

The carriage I took was not the most comfortable and once we left the town roads, many of the country roads were so rutted up by carts that I was fairly shaken to pieces before we had gone many miles. I was thankful when the driver stopped at an inn on the Chester road to water his horses. It also gave me chance to compose myself and put straight my bonnet which had slipped during the unmerciful bumping about that I had endured.

Country inns are so different from town inns. There is nothing much going on until the coach arrives and then it is all activity. One of the London coaches arrived while I was there. It was headed to Liverpool by the sound of the voices, a very unnatural accent to my ears. The Manchester accent is flat enough but the Liverpool voice is such a mix of accents from all over the world that it sounds as though it isn't sure which continent it belongs to.

I was grateful when I was back in the privacy of my own coach and very soon we were in sight of dearest Arley Hall. What a delight to the senses it was as we drove through the village, people craning their necks to see who it was in the fine carriage. I saw Mary Burgess pass by and I know she was shocked when she saw it was me in the carriage. She recovered herself in time to return my nod before we had passed by. I doubt it took much time before the whole village knew I had arrived in a fine carriage.

I had instructed the coachman to drive direct to the stable yard even though Lady Betty had very kindly offered that I would be welcomed as an honoured guest. When it came to the moment I did not feel it was right for me to call at the front door. I went directly into the servants' kitchen where I knew my way.

Oh what a shock to the senses to be back in those familiar surroundings again! Nothing had changed and I felt an overwhelming nostalgia for the fineness of what I used to have at my disposal. Manchester has nothing on the level that Arley possesses, not even in the home of Sir Thomas Egerton, Knight of the Shire. I felt tears welling up within me and it was all I could do to keep my composure. Everything was so familiar yet everything was changed; the scents of the hallways, of polish mixed with cooking smells; the sight of the old familiar chairs at the kitchen table; the gleam of the copper pans hung on the walls, though I might say not as much of a gleam as when I was there. This was not my home any more.

The room was all bustle as I entered. An older woman was shouting orders to two young maids as they were preparing dishes for Lady Betty and her guest. They stopped work to look up at me but I did not recognize any of their faces. The cook, for such she told me she was, passed a few pleasantries with me then bade me wait in the housekeeper's sitting room while she sent one of the girls to fetch Mrs. Taylor, the current incumbent. I confess, having read Ann Worsley's pen portrait of the woman I was keen to meet her.

Of course I knew where the room was but I felt quite taken aback to be standing outside my old room, my domain. Once more I felt myself at risk of being overcome by tears. I felt so out of place, so wrong to be there as a guest that I could almost have wished the clock turned back three years and nothing changed. It was only the remembrance of my beautiful babies at home and my success in business that brought me to myself. I could not wish those away and I held my head high.

The sitting room was not as I had kept it, of course. It was dressed in the fussiest style with touches of lace everywhere and the most garish colour of green on the chair cover. Thankfully Mrs. Taylor wasn't there, of course, she would no doubt be supervising the upstairs maids. I quickly looked around for the receipt book that I knew must be in her safekeeping, but before many minutes had passed one of the maids was back with a message for me. As I knew the way, I was to take myself to the front hall where the butler Mr. Taylor was waiting for me. Well! It seems I'm neither fish nor fowl in this house! I went straightaway to the hall where Mr. Taylor stood, haughty and mute. At least he had the manners to take my outdoor clothes before he took me in to meet Lady Betty.

He showed me into the sitting room and I was pleased to see my good friend Ann Worsley sitting with Lady Betty. She has become a good companion rather than simply a lady's maid. It is not Lady Betty's way to stand on ceremony all the time and she greeted me warmly, as she might an old friend. She is a good-hearted woman and my visit made me realize how much I miss her and Ann.

She was graciousness itself and made enquiries after Mr. Raffald and my girls. She was very interested in hearing how I had adapted to working in a trade. I answered her to my best endeavours and returned her enquiries with my own about her dear children.

I was honoured after our lunch to meet again her younger children, Emma and Harriot, grown to be pretty girls of seven and eight years with manners a credit to their mama although they did not seem to recognize me. I did not see the older children. At twelve and thirteen Peter and Margaret were at their studies, and Anne at seventeen was all grown up and nearly married, although Lady Betty confessed to me that she was being headstrong, just like her grandpapa. She was refusing all potential suitors as inadequate. Lady Betty was quite despairing of getting her settled at all, especially when Anne kept taking to her bed with mysterious pains.

My visit was nearly at an end and I knew I must put my request before I left, but I could feel my courage slipping away. I felt embarrassed to ask but I knew it would be money spent for naught if I did not use this opportunity. I waited until the children had returned to the nursery and thankfully Ann gave me the nudge I had needed. She very kindly asked about my plans for a book of cookery recipes that I had written to her about, and there in her hands she held the housekeeper's receipt book which she had taken from Mrs. Taylor before my arrival.

I was delighted and feigned an idle interest in it, for old time's sake. As I turned the pages I made mention of some that I knew to be Lady Betty's favourites, begging her permission to copy them down. She was then all keen interest and after she made some suggestions of improvements which I took gladly. It gave me the chance to ask her if I might presume to dedicate my intended book to her, in grateful thanks for all the useful insights I gained from her in my time as her housekeeper.

I flatter myself that she was delighted to be the patron of the book as she knows mè well enough to be confident that I shall make it the best book of its kind on the market, and as a member of one of the first families in this area it will give the book the necessary entry into the best society. Of course she would never mention money but I felt it only right to offer her a copy of the book and asked only that she might mention it to such of her acquaintance as may appreciate the knowledge contained therein. She agreed readily and only asked for a further four copies, that her daughters may each have one for their future as ladies of great houses. It was a concession I readily granted.

It was with a heavy heart that I took my leave, lingering longer than I should have done to say my farewells to the servants I remembered. There were so few left now, only Hannah Bushell and Elizabeth Woodcock have stayed, and they look set to stay longer I fancy, for I know Ann Worsley thinks highly of them both. It was hard to leave that place where I have so many happy memories and a time I will always treasure, but it was soon time to return to my future, to get busy on my great endeavour.

It was decided for me when the coachman, rough fellow that he was, called out to remind me I would pay extra if we were not back by evening. It was a perfect summer's evening as we drove away and I will forever have a picture in my heart of the Hall framed perfectly by the immaculate gardens and grounds and lit by the afternoon sunlight. Once we were through the village and out on the open road I allowed myself to shed the tears I had contained all day and they flowed freely, grieving for the ordered life lost.

1766 Aug 16th Marketplace shop

Since I returned from my visit to my dear Lady Betty I have not had a moment to think about my book. I intended, of course, to start on it the very next day but John came rushing in to tell me of a conversation he had chanced to overhear in the Market-place. Two distinguished gentlemen had been talking behind the stall, discussing the troubles of Mr. Thompson, the bookseller, whose shop on the Market place would be to let very shortly.

Poor old Mr. Thompson, it seemed had fallen behind with his payments after his son had borrowed some money from him to invest in a new cotton spinning invention. Not understanding the intricacies of the trade, Mr. Thompson had trusted his son's judgement but had come unstuck when the invention was quickly improved upon by another inventor. All the original subscribers had lost their money and Mr. Thompson was now in debt with no resources to call upon. He would need to sell up his shop as soon as possible. It was a sad story and I certainly would not wish to profit from another's misfortune but, as it meant a highly desirable shop was becoming available, a fast deal would be needed.

Here was an ideal opportunity placed at my feet that and I could not ignore it. The shop was exactly what I required to improve my business. It is unfortunate that we are still committed on the lease here at Fennel-street but if I am diligent we may be able to sell that on at the earliest opportunity.

That same day I called on Mr. Thompson, on pretext of

discussing the printing of a book such as I had in mind. He soon confessed his situation to me for he did not have the heart to pretend, knowing his story was all over the market place, and the poor man was so broken by his son's honest mistake.

He was not sorry to have backed his son. He believes so completely in him that he backed him with everything he had. He was sorrowful on his son's account who had taken it hard, losing his father's money. He had taken a boat to Liverpool, from there to take a ship to the cotton fields to try to make back the money he owes his father.

All the trouble has left Mrs. Thompson in a poor state of health, unwilling to take part in daily life. Poor Mr. Thompson was glad when I made him my offer and we struck a deal immediately. I offered him a fair price and used my influence with Mr. Harrop to recoup him some value for some of his presses. I did what I could to help him and in consequence I am soon to move to my very own shop in the Market Place, the beating heart of Manchester.

1766 Sept

So much has happened since my visit to Arley that it begins to seem like a dream. We are in September and I have so much else to take my attention that I still cannot put my hand to the book as yet. The book will have to wait until I have my new shop established. That must take priority now, along with finding someone to take on the lease of our premises on Fennel-street.

It was clean when we left, I made certain of that. I also saw to the cleaning of the shop before I could trade from it, for Mrs. Thompson was not in any fit state to do it and Mr. Thompson had no one else to call on to help him. It is invidious how his friends have deserted him. In business one only has oneself, I can see that.

I consider myself fortunate that I have a strong husband and dear sisters to call upon. With this venture I believe I will need to call on them for more aid than I would like and sometimes I wonder if it is the right thing to do. It is a big undertaking and I am sure I can do it. The time is right for me to move up in the world, it will be good to be closer to John during the daytime, and he may be useful to me. My standing in this town is growing with each enterprise I undertake. Sometimes I feel that I am running everyday, but I know I must continue to improve or I may lose what reputation I have gained.

1766 Oct 10th

I have so much work to do now that even with two extra kitchen maids and a scullery maid I am kept busy all the hours there are. My shop is doing very well and it is all I could have hoped for. My customers from Fennel-street have followed me, and I have gained many new ones in the new location. As well as continuing the Register Office, I have at last added a school to my list of businesses.

I first made sure to mention it to as many of my customers as I thought would make use of the opportunity, and pretty soon had my first three girls at fifty pounds each per term. My scheme is for them to spend twenty weeks learning the refinements expected of a lady of quality. To this will be added time spent working under my instruction in my kitchen. I can teach them all they need to know about running a household, joining economy with elegance. Their accomplishments will be certain to earn the admiration of important men as future husbands.

My name will carry with it a guarantee of a high quality, of course. It would not surprise me if, before too long, I do not find more pupils preferring my school to that of certain other people, including that Mrs. Blomely. Before now she may have thought she was the best in Manchester but once my school is established I think I might claim that prize spot for mine. It is certainly possible as her grasp of the finer points of society life is not quite as nice as the one my experience gives me.

1766 Nov 7th

I thought I had found a suitable tenant for the cellar at Fennel-street but was soon vexed when, after haggling over the price for half an hour, the wretched man said no. I know I can drive a hard bargain but I like to think I am fair and I will not be twisted out of a fair price by a charlatan who thought he could take advantage of a woman. Better no tenant than one who starts out by being such a weasel.

Thankfully my school is having better fortune and I have gained a further two young ladies this month. My first ladies are doing very well and generally I am pleased with their progress but one of them is causing me some disquiet. Miss Jameson is such a tomboy and a real trial to teach the proper decorum. If she cannot learn the lessons I set I will be forced to write a letter to her father. He may be able to exert some influence on her or she will have to leave. I will not have one bad apple give my school a bad name.

1766 Dec

Mr. Green has become a veritable tower of strength to me and he is proving what a good judge of character I am. His appointment as writing master to my little school has repaid me handsomely and his skills add to the reputation I have gained. He has even saved me having to write to young Miss Jameson's father by taking extra time with that young lady to educate her on the value of good decorum. The effect on her has been nothing short of miraculous and she is beginning to blossom into an accomplished hostess fit for any society.

Yet another three young ladies are waiting to be taken on when I have the room. They daily come up to me begging me to find a place for them in my school, telling me it is already considered superior to any other. It is very gratifying but I have always thought that if I ever applied myself to teaching that I would be very good at it.

I have never given voice to high blown style. My way is to state plain what needs to be said to communicate properly. It is sometimes the simplest things that are hard to grasp and not everyone understands things the same. Of course, I am also very thorough and I have years of valuable experience. The families I worked for may not always have noticed me, for that is the way it should be, but they knew they could reply on me to provide what they needed. My young ladies will have the benefit of what knowledge I have to give them and they will do well, of that I am certain.

1767

1767 Jan

Well! Today I was faced with that woman again. She flaunts her school in my face and thinks she has the better of me because she has eight young ladies to my five, but I think my ladies will make better matches than hers when it comes to the skills that matter.

Today she sent her pupils out to walk down Dean's-gate at just the time she must know that mine would be there. It is really most inconsiderate on her part. There were so many parading at the one time that one of my young ladies was pushed to walk into a deep, dirty puddle. Poor girl was most distressed, as she had every right to be. Even with pattens on her shoes her feet were sodden through and soaked in mud when she returned to school.

It is one thing to accustom my young ladies to the jostle and stares of the Manchester people but to add in the indignities of the filthy roads may be more than they need. Mr. Fischar ought to have thought to take a different route when he saw the other school coming towards him. It is no use being able to teach them to dance if he cannot teach them how to avoid uncomfortable encounters.

He ought to have crossed them over to the other side of the road before they met, and I hope he took heed of my advice to do just that should the occasion arise again, as I am certain that it will. That is, if he does not desert my school for hers, for I know she has tried to coax him over.

That woman can be so wicked. She is aware he is superior to her own dancing master in so many ways. Her school is beginning to suffer in comparison to mine. I teach the essential skills for young ladies who wish to be deemed fit to be the hostess for a man of rank in society.

1767 Feb returning to the cookbook

Today I was able to return at last to my plan of producing a book of my own recipes, something I can increasingly see will be a most useful item. The girls in my school have all written out their own copies of my recipes as I taught them but not all the girls are quite so diligent at following exactly my instructions. As ladies of good families it is not for me to chastise them overmuch or their father's may take it into their minds to take the them, and their fees, away from my school.

One thing I have noticed from the young ladies in my school is just how ignorant and frankly dim-witted some girls are who are destined to run the households of some of our town's greatest men. I must write my book in as plain a style as possible to be understood by the weakest capacity.

It will be a heavy enterprise, I make no mistake of that, and I am already as busy as a body can be between the shop, the office, the school and my babies. John complains constantly that he does not have any of my time though he is always glad of the money that comes in. It does not seem to stop him finding me in bed when I am fit for nothing but sleep.

I knew he was a lusty man before I married him but after four years of marriage and two babies I had thought he would be less demanding. He is a man of forty years now but he has not slowed down. Since he gave up the manual labour of the gardens at Arley Hall he has had more energy for mischief. I must speak to his brother James to see if he can provide him with some hours of toil in his gardens to keep him as worn out as I am.

For now I think the damage is already done. I woke this morning feeling sickly again, a sure sign that I have come to dread. Young Emma has barely been weaned from me but another six months and I am likely to be a milk cow again. If I am to work on a book as well as my other businesses I must look into finding a wet nurse substitute for this next one. One of my shop girls is sure to know of someone.

The morals of many in this town are not the highest and girls are always pregnant. It must be something in the air for I never expected to fall pregnant as often as I do. I will not have my child suckled in an immoral home, however. A married woman must be found. However, there is time for that later. First I must set out my plan for my cookbook. I will start tomorrow; there is no time to waste.

1767 March a title for the book

I have given my book some considerable thought and have now decided how I want my book to look. Perusing others that are already in print I can see there are some conventions worth following. It must contain sections devoted to those dishes that are most useful, in the order they may be served at a dinner. I shall begin with soups then fish and fowls, roasting meats and made dishes (for no household can afford to live on roasted meats all the time, nor is it good advice to do so.) To give the dishes in their order of serving, I think makes the most sense. But how do I include all the necessary skills to produce the dishes correctly, I wonder? I could write one book just on pickling alone, it is such an essential skill for a competent housekeeper.

I am undecided what I shall give it as a title. One idea is 'A Complete Companion for Cooks, Housekeepers and Ladies, to make Household Management of the most Ease and least Expence'. Maybe that's a little too much, but if I simply call it 'A Cook's Companion' then I will not reach the fullest audience and the ladies who it will chiefly benefit will not deign to look at it.

Perhaps I should call it 'A Lady's Companion'? That seems to suggest something else altogether. I wish it to have the name Lady in the title but also something to indicate it contains the wisdom of an experienced housekeeper.

It will be a book of useful recipes and I can include my advice on the setting up of a grand dinner table, the buying of foods in their right seasons, etc, but I will not venture into physical remedies or household management. I will keep myself to advice on foods that I have found acceptable to the English palate. Some of the recipes I have seen in French cooks' books would not suit the rougher English tastes. I should like to include that it is written by a Yorkshire woman but I will let Mr. Harrop guide me on that count.

Let me see what I have got so far,- 'A Housekeeper's Advice on Oeconomy for Ladies'. No, that sounds a little presumptuous. Perhaps 'A Yorkshire Housekeeper's Guide for the Ease of Ladies' would work. It sounds better but anyone may become a housekeeper. It does not follow that they have advice worth following. I have fifteen years experience which should be noted. 'A Guide from an Experienced Yorkshire Housekeeper for the Use and Ease of Ladies'. That sounds quite good. I will speak to Mr. Harrop and I know he will give me the benefit of his advice.

1767 April

Mr. Harrop approved wholeheartedly of the last idea for the title, with one small change. I am not convinced he is right but I must bow to his experience. Reluctantly I agreed to his suggestion to change Yorkshire to English. He believes it will give my book a wider appeal. I certainly would not want customers in London turning up their noses at my work because they may perceive it as the work of a country cook, rather than that of a well educated and experienced housekeeper and businesswoman.

He also advised that it should be 'the' rather than 'a'. Using the word 'the' gave it more prominence to indicate that it was the only one of its kind, he recommended, where 'a' suggested it was one of many. And so it will be called 'The Experienced English Housekeeper, for the Use and Ease of Ladies', rather a distinguished title I feel. Now we have begun in earnest and I must set to finding sufficient recipes to make my book the best of its kind.

1767 May observations on soups

When I began to look through my recipes I realized that there are some instructions that apply in general to sections of cooking., such as soups, pickling, etc. These general skills will apply to every dish in the section to improve the finish and taste of many dishes included. It will be useful to set out my observations in an introduction at the beginning of each section beginning with soups.

Observations on Soups

WHEN you make any Kind of Soups, particularly Portable, Vermicelli, or brown Gravy Soup, or any other that has Roots or Herbs in, always observe to lay your Meat in the Bottom of your Pan with a good lump of Butter; cut the Herbs and Roots small, lay them over your Meat, cover it close, set it over a very slow Fire, it will draw all the Virtue out of the Roots or Herbs, and turns it to a good Gravy, and gives the Soup a very different flavour from putting Water in at the first: when your Gravy is almost dried up fill your Pan with Water, when it begins to boil take off the Fat, and follow the directions of your receipt for what Sort of Soup you are making: When you make old Pease Soup take soft Water, for green Pease hard is the best, it keeps the Pease a better Colour: When you make any white Soup don't put in Cream till you take it off the Fire: always dish up your Soups the last thing; if it be a Gravy Soup it will skin over if you let it stand; if it be a Pease Soup it often settles, and the Top looks thin.

I am very pleased with that though no doubt will find more to say once I have thought about it. I must leave the book there and apply myself to finding more help for my kitchen. Last week I saw an advertisement in Mr. Harrop's Manchester Mercury that quite tempted me for a little while but in the end I thought better of it.

> Any gentleman, or lady, wanting to purchase a Black Boy, 12 years of age, with a good character, has had the smallpox and measles. Whoever this will suit, may, by applying to the Higher Swan and Saracen's Head, in Market Street Lane, Manchester, meet with a Proper Person to deal with them on reasonable terms.

I have heard that they are excellent workers if you can find one of good character, but who is to say he will be one of those? Finally I decided against enquiring further. The idea of owning another person does not sit well with me and there are many willing workers in this town who will work for the least pay that I do not need the responsibility.

1767 May 26th observations on fish and finding subscribers

I have applied myself to compose my observations for the next section of my book which will be on cooking fish. It is a section which has many general rules to apply.

Observations on Fish –

WHEN you fry any Kind of Fish, wash them clean, dry them well with a Cloth, and dust them with Four, or rub them with Egg and Bread Crumbs; be sure your dripping, Hog's-lard, or Beef-suet, is boiling before you put in your Fsh, they will fry hard and clear, Butter is apt to burn them black, and make them soft; when you have fried your Fsh, always lay them in a Dish or Hair Sieve to drain, before you dish them up; Boiled Fish should always be washed and rubbed carefully with a little Vinegar, before they are put into the Water; boil all Kinds of Fish very slowly, and when they will leave the Bone they are enough; when you take them up, set your Fish-plate over a Pan of hot Water to drain, and cover it with a Cloth or close Cover, to prevent it from turning their Colour; set your Fish-plate in the inside of your Dish, and send it up, and when you fry Parsley, be sure you pick it nicely, wash it well, then dip it in cold Water, and throw it into a Pan of boiling Fat, take it out immediately, it will be very crisp and a fine green.

Mr. Harrop has told me that if I am seriously to make my book a success then I need to busy myself to raise some subscribers. Without some advance orders, it will not be worth Mr. Harrop's while making a run of it. The amount of the paper fee he requires is so steep I could not possibly pay it myself, so I will apply myself to writing to places where they may raise subscribers.

The first one to mind was dear Mr. Seth Agur in York. His most excellent confectioner's shop is just the place where ladies will enquire for the newest recipes. He was always so kind to me when I was housekeeper at Escrick, and I was glad to recommend him to Mr. Postlethwaite's household, from which Mr. Agur gained some valuable patronage.

Mr. John Wetherall in Hull will also remember me, I am certain. He is such a gentleman I can rely on him to promote my interests. Mr. Tindall's confectioner's shop in Leeds would also be useful if not quite as fashionable. I can supply him with my book at reasonable cost, for Manchester has a regular carrier to there. I am certain that if I take the carrier's book keeper, Mr. Bullough, a nice Hottentot pie he will make sure my books are kept safe and dry for a good price.

There is also Mr. Kendall, at the Peacock, in Derbyshire, and Mr. Eaton in Doncaster would take it at his Silk Merchant's shop. He is such a helpful man and if there is a commission in it for him I know he will take the opportunity. I will write to them all and maybe that will suffice. I will speak to Mr. Harrop tomorrow and take his advice. Now I must think how to phrase the letter.

Dear ----,

I trust this letter may find you and your family in good health and prosperous business, and I wish to thank you for the many happy years I had of dealing with you when I was Elizabeth Whitaker, housekeeper to (and here I will insert the house where I worked appropriate to the town). I always found you to be honest, reputable and trustworthy and thank you for your help during my service there. If I may presume on your attention a little longer I have in mind now an arrangement which I am certain will be of mutual benefit.

Encouraged by a great number of friends here in my new abode of Manchester, I am preparing a useful collection of recipes that I have found to give good results in preparing the most elegant dishes suitable for the most genteel families. This collection is to be printed as a book by my good friend Mr. Harrop, a printer of some repute, and it will be sold for a good sum. Mr. Harrop has suggested five shillings, which seems to me a good amount and I will endeavour to put my best into it to make it worth the value.

My purpose in contacting you is to ask if you would consider in the first instance raising subscriptions for me at your shop in York, then to take finished copies for sale, terms to be agreed once the final price is known, of course. If you are agreeable I will send some sample pages to be viewed at your premises.

I know you to be a fair man and I would not presume on our friendship if I did not know you to be the most excellent of men who will deal fairly with a woman asking for his help.

    I remain,

        your most humble servant,

           Elizabeth Raffald.

That will do nicely, with a little adjustment for each place that I have in mind. I shall have Joshua copy that out three times for me to sign. He has the best hand of all my nephews and is so trustworthy he is sure to do a good job of it.

1767 July 1st replies

Today I received the first reply to my enquiry for subscribers and it was from Mr. Agur, a positive reply of course. Such a good reply I shall include it here

> "My dearest Mrs. Raffald, Firstly allow me to belatedly send my happy felicitations to you and your husband on your marriage. I and Mrs. Agur are exceedingly happy that your life has taken such a fortunate turn. We fondly remember negotiating sales with such a fair-minded woman as you. We trust you are settled in your new town and wish you all success, although your absence from York is much regretted.
>
> With regard to the business, of course we will help in whatever way we can. A new book of household management will be eagerly sought by the ladies of York and I have no doubt of the quality when produced by your own fair hands. If you can send me some examples of the pages it will help me to whet the appetites of my customers. I await your next letter when you have firm details of the price, etc. I am yours, etc., Seth Agur."

Such a good letter, I could hardly have hoped for a better reply. I must set to work on a few of my best recipes to send out as sample pages. My Portable Soup for Travellers is a good one, and Bride Cake is very popular here. I must also add one which shows the skills of making decorations for table with the greatest economy and least expence. Ladies of Yorkshire will appreciate the refinement.

1767 Aug 10th Sample recipes

Finally I have written out the recipes to be printed as sample pages. Mr. Harrop assures me that he will have them ready within the week for me to send out to those shops willing to take the names of subscribers. It was most difficult to decide which ones to use and which to leave out, but I am confident of the few I selected. Together with the first Observation paragraphs these will give a good account of the skills to be gleaned from my book, and should create some interest in my work of cookery. The first recipe, of course, is Soup for Travellers, most useful for making best use of meat before it goes off;

> *To make* Portable Soup *for Travellers.*
>
> *TAKE three large Legs of Veal, and one of Beef, the lean Part of Half a Ham, cut them in small Pieces, put a Quarter of a Pound of Butter at the Bottom of a large Caldron, then lay in the Meat and Bones, with four Ounces of Anchovies, two Ounces of Mace, cut off the green Leaves of five or six Heads of Celery, wash the Heads quite clean, cut them small, put them in with three large Carrots cut thin, cover the Caldron close, and set it over a moderate Fire; when you find the Gravy begins to draw, keep taking it up 'till you have got it all out, then put Water in to cover the Meat, set it on the Fire again and let it boil slowly for four Hours, then strain it through a Hair Sieve into a clean Pan, and let it boil three Parts away, then strain the Gravy that you drawed from the Meat into the Pan, let it boil gently (and keep scuming the Fat off very clean as it rises) till it looks thick like Glew; you must take great Care when it is near enough that it don't burn; put in Chyan Pepper to your Taste, then pour it on flat Earthen Dishes, a Quarter of an Inch thick, and let it stand till the next Day, and cut it out with round Tins a little larger than a Crown piece; lay the Cakes on Dishes, and set them in the Sun to dry; this Soup will answer best to be made in frosty Weather; when the Cakes are dry, put them in a Tin Box with Writing Paper betwixt every Cake, and keep them in a dry Place; this is a very useful Soup to be kept in Gentlemen's Families, for by pouring a Pint of boiling Water on one Cake, and a little Salt, it will make a good Bason of Broth. A little boiling Water poured on it will make Gravy for a Turkey or Fowls, the longer it is kept the better.- N.B. Be careful to keep turning the Cakes as they dry.*

I am including the recipes for Bride cake and for the icing. I make good business in this town with this rich fruit cake. It is a decided improvement on Bride Pye, especially with the double icing layer which I have devised, using almond under the sugar icing. It is a cake fit for royalty.

To make a Bride Cake.

TAKE *four Pounds of fine Flour well dried, four Pounds of fresh Butter, two Pounds of Loaf Sugar, pound and sift fine a quarter of an Ounce of Mace, the same of Nutmegs, to every Pound of Flour put eight Eggs, wash four Pounds of Currants, pick them well, and dry them before the Fire, blanch a Pound of sweet Almonds, (and cut them length-way very thin), a Pound of Citron, one Pound of candied Orange, the same of candied Lemon, half a Pint of Brandy; first work the Butter with your Hand to a Cream, then beat in your Sugar a quarter of an Hour, beat the Whites of your Eggs to a very strong Froth, mix them with your Sugar and Butter, beat your Yolks half an Hour at least, and mix them with your Cake, then put in your Flour, Mace, and Nutmeg, keep beating it well till your Oven is ready, put in your Brandy, and beat your Currants and Almonds lightly in, tie three Sheets of Paper round the Bottom of your Hoop to keep it from running out, rub it well with Butter, put in your Cake, and lay your Sweet-meats in three Lays, with Cake betwixt every Lay, after it is risen and coloured, cover it with Paper before your Oven is stopped up, it will take three Hours Baking.*

To make Almond-Icing *For the* Bride Cake.

BEAT *the Whites of three Eggs to a strong Froth, beat a pound of Jordan Almonds very fine with Rose-water, mix your Almonds with the Eggs lightly together, a Pound of common Loaf Sugar beat fine, and put in by Degrees; when your Cake is enough, take it out, and lay your Icing on, then put it in to Brown.*

To make Sugar Icing *for the* Bride Cake.

BEAT *two Pounds of double refined Sugar, with two Ounces*

> *of fine Starch, sift it through a Gawze Sieve, then beat the Whites of five Eggs with a Knife upon a Pewter Dish half an Hour to beat in your Sugar a little at a Time, or it will make the Eggs fall, and will not be so good a Colour, when you have put in all your Sugar, beat it half an Hour longer, then lay it on your Almond Iceing, and spread it even with a Knife; if it be put on as soon as the Cake comes out of the Oven it will be hard by the Time the Cake is cold.*

I may include Bride's pye, for I know that is still popular in many parts of Yorkshire, although I feel it will go out of favour once they hear of Bride cake.

> ### A Bride's Pye.
>
> *BOIL two Calf's-feet, pick the Meat from the Bones, and chop it very fine, shread small one Pound of Beef Suet, and a Pound of Apples, wash and pick one Pound of Currants very small, dry them before the Fire, stone and chop a quarter of a Pound of Jar Raisins, a quarter of an Ounce of Cinnamon, the same of Mace and Nutmeg, two Ounces of candied Citron, two Ounces of candied Lemon cut thin, a Glass of Brandy and one of Champagne, put them in a China Dish with a rich puff Paste over it, roll another Lid and cut it in Leaves, Flowers, Figures, and put a Glass ring in it.*

Mr. Harrop has recommended that I include an introduction to give an idea of myself but I do not wish to put myself so forward. I would rather my cooking speaks for me. He says I must include a list of what can be expected in the final volume to encourage subscriptions. The whole endeavour has already become such a lot of work that I sometimes wonder if I should ever have begun. Perhaps I will talk with Mr. Harrop and propose a smaller volume than the one we originally envisaged.

1767 Sep extra pages, pregnancy issues

Mr. Harrop has asked that I include with my sample pages a direction for a table decoration, to show what can be done with a little imagination. He says I am well reputed for the excellence of my displays and so I will include my recipe for a Fish Pond set in flummery, always an entertaining addition to the best of dinners.

I have looked at other examples of decorations but I think that is a pretty one, and very effective. I could have given directions for gold or silver globes but I must be satisfied with what I have or I will be forever writing out samples. I have not included my observations in general for preparing flummery but that can be a reason for ladies to buy the whole book.

Comparing what I wish to say with other cookery guides, and to remedy what I see as their lack, I have settled on eighteen sections for my book. When I feel more comfortable I will write them out here. It is always clearer to see any omissions when it is written in front of me.

I do not have many days, however, when I feel able to sit to write at all. This baby sits very heavy on me, not at all like the first two. Please God this one is a boy and then maybe I can be done with all this pain and discomfort, for carrying babies is not at all an easy thing to do while working, and once they are born I have less time to do everything that is needed. I am indeed blessed with the two girls we already have, and I am very proud of them, but t I am struggling to make time for my businesses. If this can be my last baby I will be very glad, and then I can have time to build my strength and put my efforts into my businesses. I feel certain that I am very close to becoming the premiere confectioner in Manchester.

1767 Oct 8th flood and section of the book

What a dreadful day today has been. We have had water everywhere and no let up all day. Local people are saying it has been the greatest flood ever known at Manchester. The rivers Mersey and Irwell have overflowed into several fields on each side their banks; large quantities of hay and corn were borne away, and many of the cellars around Fennel-street are flooded. I am glad we are not still living there.

I was also told that damage has been sustained at Salford-Quay, in sugars, spirituous liquors, dye stuff etc. So much damaged and destroyed, it is supposed to amount to several hundred pounds, although reports say that the Duke of Bridgewater's canal has received no damage. For myself it has been difficult enough to keep the water at bay from my shop here in the Marketplace. Every time I bend down to sweep out yet more mud I get a most painful strike from this baby. He is lying so low on my groin that I fear every pain will be the one to herald his arrival into the world.

Business was so slow today that after a few hours struggle against the mud I was forced to rest for fear I would deliver before the due time right there on the shop floor. I did not waste my time however. I sat with pen and paper and wrote out the titles for the sections of my cookbook, dividing the book into three parts.

Part I
I Soups
II Dressing Fish
III Roasting and Boiling
IV On Made Dishes
V Pies
VI puddings
Part II
VII Decorations for a Table
VIII Preserving
IX Drying and Candying
X On Creams, Custards and Cheesecakes
XI Cakes
XII little Savoury Dishes
Part III
XIII Potting and Collaring
XIV Possets and Gruel

Once I had all the sections written out I knew I must find a short way to list what was in the parts to entice subscribers. I wrote out a different list, to be sent out with the sample pages.

PART FIRST, Lemon Pickle, Browning for all Sorts of made Dishes, Soups, Fish, plain Meat, Game, Made Dishes both hot and cold, Pyes, Puddings, &c.

PART SECOND, All Kinds of Confectionary, particularly the Gold and Silver Web for covering of Sweetmeats, and a Desert of Spun Sugar with Directions to set out a Table, in the most elegant Manner, and in the modern Taste, Floating Islands, Fish Ponds, Transparent Puddings, Trifles, Whips, &c.

PART THIRD, Pickling, Potting, and Collaring, Wines, Vinegars, Catchups, Distilling, with two most valuable Receipts, one for refining Malt Liquors, the other for curing Acid Wines, and a correct List of every Thing in Season in every Month in the Year:

1767 Nov 15th Grace is born

I have another daughter who we have called Grace. Praise be she was delivered safely and she is a beautiful baby but I cannot help feeling a little disappointed that she was not the son that John and I so wished for. Still, a healthy baby and a successful pregnancy is something to be grateful for.

Although the passage of the birth was swift it has left me feeling ill used. Mrs. Withnall says it will pass with the application of some poultices but I do not feel right down there at all. I think John and I must reconcile ourselves that we are not meant to have a son. I do not wish to go through that experience one more time. Each time is taking more out of me and leaving me weaker every time

1768 Jan observations on roasting and boiling

How time has passed since I last had time to write. With three young babies to care for, businesses to keep going my eyes are barely open before they close again, or so it seems. My load is finally lightened since I secured a young girl to help me with the children.

She is clean and intelligent and very experienced with little ones, having had six little brothers and sisters to care for since her mother died. She has been freed from those duties by her younger sister, who is now old enough to take them on, and by the loss of two of her brothers who died, she assured me, from a weakness they were born with, having had a very poor start in life. They were born at a time when their father was short of work and so the family all but starved. If I had known them I would surely have helped but it is too late now, even though I am the one to benefit from her loss.

She is called Jane and is a good girl, diligent and attentive to the children, not needing any direction from me during the day. She repays her wages several times over with the love she gives the babies and little Grace is very well behaved for her.

It has given me the time to return to my book and I have already made good progress on my Observations on Roasting and Boiling meats. It is a much longer section than I intended but it is an important part of every menu and cannot be skimped.

Observations on Roasting and Boiling

WHEN *you boil any Kind of Meat, particularly Veal, it requires a great deal of Care and Neatness; be sure your Copper is very clean and well tinned, fill it as full of soft Water as is necessary, dust your Veal well with fine Flour, put it into your Copper, set it over a large Fire; some chuses to put in Milk to make it White, but I think it is better without; if your Water happens to be the least hard it curdles the Milk, and gives the Veal a Brown Yellow cast, and often hangs in Lumps about the Veal, so will oatmeal, but by dusting your Veal, and putting it into the Water when cold, it prevents the foulness of the Water from hanging upon it; when the Scum begins to rise take it clear off, put on your Cover, let it boil in Plenty of Water as slow as possible, it will make your Veal rise and* plump: A Cook cannot be guilty of a greater error than to let any Sort of Meat boil that it hardens the Outside before the Inside is warm, and discolours it, especially Veal; for Instance, a Leg of Veal twelve Pounds Weight, will require three Hours and a half boiling, the slower it boils the whiter and plumper it will be; when you boil Mutton or Beef, observe to dredge them well with Flour before you put them into the Kettle of cold Water, keep it covered, and take off the Scum; Mutton or Beef don't require so much boiling, nor is it so great a Fault if they are a little short, but Veal, Pork, or Lamb, is not so wholesome if they are not boiled enough; a Leg of Pork will require half an Hour more boiling than a Leg of Veal of the same Weight; when you boil Beef or Mutton, you may allow an Hour for every four Pound Weight; it is the best Way to put in your Meat when the Water is cold, it gets warm to the Heart before the Outside grows hard, a Leg of Lamb four Pounds Weight will require an Hour and half boiling.

When you roast any Kind of Meat, it is a very good Way to put a little Salt and Water in your Dripping Pan, baste your Meat a little with it, let it dry, then dust it well with Flour, baste it, with fresh Butter, it will make your Meat a better Colour; observe always to have a brisk, clear Fire, it will prevent your Meat from dazing, and the Froth from falling, keep it a good Distance from the Fire, if the Meat is scorched, the Outside is hard, and prevents the Heat from penetrating into the Meat, and will appear enough before it be little more than half done. Time, Distance, Basting often, and a clear Fire, is the best method I can prescribe for roasting Meat to perfection; when the Steam draws near the Fire, it is a Sign of its being enough, but you will be the best Judge of that from the Time you put it down. Be careful when you roast any Kind of Wild Fowl, to keep a clear brisk Fire, roast them a light Brown, but not too much; it is a great Fault to roast them 'till the Gravy runs out of them, it takes off the fine Flavour, — Tame Fowls require more roasting, they are a long Time before they are hot through, and must be often basted to keep up a strong Froth, it makes them rise better, and a finer Colour. — Pigs and Geese should be roasted before a good Fire, and turned quick. — Hares and Rabbits requires Time and Care, to see the Ends are roasted enough; when they are half roasted, cut the Neck Skin, to let out the Blood, or when they are cut up, they often appear bloody at the Neck.

1768 Feb 2nd earthquake

Oh, what a day today was! Just as I was lifting a pan of soup from the fire, the floor began to move and shake so much that I was feared to death the house would fall down. I managed to set the pan down without scalding myself and I held onto a chair for support.

Only a little of the soup was lost though it slopped in the pan like a stormy sea. Pots fell from their shelves with such a clatter it made the kitchen maids scream even more than they had been. We were all of a dither for quite some time after the shaking had stopped.

John soon came rushing in to check we were all safe and to help clear up the mess that had been made. Jane had brought the babies into the kitchen, for fear of being separated from everyone, but the babies were fine, thinking it a funny game that mamma was playing. It was no game to clean all the dust and grit from the pans and tins before we could use them again. The broken dishes will need to be replaced at my earliest opportunity though I do not know when that will be.

It took me the rest of the day to catch up on the order for Lady Assheton. Her man had to call back twice before it was ready, and even though I offered to send it as soon as it were done he insisted he would not return home again without it.

It was a relief from the day's drama to sit this evening with a letter from Arley from my dear friend Ann Worsley. It was not good news however, for Lady Betty had told her that she might need to step down from her post as her maid, in favour of young Hannah Bushell.

I confess myself torn between my friendship for Ann and my pride in seeing Hannah advance so well. She was always a keen worker and deserves a chance to progress. I tried to give my best reply to help them both, and though I must prefer Ann, as a good friend, even she must see that the time will come soon enough when she cannot continue to work. I hope she has some money set by.

1768 March Ann retiring

Ann has written again to tell me she has agreed to accept the change. She writes of the suffering she has with the stiffness in her fingers that no amount of massaging with oils and herbs will soothe. She so frequently had need of Hannah's help to button up

Lady Betty's gowns that I do not wonder she has made the decision.

In view of Ann's age and familiarity she is being kept on as companion adviser to Lady Betty. They have been together a long time those two and I know Lady Betty loves her as she would her own mother. Ann feels badly about being unable to continue but she can still serve her ladyship in other ways. When visitors are infrequent or there are people she is unable to confide in, she appreciates the value of the ear of a friend she can trust to be discreet.

Poor Ann, her letter shows that she feels her age now, and the list of her complaints is a long one. I fear she is sickening and beginning to give up completely. It is such a blow to her to give up her position. She lived only to serve Lady Betty and I have seen before in long time servants, especially those in senior positions that once their role is taken from them they seem to have no more will to carry on.

It is precisely that thought that spurred me to take action while I was still able, although I might not have done had I any idea of the amount of work I had chosen. I pride myself that I was never afraid of hard work but now it is morning, noon and night. One never knows when another order will arrive with instructions for it to be ready the next day. It is all uncertain except for the certainty that I must work hard.

My dear papa was wont to say that hard work ne'er killed a man but some days I wonder. Perhaps that is not the same for women who often work for longer and for more effort for less recompense. John at least has time to relax with other men for company, I would not dare to take the time out, there is always more to be done. Only writing in my diary is my luxury, with a tiny nip of brandy to keep me warm on these cold nights.

Ah well, I must not complain that business is too good. My book should be ready by year's end and that may bring me sufficient profit on which to move us all to a decent living in my dearest Yorkshire. That is a thought to raise my spirits, I will write back to dear Ann with some thoughts that may raise hers.

1768 April 4th Cotton machinery issues

Well I said that the name Thomas Highs would come into the news again and I have been proved right. Unfortunately the man has not managed to keep his inventions a close secret and he is being copied by everyone. It has now come about that a rough weaver from Blackburn, one James Hargreaves, is claiming that he has made a better machine than Mr. Highs, when all he has done is take the same design and add two more spindles, making eight instead of six that Mr. Highs had.

Mr. Hargreaves claims he had the idea by a happy accident and named his new machine, the Spinning Jenny, after his daughter, but I have it on good authority from a chapman who travels that way that Mr. Hargreaves does not have a daughter Jenny.

Mr. Highs was unable to take any action but Mr. Hargreaves has had his comeuppance in a strong way, at the hands of the very people he worked with. It is sad and a sign of most people's reluctance to grasp the benefits of progress, but Mr. Hargreaves' machines caused such jealousy and fear among his neighbours that last month an irate mob gathered at Blackburn's market cross and marched on his barn at Stanhill where he had his workshop.

They smashed the frames of 20 machines he was building for the cotton manufacturer Mr. Peel. The machine breakers then marched on to Brookside Mill and finally to Mr. Hargreaves' home at Ramsclough. Here, if reports are to be believed, one of the rioters placed a hammer in Hargreaves's hands and forced him to destroy his own machinery. What torment, but a true lesson in reaping what you sow though a sad day for progress. It's said that Mr. Hargreaves plans to leave the area altogether.

There are high prizes to be won in this cotton trade which is gripping Manchester like a fever. Everywhere is about cotton and fortunes are there to be made.

I begin to feel I am in the wrong trade for making my fortune but it is consolation to me that these men and their families will always need to eat and are happy to spend money to eat well, so perhaps this trade can be good for me too. It has inspired me to work more on my book, and to write down my ideas so that if they are copied I can point to these dates and say, 'there, this is when I wrote it, not copied from anyone.' I have produced more observations to take my total to four sections complete now, this time it is for Made Dishes, a very useful section.

Observations on Made Dishes

BE *careful the Tossing Pan is well tinned, quite clean, and not gritty and put every Ingredient into your White Sauce, and have it of a proper thickness, and well boiled, before you put in Eggs and Cream, for they will not add much to the thickness, nor stir them with a Spoon after they are in, nor set your Pan on the Fire for it will gather at the Bottom and be in Lumps, but hold your Pan a good Height from the Fire, and keep shaking the Pan round one Way, it will keep the Sauce from curdling, and be sure you don't let it boil; it is the best Way to take up your Meat, Collops, or Hash, or any other Kind of Dish you are making, with a Fish Slice, and strain your Sauce upon it, for it is almost impossible to prevent little Bits of Meat from mixing with the Sauce, and by this Method the Sauce will look clear.*

In the Brown Made Dishes take special Care no Fat is on the Top of the Gravy, but skim it clean off, and that it be of a fine Brown, and taste of no one Thing particular; if you use any Wine put it in some Time before your Dish is ready, to take off the rawness, for nothing can give a Made Dish a more disagreeable Taste than raw Wine, or fresh Anchovy: When you use fried Forcemeat Balls, put them on a Sieve to drain the Fat from them, and never let them boil in your sauce, it will give it a greasy look, and soften the Balls; the best Way is to put them in after your Meat is dished up.

You may use pickled Mushrooms, Artichoke Bottoms, Morels, Truffles, and Forcemeat Balls in almost every Made Dish, and in several, you may use a Roll of Forcemeat instead of Balls, as in the Porcupine Breast of Veal, and where you can use it, it is much handsomer than Balls, especially in a Mock Turtle, collared or raggooed Breast of Veal, or any large Made Dish.

1768 May 12th

I have received another missive from Ann. I did not expect a reply so soon but she wrote to tell me she is most happy with her new position and quite settled. She had a very lively story to tell me that she heard when she went with Lady Betty to visit her sister Margaret in Knutsford, where everyone is quite scandalised.

The story concerns one of their residents, an Edward Higgins, whose tale began when he gave his status as Yeoman at his marriage to one of Knutsford society's daughters in the year 1757. His new wife, Katherine, was no doubt satisfied when told that

Edward owned property in various parts of the country and lived on the rents. A dutiful wife would never enquire further into her husband's background. He lived in the style of a gentleman, riding to hounds with the gentry and owning several horses of his own. As time went by there were five children to add to the household of Squire Higgins, and he was reputedly very fond of his growing family.

What the folk of Knutsford did not know at the time was that, for his past activities in the year 1754, he had been convicted of housebreaking in Worcester and sentenced to transportation for seven years. He had gone but the American colonies could not reform Edward. Soon after his arrival in Boston he had stolen a large amount of money from the house of a rich merchant and bought himself a passage home. He was back in England a few months after being transported.

For a while he lived in Manchester, where I am glad not to have met him, though I am sure he would not have hoodwinked me. He then moved to Knutsford where he bought the house known as the Cann office, on account of it having once been the place in which scales and weights were tested. Life in Knutsford's genteel society was of course placid and orderly. Higgins and his wife dined with their neighbours and he hunted, fished and shot with them.

Such a life gave him the chance to become familiar with the layouts of the houses of his hosts, and he would sneak back for a spot of burglary. On one occasion when Mr. and Mrs. Higgins were guests of the Egertons, Sir Peter Warburton's relatives, in their house at Oulton Park, Mr. Egerton's jewelled snuff box, left in plain sight on the table, was stolen. Of course the Egertons had no idea of their guest's true nature, and there was no question of searching the guests. Ladies and gentlemen did not do such things! But now it seems quite likely that it was Higgins that took it.

When he was finally caught, he confessed all including one dreadful occasion when, wandering along the Rows in Chester late at night, he saw a ladder that some workman had left against the wall of a house in Stanley Street. He climbed up and into a bedroom where a young woman lay asleep. She had returned from a ball and her jewellery was scattered on the dressing table. Higgins calmly pocketed his good fortune, held his breath when the girl turned over in bed, and then made his escape. He said "Had she awaked I would have had no choice but to murder her." He truly was a dreadful scoundrel. Transportation was too good for him.

Besides burgling the homes of his friends in Knutsford, Higgins also went out some nights, muffling the hooves of his horse so as not to disturb the neighbours and held up a coach or two on the Chester Road. The area between Knutsford and Chester is rife with highwaymen and often called "Indian country" in which the law could not be enforced. Higgins found it easier to hold up a coach than to burgle a house but he finally came to his end last year.

He had taken a journey into Wales, telling his wife that he would be away "collecting the rents," but his luck had run out at last. He was caught breaking into a house in Carmarthen and, once identified as an escaped prisoner, his fate was sealed. After being sentenced to death he wrote,"I beg you will have compassion on my poor disconsolate widow and fatherless infants, as undoubtedly you will hear my widow upbraided with my past misconduct. I beg you will vindicate her as not being guilty of knowing about my villainy."

Squire Higgins died on the gallows at Carmarthen on 7 November, 1767. My heart goes out to his innocent children who must bear the shame of their father's name.

1768 Jun 2nd

Once again I am beginning to have the familiar sickly feeling that means only one thing, that I am pregnant again. I really do not need this at this time. I am getting several commissions for public dinners from Mr. Budworth at the Bull's Head, and Mr. Harrop is pressing me for the final pages for the book. I have enough work to need yet another girl for the kitchen and need to find some more reliable delivery boys. My sister Jane may send me another of her boys to help me. Her last letter despaired of finding work for him in Howden, there are so few opportunities there.

Another child, Heaven help me, I pray that this one may be a boy. Surely three girls is enough for any family. It must be a boy next. If I am to have any business for my children to inherit I must press on with the cookbook for that is a task that only I can do.

I have written out my Observations on Pies and Puddings, another long piece but I will copy it out here so I may check that I have everything I wish to say included.

Observations on Pyes

RAISED Pies should have a quick Oven, and well closed up, or your Pye will fall in the Sides; it should have no Water put in, 'till the Minute it goes to the Oven, it makes the Crust sad, and is a great Hazard of the Pye running. — light Paste requires a moderate Oven, but not too slow, it will make them sad, and a quick Oven will catch and burn it, and not give it Time to rise; Tarts that are iced, require a slow Oven, or the Icing will be brown, and the Paste not be near baked. These Sorts of Tarts ought to be made of Sugar Paste, and rolled very thin.

Observations on Puddings

BREAD and Custard Puddings require Time, and a moderate Oven, that will raise, and not burn them; Batter and Rice Puddings a quick Oven, and always Butter the Pan or Dish before you pour the Pudding in; when you boil a Pudding, take great care your Cloth is very clean, dip it in boiling Water, and Flour it well, and give your Cloth a shake; if you boil it in a Bason, Butter it, and boil it in plenty of Water, and turn it often, and don't cover the Pan; when enough take it up into a Bason, let it stand a few Minutes to cool, then untie the String, wrap the Cloth round the Bason, lay your Dish over it, and turn the Pudding out, and take the Bason and Cloth off very carefully, for very often a light Pudding is broken in turning out.

Yes I am quite content that I am making progress now. That is the instructions for the first section of the book finished. Now I will move onto my favourite section, dressing the table and creating impressive confectionery dishes.

1768 Jul 20th

I was pleased to receive yet another letter from my friend Ann at Arley Hall, although from now on I must find another way to refer to her. She has had to give up completely and has gone to live with her sister in Great Budworth. Her health got so bad and she writes that her letter was written by Hannah because her hands have got so crooked and painful that she can no longer hold a pen to write with.

Poor Ann, I cried a few tears over her predicament. Not even a widow with children to support her, she is cast into poverty, dependant on charity from her sister's family.

She says that Lady Betty presented her with a handsome parting gift and a little extra on the wages she was due, so she must make that last as long as she needs. It has made me thankful that I took the chance to marry John and leave service, or I too could have been in that predicament. My hands are forever active and I am glad to say showing no signs of seizing up for that would be calamity for this business.

I will send Ann a little gift and tell her she must write to me if she ever needs my help. I would not see her destitute for she is the closest I have ever come to a good friend. I am pleased for Hannah that she has been able to advance but it is sad that it is at Ann's expense.

Ah well, I cannot dwell on it for I must move on with my cookbook. Mr. Harrop wants to get the book finished by December and if I do not comply he may print a half finished book. I have now started on the second part, beginning with the Observations for the section on making Decorations for a Grand Table.

Observations On making Decorations *for a* Table

When you spin a Silver Web, or a Desert, always take particular Care your Fire is clear, and a Pan of Water upon the Fire, to keep the Heat from your Face and Stomach, for fear the Heat should make you faint; you must not spin it before a Kitchen Fire, for the smaller the Grate is, so that the Fire be clear and hot, the better able you will be to sit a long Time before it, for if you spin a whole Desert, you will be several Hours in spinning it; be sure to have a Tin Box to put every Basket in as you spin them, and cover them from the Air, and keep them warm, until you have done the whole as your Receipt directs you.

If you spin a Gold Web, take care your Chafing Dish is burnt clear, before you set it upon the Table where your Mould is, set your Ladle on the Fire, and keep stirring it with a Wood Skewer 'till it just boils, then let it cool a little, for it will not spin when it is boiling hot, and if it grows cold it is equally as bad, but as it cools on the Sides of your Ladle, dip the Point of your Knife in, and begin to spin round your Mould as long as it will draw, then heat it again; the only Art is to keep it of a proper Heat, and it will draw out like a fine Thread, and of a Gold Colour; it is a great Fault to put in too much Sugar at a Time, for often heating takes the Moisture out of the Sugar, and burns it, therefore the best Way is to put in a little at a Time, and clean out your Ladle.

When you make a Hen or Bird Nest, let part of your Jelly be set in your Bowl, before you put on your Flummery, or Straw, for if your Jelly is warm, they will settle to the Bottom, and mix together.

If it be a Fish Pond, or a Transparent Pudding, put in your Jelly at three different Times, to make your Fish or Fruit keep at a proper Distance, one from another, and be sure your Jelly is very clear and stiff, or it will not shew the Figures, nor keep whole; when you turn them out, dip your Bason in warm Water, as your Receipt directs, then turn your Dish or Salver upon the top of your Bason, and turn your Bason upside down.

When you make Flummery, always observe to have it pretty thick, and your Moulds wet in cold Water, before you put in your Flummery, or your Jelly will settle to the Bottom, and the Cream swim at the top, so that it will look to be two different Colours.

If you make Custards, do not let them boil after the Yolks are in, but stir them all one Way, and keep them of a good Heat 'till they be thick enough, and the rawness of the Eggs is gone off.

When you make Whips, or Syllabubs, raise your Froth with a Chocolate Mill, and lay it upon a Sieve to drain, it will be much prettier, and will lie upon your Glasses, without mixing with your Wine, or running down the Sides of your Glasses; and when you have made any of the before-mentioned Things, keep them in a cool, airy Place, for a close Place will give them a bad Taste, and soon spoil them.

My reputation for a good dinner table is unrivalled in this town. The business of putting on a good dinner cannot be underrated in its effect and it is good for my business that more people are realizing how useful I can be to their business.

I have an idea that I could be of use to Mr. Budworth at the

Bull's Head. He has many public dinners and I am certain we could work together for some mutual profit. His premises being next door to mine certainly make it convenient.

1768 Aug 18th

Mr. Budworth was very receptive to my suggestions for his formal dinners. He has some very important ones in the coming few months, especially at the beginning of September next when he is hosting the young King of Denmark, King Christian, and his retinue. That will be exciting, although I have heard some rumours of the young king's strange behaviour. No matter, he can act as he likes as long as I am paid for the handsome dinner I will put before him.

I have a more interesting dinner to prepare before that, however, for the local businessmen who will be meeting to discuss our town improvements. Now those are the meals that interest me. I want to know what is being planned and what opportunities are coming that I may grasp.

I have progressed with the sections on my book and think I now have ready Observations on Preserving, Drying and Candying. I will write them out separately first to see what they look like. I can always amend the presentation later.

Observations on Preserving

WHEN you make any Kind of Jelly, take Care you don't let any of the Seeds from the Fruit fall into your Jelly, nor squeeze it too near, for that will prevent your Jelly from being so clear; pound your Sugar, and let it dissolve in the Syrup before you set it on the Fire, it makes the Scum rise well, and the Jelly a better Colour: It is a great Fault to boil any Kind of Jellies too high, it makes them a dark Colour; you must never keep green Sweetmeats in the first Syrup longer than the Receipt directs, lest you spoil their Colour; you must take the same Care with the Oranges and Lemons, as to Cherries, Damsons, and most Sorts of stone Fruit, put over them either Mutton Suet rendered, or a Board to keep them down, or they will rise out of the Syrup and spoil the whole Jar, by giving them a sour bad Taste; observe to keep all wet Sweetmeats in a dry cool Place, for a wet damp Place will make them mould, and a hot Place will dry up the Virtue, and make them Candy; the best

Direction I can give, is to dip Writing Paper in Brandy, and lay it close to your Sweetmeats, tie them well down with white Paper, and two Fold of thick Cap Paper to keep out the Air, for nothing can be a greater Fault than bad tieing down, and leaving the Pots open.

Directions for Drying and Candying

Before you candy any Sort of Fruit, preserve them first, and dry them in a Stove or before the Fire, till the Syrup is run out of them, then boil your Sugar, Candy Height, dip in the Fruit, and lay them in Dishes in your Stove till dry, then put them in Boxes, and keep them in a dry Place.

1768 Sep 8th The king of Denmark's visit

What an occasion was the visit of the young King of Denmark. It was a real feather in my cap to have provided the food for him at the Bull's Head, and a very handsome purse I picked up too. The young royal was very generous with his bounty, although the manners of some of his nobles were disgraceful. I was glad to stay safely in the kitchen but the stories of the ribald comments passed in front of the young maids who waited on them made my cheeks blush.

It certainly tested my skills, getting the food from the fourth floor kitchen down to the ground floor dinner room. I had need to scold one or two servants for dawdling. It meant the food was sent back on an occasion or two. I will not have it said that my food was not good enough for the King of Denmark. Mr. Harrop put such a good report of the visit in his newspaper I had to paste it here for remembrance of a big occasion in my life.

On Friday last this Town was honoured with a sudden and unexpected Visit of the King of Denmark, accompanied by many foreign dignitaries; the King's Pages; Chief Physician; Chief Surgeon and several other Domestics and Attendants, to the amount of nearly Fifty Persons.

About five o'clock in the Evening before, one of his Majesty's deputies (attended by an

Interpreter), arrived at Mr. Budworth's, the Bull's Head Inn, notifying the King's intentions, and desiring Fifty-one horses to convey him and his Retinue from Rochdale. Immediately Three Post Chaises and the horses desired (with those of several private Gentlemen, out of Respect and Compliment to his Majesty) were sent to that Place, expecting his coming here that Evening. On the first Report of his Arrival, the Regiment of Dragoons, (commanded by the Marquis of Lothian), quartered here, were under Arms but were immediately dismissed by his Majesty, with genteel Compliments. After Breakfast, his Majesty very politely shewed himself at the Window, and complaisantly bowed to a very brilliant Appearance of Ladies in the Neighbouring Houses (although he straight afterwards asked to be moved to a room away from the noise of the Marketplace as the pillory and stocks were both noisily occupied). Soon after, Edward Byrom, Esq; was introduced to his Majesty, (by a Recommendation from Lord Morton, President of the Royal Society), to accompany and to view the Duke of Bridgewater's Canal, and the Manufactories peculiar to this Town. Accordingly, about eleven, his Majesty, (attended by his Nobles and several Gentlemen of the Town), was conducted to the Boats than in waiting for him; the King went to the Head of the Canal and down in further Boats to the Head of the Trench cut in the Rock, (two Miles under-ground) lighted all the Way by Candles. His Majesty much admired the Greatness of the Undertaking, expressed great satisfaction at the Ingenuity Facility with which the whole is conducted and was pleased to give the Workmen a handsome sum of Money on his Return from Worsley, he then proceeded to the Warehouses here, where he was highly celebrated and much admired the Beauty and

Elegance of the several Manufactories shewn to him, purchased large Quantities of Velvet, Gold and Silver for Waistcoats, and other Goods manufactured here. He then returned to the Inn about seven, and being much fatigue, chose to dine by himself. His Majesty very politely excepted the Call of a Ball, or to have any other public Acknowledgements paid him, as he chose to travel as privately as possible.

He lay at the Bull's Head Inn, where he and his Attendants were very commodiously entertained, which he was pleased to acknowledge when he went away. At his departure on Saturday Morning, his Majesty returned his Compliments to the Gentlemen of the Town for their respectful Attendance and Civilities shewn to him and very obligingly declared that he should ever retain a most grateful sense of their honour.

On Friday evening Signior Copli the Venetian and his Children had the Honour to perform at the Bull's-Head in this Town, before the King of Denmark, and the Noblemen who attended him, and met with universal Applause.

I fancy that will put the name of Manchester in a good light on the Continent. I hope the young king will also take away a memory of the excellent creams and cakes that he ate, for I am content that he tasted the finest that I could make. This puts me in mind to write out my Observations for the making of these delicacies for they are easily ruined.

Observations upon Creams, Custards and Cheesecakes

When you make any Kind of Creams and Custards, take great Care your Tossing Pan be well tinned, put a Spoonful of Water in it, to prevent the Cream from sticking to the Bottom of your Pan, then beat your Yolks of Eggs, and strain out the Threads, and follow the Directions of your

Receipt. – As to Cheese-cakes they should not be made long before you bake them, particularly Almond or Lemon Cheese-cakes, for standing makes them oil and grow sad, a moderate Oven bakes them best, if it is too hot it burns them and takes off the Beauty, and a very slow Oven makes them sad and look black; make your Cheese-cakes up just when the Oven is of a proper heat, and they will rise well and be of a proper Colour.

Observations On Cakes

When you make any Kind of Cakes, be sure that you get your Things ready before you begin, then beat your Eggs well and don't leave them 'till you have finished the Cakes, or else they will go back again, and your Cakes will not be light; if your Cakes are to have Butter in, take care you beat it to a fine Cream before you put in your Sugar, for if you beat it twice the Time, it will not answer as well: as to Plum-cake, Seed-cake, or Rice Cake, it is best to bake them in Wood Garths for if you bake them in either Pot or Tin, they burn the Outside of the Cakes, and confine them so that the Heat cannot penetrate into the Middle of your Cake, and prevents it from rising: bake all Kinds of Cake in a good Oven, according to the Size of your Cake, and follow the Directions of your Receipt, for though Care hath been taken to weigh and measure every Article belonging to every Kind of Cake, yet the Management and the Oven must be left to the Maker's Care.

1768 Oct 18th

In the Mercury today was a report of a commotion that had been heard all over town on Sunday last. A poor woman of Mrs. Withnall's acquaintance had been proved wrong in her belief that her husband was cheating on her. Mrs. W told me that the man was a known rogue and had probably been guilty of the crime as charged but he was quick with his story, and made his wife out to be a fool. Not the first time, Mrs. W told me yesterday. The matter resulted in the following notice in the Mercury by Mr. Mainwaring.

'Whereas a great Number of People was

> tumultously gathered together in the Evening of Sunday the 9th Day of this instant October, at the Upper End of a street called Deansgate, in Manchester, occasioned by a strange Woman pursuing a man, whom she called her Husband, and charging him with having taken a Basket of Bottles, then found in his Custody, out of the Dwelling-house of Mrs. Jodrell, and that one of the Servants of that House was his Sweetheart, and about to be married to him. Now I do hereby certify, that having properly examined this Matter, I am convinced at the Basket of Bottles did not come from the said House, and upon due Enquiry, it does not appear to me that the said Man had any Connection or Acquaintance with the Servants of the House. Peter Mainwaring'

Another poor woman duped by a fast talking man, who has also managed to fool a magistrate. She is in a sorry way, Mrs. W. told me, but she is a little simple and very hard to help. She is convinced the man is hers, when it is plain he is not. I fear she is destined to suffer her whole life long.

If I do not soon finish the work needed for my book I too will be a sorry woman. Mr. Harrop is fast losing patience with me. He has no idea how busy a woman can be with babies, three businesses and a reputation to keep up. It is madness to add a book to my load but once I have started on a path I will not give up. I think I have ready my Observations on Potting and Collaring, Possets and Gruels &c., and Wines, Catchups and Vinegar. Once I have them ii will soon finish.

Observations on Potting *and* Collaring

Cover your Meat well with Butter, and tie over it Strong Paper, and bake it well, when it comes out of the Oven pick out all the Skins quite clean, and drain the Meat from the Gravy, or the Skins will hinder it from looking well, and the Gravy will soon turn it sour, beat your Seasoning well before you put in your Meat, and put it in by Degrees, as you are beating; when you put it into your Pots, press it well, and let it be quite cold before you pour the clarified Butter over it. --In collaring be careful you roll it up, and bind it close, boil it 'till it is thoroughly enough, when quite cold, put it into Pickle with the Binding on, next Day take off the Binding when it will leave the Skin clear; make fresh Pickle often, and your Meat will keep good a long Time.

Observations On Possets *and* Gruels *&c.*

In making Possets, always mix a little of the hot Cream or Milk with your Wine, it will keep the Wine from curdling the Rest, and take the Cream off the Fire before you mix altogether. – Observe in making Gruels, that you boil them in well-tined Sauce Pans, for nothing will fetch the Verdigrease out of Copper sooner than Acids or Wines, which are the chief Ingredients in Gruels, Sagos, and Wheys; don't let your Gruel or Sago skim over, for it boils into them, and makes them a muddy Colour.

Observations on Wines, Catchup, *and* Vinegar.

WINE is a very necessary Thing in most Families, and is often spoiled through mismanagement of putting together, for if you let it stand too long before you get it cold, and do not take great Care to put your Barm upon it in Time, it summer-beams and blinks in the Tub, so that it makes your Wine fret in the Cask, and will not let it fine; it is equally as great a Fault to let it work too long in the Tub, for that takes off all the Sweetness and Flavour of the Fruit or Flowers your Wine is made from, so the only Caution I can give, is to be careful in following the Receipts, and to have your Vessels dry, rinse them with Brandy, and close them up as soon as your Wine has done fomenting.

1768 Nov 1st The Bull's Head, Manchester

Once again I was given the commission to cook for an important dinner at Mr. Budworth's inn. This time it was not such a prestigious company but I still did my reputation a lot of good among men who may recommend their wives to come and shop with me in future. Mr. Edward Byrom, he that is honouring his sainted father, Dr Byrom, with a church named for him, St John's off Deansgate, paid handsomely for a meal for all the workmen who had finished the building in good time.

There were so many of them and as the company was not so fine as my last meal I made sure to show myself so that they may know whose food they were eating. The occasion also gave me a better chance to see the full extent of the Bull's Head, for it is a sprawling building with a generous stable yard. When I was here for the meal for King Christian they had fifty horses in the yard. The stench that rose up the four floors to the kitchen window was almost unbearable.

The front entrance comes off the Market place of course, with a long corridor along the rear of the front rooms on the ground floor. On the left of the entrance is a snug bar parlour, very genteel; on the right is a long bar room, with black oak rafters. This room houses Prince Charlie's chair, a massive mahogany chair with finely curved handles and a high back which is topped with a carving of a bull's head. This chair is the High seat at all the important gatherings, I was told. There is a story that the young Pretender visited Manchester in secret, but that can be a story for another time. At the end of the long corridor is a smoke room, in a projection at the front of the building, it forms a curious recess from the other part of the house and is used for breakfast or lunches for the coaching passengers.

When I called in to prepare the food a gentlemen was in that room having his hair attended to by Mr. Hurst, the barber and peruke maker. He was sitting near the window, on one of the settees which are placed all around the room, underneath oak rafters with carved supporting brackets. It is a very fine room with engravings hanging on the walls and I suspect that much business is transacted here without having to step across to the Exchange.

Towards the end of the long passage is a door to the bar parlour which opens out into Blue Boar Court. At the very end of the long passage is the fine oak Jacobean staircase with its sweeping curves leading to the Great Room, the banqueting room put to use for so many important functions. It is long, low and spacious with black oak rafters and a long dining table with many seats and old windows on one side only which overlook the rear yard. The staircase, with steps of oak, plain rails and balusters, extends from the ground to the top of the four storey addition, giving access to all the bedrooms and the kitchens at the rear of the fourth floor.

It must be the premier place in Manchester and it has become my domain now, thanks to Mr. Budworth's need for high quality cooking. I must work with the old fashioned open arch, however, and not a modern coke oven which I could wish for. They are becoming all the fashion now and seem very efficient to work with. I shall certainly include details of them in my cookbook if Mr. Harrop can arrange an engraving for me. First I must finish the final Observations then I can keep my promise to Mr. Harrop to have it finished before the end of the year. I have only sections on Pickling, keeping Garden Stuff and Distilling to add. I must then add a section on Grand Table setting together with some useful engravings of a table set for two courses. That will come at the very end where it will be easy to find.

Observations on Pickling.

PICKLING is a very useful Thing in a Family, but is often ill managed, or at least made to please the Eye by pernicious Things, which is the only Thing that ought to be avoided, for Nothing is more common than to green Pickles in a Brass Pan for the Sake of having them a good Green, when at the same Time they will green as well by heating the Liquor, and keeping them on a proper Heat upon the Hearth, without the Help of Brass, or Verdegrease of any Kind, for it is Poison to a great Degree, and no Thing ought to be avoided more than using Brass or Copper that is not well tinned ; but the best Way, and the only Caution I can give, is to be very particular in keeping the Pickles from any Thing of that Kind, and follow strictly the Direction of your Receipts, as you will find Receipts for any Kind of Pickles, without being put in Salt and Water at all, and greened only by pouring your Vinegar hot upon them, and it will keep them a long Time.

Observations on keeping Garden-Stuff *and* Fruit.

THE Art of keeping Garden-stuff is to keep it in dry Places, for Damp will not only make them mould, and give again, but take off the Flavour, so it will likewise spoil any Kind of bottled Fruit, and set them on working; the best Caution I can give, is to keep them as dry as possible, but not warm, and when you boil any dried Stuff have plenty of Water, and follow strictly the Directions of your Receipts.

Observations on Distilling.

IF your Still be a Limbeck, when you set it on, fill the Top with cold Water, and make a little Paste of Flour and Water, and close the Bottom of your Still well with it, and take great Care that your Fire is not too hot to make it boil over, for that will weaken the Strength of your Water; you must change the Water on the Top of your Still often, and never let it be scalding hot, and your Still will drop gradually off; if you use a hot Still, when you put on the Top, dip a Cloth in White Lead and Oil, and lay it well over the Edges of your Still, and a coarse wet Cloth over the Top : it requires a little Fire under it, but you must take Care that you keep it very clear ; when your Cloth is dry, dip it in cold Water and lay it on again, and if your Still be very hot, wet another Cloth, and lay it round the very Top, and keep it of a moderate Heat, so that your Water is cold when it comes off the Still. — If you use a Worm-still, keep your Water in the Tub full to the Top, and change the Water often, to prevent it from growing hot; observe to let all simple Waters stand two or three Days before you work it, to take off the fiery Taste of the Still.

1768 Nov 8th

John and I came to an arrangement this last month that we will sell seeds and such in the shop. It means he will join me to work in the shop rather than standing out in all weathers, which he is finding bad for his back. In reference to the change I decided to change the title of my regular advertisement in the Mercury to say 'RAFFALD'S SHOP Near the Exchange, Manchester', which is how I hear it referred to all the time.

Many people assure me they will only shop at Raffald's to be sure of getting good food. I am not sure I approve of the informality but if it reaches more people I must be guided by my customers. I made sure I included a full list of my products so that there would be no mistaking whose shop it was.

Canterbury, Shrewsbury and *Derbyshire* Brawn, *Newcastle* Salmon, *Yorkshire* Hams, Tongues and Chaps, Potted Woodcocks, Char and Potted Meats, Portable Soup for Travellers, also a large Quantity of fresh Mushroom Catchup, Walnut Catchup, Lemon Pickle and Browning for Made Dishes; Pickled Mushrooms, Barberrys Mangos and other Sorts of Pickles; dry and wet Sweetmeats, Plumb Cakes for Weddings, Christenings, and all Kinds of Cakes; Mackroons and Biskets, Jellies, Creams, Flummery, Gold and Silver Webs for covering Sweetmeats, and all other Decorations for cold Entertainments; Morells, Truffles, Maccaronys, Vermacelli, Capers, Anchovies, Chyan Pepper; Sagoe, Isinglass; best Durham Flour or Mustard; *Jordan* and *Victoria* Almonds; Salt Petre, Bay Salt, Poland and Common Starch, Lemons and Oranges, &c. &c.

NB The REGISTER OFFICE continued as usual. Several good Cooks for large Families are wanted.

Likewise just received to be sold Wholesale and Retail, a large Quantity of best *London* Split Peas, and all Sorts of Garden Peas and Beans, Canary and Hemp Seeds; where Country Gardeners, Shopkeepers and others may be well supplied with as good and as cheap as in *London*, with good Allowances to those that sell again.

1768 Dec 6th canal meeting and finishing the book

The world just never stands still. Today I heard tell of an exciting meeting that was notified in this week's Mercury. It seems Mr. Brindley, the man who designed the Duke of Bridgewater's canal, has done research on extending a canal route all the was from Leeds to Liverpool, clean across the country! On December ninth at twelve noon he has called for all gentlemen desirous of promoting the canal venture to attend the Golden Lion in Liverpool on that day. What a wonder it would be if that was done. Mr. Brindley is certainly the man who knows how to do it.

Well I have my own engineering to focus on and that is to engineer a finished manuscript for Mr. Harrop before the end of the year and before this next baby arrives. It is only the Observations for a Grand Table to finish, and the table settings engraving, which Mr. Harrop will arrange for me once I give him my own drawing.

Directions for a Grand Table.

JANUARY being a Month when Entertainments are most used, and most wanted, from that Motive I have drawn my Dinner at that Season of the Year, and hope it will be of Service to my worthy Friends; not that I have the least Pretension to confine any Lady to such a particular Number of Dishes, but to choose out of them what Number they please; being all in Season, and most of them to be got without much difficulty; as I from long Experience can tell what a troublesome Task it is to make a Bill of Fare to be in Propriety, and not to have two Things of the same Kind; and being desirous of rendering it easy for the Future, have made it my Study to set out the Dinner in as elegant a Manner as lies in my Power, and in the modern Taste; but finding I could not express myself to be understood by young House-keepers, in placing the Dishes upon the Table, obliged me to have two Copper-plates; as I am very unwilling to leave even the weakest Capacity in the Dark, being my greatest Study to render my whole Work both plain and easy. As to French Cooks and old experienced House-keepers, they have no Occasion for my Assistance, it is not from them I look for any Applause. I have not engraved a Copper-Plate for a third Course, or a Cold Collation, for that generally consists of Things extravagant; but I have endeavoured to set out a Dessert of Sweetmeats, which the industrious House-keeper may lay up in Summer at a small Expence, and when added to what little fruit is then in season, will make a pretty Appearance after the Cloth is drawn, and be entertaining to the Company. Before you draw your Cloth, have all your Sweetmeats and Fruit dished up in China Dishes or Fruit Baskets; and as many Dishes as you have in one Course, so many Baskets or Plates your Dessert must have; and as my Bill of Fare is twenty-five in each Course, so must your Dessert be of the same Number, and set out in the same Manner, and as Ice is very often plentiful at that Time, it will be easy to make five different Ices for the Middle, either to be served upon a Frame or without, with four Plates of dried Fruit round them; Apricots, Green Gages, Grapes, and Pears — the four outward Corners, Pistachio Nuts, Prunelloes, Oranges, and Olives — the *four Squares, Nonpareils, Pears, Walnuts, and Filberts — the two in the Centre, betwixt the Top and Bottom, Chestnuts and Portugal Plums — for six long Dishes, Pineapples, French Plums, and the four Brandy Fruits, which are Peaches, Nectarines, Apricots, and Cherries.*

That must now be the last word. I have written almost every recipe I know of. Just a few more and then it will be complete. I must press on with this endeavour even though I feel it is really too much for me in my current condition.

I am weary with work and this baby is sitting so low down it is painful wherever I sit. I will finish my book, I am determined, however weak I feel. Then Mr. Harrop will be satisfied and he can go ahead with the printing of it and I can dedicate myself to getting back into my business. Perhaps if the book does really well I may make enough money to quit the shop.

1769

1769 Jan 28th

At last I have been delivered from the pain and weariness of pregnancy but I am still weak from this last childbirth. Despite Mrs. Withnall's best attentions it was a difficult birth and the baby was so sickly that John took her straightaway to be christened. We have called her Betty, after Lady Betty of Arley, and in honour of the book being born this year too. We will have a little christening cake once I feel well enough to hold a whisk once again. Just now it is all I can do to scrutinize the proof sheets for the book that Mr. Harrop sends me at regular intervals.

It has been helpful having John in the shop, although he does not have the best manner with some of my good customers. Mary is always at his side, however, and she knows how to soothe any ruffled feathers. We also have some good kitchen maids who can be trusted to keep up the standards of our baking without needing to be watched every minute.

1769 Feb 1st Manchester's nude male race

Oh my, what a day it was today! It was the naked male race over on Kersal Moor and I had hoped to take a stand there, but the competition for the spaces was too fierce. I had to be content to sell what I could from my shop, though I made sure to take a basket of goods with me and I managed a brisk trade thanks to William's help, running back and forth to the shop for more goods when I needed them.

I found a ready market for my made dishes and John did well selling his posies too, which saved him from staying the whole day in the Bull's Head. He really is getting in thick with Mr. Budworth, the landlord there. I do hope he is not making a nuisance of himself as I find it a good source of business since I catered for the dinner for King Christian, and I am hoping for more.

The race crowd was in a very jolly mood thanks to all the handsome young military men joining in the race, especially the big, brawny Scotsman, Captain Roger Aytoun who won himself a bride. Mrs. Mynshull was judging the race but took her duties a little too seriously, I think. She presented the captain with his purse of money and a deal was made between them.

He claimed her hand in marriage as his prize, and she did not refuse him. I could not believe it when I heard. I have always thought Mrs. Mynshull such a respectable lady. How she could lower herself to be part of such a spectacle I do not know, and at the age of sixty-four she is surely old enough to know better. Her friends tried to advise her but it seemed her mind was set on the Scotsman. His charm tempted her but I fear she will suffer the consequences of a young husband who, I hear, has quite questionable habits.

The wedding will be tomorrow and it cannot go well. John tells me that Captain Aytoun was in the Bull's Head all the rest of the day, drinking with his acquaintance. I could hear enough of the men from our window, making terrible noises all evening, loud enough to wake my poor babies. I sent word to John to beg them to calm their behaviour, but it did not abate. John did not come back till much later and he was so drunk he fell asleep in a chair. He managed to tell me that the young man was having second thoughts about the wedding and had told everyone around that he would be staying at the Bull's Head forever more, he was so disinclined to marry that old woman.

I hope reports of his behaviour reach Mrs. Mynshull's ears so that she may think better of it. It is such a lewd business altogether and it is wrong to use marriage vows to satisfy wanton lust, which is all it can be on her part. On his side it can only be greed, to be bought like a prize bull at market. Neither of them are showing due reverence and I think they will both get what they deserve.

1769 Feb 2nd Aytoun/Mynshull wedding

I went along to see the wedding of Captain Aytoun to the widow Mynshull, as a good Christian should, to support two people making their vows before God but more in hopes that one or other would come to their senses in time to repent. I am not sure how the vicar could perform the service and keep his position. It was certainly a travesty.

The young man had kept to his promise to keep drinking and was so dead drunk that he was only upright because he had a stout fellow on either side lifting him up. They had half carried, half dragged him down the aisle and sat either side of him in the pew as they waited, but I saw him fall forwards twice as we waited for the bride to arrive.

Of course she was there promptly and I fancy she was surprised to see that he had turned up. Maybe she had second thoughts herself. Her face was a picture of doubt but for her own reasons she pressed on with the ceremony with determination. When the vicar asked if anyone knew reason why they should not marry, I could hear the whispers ripple around the church. Everyone looked at their neighbour, and Captain Aytoun's head suddenly jerked up, his eyes wild as he turned to us in the congregation. I thought someone should point out the wickedness they were committing but it was not my place to do so.

We all minded our peace and the wedding ended with the young men dragging the groom off in the direction of the Bull's Head yet again. He may be married in name but he will surely be dead before long if he tries to keep his promise to stay drunk. What a waste of a good fighting man. He was believed to have a good career in front of him but what will happen to him now?

The bride departed the church in the opposite direction with what few friends had come to support her. It was notable that none of her children had attended the service. Once they hear of it they may try to have her committed to the Lunatic Asylum, and maybe she would benefit from a stay there. I cannot foresee a happy marriage for either of them.

1769 March 6th

Today I drafted my advertisement for my new cookery manual. Mr. Harrop has been most helpful in deciding which words to emphasise. He really is a most excellent friend. I must send his wife a dish of my specialty, fricando of veal. It is a particular favourite of his, I know. He says his mouth waters so much when he reads over the proofs of my pages that he often ruins a page and has to order a new one to be run off. He is such a wit, such a clever man and generous with his time and skill. I doubt my poor efforts would have turned into such an excellent book without him.

I wanted the advertisement to be bold, but not showy. It needed to be eye catching and distinctive. I am very pleased with the title of the book. That I must credit to dear Mr. Harrop. I simply wanted to call it the Experienced Housekeeper but he insisted on adding the word English to give it a touch of class and substance. I was not completely in favour of the amendment for I am a great believer in the excellence of French cuisine, or the common sense of Yorkshire housekeepers. However, I could not dispute that I was for many years an English housekeeper, and it was for families without the benefit of one such as myself, with the valuable experience I have gained, that I wrote this book.

It is for the many newly rich families, new to Society who will not have the knowledge of how to keep a good table, and my recipes are intended for the young ladies of the town. Ladies who are not brought up to run a great house as it should be run, will have need of the guidance my book can provide. There are certainly not many as knowledgeable as my own dear Lady Betty of Arley. Now she is a great lady and I learned many of her shrewd ways of food management. I hope she is not disappointed with some of the adjustments I have made to some of the dishes.

1769 April 4th

Mr. Harrop was very kind today and handed me a print of today's Mercury advertisement for my book. I think it looks very well, and for the amount it costs me I hope it brings in a good number of subscribers, for I am nearly one hundred short of making the total needed to cover all the costs and make a little bit of profit for myself.

The notice had to contain all the benefits to be gained to reach the desired subscribers. I know that my expertise will be worth the investment, all my knowledge is poured into this endeavour, but the notice needs to convince enough people to buy it.

'Ready for the Press and speedily will be Published,
An entire new work,
Wrote for the Use and Ease of Ladies, House-keepers,
Cooks, &c, entitled
The EXPERIENCED ENGLISH House-keeper,
by Elizabeth Raffald,
Wrote purely from Practice, and Dedicated to the
Hon. Lady Elizabeth Warburton,
Whom the Author lately served as House-keeper
First Part lemon Pickle, Browning for all Sorts of made Dishes, Soups, Fish, plain Meat, Game, made Dishes both hot and cold, Pyes, Puddings, &c.

Second Part, All kinds of Confectionary, particularly the Gold and Silver Web for covering of Sweetmeats, and a Desert of Spun Sugar, with Directions to set out a Table in the most elegant Manner, and in the most modern Taste, Floating Islands, Fish Ponds, Transparent Puddings, Trifles, Whips, &C.

Third Part, Pickling, Potting, and Collaring, Wines, Vinegars, Catchups, Distilling, with two most valuable Recipes, one for refining Malt Liquors, the other for curing Acid Wines, and a correct List of every Thing in Season in every Month of the Year.

N.B. At every Place where the Subscriptions are taken in, the Contents of the Book may be seen

CONDITIONS

I. The Work shall be printed with all convenient speed, and a good Paper, and with a new Letter, in a large Octavo

II. Price to Subscribers, Five Shillings, neatly bound.

III. After the Subscription is closed, the Book will be advanced to Six Shillings.

IV. The Book to be signed by the Author's own Hand-writing, and to be entered at Stationers Hall.

Subscriptions to be taken in by Messrs Fletcher and Anderson, Booksellers, St Paul's Churchyard, in London; Mr. Ager, Confectioner, in York; Mr. Eaton, Silk Mercer, in Doncaster; Mr. John Wetherell, in Hull; Mr. Tindall, Confectioner, in Leeds; Mr. Kendall, at the Peacock, Derbyshire; Mr. Ashburner,

> Bookseller, in Kendal; Mr. Ashburner, Bookseller, in Lancaster; Mr. Stuart, Bookseller, in Preston; Mr. Dunblain, Printer and Bookseller, in Liverpool; Mr. Poole, Bookseller, in Chester; Mr. Leigh, Bookseller, in Northwich, and by the Author, Elizabeth Raffald, Confectioner, near the Exchange, Manchester.'

1769 May funny news story

There was such chatter going on in my shop today, and such laughter that no work was done for a full half an hour while we were told this story. It was not funny for the poor unfortunate who was the victim but it is reassuring that one can rely on gentlemen to protect the ladies against highway attacks. Once it was known that all were safe and unharmed it was a pleasure to laugh about it.

Mr. Wainwright gave me his copy of the newspaper with the item as it was reported. His friend had been in the coach, and had told him how the company had laughed and cursed when they found the results of their heroics had resulted in nothing but an attack on an innocent person. Mr. Wainwright said his friend would be better prepared when he next made that journey.

> "The Leeds coach was stopped at Helsbury on Tuesday Night Last about twelve o'clock by a single Highwayman who was shot at and wounded by one of the Passengers but escaped; his Horse however was secured. The Passengers thinking they had wounded him, got out of the Coach and in the Confusion and Darkness of the Night seized one of their Fellow Travellers, tied him Hand and foot and threw him in the Basket behind the Coach where, in spite of all the Assurances of a Companion, he was obliged to lie until they arrived at the next Stage, when after several Interrogations, they were convinced of their Mistake and released him."

1769 June

My advertisement for the book has run several times more now, and it is bringing in more requests for my book, which is a great relief, for I was afraid I may not raise enough subscribers. Mr. Harrop assures me not to be concerned, he sees this all the time. An idea can be slow to catch on, then it reaches more people and becomes talked about as a thing to be greatly desired, and before you know it another print run is required to satisfy demand. I do not expect to reach those heady heights but I will be glad when I have some profit in my hand and not a debt. We do not have any money to spare at the moment. Any extra I have made this last twelve months has been spent on investment for the book. It must do well or I am undone.

1769 July another baby

Mrs. W tells me I am working too hard and if I do not take some rest it could be dangerous to me. She confirmed what I already knew, that I once more am carrying a child. Her advice is that I must take more care or risk both my life and that of this baby. I do not see that I have any choice. I must work or there will be no money to keep my family, and the baby must take his chance.

John is bringing in less money every week, having lost his passion for work and finding one for the cockpit, where he is convinced he will make his fortune. I know he misses working on the fine gardens of country houses and is wishing he had never left Now he says that business does not suit him at all, something he ran away from on his father's land when he went to apprentice himself at Perfects in Pontefract.

It was always his ambition to be in charge of a great garden, he is such a man of the outdoors. When he had his position at Arley he was convinced he could make more money in business. Now he has had experience of both he does not know what he wants and hides his shame in his hopeless attempts to make fast money. It will never come but he cannot see it. Once this baby is born, if I have my strength back, I will look for better opportunities for him, ones that will keep him well away from the cockpit.

1769 August

Today I heard some talk from Mr. Artingstall, the journeyman for Thwaite and Moresby, about a scandal brewing in the growing trade in cotton spinning. He sat in my shop and ate some sweet patties before he went onto his next call and was quite in the mood to tell all and sundry what was going on. Two days ago he had been at Preston, where they do some of the finest spinning, and had heard the scandal there.

A man named Richard Arkwright, known as a barber and

peruke maker, was turning his interest to the money he might make from spinning, though he had no knowledge of the process at all. He was known to be an enterprising man and had come across one John Kay. He got him to talking about the new spinning machine he was building for Mr. Highs and Mr. Arkwright managed to possess himself of a model.

That nice Thomas Highs, who was such a clever man, had last year had John Kay build him his first spinning machine which was also stolen from him., Now Mr. Highs has improved on that first machine and invented one called a Water Frame, which Mr. Kay had built for him. Mr. Highs named it a Throstle and it is for the spinning of twist by rollers to run on water power. It sounds ingenious to be sure, but once again Mr. Highs is likely to be cheated out of his success by an enterprising man. I am all for progress but it should not take away another man's trade.

Mr. Artingstall was all excited about his story, for in his trade it is an important development, promising riches to the winner, and he expected trouble to ensue. Stealing of inventions is very much frowned on, although it happens such a lot.

I wondered if they might find a machine to replace his work as he spent so much of his day sitting in my shop, but he was confident they would not find a machine that could ride a horse from Preston to Manchester without being shook to pieces.

1769 September

What a day, what a day! I almost thought I would not make it through when one of the new kitchen maids dropped a whole tray of spun sugar globes just as I was ready to dress them up for the table! I thought I was ruined, the pièce de resistance of the dinner gone. I had to set to with some of the silver globes together with the few golden ones we could rescue. Dredged in triple refined sugar they looked good enough to send out so the loss was not missed. I daresay they may have looked better but I declare I was for to drop by the time we finished.

These dinners at the Bull's Head are a feather in my cap and no mistake, but I fear they will be the death of me if I cannot train more girls in my ways. I will be glad when my book is published and all can avail themselves of my methods.

Mr. Harrop promises me it will be ready soon but cannot give me a date yet so I must only advertise it in vague terms. It is no use continually promising it will be soon, I fear, for others may have the same idea and have theirs ready before mine. Mrs. Blomeley, I am sure, is thinking of it. It won't be as good as mine, of course, but she is better at making a noise about things than I am, the woman has no idea of discretion. I must read through another ten sheets of proofs tomorrow to check all is as I require but I fervently hope they are the last.

Little Betty is still fiercely suckling, I have no fear of her health anymore, unlike poor little Grace who clings to me so fretfully whenever she sees me. I am constantly in fear of her catching a fever in this damp, muddy environment which is Manchester. At least I have no such worries of Sarah and Emma who behave beautifully and show promise of being graceful young ladies. Their natures are all that I could want.

If only I could give John the son he so desperately needs to carry on the business. Then he may regain some of his pride in his work. Thankfully he has stopped going so much to the cock pit and has turned back to helping his brother James in his garden so he is once again bringing in more money than is lost in gambling. Perhaps God will grant us the boon of a son with this one I carry now.

I also hope He grants me the boon of an end to my child bearing. Each one drains me of so much strength. I am beginning to think I may not be able to have boys, but we are in God's hands. Please God this one I carry will have the strength his papa needs.

1769 late October The Experienced English Housekeeper first issue

Mr. Harrop had promised my book would be ready and so it was. I cannot believe that as I sit here I hold a copy of my book, my own book, produced by me, with a little help from Mr. Harrop. To be sure, no book would be produced without the skills of the printer and his dark mysterious arts, just as a meal does not assemble itself from the raw ingredients. Without the skill of a good cook such as myself it can be a lumpen, tasteless disaster.

Now everyone can learn the skills that I have perfected. With my book I can teach more than I could ever have hoped to accommodate in my little school. More than Mrs. Blomeley can too, however she may boast. I say put it down in a book, Mrs. Blomeley and then we may judge whose methods are superior. Her girls can never produce the delights that I have learnt over the years. One needs 'the touch' and she definitely doesn't have it, certainly not with flummery, of that I am sure.

Of course I must be reconciled that now Mrs. Blomeley may read my book herself and gain the knowledge from me but I doubt she will ever say so. I am sure that she would never admit to buying a copy although it would give me great satisfaction to sign one for her. I can be gracious in my victory.

She always professed to be writing a book herself but she does not have the grasp of language that is needed to converse with the truly genteel classes that I flatter myself I have. Not for nothing were my years spent in service at some of the finest houses in Lincolnshire and Yorkshire, or the years spent learning at my father's knee. My dearest papa, I always give thanks for his love and dedication.

1769 Nov 9th

Today I was able to insert my final advertisement for subscribers to my book, The Experienced English Housekeeper, (oh how I like to write that, it sounds so grand), which will be available Wednesday next. It was posted in the York Courant, an excellent paper which will reach all the people of substance in York and around.

My arm aches worse than when I have made fifty spun sugar globes for table decorations, and yet I have not cooked at all today. For the last few weeks I have been continually signing copies of my book and have finally signed all eight hundred of them. Mr. Harrop had suggested I take only fifty at a time but if a job needs to be done them I get on and do it. I needed to finish for I am catering a most important dinner on Friday, so I did not have the time to dilly dally.

Finally all the books are signed and I can make the arrangements to send them to all the sellers who have taken in subscriptions for me. Mr. Harrop kindly offered to do it for me but he wanted a rather extravagant fee for doing so. I prefer to do it myself and know that the correct quantities have gone to the right people.

I am pleased that so many places agreed to take my books although some have demanded a bigger fee than others. Mr. Fletcher, of Fletcher and Anderson booksellers, in St Paul's Churchyard, London, was the most demanding but he knows it is critical for one to have a presence in the capital so he could demand more. Thankfully Mr. Ager's confectionery shop in York is just as important in my view, and he was less grasping, simply fair. I am glad to have so many offices acting on my behalf but it is also a benefit to them not only to take a share of the profit but to add to their stature in having such a knowledgeable book on their shelves. I think I should still stay in profit even if it is less than I had hoped.

Mr. Harrop has assured me that, if this volume of sales can be continued, a second volume will be more profitable. He will be able to reuse the plates so long as I do not make many changes, for of course I have noticed many omissions and a few mistakes, which must be down to Mr. Harrop's boys composing the plates wrongly.

I also have several recipes that friends have been pressing on me when they heard I was composing a book. I did not want anyone else's recipes in my book, but I can see that it may sell more volumes to the friends of those who contribute. I will consider some from those people I can trust to make them properly. Others have clearly not been tested properly and so I have quietly lost them. Only the best will appear if I have the opportunity to issue a second edition.

It has been most gratifying to see how many subscriptions my book has received. Of course I must thank Mr. Harrop for his guidance and encouragement and for the reach of his newspaper. I have had many enquiries locally but I must keep the advertisements in the newspaper if I wish to sell more.

1769 Dec 24th

It is a relief to sit down with a pen in my hand once more for I am got so busy, and I am so weary with the weight of this baby that I scarce have time or patience to sit at night with my diary. It's all I can do to keep my eyes open and my hand moving across the page but I enjoy the chance to put my thoughts down. It has been one of those days when I wonder again if I was right to marry John. I feel so alone now that were it not for Mary I doubt I could keep going.

John was always a hard worker, but he always had a capacity to find amusement quicker than I ever could. Once that amusement was whenever we two were together but now it seems that when I do get a precious few minutes to look up from my work he has found his amusement in the company of others. I cannot begrudge him his enjoyment while he brings in an income from his labours, but there are times when I could wish he could do more to take the burden of progress from my shoulders.

How will we ever secure a good future for our girls if we do not progress? They must be seen as worthy of a man of some fortune or at least the promise of one, for in this town of Manchester there are those who are raising themselves good fortunes by their own efforts. Even a humble born weaver may, by their own ingenuity and application, advance into a respectable position in this cotton trade which is all around us now.

Our girls can be the ideal mates, knowing what is needed to promote their husband's business, trained in skills of economy and elegance. They will have an opportunity I could never have had. I have proved it is possible for a woman to be a success in business but I do not wish for them the hard work of a business. It is constant work and financial juggling from dawn to midnight.

My wish for my girls is the opportunity to rise into nice society. They have been educated to be ladies, and here in Manchester they have the possibility of leaving their humble roots behind in a way never possible before. The world is opening up here, and if a young weaver can be the next tycoon, who knows what is possible? Look at Mr. Arkwright, one day a peruke maker, now a man building a fortune.

Yes, tomorrow I must speak with John on this subject; I cannot carry this weight alone. We must do more to assure our girls' success and a future for our unborn son.

1770

1770 January Dec 27th Lady B's daughter, Ann, died, 28th Hannah/Anna Raffald christened

Well it seems that yet again we are not to be blessed with a son. My new daughter, Hannah we have called her, is beautiful but it adds more burden to my shoulders. I will need to make sure all my girls will be assured of a good life.

At least with this baby I have no fear for her health. She is a strong baby with such a happy nature that she is no trouble to manage. It is just as well, for I do not know what more I could do. I already feel that I work all the hours God sends, and Mary does too.

I must look to finding more items to sell in my shop; perhaps I can stock the perfume waters that are all the rage. My nephew Joshua has shown a talent for mixing up potions and waters and he says they are nought but a bit of water with a little essence sprinkled into them. He is always late back when he delivers to Mr. Wagstaff, the apothecary, in Back square.

He tells me there are hundreds of chymicals to make into potions and waters, hundreds of different substances. He wants learn more about them and has asked Mr. Wagstaff if he may go to help him on Saturdays after he has made his deliveries.

I had to tell him that Saturday is my busy day but if he delivers quickly then I will not go looking for him and he can dream among the chymicals all the rest of the day. If he turns out to be truly useful at it I will speak to his mother about securing him an apprentice place, if Mr. Wagstaff will have him.

At least we may plan for a future for him if he is not to be cut off before he has done anything. I am thinking of my dear Lady Betty and her daughter Ann who she lost December last. It must be a great sadness to lose a child when she has reached twenty one years of age. A mother must think that her work is done by that age and all that is needed is for a good marriage to be made.

I am glad to say that my girls are growing nicely but I live in fear of some disease taking them from me. When it floods in this town the streets run nearly ankle high in dirty muddy water which can sit in some streets for weeks. The rats become ever more present and crimes seem to be worse.

There was such a wailing and a screaming Saturday last when one of the women sentenced for whipping at the Market Cross was shouting her innocence all afternoon. She was with two men who took their punishment manfully, as they should, no doubt grateful that they were not subject to transportation. The Mercury carried the report this week

> Robert Shepherd of Rochdale and James Hilton, both for Seven Years each for stealing Goods out of the shop of Mr. Jeremiah Kay and Mr. Henry Grundy. On the stocks was one William Lord for being found in the Shop of Mr. Hall on Long Miln-gate, with false keys and picklocks; Robert Wolfenden for stealing a Silver Cup, the Property of Mr. Pilling of Bury, and Mary Thorp for stealing Handkerchiefs out of the Shop of Messrs. Phillips and Greenway.

Oh, that woman screamed so loud, I nearly dropped the cake I was getting out of the oven. Thank goodness they are not all like her or I would need to move from my shop, and I do not yet want to do that. The crowds that come to view the miscreants bring good business that makes up for the occasional woman in distress. I can make good money from if I am shrewd and use this time to look around and see what my next venture may be to make more money than I do now. I already have an idea that may work.

1770 Feb 20th Mercury ad Bull's Head change of landlord

The change I had been worrying about is now official. Mr. Budworth has handed over the running of the Bull's Head to Mr. Richard Alsop and so I must negotiate terms with a new landlord for the food I supply.

They each took a notice in the Mercury this week to make it official and to tell everyone in the Town. Mr. Budworth's was a very polite thankful Acknowledgements to the Nobility, Gentry and Others, hoping they would favour his successor in the House. Mr. Alsop's notice was placed directly below his, entreating the same for the Continuance of their Favour, promising to have wines and every other accommodation that may be required.

My negotiations were helped by the insistence of the Dragoons that they would not allow of anyone else but their excellent Mrs. Raffald being engaged to supply their meals. Captain Haydock has said he has never tasted finer cooking than mine and would challenge anyone who said otherwise.

1770 March 29th burial of Grace

Tonight I am beside myself with grief for today I said goodbye to my beautiful little Grace. She was well named and I always knew she was too good for this earth but I do wish God had seen fit to leave her in my care a little longer than this. I will remember her in my prayers every night.

She was only two years old and so beautiful, with the blond curls of my sister Jane, so different to her own sisters. They all have the dark, coarse tresses of John's family. They each have a nursemaid who tussle with them daily to tame them into something presentable, but Grace's ringlets formed a veritable halo round her gentle head. She was a little beauty and showed such aptitude to learning her letters. Even at two she could spell her name.

I will miss her dreadfully, but she is with God now, I am sure she will be at his side now for she wasn't with us long enough to accumulate any sin. I am convinced though that it was the dirt of this town that made her ill. She needed to breathe some good country air and I wish now I had sent her to my sister Jane in Yorkshire, God's own county. The air there would have saved her, I am sure, but she sickened so quickly that she was soon too ill to make the journey.

I see now that I should have acted sooner but that is no use to her now. I was glad at least that she could be buried in the Collegiate Church here. I was determined her grave would be marked for me to visit. My poor angel deserved the best and we made a respectable mourning party, even John's brother George came into Town with his wife Mary.

Their younger brother James was also there of course, with his face mournful as usual, hoping he may not catch anything by being there and his wife was too sick to come he said. She does not do very well with his anxious moods, I have noticed. She would do well to ignore his worrisome ways which soon bring her down.

I had allowed my shop girls to come, provided they could look decent and had suitable clothes. My babies Sarah, Emma and Betty looked their best and their nursemaids kept them in good behaviour as they said goodbye to their sister. My baby Anna was in my arms, it seems no time since we were in that building to welcome her into the world, barely two months have passed. My sister Jane's boys made up the party, standing to attention very well I thought, a credit to their mother. Yes, I think we showed the people of Manchester that we know how to show our respect.

I insisted that Grace had the best coffin available, even if I did have to persuade Mr. Syddall to take less than his first outrageous price. And I wasn't going to let him foist any knothole riddled wood on me either. One or two were acceptable but any more is just too common. My shop girls draped the front room of the shop in black of course and we proceeded from there through the market place. I only paid for one bell ringer and the sermon by Reverend Peploe but I made sure to take them some of my newly baked pies in thanks.

One expence spared was the fee for the undertakers to carry such a tiny coffin. John carried it tenderly and looked like he would not let go of it, I saw him struggle to keep his composure too putting his favourite little girl into the earth. I will send Joshua to plant a small rosemary bush over the spot tomorrow to remember my little girl and surround her with its aroma as she takes her leave of this world.

1770 April Thomas Highs in Manchester

I saw such a strange little man today as I was walking through town. I had cause to cut through the alley to the Exchange and there, standing with his back to the wall, was a little man, staring out in front of him. I thought no more of it at first, he seemed to be in no distress, and so I passed by with no more than a nod. However, when I was making my way back to the shop, after spending an hour or two setting up a dinner for Mrs. Walker, there he still was, looking as though he had not moved an inch.

I noticed Mr. Alsop in the yard of the Bull's Head looking my way and he shook his head, gesturing for me to walk past the man. He did not seem dangerous, he was far too small a man but I was concerned for his welfare. I went over to Mr. Alsop to ask his advice. Mr. Alsop reassured me that it was just his way and was best left alone. He told me the man was no bother but got in a terrible temper if anyone disturbed him. When he told me his name I understood completely. It was the inventive Mr. Thomas Highs, a man of vision when it came to progress.

I waited a while, passing the time of day with Mr. Alsop, out of which came a very useful commission for a dinner next week, so Mr. Highs did me a good turn, although he never came out of his trance while I was there.

1770 May 8th Boston Massacre March 5th

There was such a long article in the Mercury today about a dreadful trouble in Boston, America on the fifth of March last. It is too terrible for words. Mr. Harrop had sent word to me to apologise that he would not be able to accommodate my advertisement this week due to the space needed for this report.

The front page was almost entirely given over to an article, with a dreadful letter from the Captain of the 29th Regiment who seemed to have been the main victims in a terrible act of treason. I thought it was such a serious case that I cut it from the paper and have placed it at the back of my journal.

I am very grateful that nothing of that nature will happen here now that the business of the Pretender to the throne is over. I feel safe that the Militia take seriously their duty to protect the honest citizenry.

1770 June 12 Mr. Arnold Fichar, dancing master, opens a school at Mrs. Ridge's near St Ann's church, George III's birthday

Today was such a noisy day, with bells ringing, and the gentlemen of the Dragoons firing rounds in St Ann's-square, but it was a very gay affair. With Mary's help I was kept busy all morning, cooking up sweetmeats and fancies to be sold to the crowds in Town for the King's birthday.

The bells started at eight o'clock in the morning and in the afternoon the Dragoons, along with four companies of the Royal Lancashire Militia who are currently quartered here, formed a very impressive sight. They were men with very good appetites too, though their uniform is not as striking as the Dragoons, who wore Oak Leaves in their Hats.

I just happened to have business in the square this afternoon and so I was there as they fired three rounds in salute to his Majesty the King. My, the noise was terrific; I think King George himself may have heard it in London. This evening there is an assembly for the Nobility, Gentry and Others, but I was not favoured with the privilege of providing the food. I believe the honour went to that woman. No matter, I have plenty of work to do with my shop, the Register Office, the school and book selling.

There are now so many schools in this area that I sometimes wonder if we can all stay in business. Fortunately the need for educated hostesses in this town grows as fast as the trade that is making men wealthy. The latest school to begin is at Mrs. Ridge's, near St Ann's church, where Mr. Fichar, my erstwhile dancing master, has opened his school with another at Mrs. Towler's. I wondered what he would do once he had left my school.

There is also Mr. Cleavin who has his school just around the corner, at the Lower Swan on Market-street-lane, which offers tuition in lunchtimes and evenings. Mr. Moratel is teaching a very superior kind of French in his school at the Three Tuns Tavern across the Market place on Smithy Door. He also attends at gentlemen's homes if needed and holds an evening at Crompton's coffee house on Friday evenings when only French is spoken.

I dearly wish there was such a facility that ladies could attend for I would enjoy the opportunity to talk in French with others. I must begin such sessions in my own school for my young ladies. It will give me an added advantage, although none of the other schools can already compete with my superior methods. Ladies at my school not only gain superior skills in dancing and French, but also the most important skill of producing distinguished dinners with economy. In that regard I have no equal in this Town.

1770 June Selling the copyright 1 Mr. Baldwin enquires

I have received a most interesting letter from a printing press in London. The owner, Mr. Baldwin, has seen my cookbook and was so impressed by it that he has made me an offer for the copyright. Of course I am not surprised for his is the fifth such letter I have received. I think every publisher in London has written to me in the previous month. What has intrigued me about Mr. Baldwin's letter is that he has shewn a true interest in the value of the information within the book. I must take some time to consider if his offer would be good business for me.

As he argues, I would no longer have any costs to outlay for another edition, nor would the correspondence to find new subscribers for the revised edition fall solely on my shoulders. He has even promised me that they have a process which will allow them to reproduce my signature on the page. That does tempt me, so that however many books I produce I do not have to sign every copy. My arm ached for three days after the first edition. However it does also ring a note of alarm that if he can already do this then others may do it too.

If I do not take his offer I may find that it becomes worthless to say genuine when pirate copies may look just the same. I detest those who use such low means of making money but I cannot ignore that they exist.

Mr. Baldwin also promises me a commission on every book sold. Of course it is much smaller than it should be but I shall assume that it is simply his opening bid and proceed from there. I will not sell my rights cheaply.

He does not mention what he proposes about advertising costs so I want his terms written clearly. It must be considered for if it is not promoted diligently my book would soon be overlooked in the multitudes of books now being produced.

Mr. Baldwin's offer is very promising and I shall correspond with him at 47, Paternoster Row, London, to see what may come of a little negotiation. To compare I shall give the same reply to one or two of his neighbours who also seem keen to get my business. That way I may be sure of my best offer.

I hope my dear Mr. Harrop will guide me in my choice for he does not want the work. His press is too reduced now to take on another work of this size. I had my suspicions that the work involved was too much for him but he was determined to fulfill the contract.

I know he did not expect it to be such a large book when he

agreed to it but it was most convenient for me to have my printer so close by. It was my greatest joy to be able to call into his office each day with my corrections and helpful suggestions. As production went on he was too busy on the press to see me, and it was more often Mrs. Harrop who would talk through the changes with me. She really is a woman of excellent taste, though I found sometimes she was a little slow in understanding my meaning. However, it was useful for me to see how someone of limited ability might perceive the instructions though it was better when I could instruct Mr. Harrop directly.

I will not be able to do that when it is produced in London but I am confident that the book will stand up well just as it is. It is only the additions that I propose for the next edition which need to be checked. I shall make it one of my conditions that each of the new sheets is printed first for my perusal, and then I may know how reliable he is. I set great store by Mr. Harrop's opinion but it is still my business and I must be the one to care for it. I shall negotiate with Mr. Baldwin and we shall see if he is the man for the job.

1770 July 3 3months pregnant/Officers Mess in Bulls Head/May 16th Louis 16th married Marie Antoinette

Today's news contained a report of an unfortunate ending to the wedding of the Dauphin in France. It is never good to start a marriage with such a bad omen,

> The Fireworks, which were exhibited on Wednesday Evening, in the Palace of Louis XVth, on Occasion of the Dauphin's marriage, ended in a dismal Catastrophe, by the Crowd all pressing to get away at one and the same Time. Several Persons of the First Condition, who were endeavouring to get to their Carriages, were bruised, and trodden under Foot; and so great was the Confusion, that Coaches were overturned, and Horses smothered; 137 dead Bodies were exposed the next Day, to be owned; among which are two Chevaliers de St Louis. And such are the Accounts of the Bruised, who died after they were with Difficulty carried Home, that, upon the most moderate Conjectures, at least 300 Persons are supposed to have lost their Lives on this Occasion; but

> it does not yet appear, that there are any English among the Number.

The news also contained a report from Boston where there is yet more trouble brewing, though this time of a different kind.

> Wednesday (in June) a Ship arrived in the River (of London), commanded by Capt. Scott, with returned Goods from Boston. Upon the Ship's arrival off Boston, the greater Part of the Merchants, to whom the Goods were consigned, refused to have them shored because their Right of Taxation was not removed; but some consented to take in their Goods, which it is supposed will be their Ruin, as few will deal with them. After the above Goods were housed, *An Importer of English Goods*, was wrote on the Doors of such as had taken them in, as a Mark of Contempt.

What a terrible way to treat honest businessmen, people will be ruined by their provocative troublemaking.

1770 Aug Selling the copyright 2 Mr. Baldwin's reply

I have heard back from Mr. Baldwin of London, who seems to think he is dealing with a country simpleton. He has made me a paltry offer, only eight hundred pounds for the copyright and a mere three pence off the sale of each book. When the book sells for six shillings I do not think six pence to the author is too much to ask.

Well, he shall receive my reply and then we shall see if he is still disposed to think kindly of me! I shall make certain that he knows I have other offers to consider.

Now it comes to it I am not so certain about signing it over and I certainly shall not unless it is worth my while. If I keep the ownership then I keep the right to choose who can print my book. It has sold so extremely well that I hope it may sell even more when I add the near one hundred receipts that have been supplied to me. Some I am not completely confident in but I will include only those from people I trust to know what they are doing, whoever has urged them onto me. I particularly like the one for tea crumpets.

> *To make* TEA CRUMPETS,
>
> *BEAT two eggs very, well, put to them a quart of warm milk and water, and a large spoonful of barm; beat in as much fine flour as will make them rather thicker than a common batter pudding, then make your bake-stone very hot, and rub it with a little butter wrapped in a clean linen cloth, then pour a large spoonful of batter upon your stone, and let it run to the size of a tea saucer; turn it, and when you want to use them toast them very crisp and butter them.*

Of course John has cast doubt on how many more books I am likely to sell. With the eight hundred already sold he thinks I have reached everyone who may want one. It is a point I must consider, I will admit. He is urging me to take the man's money now as he has a good idea of how to use it. I think work on a market stall is beginning to pall for him and he is always on the lookout for other work, especially for a grateful licensed victualler.

He told me of a conversation he had yesterday with his new good friend Charles Blakeley, of the Eagle and Child on Hangingditch. It seems the man is looking for someone to take over his business as he wants a smaller place to manage. John thinks he and I are the right people to take it on and the money would allow us to do that.

It is an exciting idea and would mean I would have only one business to manage instead of the present four. Just lately it has been extremely vexing when my food is being brought back to the shop because the boys cannot find the house where it is to go to. I have a need for a full list of directions for all my customers' addresses but I have no time to make one. It may be that I could ask Mr. Harrop to print me a few sheets of such details.

I am still considering Mr. Baldwin's offer, which needs more thought. I will not sell my book short, I know its worth but I must make a decision, though Mr. Baldwin must come considerably higher in his offer before I am prepared to sign my rights away.

1770 Sept beginning directory

I have given a lot more thought to the idea of a book of directions to the houses of people of certain standing in the Town and when I mentioned it to Mr. Harrop he tells me that such a thing already exists for London Town and is much in demand. I can see it would be extremely useful to a great many people in a place where everyone of any consequence has a house.

Travellers in business, journeymen and such, finding the town changed since their last visit, are always asking me in my shop for directions to such a one's house, or to Mr. So-and-so's business. While I await Mr. Baldwin's reply I will put myself to work on this new endeavour. It greatly appeals to me that I will be the first in the Town to produce such a useful booklet. It will only be the size of a pamphlet so I am certain that it will not be too much for Mr. Harrop to print for me. In the event that he does not want the work I may approach Mr. Baldwin to see if he will give me a good price on the printing.

1770 October 6 months pregnant/John working in a pub/chaise to Stockport 11s 6d

John has certainly taken to the life of work in an inn since he began helping Mr. Blakeley at the Eagle and Child. He says that the more he sees of it the more he is convinced it is for us, that we could make it into something special, the premier place in town.

For myself, I am not as convinced it is the best place we can take on for where it is on Hanging-ditch is not a favourable position for the best sort of people. It is not in the best part and it attracts a rougher sort of customer than I am used to. I also could not possibly take on one more enterprise until this baby is born.

I am having the most trouble with this baby than I had with all the others put together. He, (and God willing this time it must be a boy as I have no desire to go through this again), moves constantly. I have more fainting spells than is good for anyone, and my ankles are so swollen I can barely get round the kitchen. Poor Mary has to see to most of the work that is needed.

John, however, is so enamoured by the idea of running an inn that he has decided he must go to stay with his brother George, who will teach him what he needs to know of the work at his inn at Stockport.

John has taken his share of the peas, beans and hemp seeds that he was owed by James and given them to me to sell in our shop. He plans to visit his brother George as soon as he can go.

I am not convinced it will be worth the eleven shillings and sixpence that is the cost of a coach journey to Stockport, unless he can beg himself a lift from one of his so called friends at the Eagle and Child. I want him to wait until I am delivered of this baby before he leaves me alone to carry all the burden of making some profit.

1770 Nov John wants an inn

It is a joy to sit once more with a pen in my hand to write my remembrances. I have been so busy while John was away that I have scarce had time to keep my accounts. Tonight it's all I can do to keep my eyes open and my hand moving across the page. Some days I wonder again if I was right to marry John. So much of the time I feel so weary that were it not for Mary I doubt I could keep going. I cannot stop, however, or we might lose everything I have built up.

John went to his brother's of course, as soon as he could beg a lift, arguing that I had so many people around me he had nothing to do so might as well make himself useful. He returned with more resolve than ever to run an inn like George's.

John was always a hard worker, I do not doubt him there, but Manchester has been a bad influence on him. He is inclined to follow his fellows in rough talk and bad habits. He used to be content in my company but now it seems that whenever I get a precious few minutes to look up from my work, he has found his amusement in the company of others. I cannot begrudge him his time while he continues to bring in sufficient income to keep us, but there are times when I could wish he could do more to take the burden of progress from my shoulders.

How will we ever secure a good future for our girls if we do not make more money? They must be seen as suitable wives for men of good fortune or prospects. In this town of Manchester there are many like ourselves who are raising themselves goodly fortunes by their own efforts. Even a humble born weaver may, by their own ingenuity and application, advance into a respectable position in this cotton trade which is all around us now. My girls can be the ideal mates, knowing what is needed in social graces to promote her husband's business, taught by their mother to be skilled in economy and elegance. Tomorrow I must speak with John on this subject. I cannot carry this weight alone. We must both do more to assure our girls' success.

1770 Dec Brawn and perfumes in advert

My notice in the Mercury this week was quite impressive with the increase in my range of goods. Most important was the provision of good quality Canterbury, Shrewsbury and Derbyshire Brawn, which is just the thing for a hearty meal in this dreadful cold weather. I also mentioned the Sturgeon, Newcastle Salmon and Cod Sounds that I keep, superior to anyone else. It would be better if I was in a condition to make my own but carrying this baby just makes me so weary that I do not have energy enough to get through my normal day's work.

Thanks to Joshua's connection with Mr. Wagstaff I have now been able to add a full range of popular preparations for personal hygiene, etc. It will make my shop the very centre of things in Town. I now stock wash balls of Royal chymical, Royal marble, Joppa, Italian Cream, Marble and Camphire. To store them I have for sale French Straw boxes, lin'd with Burgamot; boxes with Swan down puffs; boxes of shaving powder; powder for the teeth; hair powder; Roll and Pot Pomatum; Syrup of Capillaire from Montpelier; essences of Burgamot, Lemon, Jessamy; true double distill'd Lavender water; true French Hungary Water from Montpelier; Honey Water for the hair; Jessamy water; Eau de Luce, de Violet and de Burgamot; fine green oil for inward or outward bruises, cuts and green wounds, extracted from English Herbs; drops for taking Stains out of Silk. I am certain these must bring in many more customers to my shop for with another mouth soon to feed I will need all the profit I can make.

I wish Mr. Baldwin would reply with his offer for my book but he seems to have forgotten all about me. Once this baby is born, and it must be not much longer to wait now, I shall write to him again and ask if he means to insult me by carrying on business in this way. I need to know, once and for all, if he means to make a serious offer for the copyright. John is pressing me daily for money to buy a licence. I wish he would do more of the work needed to earn it and then he might not press me so much. He will just have to wait however, for I am not yet entirely convinced that it will be a good business to take on. In any event, I will be doing nothing until I have got myself safely delivered of this baby.

1771

1771 Jan twins

I knew I had felt worse with this baby than my others and had thought it was the possibility of being a boy but nothing prepared me for Mrs. Withnall's news. She is a very knowledgeable midwife so I cannot doubt she is right in what she says, but I didn't know what to say when she told me I was having twins. It was lucky I was sitting down at the time or I may have fainted from the shock.

She cautioned me that they were both very small and not growing as much she would have liked. I must rest properly for the next few weeks until they arrive. When I assured her I would, she wagged her finger at me and said I did not know what rest was but I must do it this time or it would all be for nothing. She quite frightened me with the idea that I might lose the babies or even my own life if I did not take care. When Mary heard she became quite tetchy with me, shooing me to sit down while she took over the work. I used the time to write another letter to Mr. Baldwin. His money is needed more than ever now with another two mouths to feed.

1771 Feb 3rd Mary & male born

I am weary of body and soul and do not feel much like going on. After a dreadful labour which drained every ounce of life from me, our babies were born. Just when I thought I had been split apart by the struggle with one baby, Mrs. W told me to gather my strength for another. Both babies were not in the correct position and she had to wrestle with the first one for what seemed like hours. She needed to free it from the cord which was wrapped round its poor little neck.

Then I was in agony for another age while Mrs. Whitnall wrestled the second child to be born. I say child but I am told it could hardly have been given the name. It, or rather he, for that was the only thing to be certain of, was deformed in so many ways that he had not have survived. He never took a breath and Mrs. Whitnall quickly wrapped him in some rags without letting me look. She said it would have been too distressing for us to see him.

She went with John to baptize him and promised to see to the burial of his body. He had been born but never lived so we could not bring ourselves to give him a name. What sorrow, what despair, I felt at the only boy I could produce being so weak, unable to survive. I know now that I am destined not to have a son.

The girl baby, who we called Mary after my sister, was weak and sickly. She was perfect in body but her breathing was shallow and she did not cry. John and Mrs. Withnall took both the babies straight to the church to be christened for we feared for Mary not lasting the day, and we were proved correct. Poor little Mary breathed her last an hour ago and she will be buried along with her nameless brother. They will not be parted from each other in life or death.

I am bereft, weak and weary and hope that is the last time that I ever go through that again. I no longer care whether John would like a son, one more labour like that one and it would do away with me. All that pain for nothing. I have been robbed of the child I had a right to expect would live. I can only put my trust in God and believe that He had a reason to take them from this world to be with Him.

Now I will turn my attention in a new direction and put my energies into my new book, a directory for the Town, as well as working my way through the receipts that ladies are pushing onto me to include in my second edition of the cookery book. I have also found that an enterprising man has devised a new kind of Fire Stove, in which may be burned any common fuel instead of Charcoal. That must be included in my new book, for it will be such a useful improvement for the work of the cook. This must keep my mind from dwelling on unhappy times. Hard work is a cure for what ails you, as my papa used to say, and so I must hope it cures me.

1771 March 23rd Prescotts journal launched

How exciting that today saw the first edition of a new newspaper in Manchester, Prescott's Journal. To think that I had some little hand in the matter is very gratifying. I dare not let John hear of my investment or he would get very angry that I had not handed the money over to him.

I have already learnt that money given to John is a gamble, usually money lost forever, for no return, but Mr. Prescott assures me that each subscriber to his newspaper will receive excellent dividends once it is established. That is a gamble more to my liking and it pleases me that I am being part of the positive forces of the town. It might make Mr. Harrop become more dynamic again if he has a rival.

1771 April Selling the copyright to Mr. Baldwin 3 an agreement

Finally Mr. Baldwin has replied to me with a better offer of twelve hundred pounds for the copyright but, although I am minded to take it, I have an idea I can raise him higher still. I have also thought of something that may appeal to him and is a good business offer to benefit us both.

I am replying to him that he can have the commission to print the second edition of my cookbook and, if that is done to my satisfaction, he may buy the copyright from me for a decent sum. I am thinking of fifteen hundred pounds. I am also including the chance to print my new Directory which is nearly finished, extra business that I think he will appreciate.

I am finding poor Mr. Harrop is less and less able to take on any commissions, and I fear he may not be in business much longer, which would be a great pity. I hope the gentlemen of Manchester will rally to his aid if needed. He has been a tireless provider of information for nearly twenty years. Many of these men of business would have been put to some trouble to otherwise obtain their news of events in London and abroad.

1771 May selling the copyright 4

At last I have reached an agreement on the price for my copyright. I had thought Mr. Baldwin was stuck on twelve hundred pounds but by throwing into the deal the publishing of the Directory, he has now agreed to pay me fourteen hundred pounds, which is much closer to my idea.

I am glad we have reaches an agreement for I am keen to bring out my improved edition with the extra receipts. If people thought eight hundred receipts was good value, they will be overwhelmed by the near nine hundred in my new book.

Once I see my copy of it I will send the manuscript for the directory to Mr. Baldwin to print. John, of course, is chafing at the bit to get the money in his hands but I was not to be rushed into making a poor decision by him or any man.

John is afraid we will lose our chance to get the Eagle and Child. He thinks we may have already missed out but that is an opportunity that I am happy to miss. The Eagle and Child is not at all the kind of establishment that I would want to have.

The place I want would be the Bull's Head, but Mr. Alsop shows no inclination of giving it up and in fact is making a handsome job of it, better, dare I say, than Mr. Budworth before him. He is certainly doing a better job than John could do. The landlord of the Bull's Head needs a certain dignity about him, an ability to deal with persons of the highest ranks without presuming to be too familiar, which is exactly how my John would go about it, of that I am sure.

I will not be rushed into fulfilling John's whims but now he has acquired some proper knowledge of the trade I think that together we could soon build a good reputation for fine wines and good food. I have an idea that we may have to look to Chapel-street on the other side of the River Irwell. Or perhaps somewhere on Dean's-gate, both places where the London coaches arrive, bringing sophisticated people into Manchester and Salford, people who will appreciate some refinement in their accommodation. I think there are one or two inns there that may suit our purpose and John must search them out for us. I will tell him when he finds one that is suitable.

1771 Jun genteel lodgings and cellar to let

I have bethought me that it is time to cut down on my stores of stock if we are to take on a new premises, and with that in mind I have advertise for our front cellar to let, also genteel lodgings. It will be very useful to start looking for new tenants before they are needed, to release us from the burden of the lease. The boys will be happy enough sharing the back cellar, and Mary can share the attics with us. That way I can make some money from the rooms in between. It cannot be helped and may only be for a short time. Any extra we can get towards our next great endeavour will be money well saved.

1771 July receiving a proof copy of The Experienced English Housekeeper no. 2

Today was very exciting for I received my advance copy of the second edition of The Experienced English Housekeeper from Mr. Baldwin. I am very impressed with the quality of the paper, a tiny bit finer than that from Mr. Harrop. I daresay they have higher standards in London than we do here in the provinces, although I must be loyal to Mr. Harrop. He made up for any lack of finesse with an excess of personal attention, something I am unlikely to receive from Mr. Baldwin, being at two hundred miles distant.

The print is good and I struggled to find any misprints or spelling mistakes within the type. I imagine that he has had this copy set in plenty of time, expecting my agreement from the very first day he set out to get my business. Mr. B strikes me as a very determined man and if this is the quality I can expect for my Directory I am well satisfied.

Mr. B's letter, which he enclosed with the book, has stated that as soon as I send him my written agreement to proceed he will pay me the agreed sum for the copyright, as negotiated earlier. I can see I am dealing with a man confident of success and I look forward to greater rewards than I ever dreamed of. I will write to him by return to accept his terms and advise John that he can begin to plan for a brighter future for us and the girls.

1771 Aug 10/13th The Experienced English Housekeeper no.2 advert

Finally the notices are in all the newspapers for the second edition of my book. Mr. Baldwin assures me it is in the Derby Mercury and the Newcastle Courant so he expects to sell all that he has printed.

I fear however, that Mr. Harrop is not on such good terms with me these days. When I passed him yesterday he gave me quite a cold look which I did not like at all. I do not see how he can complain because it was his rejection of the work that sent me to another printer. I hope he does not bear this grudge for long. It could be that he is having problems with the other newspaper in competition with him, but I hope he will rally himself.

It was unfortunate for him that as part of that rejection he has also lost the work of printing my Directory, but I still have a great deal of respect for him. I hope we will work together again in the future. I already have ideas for more works of reference that I think are needed in this Town if not in the whole country.

The sales I have had so far for the cookbook have shown me that people have the same needs in towns all over the kingdom. I will make an appointment to see him at his earliest opportunity and discuss with him which of my ideas he thinks would be best to pursue.

1771 Sep meeting Mr. Harrop

At last I had an opportunity to have a meeting with Mr. Harrop and was distressed to hear his predicament. The arrival of the new newspaper has caused him considerable loss of business and he is looking for investors to keep him afloat or he will be out of business in a year. Of course I was delighted to offer him some investment. Ironical that it should come back to him courtesy of a rival printer, but I have promised him that when I receive the money from Mr. B I shall invest a portion with him, as I am sure would many others in this town who respect him greatly. He was very receptive to my idea of a book of midwifery, knowing that I have been through a range of experiences so would talk with some first hand experience in guiding others. He suggested to me that I contact Mr. Charles White, the eminent surgeon who has begun the idea of a Lying-In hospital in Salford. He knows him as a very good sort of a man and is sure he will guide me in what to write in the book. He offered to write me a letter of introduction for which I was most grateful.

1771 Oct Mr. B and the copyright money

Well Mr. Baldwin is going down in my estimation and I am beginning to be sorry I sent him my signed agreement to allow him the copyright on my book. He is being most dilatory in bringing the payment to me. He writes to say that business is very business and he is sorry for the delay, etc, etc, but these honeyed words do not hide the fact that this man is making profit from me and not paying the bill. I will write him a very strongly worded letter that if I do not receive my payment within the next month that I will consider our agreement void. Thankfully the delay has served to lose us the opportunity to take on the Eagle and Child, which John was persistently hoping we would take however often I refused. He would tell me that any money of mine belonged to him by law but I would not let that sway me. 'It might be yours under the law, John Raffald,' I said to him, 'but it's mine by rights and if its in my possession then there it will stay until I can see good reason to part with it, no matter what the law says. And if you try to drag me in front of a court or committee I will tell them all about your little activities that are outside the sight of the law.' I think it surprised him that I knew about them but I hear a lot in my little shop, much that I was not supposed to hear no doubt, but I keep quiet what I know and use it as I must. I have a feeling that if I do not take some precautions with my money that he would spend it all in the shortest time and leave us fit for the workhouse.

1771 Nov

Mr. Baldwin has promised to bring me the money himself and in his reply he states he will be here within the week. Of course now that he is coming in person I must set to with finishing the Directory pages. I have made very little progress with it in the last month due to an increase in business, which is very gratifying but is making my head spin with everything I have to think about. I will need to make certain that John does not see all the money that Mr. Baldwin brings as some of it is destined for Mr. Harrop and I mean to save some of it for my own purposes. I shall write to Mr. Baldwin with my acceptance tonight but tell him to leave it for a month that I may have my new Directory pages ready for him to inspect. I shall tell John that I have taken his lower offer to reduce the amount of my money that he will have spent before I can hold it in my hands.

1772

1772 Jan finalising the directory

John is becoming quite unbearable to live with, if he does not have a drink he has such bad moods that if I were a lesser woman he might think he would be able to take out his anger on me. He knows however that any action in that vein will not suit his aims, and it is not my fault if I do not have the money from Mr. B yet.

He has not yet forgiven me for losing him the Eagle and Child, as though it was ever my fault. It was my wish, for certain, but I could not give him money I did not have, and I am glad to say that Mr. Blakeley has changed his mind about selling his tenancy now. He and John had such a falling out that I doubt if Mr. Blakeley would have sold to him anyway, whatever money he had.

It is of no matter to me now, I am too busy to take much notice of John and his tempers. I am almost finished with the first draft of my Directory and must post off the pages to London at my earliest opportunity. With luck I will be able to send young Joshua to the post office for me within the next day or two.

It is such a problem to finish when everyday I hear of yet another address or another street that is being changed. It is a great trial to get all the information complete. I have decided that whatever I have in two days time will be what is produced. I can always send small amendments through the postal system to Mr. Baldwin before it is printed.

This is where Mr. Harrop had the advantage. I could call over to his press with my requirements and receive my answer within a few minutes. I am not too happy with this printing at a distance where every change takes such a long time to effect. However, it is being done for a good price. That is, if I ever receive the money. I am becoming impatient with Mr. Baldwin but Mr. Harrop assures me that he is utterly trustworthy and a much respected man in the business.

1772 Feb Directory proofs

Mr. Baldwin may not have come through with my money yet but I am happy that he produces good work. Today I received the proofs for my Directory and it looks very well. The front page is direct and says what to expect to find inside.

> THE MANCHESTER DIRECTORY, FOR THE YEAR 1772, Containing an Alphabetical List of the MERCHANTS, TRADESMEN, and PRINCIPAL INHABITANTS in the town of MANCHESTER, with the Situation of their respective Warehouses and Places of Abode, also SEPARATE LISTS of The Country Tradesmen, with their Warehouses in Manchester. The Officers of the Infirmary and Lunatic Hospital. Of the Excise. The Principal Whitsters. Stage-Coaches, Waggons, and Carriers, with their Days of coming in and going out. The Vessels to and from Liverpool, upon the Old Navigation, and Duke of Bridgewater's Canal; and their Agents. Manchester Bank and Insurance Office. His Majesties Justices of the Peace, in and near Manchester. AND THE Committee for the Detection and Prosecution of Felons, and Receivers of Stolen Goods.'

Mr. Baldwin has taken some of my own words and made them into a most elegant front page. My note was to answer those who would wonder why I would presume to compose this useful guide to the Town.

> The Want of a DIRECTORY for the large and commercial Town of MANCHESTER, having been frequently complained of, and several useful Regulations being lately made; I have taken upon me the arduous Task of compiling a *Complete Guide*, for the easy finding out every Inhabitant of the lest Consequence; as also most of the Country Tradesmen, and the Places where their Warehouses are situated; likewise an Account of the Stage-Coaches and Carriers, with the times of their coming in and going out of Town, etc, etc.

I took it to show Mr. Harrop for his professional opinion. We are once more on good terms. The problems he had were not with me but with the poor state of his business. Happily he has averted the disaster that was confronting him with help from several of his friends in Town. I have promised him a generous donation to come once I have my payment and together it should be enough for him to continue in business.

I will always prefer to do business with him over Mr. Baldwin and I told Mr. Harrop this today. Any of my future manuscripts will go to him to print and to no one else and I made him that serious promise today. He was most appreciative of my support. I swear I saw his eyes brim with tears but he remained dignified. In return he has promised to write to Mr. Baldwin on my behalf to approve the proof, with a few notes on type that he thinks will be helpful, and demand that he sends his due payment at his earliest opportunity.

It was gratifying to once more be held in his regard. I may not belong in the first order in this Town but I believe I am one of the genteel sort among the smaller businesses. If only John were more respectable we might have a better sort of society.

He is more certain than ever that we should take on an inn, and I am becoming convinced that it may work out better for us than a shop. Perhaps if we have a high class establishment I can convince him to behave better, then he must surely be accepted by more of the better sort of people in Town.

1772 Mar 17 More perfumes

Another feather in my bonnet today, I have obtained through Joshua a small supply of fine flask Florence oil, which cannot be purchased easily everywhere. Mr. Wagstaff was very amenable to supplying me with a regular stock together with the perfumes he already supplies.

My customers say that the preparations they buy from me are superior to all others, which of course they are, thanks to my nephew Joshua. He has shown such aptitude for making the perfumes that he now does much of the dispensing for Mr. Wagstaff.

He has quite left my service now, for which I am disappointed, but after he has completed his training he may find a better employment than he would with me. His talents have provided me with a good income from the products he makes and, as they do not involve me in any work beyond that of selling them, they are a valuable item of stock for me now.

1772 Mar 31st first trade directory published by Baldwin

At last my Directory for Manchester is a reality. I placed the first notice in today's Mercury, only a simple notice for I have no idea yet how popular it may be. It may be a complete waste of my time and I am beginning to wonder if I have presumed too much.

This Day is Publish'd, Price 6d,

A NEW DIRECTORY, for the Town of MANCHESTER. Containing an Alphabetical List of the Merchants, Tradesmen, and principal Inhabitants, with the Situation of their respective Warehouses and Places of Abode. Also separate Lists of the Country Tradesmen, with their Warehouses in Manchester – Officers of the Infirmary and Lunatic Hospital – Officers of Excise – Principal Whitsters – Account of the Stage Coaches and Waggons, with their Days of coming in and going out – Lists of the Vessels to and from Liverpool, upon the Old Navigation, and the Duke of Bridgewater's Canal, with their Agents – Manchester Bank and Insurance Office – Justices of the Peace in and near Manchester, and the Committee for the Detection and Prosecution of Felons, of Receivers of stolen or embezzled Goods.

Printed for the Author, and sold by *R. Baldwin*, No. 47 Paternoster-row, and by the Author, *Elizabeth Raffald*, in the *Market Place, Manchester,*

Mr. Baldwin has still not sent his promised copyright payment and I am quite losing patience with him. If he were not so far distant I would go to see him. I will write to him again, a very strong letter this time. I believe I may be able to take action against him for breach of promise if he does not pay soon.

It is really too bad of him to take so long over paying his debts. I have already decided that this will be our only transaction. The Directory looks well enough but all the trouble of communicating with him in London has taken its toll on my nerves. It is much more preferable to deal with my friend Mr. Harrop. I feel I am justified in calling him my friend now and I trust he considers me a friend of his, too. He is confident the directory will be a great success and has suggested that I should consider beginning work on the next edition which he would be honoured to produce. I already have nearly ten pages of names to add, so many people are moving into this area it changes every day.

1772 April declining the shop (7/ 14/21 April, 5/12/26 May, 2/9/16 June)

Mr. Harrop will have to wait for his new manuscript for we are all excitement now at a great opportunity before us. I can hardly bring myself to put it down on paper for fear it jinxes the enterprise. I have straightaway put a notice in the Mercury to advertise our stock for sale.

> ### To be Let, and entered on Immediately,
> A Good and well-accustomed Seed and Confectioners SHOP, situate in the *Market-place, Manchester,* now in the Possession of *John Raffald,* Seedsman, and *Elizabeth Raffald,* Confectioner, who are declining those Branches, and entering into a different one.
>
> N.B. The Stock in Trade to be disposed of, consisting of a large Quantity of pickled Hambro' Sturgeon, Olives, Catchup, Lemon Pickle, Browning, fine Teas, double refin'd Sugar, Spices, all Kinds of Groceries, &c. now selling at Prime Cost, and will continue till all be Sold.
>
> For further Particular Enquire of the said JOHN RAFFALD.

The new business is almost a sure thing and I have had a solemn promise from the current owner that he will keep it for us. It is an opportunity that suits me as well as it suits John. He soon recovered from his doldrums over the Eagle and Child once I put this offer in his way.

It means that I need to find a new tenant for the shop in a hurry. We will not be able to manage this and our new business. John is doing well on selling my Directory and it is having a good effect that when he is busy doing that he is not spending time drinking with his cronies, so we both benefit. The only drawback to it is that he sees exactly how much I am making from the sales and I struggle to hide any of the takings from him. It will not matter soon, he will have more than enough work to keep him busy and out of mischief.

1772 May selling up

I am beside myself with worry over what I have signed my name to. Mr. Baldwin still has not arrived with the money for my copyright and we were depending on that money to set up our new establishment. There is so much that needs to be done to the insides to bring it up to what I expect for my customers.

I am sick with worry over selling on my stock here at the shop. I have had no decent offers for it at all. I had to ask Mr. Harrop to extend my advertisement to include details of just what stock is involved in the transfer. I need us to clear a decent price for everything or we may need to approach an office I have heard of in Liverpool. It is a Register Office owned by a Mr. Moorfield, who has extended his reach to include supplying people, possessed of a certain Income, with Sums of Money, to any Amount He promises the utmost Secrecy and Dispatch. I hope I can avoid coming to that but I am more than ever dependant on Mr. Baldwin delivering on his promise.

1772 June horse racing

John has fair driven me to distraction today with his talk of the races. All he can think about is how he is going to solve all our money problems by placing money on Mr. Fernyhough's bay mare to win its race next week in Kersal. He declares it is well known around the stables that his is the certain winner. Everyone I know is saying that Mr. Radcliffe's bay mare, Shepherdess, is the favourite horse to win but John is convinced he is party to some inside knowledge that will make us a packet of money. He has not learnt yet that it is the holders of the books who are the only winners.

There are going to be three days of the races, on the tenth, eleventh and twelfth of this month, and I cannot wait for them to be over, for until they are finished John will keep up his incessant babbling about conditions and runners and whatever else. I know he has good intentions at heart but his babbling wears me down.

My own heart is sore that I did not think of the opportunity that Mr. Deaz from the Old Coffee House did. He has arranged with the Stewards of the Races to provide Breakfast Al Fresco, a public Breakfast, a novel idea for Ladies and Gentlemen, and it has to be a certain moneymaker. He is having pitched Tents for the Accommodation of the Company, with a Band of Music at half past Ten o'Clock on Thursday Morning, upon the Bowling Green at Chetham Hill. I will go if only to observe how the idea is received.

1772 July 14 new patten maker

Young Roger Parkinson has finally managed to open a patten making business of his own and I am well pleased for him. He is such a well mannered young man and he has opened his shop in Hanging Ditch, opposite the shop of Mr. Finney the grocer and Tea Dealer, and near Mr. Mayers' shop of Tobacconist and Snuff-maker.

Roger put a nicely worded notice in today's Mercury

announcing the end of his apprenticeship with Mr. Paul Harris and the beginning of his business in all its various branches. He has set up with stock of the best and most fashionable Goods on very reasonable Terms, humbly presuming he has it in his Power, as it will ever be his Study, to serve those as please to favour him with their Custom, on such Terms, as will meet their Approbation for a Continuance of their Favours. Quite correctly, he returns his sincere Thanks to his Friends for their Kindness already conferred on him, and to those Persons who please to Countenance him with their Orders, may be assured of having them executed in the neatest and best Manner, and with the utmost Punctuality and Dispatch.

I wish him success of his venture as he is a man with the greatest attention to his customer's needs. He is an upcoming, enterprising man, just the kind I would hope to take a shine to one of my daughters.

1772 Aug25 first ad for Kings Head

At last I can speak of our new venture, now it is a certain thing. We have possession at last of our great enterprise, The King's Head Inn, Salford. I had begun to think it would not happen but we have done it, we are now moved in.

How fine our advertisement looked at the top of the Mercury's front page today. With Mr. Harrop's help it was composed in a most genteel style and I am so proud to announce it to the world.

King's Head, Salford, Aug. 25, 1772

John and Elizabeth Raffald

Desire to acquaint their Friends and the Public

THAT they have taken and entered upon the old accustomed and commodious Inn, known by the Sign of the KING'S-HEAD, in SALFORD, MANCHESTER, which they have fitted up in the neatest and most elegant Manner, for the Reception and Accommodation of the Nobility, Gentry, Merchants, and Tradesmen, who shall please to honour us with their Company, where they may be assured of the utmost Civility and good Treatment, they being determined to make it their Study, as it will always be their Interest and Inclination, to merit the Approbation of their Friends.

They likewise take this Opportunity of returning their sincere Thanks for all Favours conferred on them whilst they kept the Seed and Confectionary Business.

It was only at the last minute that we were sure of our plans to begin a Card Assembly through the winter Season so John had to run over to Mr. Harrop's to add the notice. Unfortunately it had to be squeezed onto the last page of the paper. We were not going to pay the extra to put it on the front page.

Notice is hereby GIVEN,
THAT THE
CARD ASSEMBLY,
Will be opened at *John Raffald's*, the *King's-Head*, in *Salford*, upon *Thursday* the 14th of *September* next, and to be continued every *Thursday* Fortnight during the Winter Season.

Card Assembly was at least in large type although the location was only written small. It was typical of John that it was put so plainly. There was not the slightest attempt at gentility or elegance. I will need to educate him to mind his manners with our customers though for now I am enjoying our new importance.

1772 Oct Selling the copyright 5 Mr. Baldwin arrives

Today, finally, Mr. Baldwin of London came purposefully to call on me with the payment he promised. He brought news that he has already made a great number of sales of my cookbook at his business in London.

It is very gratifying to be noticed by the grand people of London in such a way, but then I suppose my name must be pretty well known after so many books have been bought. I have lost count now of the number of books that have sold but it must number near a thousand.

I am sure my father would never have dreamed that one of his daughters would be so well known, although he would chide me for being so proud. Whenever I sought to be recognised he would tell me I was only doing God's work and any glory was due to Him. My choice was to be grateful to be the chosen instrument.

Dearest papa, I see now he was such a dreamer, his head always in books seeking more knowledge that he might understand the world better. I have learnt that it is hard work and industry that matters in this world, without it there are no riches with which to bless His name or do good to those less able than ourselves.

Mr. Baldwin arrived at an unfortunate moment in the day, just as I was at my desk in the snug bar giving instructions to young Joshua. I had not finished when Mr. Baldwin was shown to the door and Joshua would have left, discreet young man that he is, but I knew I could trust him not to gossip so I bade him stay till we were finished. I was also keen to have a witness to our dealings. Perhaps the man thought he may be dealing with country bumpkins not knowing that I am fully of aware of the sharp practices that are used against the unwary. I made sure I had his letter on my desk where he clearly stated that he would pay me fourteen hundred pounds. I wanted to be sure he knew that I knew what I was about.

Mr. Baldwin was rather dusty from his journey having just stepped from the coach outside the Spread Eagle. He had not even taken the time to call in to that establishment that he might refresh himself but had come straight to see me. He did seem a little nervous and after a glass of small beer to slake his thirst he was keen to hand over the roll of notes that he carried. I will confess that I felt a mild hysteria coming over me as he counted out more money than I have ever seen in my life.

He suggested that he should go with me to put my payment into a banking house, as they do now in London. I forbore to tell him that a married woman such as me would not have any use for putting money in a bank. It was of no use to lose all say over it to a husband, especially one such as mine who would spend it quicker than a wink. It would be out of my hands and I would have to go begging for it back.

I told him in no uncertain terms that the notes would be safe once placed in my hands. I did not tell him that most of the amount was already spent, it having taken him so long to pay me. I simply thanked him for his concern and after he had counted the money out I called Joshua over and asked him to count it again for me. The poor lad was trembling like a leaf at holding so much money as I was but I did not want Mr. Baldwin to see my hands shaking. He counted quietly then nodded as he handed the notes back to me.

I have never seen so much money altogether in my life, and to think it all belonged to me was a little overwhelming. I felt as if the room was fading away from me and it was just me and this money in front of me. Whatever else happens in my life I doubt I will ever have as great a moment as that again. To think there are people in this town who deal in amounts bigger than that as if it was nothing but to me it was a fortune.

I quickly gathered my wits as Mr. Baldwin began speaking again, asking me to sign his receipt. I kept my voice steady as I thanked Joshua and bade him wait in the corner while we concluded our business. I told him to forget what he had just seen, I I know I can rely on him not to breathe a word to anyone. I will need to find a good home for this money before John finds it. I fear John is getting to know my hiding places and he will ask about this visit so I must have a good answer to ensure that he gets his hands on as little as possible.

I had thought to bid Mr. Baldwin goodbye once our dealings were complete as he had mentioned that he had other business in Manchester, but it happened that he had a little more to say. He had received complaints from several purchasers that they could not understand some of the terms used. He suggested that my book needed some adjustment for the London customers.

Now I could have answered a little more kindly but for an untrained man to question what I had set down in my instructions I found it insulting. He had already confessed to me that he knew nothing about these matters then had the temerity to suggest that terms such as garth were too particular to the North. I thought that was ridiculous and I had to say so.

I drew myself up with as much dignity as I could muster and told him, in as polite a tone as I could muster, that what I had written, I proposed to write at the time, it was written deliberately and I could not admit of any alteration. I put the notes securely into my bodice and wished him good day.

Once my visitor had left I made sure to put a little portion away for my poor old ladies of the parish. They shall have a pretty parcel from me this week. Of course it was such a large sum that I needed to tidy it away before John could cast his eyes on it. He is splashing our money like cheap beer since we began to run this inn.

1772 Nov Mercury notice of theft

I had promised to invest a portion of my money into Mr. Harrop's newspaper printing business and so I kept my promise and took him my contribution. That man works tirelessly to keep the people of this town informed about what is happening outside of it. He is the only man prepared to put himself out in such a way and he deserves to prosper. His work is always of an excellent standard, much the best of all the booksellers in the market place.

Perhaps I shall write another book for him to print for me. I do certainly see a need for a manual on midwifery practices. There are some dreadfully backward ideas in this town and too many babies and mothers are perishing for want of proper treatment. I attended a talk by Mr. Charles White, the eminent surgeon, a most knowledgeable man and very interested in the subject. He has proposed a Treatise on the Management of Pregnant and Lying-in Women which I think must change current thinking. I shall write to him and ask his opinion.

There was such fuss today over a suspected thief appearing at the door of our inn. Only one day since the article appeared in the Mercury, it is thought the very persons tried to sell a feather bed to John in the bar room. The article in the newspaper stated that the persons were rambling about the Country, supposed to be gone to Rochdale but it seems they were not yet give up on Manchester and were keeping themselves low here in Salford. In the article they were named as William Coe, and a Woman who passes for his Wife. Coe is a very little Man, with Crooked Legs, the Woman, middle-sized, slender, and pale faced, follow the Business of making and selling Carpets. They lately left their Lodgings in Manchester, taking with them the Feathers from the Bed and Bolster.

This just fits the description of the people here today but John simply scolded them out of the bar and sent them on their way so I am none the wiser. I would have turned them in myself if I had seen them. Fancy robbing an honest householder of a valuable feather bed! If any of my tenants did that to me I would take after them with a hot tossing pan.

1772 Dec 1 Mercury notice of a break-in

John Holbrook, the carrier, was in such a rage today over a theft from his yard. He was in the public bar talking to John, bemoaning his bad luck at losing some very valuable parcels due to a break in at the warehouse. He was raging so loud I had cause to go through to remonstrate with him.

We do not have that kind of establishment, but he is normally such a calm man that I thought it only right to take pity on him. I brought him back into my snug bar to sit him down with a brandy while he calmed himself. He had placed an announcement in the Mercury but he was not very hopeful of recovering the property. He showed me the article and the list was dreadful.

> "Broke open, on Thursday Night the 26th Inst., A Carrier's Warehouse in the White Lyon Yard, Deansgate, Manchester, and the following Things stolen, three Pieces of Saddleworth Plain; a Truss about 31lb weight, containing Printed Cotton Gowns and Handkerchiefs; a large Truss upwards of a hundred Weight, containing Kendal Goods, supposed to be Linseys or Stockings, or both; several smallish Parcels, containing Manchester Goods, and some Hams, Cheeses, and other Things. This Felony, from several circumstances, is supposed to have been committed by a Gang of Fellows, who travel about the Country and live by House-breaking, etc, having with them Picklocks, Handspikes, Chisels and other proper Tools for opening Doors and Windows. They are supposed to be still in Manchester. Besides the several Parcels of Goods mentioned above, there are several other Parcels missing, containing Baizes, Frizes, Checks Fustians, Tammies, Camblets, half-Camblets, etc, etc
> Whoever can apprehend the Person or Persons who stole the said Goods, so that they may be convicted of the same, shall receive a Reward of Five Guineas, by applying to John Holbrook, Shrewsbury Carrier, at the White Lyon, in Deansgate, or to John Lawrenson, his Book-keeper."

Finally Mr. Holbrook calmed himself down and thanked me for my patience with him. He had my sympathy as a fellow business person. Losing any business is like taking money out of the mouths of your children.

I was interested to sit with the Mercury and see what else was happening in the world. I found this article about France most troubling. We have had our own problems with supplies in this town but the struggles of the French people sound most alarming.

> Extract of a letter from Paris, Nov 15 1772
> "A Report prevails here, that several People in the Southern Provinces of France have taken Arms, and declare for a Change of Government, as the present arbitrary Mode (they say) is insupportable. True it is, that the late Proceedings towards the Princes of the Blood, has raised the greatest Murmurs amongst the whole Body of People, but it is most prevalent amongst the military, which is extremely singular. The greatest Confusion reigns, and bitter Execrations are hourly uttered against the King and

Ministry. Many People have been taken up for their Freedom of Speech, and some of those of distinguished Rank, but this cannot repress the Indignation of the Populace, nor stop their just Complaints. Taxes have amazingly encreased, Provisions are immoderately Dear, and the repeated tyrannous Proceeding of the Ministry are really insupportable. In short, if some Method is not shortly taken, and those very spirited too, dangerous Consequences will immediately attend. It is reported that the Count d'Artois is confined to his Apartments."

In another article Private Letters from France speak of some dangerous Combinations that have lately been discovered in one or two of the Provinces of that Kingdom, and it is even insinuated that a general Insurrection is apprehended.

Times are hard in this country but it sounds that starvation is the same the world over, causing men to break into fighting and lawlessness. When the sovereign shows such disregard for their people by spending extravagantly on finery, while working people have no bread to live on, it is bound to excite strong feelings.

1772 Dec 29 canal

There is good news today in the Mercury, although I pride myself that it was I who gave Mr. Harrop the hint that this was about to happen. I had heard from my suppliers that some goods would be getting cheaper, thanks to a new ease of transport between here and the port at Liverpool.

Extract of a letter from Warrington, Dec 17
"Tuesday next the Duke of Bridgewater will finish all his Locks at Runcorn, and on Wednesday will open his Navigation, and receive Vessels from the Mersey, by which Merchandize will be carried from Liverpool to Manchester. On this Occasion an Ox is to be roasted whole, and about eight hundred Workmen will be entertained with a dinner, Ale, etc. through the Course of this Navigation, which is thirty-four miles long, all Difficulties have been surmounted, one small Piece of Land only excepted, which is the property of Sir Richard Brook, and lies as yet undermention'd how it shall be cut, which will oblige the Duke to draw his Goods via Carts over this Tract of Land. The Gentlemen and Tradesmen of this Country wish to see this Nook cut through, as the Land Carriage will annoy the

> Baronet, and bring an additional Expence of Eighteen Pence per Ton upon the Merchandize."

Nothing is more certain than that men of enterprise will find a way to resolve this problem before long. Everywhere around me there springs ideas to solve every problem and even to provide answers to some problems that have not yet been thought of.

The clever Mr. Highs has been designing yet again and his son has won a prize in the sum of two hundred guineas for showing his father's latest invention, a double jenny, to the men of the Exchange here. I hope that he may finally win the acclaim he deserves.

1773

1773 Jan, collating the new Directory

I must make progress on my new Directory. I have had so many complaints from people omitted from the first book that I had no idea that it would be taken so seriously. Even people from out of the area demand to be included. Demand! Of me! Some of them soon went quiet when I mentioned that payment of a fee may persuade me to include them, but for others it was no issue because they took it as a mark of success.

I do wish I had thought of that for the first directory, but it will certainly feature in this one and in any future ones I may produce. I make an exception for widows, however, for I will not take their little all from them. Any widow managing to keep a livelihood going without a man to earn for his family merits my utmost compassion.

Mr. Harrop has been all kindness in helping me with this endeavour, and it is so much easier to be working with him rather than with Mr. Baldwin. I didn't care for his London ways of treating people with whom he does business, leaving them in ignorance for months before answering their justified concerns, sometimes only after five or six letters have been sent.

Sometimes I wish I had never sold him the copyright for my cookbook. He does not have the correct respect. His last letter asked me for permission to include physical remedies in his next edition as a way to widen the book's appeal. I replied very firmly in the negative to that. I reminded him to look at my preface to the Reader where I state quite clearly that I do not presume to meddle with physical receipts, leaving them to the physicians' superior judgment, whose proper province they are.

We live in modern times now, when scientific discoveries are making homespun peasant quackery outdated. I have witnessed some ridiculous practices but I will have none of it in my home. In Manchester we have men of such talent and ingenuity, constantly making advances in our knowledge. I refused to be associated with any backward remedies and left him in no doubt as to my preferences.

He constantly tries my patience, so unlike my own dear Mr. Harrop. I must have the new Directory ready for him to print soon or I fear even he will lose patience with me.

1773 Feb still preparing the Directory

This new Directory is becoming impossible. My pages are so muddled that I wonder if it would be easier to have a separate Appendix to add to the first directory. Mr. Harrop, however, says not, that it needs to be set as a whole new book from the beginning.

Just when I feel certain that I have added as many names as are needed, someone new moves into the town and I have to adjust the list again. I can see that I will never be finished with this task. Sisyphus rolling that rock eternally up the mountain might have sympathy for me. I begin to feel an inkling of how he must have felt.

Already I have added fifteen more pages but whenever I take them to Mr. Harrop he spots another name that I have missed, or a new carrier route that has been added.

He has suggested that he will help by sending out his apprentices when work is quiet, to go round the town and make proper enquiries. If I will draft a notice to go in his newspaper to ask people to comply with these proper enquiries he will charge me only half his usual rate and no charge for the apprentices' time. He promises to run the notice at the top of a column for extra effect.

I have the utmost faith in my dear friend so am glad to accept his help. I will let them come to me, and any I do not have in two weeks will have to wait for the next book, if I ever have the strength to do another.

1773 March 16/23 & April 6/13 appeal for entries in Directory 2

My notice calling for Directory entries made its first appearance in today's Mercury. It looks very well and was, as promised, at the top of the column. I just had to clip it from the newspaper to keep as a memento of yet another step on my path to success.

> ### To the Inhabitants of MANCHESTER
> A New Edition of the MANCHESTER DIRECTORY being intended to be published with all convenient speed; it is proposed, in order to make such an useful Work as correct as possible, to send proper and intelligent Persons round the Town, to take down the Name, Business and Place of Abode of every Gentleman, Tradesman, and Shopkeeper, as well as of others whose Business or Employment has any tendency to public Notice; the Proprietor therefore humbly requests, that every one will please to give the necessary Information to the Persons appointed, that she may be enabled to give an accurate Edition of a Work so Advantageous to such a large populous, and trading Town as this is; in the Completion of which, she can assure the Public, that no Labour or Expence shall be spared to make It worthy of their Approbation, as an easy and sufficient Directory, not only to Strangers, but likewise to the Inhabitants of the Town.
>
> ELIZABETH RAFFALD
> At the *King's Head, Salford, Manchester*

Mr. Harrop has persuaded me to run it for four weeks altogether in order to reach all the businessmen who travel in and out of the Town all month. I would have preferred only a two week run but thanks to Mr. Harrop cutting his rate that is only what it is costing me, so I am satisfied.

Already I have received several notes brought to me by the lads who work for John in the bar room from businessmen wishing to be sure their details in the new Directory are correct. My newest enterprise has had the double effect of bringing in more trade to the inn, which I hope John appreciates.

I am not certain that our takings are as full as they ought to be for the number of customers staying longer in the bar room and the noise they make. Of course John will not hear of me interfering so I must leave it to him, it is his domain, as the food is mine. However, I will ask my nephew William to keep his wits about him when he works for John, to watch who pays and who does not. He will certainly tell his Aunt Raffald the truth. If I find that John is giving away drinks I will take him to task. Our fortunes depend on each other and I will not allow him to squander mine.

1773 April daughter's speech

I was so proud of my darling Anna today. She really is a remarkable girl, tall like her father, beautiful like her Aunt Emma, and with a mind like her mama's. Such a clever child, I can see that I will have a worthy successor for my businesses. She stood before her papa, her Aunt Mary and me, and recited without a pause or hesitation, her Lord's Prayer.

She was turned out so tidily in a clean white dress with a matching white ribbon in her golden hair which shone like a little halo. She looked perfectly angelic with her head bowed and her hands clasped tightly together. She even managed a little curtsey to us at the finish, with only a tiny wobble.

I gave her a penny for her efforts and bade her save it for her future but the little dear returned it to me saying no mama, you must keep it and make some more money from it. Her solemn little face was more than I could bear and I had need of my kerchief to hide the tears in my eyes. To be only three years old and to have such a clever mind, it was too much to hope for. God willing she is allowed to survive the dirt and diseases of this town.

I think I must take her from her nurse soon and enrol her at the school in Barton-upon-Irwell with her older sisters. There she will be in good country air and she can learn more than her nurse can teach her. A mind like that must not be wasted and her education must be a cause worth the expence. Soon I will have finished the next Directory and some of the money from that will be well spent on Anna. This town is growing so big she must have whatever advantage I can give her.

The Reverend John Whitaker gave a talk last week about the totals of his recent enumeration of the people of Manchester and Salford. He astounded us with his figures, and he is a serious man so we can trust his judgement. He gave the number of people now living in Manchester to be 22,481, made up of 5,317 families with a further 4,765 here in Salford, 1,099 families, and 13,756 in over 2,500 families living in the outer townships, all of them depending on Manchester for their livelihoods.

All these people are housed in less than 7,000 houses. It is no wonder we feel full to bursting, and I am certain that soon there will be a limit on people allowed to move here or life will become intolerable with overcrowding. Some buildings are already dilapidated and badly kept.

1773 May 10 Tea Act issued to protect the British East India Company,

There is talk about the market that Parliament is planning laws to protect the cost of tea shipped by the East India Company. From what I hear they have large stocks of tea in their warehouses in London and the company is struggling. It does not seem to have reduced the cost of tea, however. It will be hard for the colonists in America. Illegal tea is being smuggled into the British American colonies.

The Tea Act granted the East India Company the right to directly ship its tea to North America and the right to duty free export of tea from Britain. In the colonies a coalition of merchants, smugglers and artisans has mobilised opposition to the delivery and distribution of the tea and many colonies have prevented the tea from being landed. Some of the stories I have heard sound criminal.

I understand about cutting corners to stay in business but I pride myself that I have only ever used the best produce in my recipes. I have had times where I have needed to make a little go a long way but economy with elegance has always been my guide.

I can think of nothing more elegant for ladies than to enjoy a pot of a delicately flavoured tea in a fine china cup with genteel discourse. I have been thinking that there might be interest in a genteel ladies' meeting for the widows of the parish. So many ladies have been left in poverty by the early death of a husband but still with the wish to engage with polite society. They would not want to visit here at the inn but it may be possible to meet in the cloisters of the Collegiate Church.

I of course would supply the tea and a selection of dainty confectioneries and for payment of a small fee, any lady may join in. It would be the perfect answer for many of the widows I know, who are genteel but without a place in society. We could institute meetings with perhaps a bible reading or other instructive lesson, a great opportunity to exchange knowledge and polite conversation. It is something I would enjoy and it may help me make a little money too. I will put the case to the Warden at the Collegiate Church and ask for his help.

1773 Jun 29 2nd & 6/13 July, 3/10/17/24/31 Aug directory published

At last the Directory is finished and can start to bring me in some money. Mr. Harrop assures me that he has had numerous customers asking for it, putting pressure on him to publish it. I am more than pleased that it is finished and I can spend time on my business again.

In that regard I am pleased about the progress with my Ladies' Tea Salon that I have proposed. I had a very good conversation with Reverend Wakefield about such a gathering that, although he disapproved most strongly of the decadence of the 'ladies aping men's habits', as he put it, he did relish the chance to lecture a group with a bible reading.

Ladies are to make a donation, from which I may take an amount to pay for the produce I supply and any surplus will go to the church's funds. We have agreed that once every month will be sufficient and our first meeting can be on the last Wednesday of July. A satisfactory arrangement all round and I will send invitations to those ladies who I am sure will enjoy a salon, and more importantly, whose conversation I will enjoy.

1773 Jul interest in coach hire

Oh me, our business has dwindled to a trickle. I knew when we took on this inn that there is very little money to be made in the summer. Once the winter season is finished most of Society have left town for the country but I thought we would have more customers than we do have. The inn has bills to be paid and no income with which to pay them.

Mr. Harrop has not yet calculated my profits from the sale of the new Directory so I must put my mind to new ways of making some extra money. John tells me we are not making best use of our stables here and he has had a good offer from Mr. Swain, of the Spread Eagle, who is keen to expand his carriage hire business. I know he has run that business for a long time so he must know how to make it pay.

John is convinced it is an easy way to make money and he can easily manage it. Once we have bought one or two carriages they will cost very little to maintain and all will be profit. That's as maybe but I don't know how he presumes we have the sum of money to buy even one carriage. He says Mr. Swain is happy to rent them to us at a very easy price but I saw the flaw in that straight way. So Mr. Swain will make money whether we do or not. I do not think that a good bargain and I told him so.

I think that Mr. Swain should provide the carriages and we provide the stabling and the costs of the advertising and then we both share the profits. I have left him to put that business proposition to his chum, but I am not hopeful of a good outcome. Sometimes I do despair at John's lack of business sense. I am beginning to think he has none.

1773 Aug 23 carnation competition, report of first ladies' salon

Today was a day to celebrate, as we held the first ever competition for Carnations at our inn. While we wait for Mr. Swain to discuss favourable terms with us, I persuaded John to return to a skill he possesses in excess of anyone. I have never seen a match for his talent in producing the best ever carnations.

We had so many entries to the competition that he was forced to withdraw his own entry. He did try to persuade his brother James to enter them as his, but James was too proud and insisted that he could grow better ones than John. I do not think they are as good and the judging will see if I am right.

We provided prizes for best perfume, best colouring, and best leaf forms, and if one particular carnation can win all three categories the grower will earn a bottle of best French brandy.

Of course everyone enjoyed the feast I prepared, the table decorated with several Solomon's Temples in flummery, each tower adorned with an example of John's carnations. This feast has been a great success and I am sure it will prove a vital part of the Manchester social calendar.

I cannot say that my Ladies' Tea Salons will be equally successful. I am quite disheartened that our first one was tedious in the extreme. Reverend Wakefield held forth for over an hour on his favourite subject, the evils of indulgence. Only three of the invited ladies attended the meeting, and it was not until Reverend Wakefield was fortuitously called away that we were able to relax and enjoy the tea and dainties I had provided.

The Jumballs I had made were well received and all the ladies asked me for the recipe and way of making them, which was most gratifying. I was happy to explain my methods, if only to prevent Mrs. Knight from dominating all the conversation. It also gave me a reason to mention that the printing of the third edition of my cookbook was to be printed next month.

Mrs. Anderson was a joy to speak to but Mrs. Knight would keep interrupting with her opinions which were of no real value at all. Widow Johnson was happy just to listen, poor soul, she is not in the best of health and was glad of an outing for any reason.

One thing we all agreed was that we should perhaps ask one of the other Collegiate Church Wardens to speak to us next time, one who is a little less dogmatic in his beliefs. We agreed that I should speak to Reverend Ainsworth for next month. Mrs. Knight thought that she should be the one to ask him, but I insisted that as it was my salon it was my duty to arrange the speaker. If Mrs. Knight took it upon herself to speak to anyone I fear we would never persuade anyone to speak to us.

Without wishing to put myself forward unduly, I mooted the suggestion that in future we might ask if other learned men might think it worth their while to speak to us. The other ladies decried the idea as unlikely. What man would think women worth educating, they asked in surprise. I replied most fervently that my father had educated all his girls and taught us to know that women had just as much intelligence as men. I myself had proved that I had more business sense than my own husband and we have all heard of women who can outthink a man, I said.

Of course Mrs. Knight had an answer to it all. She suggested slyly that a woman can use low cunning to get her way but it is not the learned cleverness that men possess. Well, I had not the patience to educate her and left it at that. A closed mind never sees the open door, as my papa always admonished when we girls refused to accept a new idea. Have an open mind, he would say, and you will see that so much is possible. Mrs. Knightly has got the most firmly closed mind of anyone that I have ever met. I doubt she even accepts that there is a door to be opened. I do hope she does not come to our next meeting.

1773 Sep 21/28 card assembly advert

At last we are opening our Season again. It has been terribly quiet in the bar over the summer, so many of Society have been out of town this year that it seemed we might have no money coming in at all. The notice for our Card Assembly which begins next week was finally placed in the Mercury today. John has a few names enrolled but I do wish he would let me write the notices. His are so blunt and without any gentility.

I now must look to engage the appetites and ensure they see a good reason to return every fortnight. How to do that, before the money is paid, is where I will need all my skills. I shall probably need to have recourse to my little funds put aside which John must never know about. I am sure I can manage a good Vermicelli soup to start which will take the edge of most appetites. I will consult with Mary tomorrow and see what she advises.

NOTICE is hereby GIVEN
THAT THE
CARD ASSEMBLY
Will be OPENED
At JOHN RAFFALD'S
The King's-Head, in Salford
On Wednesday the 29th of Sept. Inst.
And to be continued every *Wednesday* Fortnight during
the Winter Season.

Thankfully my second Ladies' Tea Salon was much better than the first. Reverend Ainsworth was a joy to listen to, such a friendly, humble man, a true believer and so human in his beliefs. He was more in touch with the real life that his parishioners lived. His talk was enjoyed by us all, even Mrs. Knight. That lady was there again, ready with her opinions on everything but Reverend Ainsworth gently guided her away from her continual complaining.

Widow Johnson did not attend for which I am sorry and I will make sure that I call on her tomorrow to check she is not ill. We did have four new ladies this time and the discourse was most pleasant, helped along by my delicate macaroon cakes. One of the new ladies, Mrs. Abbot, offered to engage Dr White, the Man-midwife, to talk to us next month. It will be a tremendous boost for our little group if she does but she claims some acquaintance with him so we shall see.

1773 Oct 12 first ad for 3rd The Experienced English Housekeeper

There was such a to-do in the Card Assembly this week. Mr. Ratcliffe accused Mr. Wainwright of cheating and caused such a stir in the room that nothing would calm him and John was forced to ask both the gentlemen to step outside. One thing I will not countenance on any premises of mine is the possibility of low, base behaviour. Those gentlemen that think they can act in that way will not be allowed through our doors, no matter how much they may spend.

I sent a gift the next day to Mr. Ratcliffe of a parcel of sweet patties, his favourite delicacy, in the hopes of sweetening his view of our assembly. I did not wish him to speak ill of us all over town for he is a man of some influence. Mr. Wainwright, however, will have stern words spoken to him if he dares to return.

As I walked along Smithy Door today to the Market-place I met up with Widow Johnson from my first Tea Salon. She is such a frail woman she looks as if a good puff of wind will blow her away. After the necessary pleasantries I asked her if we might have the pleasure of her company at another Salon, but she shook her head sadly. It seems that her son heard about our little gathering and has forbidden her to go again. He had called it an unnatural connivance, fit only for women of low repute and not for decent women. She looked most uncomfortable so I simply said that I understood and changed the subject and made my polite regrets, etc., hoping that my face did not betray the anger I felt at her son's rudeness to me.

That he should suggest that I, Elizabeth Raffald, would be involved in something not of the highest standards or the most respectable motives is an insult. There are times when I despair of men's attitudes to women, that their violence, neglect and mistreatment are forgiven by the church, just because a man is given more privilege than a woman. Was it not a woman who gave birth to the Saviour? Is not the bountiful earth described as Mother Nature? Why then does church and government treat women as second class or even as waste? I have worked more businesses than John, made more income than he will ever make and yet because I am married to him, the law says that everything I have is his.

In my house what I make is mine and I will only allow John that portion that he dares to ask for, and then only from the portion that I allow him to know about. Why, if I left it to John we would be living on the poor rate. I thank my parents that I was born with a good brain and a good education. Life has taught me that what I have is hard come by and the law will have to be up earlier than me to take it from me.

I was so incensed at Widow Johnson's comments that I paid a full seven shillings and sixpence for a cucumber, an expence I would never normally go to, but I will make it pay for me at this week's Card Assembly. My dinners always receive the nicest comments from our customers and I hope Mr. Johnson hears about it and regrets the penance he puts upon his mother. I would not allow my daughter's husbands to dictate so to me if I am a dependant widow woman.

1773 Nov carriage hire

We are decided now that to go into business with Mr. Swain, although I am not pleased that he has claimed first billing in the endeavour. He did make a persuasive case that his name was better known for coaches and would command more respect than one known for the quality of its food. He quite threw me off with his flattery but not so much that I forgot to insist that all business would come through me only.

I do not trust these two men to have any business sense for I know John has none, and if Mr. Swain was so good at it he would never seen the need to approach John to share it with him. He tried to say it was because there was too much custom for him to handle on his own but I can see straight through his thin story.

There is work needed on this enterprise, of that I have no doubt, and I am certain that with the Elizabeth Raffald touch I can lift it above the ordinary and attract the better kind of customers. The people with the money in this town appreciate the kind of attention to detail for which I am renowned. I certainly have a good deal of work ahead, for John would not be persuaded to begin with just one chaise.

He was fixed on taking three coaches, for which we have the room, because with three we would always be sure of having one ready for hire at the shortest notice. I was not convinced that three sets of horses all needing to be fed and groomed was an expense we could manage at present. He was not easily persuaded but I would not hear of it no matter how much Mr. Swain flattered and cajoled me.

There is something about that man that sits ill with me. I see how John is juggled by him but he will not trick me and John knows not to challenge me when I have made up my mind. I saw the two men nudging each other and laughing together as they went into the bar room, but if they think they will get one over on Elizabeth Raffald they will discover their mistake soon enough.

1773 Dec 11th Carriages ad in Manchester Mercury

Now it is official that the Raffalds have added carriage hire to our list of enterprises. The first notice has appeared in the Mercury for all to see and I have another clipping to add to my collection.

It does grieve me to see our name in second place but it cannot be helped. If this goes well we will have our own carriages before long. I am confident that word will soon spread of the superior nature of our carriages.

My scullery maids scrubbed and polished the ones we received from Mr. Swain, until they were to my standards, which are evidently higher than Mr. Swain's. The extra work with the horses has kept John busy and it is good to see him working outdoors again. He is much happier when he is working with nature and the horses respond well to him.

My nephew William reports that he is gambling less since the carriages came, and of course, the less he is in the bar, the less he is able to give favours of free ale to his hangers on, those lacklustre men who loiter and abuse our hospitality.

1774

1774 Jan 1 & 18th ad for 3rd The Experienced English Housekeeper

Some people in this town will use any opportunity to favour their business. I saw a notice in the Mercury today about the Weighing Machine, at Alport Town, which has been for some time unattended, owing to former Neglects, Mistakes, and Mismanagement. John Gooden, that clever innkeeper at the Half Moon inn close by the machine, has taken it upon himself to run it, with strict impartiality, he says.

I think he is being a little incorrect when in this notice he states, after declaring all Propriety in Tallies are kept, that by the by, he has a convenient Public House near the Machine, where a good Stock of

Liquors will be kept, and good Order observed.

Which inn can say they are a stronghold of good measure and propriety? Not even my own, although I lay that blame squarely at John's feet. He will try to overcharge the travelers that come to us and although I do my best to give them good measure in the foods I supply, they will not return to us if they feel cheated. When I say this to John he just scoffs at me and says there are plenty more of them all the time. There are plenty more inns for them to choose, I tell him, and they will talk to each other and give recommendations. He would not listen to me, only shrugging his shoulders, as if that was any answer.

1774 Feb 1st meeting for cotton manufacturers

Such a meeting there was tonight over at Crompton's Coffee House. It was attended by several of the travelers in cotton who were staying with us and from what I heard of their conversation it was on the serious matter of Security for the Cotton and Linen trade.

There have been so many thefts and burglaries in this region that the losses are likely to drive away the traders and with them their money and work for others who depend on their trade. It is not just the cotton manufacturers who benefit but also all the little businesses that work for them; the domestic servants, leatherworkers, cabinet makers, ironmongers, and everyone else who thrives here, even our own inn which benefits from the trade.

I was alarmed to hear their views for these are serious men, of discerning tastes, who appreciate fine rooms with good wine in stock. I make it my business to keep my customers away from John's grasping hands and thanks to my nephew William's help I am able to procure wines worthy of the name. If John will not take care of his bar room it is upon my shoulders to take extra care of my good customers. My gentlemen will return for more of Mrs. Raffald's mouthwatering meals and not for Mr. Raffald's rough ways.

The Captain of the Dragoons has offered to me that he will have words, or worse, with John but I cannot allow that. I will not have someone else minding my marriage. To John I am wed and so we will be to our dying days, though god willing that will not be for years yet. I have so many ideas of ways I can make changes to improve our lives. No, I must be the one to take John in hand, even though he frightens me a little when he is roaring drunk. When he is sober he is a different man and that is the one I will talk to.

1774 Mar 8 cotton regulations

It is good to see that the authorities here in Manchester are taking swift action on the threat to our cotton trade. In the Mercury today there was a notice that they have appointed a Committee of Gentlemen to look into the problems of the cotton and linen manufacturers. They have introduced several Measures relative to the present State of Trade, which it is hoped, may have the most beneficial Consequences. They are acting in a most formal manner with all Proceedings regularly minuted, and Copies taken of all Letters sent and received by the Committee. This must encourage our gentlemen of business to make Manchester the centre of their Trade. I do not think anywhere else is taking such care.

It is in direct contrast that another notice told of the card sharpers who are plaguing every inn and coffee house in Manchester. There are four of them, acting as if unknown to each other, all ill looking characters. They tried it here in the King's Head but we had received word from Mr. Swain at the Spread Eagle here on Chapel-street that they had been there and were heading our way, so we were wise to them.

The customers at the Blue Boar and the Cock on Market-street-lane were not so fortunate and Mr. Harrop's report says that on Friday night the four Sharpers went to the Blue Boar, along with a travelling Hosier.

> They engaged them in discourse on various subjects, and in the end one of them introduced Cards, and proposed to his Brother Sharpers, that he would cut a five with any of them for Fifty Pounds; one of them challenged the Wager, and being short of Cash, enquired of the Hosier what Money he had of him, he produced eleven Guineas, but being short of the Wager, the Villain pulled out of his pocket Pieces of Paper, which he called Bank Notes, and proposed to go and get Cash at the Bank; he desired the Hosier would go with him, which he did as far as the Bull's Head, but at the instant recollecting himself, told the Owner of the Money that he had better go and keep his Companions Company, and comply'd with his request; but to his great Surprise he found them all fled.
> The same Rascals (as is supposed) went immediately to the

> Cock, in Market-street-lane and defrauded John
> Greenhalch, of Bamford, of twenty-nine Guineas, by
> similar Pretence: One was a short stout Man, his Wig had
> many small Curls, another a tall Man, with a blue grey
> Coat, and a third was a lofty fresh looking Man, with a
> brown Coat. It is supposed they lodged at the Spread-
> Eagle, in Hanging-ditch, the preceding Night.

It makes sad reading to hear of these misbegots but I do believe it was only their own greed that put them in harm's way. If they had not thought to make money from an easy sounding wager they would not have lost anything. I am grateful they did not make it through our doors for it is just the thing that would tempt my John. He has become a gambler's dream, ready to place a wager on any possibility, believing he is due a win.

1774 March 18th Sir Peter's death, pregnant

Today I received a letter from my dearest friend, for I think I may now call her that, Lady Betty of Arley. It carried the most sad news, not too unexpected however, that her dear husband, Sir Peter had passed away on the eighteenth of March last. The poor lady is bereft without him and the baronetcy has now passed on to their son, Peter, the fifth baronet.

To think young master Peter is now a baronet at only twenty years of age is difficult for me to comprehend. She writes that he will complete his studies at Oxford before he returns home to take up his new duties. It will be left to his mother to manage the estate with Mr. Harper's help till then.

Mr. Harper has promised to stay on as estate steward until young Peter has established his own household but in truth she thinks losing his master has caused Mr. Harper to lose heart for the job. I can hardly think of that young boy as master of such a grand house, young rascal that he was, and he has some big shoes to step into after the good work that his father did. If he allows himself to be guided by his mother I know she will give him sound counsel on his duties and he will do well.

Lady Betty mentions that her spinster sister Margaret has invited her to live with her at Knutsford where she has a pretty little cottage. I remember that the village does have many amenities and a good assembly room there that would provide entertainment enough for them. I think she should take up the invitation. It will do her no good to sit about being maudlin about the past, and I can testify how good it is to have a dear sister near. My sister Mary is an excellent support for me and without her to confide my troubles in I do not know how I would fare.

John's gambling is becoming ever more of a problem but woe betide him if he ever ventures into my strongbox. It is as closed to him as my bed is, now I realise he has managed to get me with child again. I had thought my child bearing days were over and had foolishly allowed him his pleasure one night, for which I am now paying the price. To be pregnant again at the age of forty-one is just so vulgar. I can only hope that this is the longed for son, but I can say with certainty that it will be my last. I will not be so foolish again.

I am not as strong as I was the last time and that did not end well. My poor little stillborn son, if only there had been medicine to save him as well as his sister Mary. The tragedy did give me an appetite to attempt one more endeavour, my manuscript on midwifery practices. It has been such an honour to study with Mr. White. He is such an educated man, so intelligent and as keen as myself to see better treatment for all women. If I do nothing else I will have a book on better childbirth practices to match my book on better cooking practices, which I am proud to say has revolutionised cookery in this town.

1774 April 12 Indian murder in US

Such terrible news comes out of the American colonies. It is as lawless as it was one hundred years ago. Decent people are not safe in their beds. The Indian natives are continually attacking our God-fearing troops and the reports published in the Mercury are gruesome in the extreme. I shall be saying a prayer for the family of one Lieutenant Grant who met a most unfortunate demise according to the letter from Charles Town, South Carolina which was printed in the Mercury.

> "It is said that the Creek Nation in general disclaim any Knowledge of or share in, the late Murders in Georgia, which were perpetrated by fourteen Creek and three Cherokees. The fourteen Creek Indians are said to belong to a Settlement on Oakmulgnie River called the Standing Perch Tree, which is composed of Lower Creeks from the Gawer and Cussita Towns. The Number of Indians who attacked the Georgia Militia and

Rangers, are said to have exceeded seventeen in Number, the Detachment of Militia, under the Command of Captain Goudgion, was about twenty-five Men, they were joined by ten Rangers, under Quarter-master Stewart.

Lieutenant Grant was so stunned by a Ball, which grazed his Temple, that he fell from his Horse, by which Means he unfortunately fell into the Hands of the Indians, who cruelly murdered him. His Body was found tied to a Tree, a Gun-barrel, supposed to have been red-hot, was thrust into, and left sticking in, his Body; his Scalp and Ears taken off, a painted Hatchet left sticking in his Scull, twelve Arrows in his Breast, and a painted War-club left upon his Body."

Dreadful, but even the Colonists are stirring up trouble with the very people who are their only support, our own Parliament. They are becoming most belligerent in their treatment of honest businessmen, and using the cover of natives to blame for their trouble.

The truth is soon uncovered by men such as Mr. Harrop, however. His story of a most outrageous incident December last, of the waste of four hundred chests of tea, had many details. It was white men, he says, dressed like natives, who stole on board the tea ships and threw the chests over the side of the ship into the deep water of the harbour, instantly ruining the tea! Four hundred chests, what I could have done with a fraction of that amount. Someone will be ruined, of that I am certain.

At my last Ladies' Salon the talk was of nothing else. Most ladies enjoyed their tea with relish, although Mrs. Knight became very dismissive and would drink nothing but Barley water. The Reverend Mr. James Bayley gave us a long homily on the sin of greed which quite took away everyone's appetite for my lemon cheesecake. It was all I could do to persuade them that it was also a sin to waste God given goodness.

1774 May 24 new paper header, printed callicoes

Today's Mercury looked very grand with a new heading. Mr. Harrop had mentioned to me that he was thinking of making some improvements to his paper. He needs to try harder to attract the discerning businessmen now that Mr. Prescott's Journal is doing so well. I think this new look should make a good impression.

There was good news for the cotton men too this month. Last week two of my customers, travellers in cotton, calicoes, muslins and linen manufacturers, were conversing about the possibilities of Parliament removing the duty on printed, painted or stained cottons.

One of the gentlemen was adamant that it would happen as it was needed urgently to give Manchester cottons the boost it needed to compete and not be at a disadvantage. His friend was less sanguine, believing that it would not happen and he would lose his commission before the month was out for insufficient business. He was most despondent no matter what anyone could say.

It was only today that I heard that the tax had been removed so I hope the poor man retained his employment. All my travellers were cock-a-hoop tonight and spent more than they usually do on their after dinner liquors so it was good for everyone. God bless King George, I say.

1774 July 18th burglary

Such a dreadful tale has reached my ears that I am sorry for the woman concerned, even though I never liked her. Miss Towler thought her school was above mine when she tempted Mr. Fischar to come to her to give his dancing lessons. Well I wished her well of him, he was no asset to my school, How ever I disliked her this latest setback is a terrible thing. She was subject to a terrible burglary.

B U R G L A R Y

On *Friday* Night last, or early on *Saturday* Morning, the Dwelling-House of Miss Towler's, situate in *Market-street-lane, Manchester,* was broke open, and the following Goods stolen thereout, viz.,

One Crimson shag cloak,
One Scarlet broad Cloth ditto,
One Drab coloured Silk Camlet ditto
One Scarlet fine broad Cloth ditto, trimmed with White Fur spotted with Black,
One Scarlet Frize ditto,
One scarlet fine broad Cloth ditto,
One Scarlet Frize ditto,
One Crimson Shag ditto,
One Scarlet Cloth ditto trimmed with Gimp,
One copper warming Pan, with Brass Lid,
One small smoothing iron,
One large Copper Tea Kettle,

> A Copper Pan,
> A Brass Pan,
> One Irish linen cloth apron and two check aprons,
> One Scarlet frize Cloak, trimmed with squirrel skin,
> One long brown silk camlet ditto lined with Brown Stuff over the Shoulders,
> One large Scarlet Frize ditto,
> One Crimson Cloth ditto, bound with Ribband,
> One Black Silk ditto, lined with Silk Damask,
> One Scarlet Cloth ditto, trimmed with fringe,
> One Riding Petticoat of drab coloured Frize,
> Two Brass Candlesticks with Sockets to take out,
> One Brass Candlestick with a spring Socket,
> Three Huchaback Table Coths with the Mark 'T' thereon.

What a loss that must be! The cloaks will be all from her young ladies who are studying with her. Their fathers will be expecting her to replace them at no expense to themselves. She will be forced to close if she does not recover them. It's no wonder she has offered a reward of FORTY POUNDS for information to convict the person or persons guilty of the burglary.

She has even offered the reward to any accomplice in the burglary who will give up his partner in the crime. Whichever way it goes she will be hard put to continue her school. She has already had to move from St Anne's square to Market street lane, which is a sign that business was not doing well, for who would forego the genteel area for one of bustle and noise.

1774 Jul 19 cannibals

There was another report of violence in the Mercury today in a letter from the Cape of Good Hope, where one of the Ships has arrived which sailed with Capt. Cook in the South Seas.

> They explored in vain to the Southward in search of a Continent, and therefore bore up for New Zealand, where they had landed, but lost a Lieutenant and two Men, who by venturing too far into the Country, had been cut off by the Cannibals; that in Consequence of this Loss, they had dispatched a second Boat, and the whole Crew were massacred; the next Boat having only a miserable Spectacle of their Remains. From thence they sailed to the Cape of Good Hope, and speedily will pursue their Voyage Home.

No very material Circumstances further passed in the Course of their Expedition.

I do wonder what it is that propels men to leave their homes for the unknown. I am sure that Capt. Cook has a wife waiting for him, who he forsakes to roam among savages and unknown monsters of the sea. It is dreadful to contemplate the fates that await them.

1774 Aug 8 florists feast
There has been such excitement this year for John's annual Carnation Competition. We have had so many more competitors than last year. I believe we may have instituted an important event in Manchester's social calendar. Our notice in the Mercury looked very impressive.

F L O R I S T S   F E A S T.
T H E
Annual CARNATION MEETING
Will be held at
Mr. JOHN RAFFALD'S, the KING'S-HEAD, in
SALFORD, on MONDAY, the 22d Inst.
Stewards MR. JOSEPH DALE,
Mr. JAMES DRURY
Dinner on the Table at Two o'Clock

My cooking is an important element of the day, not that the men are more interested in it that the competition, but I pride myself that I am known for the best meals in town. My cooking has reached all around the country now. My book of recipes has sold in excess of a thousand copies and has just been published in a third edition.

It was just as well that my sister Mary was able to help me with the work of preparing for the dinner, for I have been almost useless with the pain from this baby. I swear it is hurting every particle of my body, there is not a bit of me that doesn't ache. It has been all I could do to stay on my feet. I will be glad when it is born, son or not, I will not go through this pain again, it would be the death of me.

1774 Sep 18 Harriet christened
My baby was born amid much screaming from her poor

mother, and was only another girl, as if I do not have enough. John was disappointed not to have a son to inherit any fortune we may make. My poor mother had only girls and it seems I am destined to have the same fate. I do not wish harm to my girls but they do not have the same rights as a man can command. In business there is no doubt that women are the equal of men but in the eyes of the law they count for nothing, especially when married.

I see such wealth growing around us and sometimes wish I had been taught the skills of cotton weaving rather than cooking. The men of business who trade in cottons and linens are getting richer and richer while we are still scratching for favours. If only I had been born a son instead of a daughter, I feel sure I could have done more.

My nephew William is as close to me as a son and shows he has the same business inclination. He is more like me than any of my daughters and I have a scheme in mind that may help us both. As a woman in business I am patronised and ignored, fit only to serve food to the men who make the decisions. I have listened to their conversations and many of them are idiots, taken in by glib talk, forging deals that will make them poorer and the other man richer. I could make business as well as them if I was just allowed to talk. But no, they will deal with John, simple man that he is, solely because he is the husband and I just the wife.

This baby has left me cranky in the extreme, making me hostage to unbearable aches and pains. I am weary of bearing babies and of working hard. It is no easy matter running an inn of this size with a profligate husband and if I am to be dependent on John's business sense I worry what will become of us.

1774 Oct John's betrayal

Alack, alas, what trouble has befallen me now, I am undone. I am aghast at the words John spoke to me tonight. I had feared moving into an inn would do John no good, but he convinced me he would make it good. Too late I have been proved correct in my instincts, would that I had not. I had thought he was acting strange and being exceeding troublesome but I have been so busy in the kitchen that I did not have the time to check his nonsense, and now it has come back to spite me.

That he was good at charming the ladies I have never doubted but I always took him as an honest man, a loyal and true husband, as I have been a loyal wife. Truth be told I have neither inclination or time to be any other. I was never sought out even as a young maid. Honest, my dear papa always said of my features. Honest is as good as one should wish for, any more is pure vanity and surely an evil in God's eyes. He chooses to make some people beautiful, however so would a little more for me have been such a trial? I have never been vain and have only my skills to recommend me, hard toil and an honest heart, a heart that is now broken completely by this news of John's. News he told me in such a hurtful way. How could he accuse me of neglecting him when all the work I am doing is for the good of us all? How can he think that I am any other than I was on our wedding day?

He has been charmed by a hussy, a woman I must see every day in the Market Place. To pass her in the road and not decry her as I want to, as my very being screams out to do, will be the hardest thing I have ever done. But I will not abase myself. I will not give them that satisfaction. But she shall not have him.

I shall keep my respectability, my reputation in this town with a husband by my side until I am a widow. And even though I know of ways that would make that day come quicker I would not risk my mortal soul over a libertine who has already risked hers. John Raffald belongs to me and he shall stay with me until death do us part as we both vowed before God and the priest.

My first action must be to hide my shattered heart so that my dear girls do not notice any difference between their dear mama and papa. I can only trust my sister Mary to confide in. She alone will know of my troubles. From her I know I will receive good counsel.

For now I shall forbid John my bed and my dinner table, let him see if his hussy can provide him with as good a repast as he enjoys here. I shall let him know what he stands to lose if he continues. I will do all I can to bring this foolishness to a swift end.

1774 Nov 8 new shop for William

John is being as stubborn as ever and refuses to beg for forgiveness. Such a wicked state of affairs but I am determined to hold my head up. He has broken my trust and our agreement that we would work together for our family. We are linked in our business and I am his wife until one of us dies, so I must make the best of it.

I cannot afford to go into business on my own but with Mary's help we may manage. I am so thankful to have my nephew William to work with. Now that he is of age he is able to take on the lease of a good shop with my backing. He has known what his Uncle Raffald was doing, how he has badly used me, his Aunt and his benefactor. He wanted to leave our service immediately, but I persuaded him that I needed him to stay and could offer him a good opportunity.

Now we have put our plan into action. We could not afford a shop on the Market-place but I got a good price on a small house at the lower end of Market-street-lane. William has a gap in the market to fill now that his Uncle James has quit his shop in Smithy Door. It was becoming too much for him in his weakened state of mind.

When he heard that his only son was lost at sea it was such a blow that he lost all heart to carry on. If he does not bear up soon he will end up in the Lunatic Hospital next door to his house. We have all lost children but the blow of losing a son must be hard to bear.

William will sell seeds and other garden necessaries from his Uncle James's garden in Salford, and all Confectioneries, from me with Mary's help, and grocery goods as I used to sell in my own shop. I can see now it was a mistake to leave my shop where I was doing so well. I do not know how I ever thought an inn would be an improvement. If I had known how it would affect John I would never have moved. Now I must start again with William but I know I can trust him to arrange the shop how I tell him, for he knows I have the experience of the business that will help him. He is happy to leave the arranging of the notices in the Mercury to my direction, knowing I can make a good deal with Mr. Harrop.

William's experience in the trade of liquors has made him keen to add Cider and Perry to his stock which I think could be useful and must make our shop the best in Town. Fortunately he has always shown himself to be a most sober, industrious young man so I have no fear that he will lapse into intoxication as his Uncle has done.

I am certain that John is regretting falling for the charms of his hussy but I will not give in to him. I am already richer for keeping my money away from him. I make sure my bills are paid, and now he can take on the burden of doing likewise for the liquors. Then he may see just how much he is dependent on me and my hard work.

1774 Dec 20 Swain carriages

I do not know if my mind was on the future I wished for, when I allowed Mr. Swain to convince me to share in the expense of a

Mourning Coach. John does frequently look starving but he will not beg for my forgiveness so I will not weaken. I do pretend not to notice when little Anna takes a pie from the kitchen. Her warm heart does her credit and it pains her to see her father looking sad.

When I was checking the receipts for the new coach it did occur to me more than once to wonder if I would soon be a passenger in it myself, but whatever grief he has caused me I do not wish harm to John. I would rather have back the good man that I married. We both need to work together to make our businesses turn to profit.

I am glad I have young William's shop to hope for. I took great pains with the notice for today's Mercury, reminding everyone that it is with the blessing of his Uncle and Aunt Raffald so they might see the quality they can expect. For anyone who may remember our shop they will acknowledge John's skills as a nurseryman and my cooking of course has its own reputation.

Our notice in the Mercury mentioned both enterprises and Mr. Harrop was kind enough to reduce the amount to pay.

First in the column was the notice for William's shop

WILLIAM MIDDLEWOOD

Begs Leave to acquaint his FRIENDS and the PUBLIC

That he has open'd a SHOP, in *Market-street-lane, Manchester*, where may be had all Sorts of *Confectionary* and *Grocery* Goods: Likewise a large Assortment of all Kinds of Garden and Tree Seeds, Garden Peas and Beans, Annual, Biennial, and Perennial Flower Seed; Seeds of Physical Herbs, and for Kitchen Use; American Tree Seeds, Hemp, Rape and Canary, ditto, Split Peas, Boiling ditto, Mats, Garden Tools, etc. Pomegranates, Seville and China Oranges, Lemons, fine Kentish, Worcester, Sussex, and other Hops, of Good Quality, and at a reasonable Price.

N.B. Likewise all Sorts of Bulbous, Tuberous, and Herbaceous Flower Roots, Flowering Shrubs, Forest and Fruit Trees that can be procured, natives or exotics, on short notice, & on the most reasonable Terms.

Just arrived, fine Sturgeon, Brawn, Mushrooms, Catchups, Olives, Pistachio Nuts etc. Likewise may be had, Mint Drops, suitable to every Taste, in different Degrees of Warmth.

The Business will be carried on in all its Branches as by his *Uncle and Aunt,* Mr. *John and Elizabeth Raffald.* He has engaged some Thousand Gallons of the best rich Herefordshire *Cyder* and *Perry*, to be ready for Sale in *March*, which will be extraordinarily good, and on very reasonable Terms.

Followed immediately by the notice for our mourning coach

Messrs SWAIN and RAFFALD

Beg Leave to acquaint their Friends and the Public
That they have fitted up in the genteelest Manner, a new MOURNING COACH and HEARSE, with handsome Furniture, able Horses, and careful Drivers. Also a handsome COACH to any Part of the Town and Country, may be had on the shortest Notice, and on the most reasonable Terms, by applying at the *King's-Head* Inn, in *Salford*.
Manchester, December 20, 1774

1775

1775 Jan 10 William's shop, sale of Aytoun/Minshull Houses

I am so proud of my nephew William and how he carries himself. He has certainly not wasted the last few years of working under my instruction. He has just the best manner of dealing with his customers to please and engage them and tempt them to call back again. He has the manners I would wish for John but which he obstinately refuses to acknowledge.

John does not appreciate the need to tempt people to return, saying that it is keeping a good cellar that will bring people in to spend their money. I knew he was a proud man when I married him but as he gets older his moods incline more to rudeness and malignity. It is a relief to leave him in the inn while I am needed to help William in the shop. It is where I feel most useful and most at home. Oh, that I ever left my dear little shop on the Market-place. That is a day I rue more with all my heart, every morning when I open my eyes and have to face another day with John in that place.

There has been gratifying interest in the Herefordshire Cider and Perry which will be soon be ready for sale, we hope. I think that

William hit upon the right idea when he added to his stock, rather than the perfumes which I sold. His brother Joshua wanted him to take a supply from his master, Mr. Wagstaff, but William stoutly refused, saying he would rather sell honest liquor that he could vouch for than dubious waters from a crazed old man. Such a row the boys had, it was hard for a loving Aunt to witness. Both boys, or rather young men, stuck to their side of the argument and it ended with Joshua vowing to leave Manchester at his earliest opportunity. He would find a situation that would prove their worth to his brother and he would make him eat his words. I advised Joshua to wait and he would be proved right when customers come to the shop seeking for the waters, as they surely would.

Such a sad notice was in the Mercury today for the sale of Mrs. Minshull's properties. Of course I should rightly say Mrs., Aytoun but I can never think of her as truly Capt. Aytoun's wife. He married her for money. That much was clear from the beginning. I said she would rue the day she gave him rights over her estate and now I am proved right. In only six years she has been reduced from a woman of some substance, with her own houses and income, to the wife of a debtor. Heaven knows what will become of her.

All her houses are to be auctioned next week. What a wicked thing it was when she picked herself a husband by watching him run naked down a hill. It is a crime, that a profligate soldier got his hands on the wealth that her good, sober husband had worked years to build. She gave it away on a whim, not even reserving much for the benefit of her children, such a scandal.

Altogether there are three good houses, with lands and appurtenances, all being sold to cover Capt. Aytoun's debts; his wife left destitute in her dotage. Her Mansion house, Chorlton Hall in Chorlton Row, only a mile out of Town, Garrat Hall and Hough Hall in Moston, with vast lands, stables, income from chief rents of at least one hundred and fifty pounds every annum. I wonder how she can bear it. She has my sympathy a little, having a wasteful husband myself I can understand, but to lose so much, to fall from such heights, it must be shaming.

Even the furniture is to be sold on negotiation, that man should be ashamed of himself. I only hope he has the decency to settle some money on his poor wife and then leave the country to follow his trade of soldier. Let him fight and seek an honourable death for he has not lived as an honourable man. Poor Mrs. Minshull, it will bring her an early death, of that I am certain.

1775 Feb 4 Changes to roads

I am so incensed with John, more than usual for his stubbornness could cost us both money. Benjamin Bower, our Boroughreeve, has called a morning meeting at the Exchange in two weeks time to consider proposals for widening the streets and removing nuisances, which is what they call the signs that we businesses need to put on the streets to draw attention to our trade.

It is intolerable to be so punished and we need our voices to be heard at the meeting. John, like a mule, refuses to budge. He says he is busy in the inn at that time. What he means is that it is his time to test the casks, by drinking generous samples.

What I wish to know is how they propose we should advertise if they take these means away from us? What will they give us to replace them, or will they compensate us for lost trade, I wonder. I am only thankful that William is sensible of the risks and understands his duty to take part. He at least intends to go, leaving the shop to my care while he is away.

1775 Mar 4 More roads meeting

Our inn has been busy today, but not unfortunately with many paying customers. After the meeting of last week about improving the environs of the town, today's Mercury carried the information that a copy of the proposed Improvements can be viewed here at the King's-head, together with the opportunity to make a subscription to the cost of the plan.

I am glad I was able to be present at this meeting, where they spoke of buying up buildings on certain streets to be demolished to make roads wider. It means I am conversant with the plan and can talk about it if consulted. This is more than John can manage, he shows no interest in it whatsoever. It does not affect us much here on Chapel-street, though our customers will be affected by the work nearby.

Fortunately William's shop is not for demolition and I agree wholeheartedly with the proposals which seek to open up the area of Old Millgate and St. Mary's-gate. The new design looks very grand, giving the town a wide open space where Ladies may walk without fear of wretches laying in wait round dark corners.

They propose to remove the houses on the Easterly side and those between the Exchange and St. Ann's-square I see as a great improvement. It will remove that dark passage which is called Dark

Entry, a most unwholesome and intimidating thoroughfare. I will walk around rather than set foot through there. Even my delivery boys are not keen on taking that route.

Mr. Crompton was at the meeting and he was pleased that at last the entrance to his Coffee House, directly above the passageway, will be considerably more elegant, but he was not pleased to think of all the mess of the work underneath his very window.

Mr. Cavendish the cheesemonger, whose shop is scheduled to be demolished, was most irate, until the Boroughreeve calmed him down sufficiently to explain that in compensation he will be offered a very nice position in St. Ann's-square at favourable rent. He soon stopped complaining when he saw the advantage to himself. I could almost have wished them to take our meagre shop but on the whole it is doing well where it is.

1775 Apr 4 news from America, beginning of revolution in the colonies

Those wicked rebels in America are stirring up trouble again for our brave soldiers stationed at Boston for the safe protection of the honest citizens wanting to live there under the protection of our King's laws.

It was in the Mercury that a Benjamin Lincoln issued an outright ban in several Towns and Districts on anyone selling goods to our troops, anything that may enable them to take the field against the Rebels or which might 'distress the Inhabitants of this Country'. Are not the English residents of that Country also entitled not to be distressed? They really go too far and I hope that the business people there do not allow the threats of being 'held in the highest Detestation, deemed inveterate Enemies to America' prevent them from engaging in honest trade.

Sometimes I despair of the men who direct countries. They take an idea and think everyone must sacrifice for their principles when often they are not the ones with a livelihood to lose. Oh no, they take no account of that. Sacrifice to the greater good, they propose. Well I will not be told who I can and cannot sell to. I will take my business where I choose, such business as I am allowed to have. Thankfully William's shop is keeping my cooking in everyone's minds, and more importantly, on their tables.

1775 May 23 Theatre closed, the Playhouse Bill, William's shop,

Dragoons

I have been kept so busy with the Officers of the Dragoons this last week with many new men arriving in a flurry of excitement. The latest arrivals are a regiment from the Earl of Pembroke's Dragoons, and they expect any day to be inspected by General Evelyn. So everyday they come back to the inn so hungry from their day's exercises that they fall on my food almost without manners.

I say almost for I am fortunate that I only see Officers who remember they are firstly gentlemen. If they forget it they are soon reminded sharply by their Manchester friends not to upset Mrs. Raffald, the best cook in Manchester.

It would help greatly if only they would remember not to leave quite so much mess of discarded oak branches about the place. It is the anniversary of the Restoration next week and so they must all have a sprig of oak to wear in their hats on the day. Their men have been stripping all the trees around to get the Officers the best sprigs. There may be no trees left surviving after May 29th.

I put it to John that he missed out on a good bit of business there, if he could have torn himself away from his casks for an hour or two, but no, he would not listen. Ah well, it cannot be helped now.

I am more pleased that my nephew is not so deaf to my good advice. I have finally prevailed upon William to see the sense of having a stock of Perfumed Waters in the shop. He does not need to believe in an item to enjoy the profit it can make him. If the customer will come to his shop to buy it, that is the only thing to believe in.

My only sadness is that it is too late to prevail upon his brother to stay. After their argument Joshua spared no effort to find a position elsewhere and he has recently left for London with a letter of recommendation from Mr. Wagstaff in his bag. Poor Mr. Wagstaff was bereft without him and said that as he felt too old now to train up another apprentice he was happy to give William the benefit of his remaining stock to sell.

He recognised Joshua's talent for the business and was happy to give him a letter of introduction to an important man in London. This man has connections with members of the King's court, where Joshua may find an opportunity to rise to a position of importance himself. If Joshua has any of the Whitaker spirit from his mother he must do well. William has already benefited from Joshua's leaving by procuring some good stock, including Clove Water, Cream of the

Kernel of Peaches and Oil of Annis, all at a good price.

Manchester Society has been much reduced this month with the closure of the theatre on the corner of Marsden-street and Brown-street. Mr. Harrop tells me that it is doubtful whether Manchester will be allowed to have another theatre at all, due to a Bill of Parliament being debated in the House of Lords this month. It is called the Manchester Playhouse Bill and is being opposed by the Bishop of London. His reason is that he says Manchester is a manufacturing town and nothing could be more destructive to the welfare of the place than the introduction of such an institution.

He might be right in some ways but when we have people of Society who wish to make Manchester their home they will want also to enjoy all the niceties that they are used to in London. This bishop should come to Manchester to see for himself how the town has grown. Life is changing for many people and a good theatre has been part of an educated civilization for centuries.

If he is allowed to forbid this, what might he forbid next, card assemblies, race meetings? Then what will we have? Nobody of nobility or gentry will ever come here and we will be a poor shadow of what we can be.

Mr. Harrop reassures me that our case is supported by the Earl of Carlisle, who spoke most eloquently, saying that because "Manchester had become a seat of Methodism he thought there was no way so effectual to eradicate that dark, odious and ridiculous enthusiasm as by giving the people cheerful amusements which might counteract their Methodist melancholy".

I do not see much of that kind of melancholy around me, it is more the melancholy of poverty but even so, I hope he persuades the other peers to his side.

1775 June theatre bill passed, 4th cookbook, tragic news item

I am glad to see I had no need to be anxious. Good sense prevailed on the Manchester Playhouse Bill. And we are allowed our theatres. A new one, the Theatre Royal, opened at the corner of Spring Gardens and York St. It was opened during Race Week with a Play and a Farce. Such a grand place, befitting a theatre dedicated to the King. I am pleased to hear that Mr. Harrop has been given the contract to produce the playbills, for he is the best printer in town.

Mr. Harrop was not very pleased with my new advertisement that I asked him to put in the paper. I had not the time to pay it my usual attention and wanted to save a little money. So many people are calling my book Raffald's cookery that I named it so in my advertisement. I must believe that my book speaks for itself and I have no need of listing everything in the advertisement any more.

This Day is published, Price Six Shillings
The F O U R T H E D I T I O N of
R A F F A L D' S   C O O K E R Y,
It is thought needless to say much upon the Use and Value of this Book, as its own Merit has proved its Worth, by the uncommon Sale it has had in so short a Time. The Author returns her most sincere Thanks for the Honour done in the kind Reception of her Work, and hopes still to merit the Continuance of her Friends and the Public's Favours, in the public Station of Life she is now in, as no Pains or Expence have been spared to fit up the KING'S-HEAD Inn, in SALFORD, with every genteel Accommodation for Travellers, &c. the best of WINES, and good ORDINARIES every Day.

Neat POST CHAISES with able HORSES, on the shortest Notice

This week we had the sad news of a young man who worked nearby. Young Jeremiah Bostock, a Tape Weaver, was found hanging in his Yard just along the road here, close by his Sweetheart's door. The evening before they had parted in ill humour and this is thought to be the Cause of his rash Action. He was a somewhat difficult boy, so the Coroner has recorded a Verdict of Lunacy. It was the only way to give his mother peace of mind but his poor Sweetheart is stricken with guilt, feeling it to be her fault. I see her most days when she passes the inn on her way to do errands for her mother. It will do her no good to carry the burden. If he would think of doing such a lunatic thing then nothing she could do would prevent it. I am glad not to be so young and foolish any more.

1775 July ducking stool moved, Lady B to Knutsford

I received such a sad letter today from my friend Lady Betty. She is leaving Arley Hall and removing to Knutsford where she will live with her sister Margaret. Her husband made a lot of money in banking, and so she is a well provided for widow with a nice home of her own. It cannot be to the standard to which Lady Betty has been accustomed, but she writes that it is too painful for her to stay at the Hall watching her son's wife rule where she once did. It has been unsatisfactory for everyone and when her sister entreated her most strongly to be her companion she accepted her offer of a home.

Margaret lives in the very centre of Knutsford with many pretty churches and frequent assemblies so I think they will live very comfortably. Sir Peter bequeathed Lady Betty a good sum for her income and she still owns properties which she, as the daughter of the eleventh Earl of Derby, brought with her on her marriage. Her nephew the twelfth Earl has been most kind to his aunt and ensured she is paid what she is due.

She has been fortunate to have so much choice and many days I have wished I was still in her service. She was always so kind to me, more so than the husband I acquired. I thought I had it hard when I was always at the beck and call of the house I worked in, but business has shown me that I have exchanged one mistress for many masters, and I must answer to them all. Even my sister Mary is more involved with William's shop than with me at the inn.

I cannot truly blame her for there are more pleasant customers in the shop than there are here, but it is hard to admit that she now surpasses me in her skill with confectionaries. The shop has become quite the place to come for the best in town. Of course she does not have the double burden of a husband and children to demand her attention.

I vow that more days than not I find myself wondering if I will become a widow soon and I cannot say whether I deem it a good or bad turn. John harasses me daily with his miseries and he will not listen to me when I advise him to stop his drinking. It is a double blow to his business when he drinks what is meant for customers.

If I am not careful to keep my temper, however, I might become a victim of the Ducking Stool which is still in use here in Manchester, to punish scolds and disorderly women. I find it curious that such a modern town has not removed this barbaric torture from its streets. I heard they were taking it away from Pool Fold and thought that a good sign, but it was only moved to Daub Holes pond near the Infirmary.

I am all in favour of keeping order but many of the poor women who are so roughly punished may be driven to their actions by the rough brutes to whom they have the misfortune to be married. Manchester should be the place to lead the way for the rights of women. It is wrong that only a man has the right in law to order punishment without question.

1775 Aug 8 US Bunker Hill, George Washington, meeting

Such a terrible report was in the Mercury today of a battle, fought at a place called Bunker Hill in America, on June 17th between our British troops and the American Provincials. It was a great victory and merited a very long report, but it came at the cost of a great many men lost. There were less of the Provincials but, perhaps in consequence, they suffered fewer losses.

There was a report of a Mr. Paul Revire carrying attested Accounts that our Regulars lost a thousand men, and the Provincials only two hundred killed or wounded, with terrible wounds. A report from Mr. Grant, one of our Surgeons, from the Military Infirmary at Boston, dated June 23rd, gives terrible details of the injuries.

> 'I have scarce time sufficient to eat my Meals, therefore you must but expect a few Lines; I have been up two Nights assisting with four Mates, dressing our Men of the Wounds received in the last Engagement: many of the wounded are daily dying, and many must have both legs amputated. The Provincials had charged their Musquets with old Nails and singular Pieces of Iron, and from most of our Men being wounded in the Legs, we are inclined to believe it was their Design to leave them as a burden on us, to exhaust our provisions and to engage our Attention.'

I do fear that the battles in America are becoming ever more serious. The Provincials have now appointed a Generalissimo of their forces in what they are calling the 'Confederated Colonies of America'. The Mercury carried copies of letters sent from a body called the Provincial Congress of the Colony of New York to his Excellency, (if you can believe that they are giving him that honour), George Washington. This New York body claims they have been reduced to the unhappy Necessity of taking up Arms to defend their dearest Rights and Privileges. I do not see how fighting is ever a Necessity between intelligent men, but only the resort of belligerent men, involving other women's sons dying for their foolish beliefs. I am glad now that I never had a son for it would pain me to watch him leave me for some foreign battlefield.

Mr. Washington does sound a reasonable man. In his reply to the petition put to him he promises every Exertion will be extended to the re-establishment of Peace and Harmony between the Mother country and the Colonies. He states very nicely that 'when we assumed the Soldier we did not lay aside the Citizen', but he adds his determination to achieve 'American Liberty on the most firm and solid foundations, and enable them to return to their private stations in the Bosom of a free, peaceful and happy country'.

These American Provincials say they are fighting in the name of the supposed Rights of Man. The right they claim is to keep the profit from their labours, and not to have to pay taxes on goods supplied to them. I do have some sympathy for their cause, for nobody likes to pay a high price for supplies. Rich men are ready to rob the poor businessman or woman and line pockets that are already bulging with wealth. Let us all have a share of the wealth, I say. A fair price is all that is needed.

I notice that the Americans are all for the Rights of Man, but say nothing about the Rights of Woman. It is not that I wish women to have power over men but simply to have an equal power over their own lives. Mr. Harrop has told me about a young girl his friends in London have heard talk on that very subject.

Her name is Mary Wollstonecroft and she is only sixteen years old but she is becoming known for her outspoken views. I do believe it cannot be long before women's voices will heard, for the time must be long overdue. In fact, to me the mystery is not why we are not yet equal in rights, but in many cases, why we are not respected as superior, and men need to ask us for permissions.

It is probably for the same reason that education is denied to so many girls, for the men are afraid that when we know as much as they do that we will see themselves for what they truly are, puffed-up braggadocios most of them. I have not met a man yet who did not believe in his own importance, but if a woman does the same she is soundly punished for the sin of pride. I thank God I was born to an educated father.

August has been such a busy month for us, I am glad to say, and our function room has been in near constant use. The gentlemen of the Reverend Mr. CLAYTON'S school were here for a very important gathering. So many of them attended, to fix upon an Inscription for their late *worthy* Master's Monument that our room was quite overflowing. So many intelligent, well mannered gentlemen I never saw before in one place. I was sent for at the close of the meeting to receive their thanks for the food I had provided. They honoured me by asking my opinion of the inscription they had chosen and I was glad to concur that it was most suitable. Of course I was in the happy position of knowing the late Reverend Mr. Clayton. He was a fine gentleman and a great speaker at one of my Ladies' Salons. I was pleased to tell them he would be gratified by their attention.

1775 Sep 6 roads meeting report, meeting at Bulls Head for force against US, letter from US

Finally we are to make some progress on the improvements that were proposed back in March. Mr. Harrop tells me that at last week's meeting, of subscribers of twenty pounds and upwards, it was agreed to implement the plan to improve and enlarge various roads in Manchester.

The *Old Millgate* will be a full ten Yards wide at each end, with buildings on the Easterly side to be taken down commencing ten Yards distant from *Mr. Turner's* and *Mr. Stephenson's* shops respectively. Also *St Mary's Gate* to be ten Yards wide at each End with the buildings on the said Northerly side ten Yards distant from *Mrs. Fox's* and *Mr. Hindley's* shops respectively.

They will also need to apply to the Right Hon. Lord *Ducie* and other Land owners to effect the changes needed on the Easterly side of the *Acker's Gates* leading into *St Ann's Square* before they can pull down the buildings standing in the way of making the present passage from the *Exchange* to *St Ann's Square* ten Yards wide. It seems that some buildings are in a Settlement or Trust and so the Committee must apply to Parliament for the ability to effectuate the Purposes intended by the Subscription. I am pleased that we do have these forward thinking committees to make improvements, for I do believe it is no use holding onto past primitive ideas when the world is fast changing.

There was another meeting at the Bull's Head this week, although I cannot see why everything must be there when we have a fine meeting room here at the King's Head. This last meeting was 'to consider the Expediency of addressing the Throne on the present "Disturbances in *America*"' and they unanimously agreed to send an address to the King, to be presented by Sir Thomas Egerton, Baronet.

To the King's *Most Excellent* Majesty

The humble Address of the Gentlemen, Clergy, Merchants, Manufacturers, and principal Inhabitants of the Town and Neighbourhood of Manchester, in the County Palatine of *Lancaster*

Most Gracious Sovereign

Actuated by an affectionate and dutiful Regard for your many Royal Virtues, and firmly attached to that Constitution, which secures to us the Enjoyment of Liberties known only to British Subjects; We presume, in the most loyal and respectful Manner, to offer our Tribute of Gratitude to your Majesty, for the many Blessings we have enjoyed under the benign Influence of your Government.

Since your Majesty's Accession to the Throne, Commerce, the great Source of Wealth, hath been not only successfully encouraged, but firmly established in this Island; and under the Auspices of Peace hath been carried to an Extent unknown to your Royal Predecessors; Manufactures flourish in every Part of your Majesty's Dominions, particularly in this Town and Neighbourhood, where they are daily advancing towards Perfection, and where the lowest of your Subjects are fully employed and are blessed with the peaceful Enjoyment of the Fruits of their Industry.

Thus happy under your Majesty's Government, we look with Horror upon every Attempt to disturb its Tranquillity; and 'tis with inexpressible Concern we behold the Standard of Rebellion created in some of the American Provinces, and our Fellow Subjects involved in an unnatural War against their lawful Sovereign. We observe with Regret, that the Lenity shewn by your Majesty towards the Insurgents hath been of no Avail, but instead of reclaiming, hath seemed rather to irritate and urge them on to more daring Acts of Violence;- And as Force is become necessary to bring them to a sense of their Allegiance, we think ourselves bound in Duty, to assist your Majesty in the Execution of the legislative Authority.

We are not intimidated at the Prohibition laid by the Americans on the Importation and Exportation of Goods to and from the British Dominions; our extensive Trade happily flows in so many different Channels, that the Obstruction of one can but little Distress, much less deter us from our Duty to our King and Country - But whatever Check our Manufactures may receive by a necessary War, we shall cheerfully submit to a temporary Inconvenience, rather than continue Subjects to lawless Depredations from a deluded and unhappy People; as we are fully persuaded, that the Trade with America can never be established on its true basis, until the Colonies are reduced to a proper submission to the Government and Laws of Great Britain.

As Englishmen, we are led by Inclination, as well as impelled by Interest, to preserve the Authority of the British Legislature, and to protect the Dignity and Prerogative of the Crown (as founded on the Principles of the Constitution), sacred and inviolate. And we beg leave to assure your Majesty, that we are ready to support, with our Lives and Fortunes, such Measures as your Majesty shall think necessary, for the Punishment of Rebelling in any Part of your Dominions, being convinced, that the Sword of Justice will be directed by the Hand of Mercy, towards such of your Subjects as have been deluded by the artful Designs of a discontented Faction.

To my understanding it means that Manchester is declaring its support for the King, which I think only right and proper. It was not so long ago that Manchester was all for the usurper Bonnie Prince Charlie, who was openly welcomed at the Bull's Head, so much so that they named a chair for him, still there today, and his men mustered at the back of the church. In fact I have observed that the one defining nature of these Manchester people is that they object to being told what to think. Tell them that it is one way and they will choose the opposite out of pure defiance.

I fear John is becoming affected by this fighting spirit for he is becoming more truculent by the day. He will not listen to me at all when I tell him he is drinking too much. He is a sad and sorry figure these days and I am at my wit's ends how to remedy it. His hussy is a long forgotten memory now and he is still my husband, so I must think of some way to shake him back to his senses. We can never be as we were but he may now admit he still needs me as much as ever. I can see that the burden of bringing him round lies on my shoulders, as if I do not have enough worries.

1775 Oct 6 24 exhibition, US trade ban, Wesley supplement

Those new Americans are thinking themselves quite above anyone else. Today's notice in the Mercury was from the Secretary of a Borough Committee in a place called Virginia, giving orders forbidding its Merchants from exporting any Merchandise or Commodity whatsoever to Great Britain, Ireland or the West Indies after the 9th September. If they interfere with the supply of my sugar from the West Indies my business will suffer, so I think it may be best to order double my usual amount this week.

It may be rather worse for the Cotton Men of this town. I expect there will be hard words said on the Exchange this week about supplies of raw cotton. India is our main supplier of the fibre, according to Mr. Harrop, as we have the rights to buy it without tariffs from there. Our manufacturers in Great Britain have a monopoly over their raw cotton and they are happy to buy back a superior finished product from us once it has been turned into fine fabrics.

I have heard some manufacturers here say that they had begun making their fortune from American cotton. Mr. Munday, of Thweat, Galley and Munday, No.1 Blue Boar Court, is such a nice gentleman and very appreciative of my cooking. He told me only yesterday, when he had cause to compliment me on my Hottentot Pye, that his business of cotton manufacturing was doing exceptionally well since he had persuaded his partners to invest in American cotton. I thought it ill advised judging by all the terrible news we hear from the Colonies but it is not for me to tell him his business. He was quite sanguine that the fighting will soon be over, and as a consequence the Americans will be grateful for anyone who will buy their exports. It is quite amazing how men and women can differ in their views.

Speaking of the Exchange, as I was a few minutes ago, I am looking forward to attending an Exhibition there in two days time. Mary of course will come with me even though she is quite frightened by the idea but she knows I would not wish to go alone and I would not ask John to go for fear he would shame me with drunken behaviour.

The Exhibition promises to be most enlightening. The speaker is a son of one Colonel Katterfelto of the (apparently) famous Regiment of Heath Head Hussars belonging to the King of Prussia. The son has spent fifteen years travelling Europe purposely to improve himself in Philosophy and Mathematics. It will be such a delight to hear an intelligent gentleman speak. He has invented a great variety of Apparatus to amuse himself and give Instruction to the Public, and generously has chosen to perform for such a price that every scholar may have an opportunity of seeing his Inventions. He is only here for one week so I was determined to attend. I am always interested to hear educated people talk of inventions. I have so little opportunity in my usual work. I feel it is a sixpence worth spending to keep abreast of progress.

In contrast I feel Mr. Harrop made an error in publishing the a supplement written by Mr. John Wesley. He rambles on for four pages, adding nothing valuable to the situation in America which we all agree must be resolved. I do fear that sometimes dear Mr. Harrop is too easily influenced by people whose politics agree with his, but if he is not careful he will lose his customers who do not share his beliefs. As wealth is passing into less noble hands, so beliefs forged from poor beginnings must result in an alternative political view.

1775 Nov 7 Meeting at Bull's Head to raise subs, £886, 27 Mcr protest over US to Lords, letter from nephew

Manchester has been diligent in opening subscriptions for the Succour of the Widow's and Orphans of his Majesty's Troops employed in America, for those who have already sacrificed their Lives or may hereafter fall in Defence. They raised nearly nine hundred pounds which they are sending to London. That will show them that Manchester is doing its part.

The Mercury this week carried a very long article on the Protest sent to the House of Lords on behalf of the Gentlemen, Clergy, Traders and Freeholders of the County Palatine of Lancaster, pleading with the King to bring to an end this dreadful war with America. I put John's name to it, of course, and I hope his Majesty takes notice to use his influence on the wicked men determined to prolong the suffering, for that is the only result.

I received a very good letter from my sister Jane this week. It was a delight to read it was such a sharp contrast to the articles in the Mercury, all about War and raising Troops. Such delightful news for she also enclosed a letter sent to her from Joshua, and it is such good news that it gladdened my heart.

I am pleased that Joshua has avoided the zeal to fight. He always was a kind, sensitive boy, gentle-natured and a little above the common intelligence. He writes that he has found a useful post working with the perfumer to the King's cousin. Of course his is only a humble role, and he would never be permitted to be in the room if the King's cousin was present, but it is gratifying to know that one of our ordinary family members has achieved such prominence. From what I know of dear Joshua he will work diligently and will surely progress higher than his present place. We truly live in wonderful times when a person can dream of reaching higher things on his own ingenuity.

I showed the letter to his brother William, certain that it would relieve some guilt on his part, and I was not mistaken. He tried not to show it, masking his emotion, with just a curt 'well done' the only comment he made, but I noticed an extra brightness in his manner as he went about the shop.

He can afford to be gracious now our shop business is doing well. He has found a ready market for his horticulture items. The connection with the Raffald name has given a guarantee of quality, though I cannot be sure for how much longer. James is having problems tending his nursery gardens and I fear his mind is playing tricks on him.

Last week he accused his manservant of stealing from him. It came out that James had simply misplaced some money but the damage has been done. His manservant has already approached me to find him another position, but I am not entirely certain of the man's character so I have told him I am no longer in that business.

It is really too much work for me to be handling any enquiries, and I do not think William has the manner to take on the business. I hate to see an opportunity go to waste and it occurs to me that perhaps my sister Mary may like to take it on as a little business of her own. I will put the idea to her and try to persuade her that with my support she could easily manage it.

1775 Dec John sober, girls' characters, novelty at the Exchange

Another Christmas season is upon us and doing very nicely for us, thank you. John has been so busy at the inn that he has had less time for drinking and it has given him pause to think. He has promised me faithfully that this is the way he will be from now on. He swore on our family bible that he will try to be more the man he used to be before the terrible craving came on him.

I hope I can trust him to keep his promise for I know he means it so sincerely, but I have seen too many men, and women, that once they have the desire to drink, all sense flies out the window, and they end in depraved poverty. As long as John lives I am in danger of surrendering what little mien I possess. My hope is that by putting my money into business with William, and next Mary, I will have some protection from destitution should he indeed succumb again.

I am very pleased that Mary is considering my idea to re-open the Register Office. I have reassured her that I will be teach her what she needs to know, and she will have something of her own after I am gone. It will be a source of income for her and such of my girls who may need her protection, for I cannot be sure that John could care for them if I were not here.

Sarah is now ten years old and is such a good girl although I cannot say she has the light touch needed for delicate dishes. She can make herself useful, however, and is doing well in her schooling, which pleases me.

Her sister Emma, at nine years old is a mystery to me. She has her Uncle George Raffald's temper, so quick to scold and stamp her foot, together with the dreamy ways of her Uncle James Raffald. She is always lost in some thought or other, then cross when she is told to mind her tasks. I can trust little Anna at five years old better than I can trust Emma to watch cakes in the oven. All I get from Emma is burnt offerings. I can only hope her schooling teaches her how to find a rich husband. She will need to be able to afford a cook or her family will starve.

With all my family worries it was a rare treat for me to attend the 'Change once more for an Exhibition of Novelties such as I had never imagined. A clever man had devised a machine in the shape of an Elephant. I once saw a real one when I was a small child. It was in a circus parade that passed through our village in Yorkshire and from memory this was most lifelike.

It was six feet high, sumptuously caparisoned and richly ornamented with several pieces of jewellery in motion. The Mechanism contained in its body was so finely contrived as to animate the Trunk, Eyes and Tail, to perform the various Motions of life as if in actual Existence. The Trunk could twist, contract or expand in a lively Manner and upon the back of the Elephant was placed a superb Tower at the top of which was fixed a large round Gallery, surrounded with railing, formed into different Divisions, in which spirals were in Motion.

The ground of the Gallery was a platform, even and regular,

upon which an Indian Nabob and a Young Lady made to go round the Gallery. The two curious Figures were animated with all the natural Motions of Life. By their side a Servant supported a large Umbrella above their Heads.

With the Elephant were two other amazing pieces of clockwork machinery though I did not consider the Lady at her Spinning Wheel to be quite as Natural as Life and she certainly could not produce thread as fast as we can already do here in Manchester. The last Machine, of an Indian Lady in her Chariot, I thought was entirely too wild. The Chariot ran round at the rate of ten Miles in an hour, the Horses appearing to gallop and the Coachman whipping them.

A slave sat at the feet of the Lady, fanning her and it was all accompanied by music from an Italian couple, Signiora Morelli and Signior Nato, playing a combination of organ, viola, tambour do Basso, French horn, etc. I found the whole entertainment most elegant.

1776

1776 Jan severe frost, frequent earthquakes, wife sold in a halter

I knew John's promises could not last but I expected better of him than one month. He swears he only took a nip of brandy to warm him after working in the cellar but I can tell he has had more than one nip. Not that I can blame him, I have needed to indulge in a nip to get some warmth myself. The cold is dreadful this year and everywhere is under a layer of thick ice. My older customers tell me it is the coldest ever known in Manchester, although I consider it mild compared to some I remember as a child in Yorkshire.

I remember a bad winter at one house near Doncaster when I had just begun my term as a kitchen maid. My mistress was so niggardly with the firewood that we servants had to freeze our fingers nearly off while cleaning the vegetables for dinner. Ice does not easily yield when there is no warmth to melt it. I still have chilblains from that time and they have been aggravated again in this bitter cold. Even with sufficient firewood I am finding it difficult to keep warm. The cold just bites into everywhere, everyone in Manchester is grumbling about it.

Today the ground gave another shaking, as though the earth itself were shivering in the cold. That makes the third earthquake in as many weeks. Some are saying it's the fault of the cotton manufacturers, pushing to make unnatural increases in the production of earth's resources. Of course that is just superstitious ignorance, some people are so primitive. I am grateful to my dear papa that he made sure I was educated, and I was taught to think rationally.

Today in the market place I saw a woman who may have benefited from an education. She was led into the marketplace by her husband, a brute of a man. He led her by use of a cattle halter round her neck, to sell her to the highest bidder. Poor woman, she looked thoroughly downcast, returned to market just like any cow or horse, to be sold just as easily. Once a deal was done she looked much happier to be leaving with her new 'husband'.

I will confess to a little envy that the separation was effectuated so easily, but I could never bear the shame of it. And if it ever crossed John's mind to attempt it I would make sure he became the laughing stock and not me. Just now I might consider taking him to the market in a halter but that would never do. We were married in the eyes of God for better or worse though I hope the better times return soon.

1776 Feb John sober,

I find I spoke too soon about John's return to drinking and he has indeed kept his promise. Now the frost has abated the Brandy has stopped and he seems to be sincerely trying to reform his ways. He has been most sober for this last week, reminding me once more of the gentle man I married.

It is sad to see the light gone from his eyes however. He used to have such a sense of fun which he has quite lost. I wonder if I have been too harsh on him, even though I have right on my side and it was he who betrayed my trust.

Perhaps I can concede that it is difficult to find time for him when I am so busy with other things, but that is no pardon for committing a sin against me and God. Perhaps God is only for those who have the time and leisure to follow Him.

I have often felt forsaken when I am only trying to earn an honest reward for dutiful work. My whole life has surely been spent in toil and I wonder when I will gain my reward. It seems the harder I work, rather than pray, the bigger that reward will be.

1776 Mar 6 shop, W Middlewood book,

I was surprised when John thought to mark our wedding anniversary by bringing me a posy of flowers. It seems he has been spending more time lately helping his brother James work on his nursery garden. They have been cultivating a new strain of carnations for which there is much demand among the gentry. To think that I have been given flowers fit for a lady of the Nobility is very gratifying. It is so pleasant to be on good terms once more with John.

Our inn is busy again and the Officers continue to have their Mess room with us. My little box of savings is growing nicely, which is what I knew must happen once John returned to his old self again. My savings will soon be used in my next venture to set Mary up in her shop.

All our preparation is done and we want only to agree on a suitable shop premises. I want her to take on my old shop in the Market Place but Mary is too timid and does not want to be too far from where I am. I do not know what she has to be afraid of. Our nephew William will be in his shop around the corner so she can be sure of his protection if it is needed.

She will not agree and it is so vexing to see the shop business that served me so well sitting vacant and me not able to take it. Ann Cooke, who was always so keen on knowing all my dishes, is also interested in the shop, but it would grieve me terribly to see her there. I cannot force Mary, however, and I would not wish to upset her. If she is not ready it cannot be for I am working every hour as it is.

She has mentioned Mrs. Radcliffe's shop here on Chapel-street which would not thrive half so well and may not ever be for sale. Mrs. Radcliffe has talked about giving up for so long that I do not believe she ever will. She is hoping that her nephew will take it over but he has been attracted by the money to be made in cotton manufacturing and will not want to stand behind a counter of a grocer's shop.

It's a good thing that was not a problem for my nephew William. He is doing so well from his shop that he has ventured into print. He has made up a Catalogue of the seeds he sells. He has such a variety of kinds that it runs to many pages. He buys seeds from Holland, Russia, America and elsewhere.

His shop is thriving and he has become such a good shopkeeper that he is respected all over town. He is doing so well that he is likely to be a greater success than his Aunt Raffald, but then, he is a man and will not have to be held back as a woman can be.

1776 Apr 2 burglary,

Such a terrible series of thefts went on last week at the upper end of Market-street-lane. We would not have noticed it, of course, but we had a suspicious person in the bar room offering to sell a collection of Ivory and Silver items which were obviously of such good quality that they could never have been genuinely acquired by such as he was. When the notice appeared in the Mercury it was even worse than I had thought.

GARDENS BROKEN

Whereas last Night, or early this Morning, several Gardens and Summer Houses, situated at the Upper End of Market-street-lane, were, by some ill-disposed Person or Persons, feloniously broke into and robbed of the following Articles, viz two Silver Tea Spoons, and one Pair of Tea Tongs, marked I G, one Ivory Tobacco Stopper topped with Silver, on which was engraved a Jockey on Horseback, marked I G 1740, in a black case; a black Japanned Cannister, full of fine Green Tea; a Looking Glass; a large Tower; a Mahogany Bottle Stand; an Enamelled Red and White China Box, lined with Green Silk, with a Set of Scales and Weights for weighing Gold in; a Cork Screw, with a Whistle to it; a Bugle Horn Snuff Box, set in Silver, with a Scotch Pebble set in the Cover; besides much damage done in the said Gardens and Summer Houses.

Any Person or Persons who will give Information, so that the Offender Offenders may be brought to Justice, shall receive a Reward of FIVE GUINEAS from the Subscribers, who have this Day unanimously agreed to prosecute, with the utmost Rigour of the Law, every such Offender for the future.

N.B. Steel Traps will be set in the said Gardens for the future.

I said John should have apprehended the man when he was at our inn but his reply was that if he did that to every suspicious deal going on in the bar room he would have no customers and a bad name.

I was shocked that this kind of thing was taking place in our establishment. A few items that may help a family fend off starvation are one thing, but on such a scale it is not to be borne. I will not admit of criminal behaviour taking place under my roof. John will hear my law on this matter and, like it or not, we will have an honest bar or none at all.

This is the limit for me and it has made me more determined than ever that Mary will set up in a shop. Mrs. Radcliffe has dithered long enough, I shall invite her to take tea with Mary and me and we shall make a deal. I am in no mood to be trifled with.

1776 May 21 new shop, Thomas Highs moves to Manchester

As I expected, Mrs. Radcliffe was no match for my negotiations. I treated her fairly and by the finish she looked grateful to have struck a good deal. Once again I have begun another business, even if it is to be in Mary's name. We are hoping to open the shop by next month.

It is so exciting for me to resurrect the best business I ever had, and so gratifying to take an opportunity before anyone else can beat me to it. The need for a Register Office is greater than ever. So many new families are setting up households in Town. There must be ten or twenty new families every month.

All this change does make putting together my next Directory a more arduous task than I had thought. Every time I think I have all the names included I find there has been another growth in the number of townspeople.

The latest newcomer was Mr. Thomas Highs, the inventor, who has moved into number six Deans-gate, opposite the Wool Pack inn. He has set up his business in partnership with a Mr. Smith so Heaven knows what inventions will be accredited to the Town of Manchester now. Mr. Highs is a modern day Leonardo Da Vinci.

I must remember to ask Mr. Harrop for some new printed character sheets to use in the new Register Office. It will not do to have the old ones with my name as proprietor. They must have Mary Whitaker as the business owner, or I can see John trying to claim the profits as his by right of being my husband. I cannot allow of that. I am determined we shall make good profits once more but they will not be for him to gamble or drink away.

Mary and I will share equally in the profits, keeping hers to secure her future and saving mine to secure my daughters an inheritance. We have talked about opening an account for her with the bank in Town. Since it was established five years ago it has become a most respectable place to put money. As a spinster she will have the right to an account in her own name, whereas I may only have one in my husband's name.

It is a wicked system, punishing hard working women who might have feckless husbands to keep, but this is a way we can make it work. I know I can trust Mary to share equally with me, she would not have it any other way. I will also have her sign a document to guarantee it, just against the possibility she may be taken over by a persuasive man.

1776 Jun 25 sister Mary's shop

Our shop is finally open and the first notice has been in the Mercury on the 25th inst.

M. WHITAKER,

At the Request of many of her FRIENDS, hath taken upon her to reinstate,

The Register Office for Servants,

And having many APPLICATIONS for SERVANTS, In GOOD FAMILIES,

Takes this Opportunity to acquaint the Public in general

THAT she will be particularly careful what Servants she recommends, as none need to apply whose Character will not bear the strictest Enquiry; And as there are at this present Time many good Places vacant for Housekeepers, Cooks, &c. any Servant duly qualified, and of an undeniable Character, may meet with Places suitable by applying to the said *M. Whitaker*, at her shop, opposite the *King's-Head* in *Salford*, where all SORTS of CONFECTIONARY may be had, and every Decoration for a Table, such as Jellies, Creams, Flummery, Fish Ponds, Transparent Puddings, Almond Cheese-cakes, Sweet-Meats, Tarts, Crawcrans, Paste, Baskets, Silver & Gold Webs &c.

> Likewise all Kinds of Catchup, Lemon Pickles, Brownings for Made Dishes; also all Kinds of Wet and Dry Sweet-Meats, Preserved or Boiled Fruits; any Lady sending her own Fruits or Pickles, may have them done in the best manner, and on the most reasonable Terms,
>
> *By the Public's most humble, and obedient Servant*
> MARY WHITAKER

We had such a flurry of activity on the first day I was unable to leave until evening. So many people commented how good it was to have me back supplying my excellent confectionaries. I must have said a dozen or more times that it was no more than my duty to help Mary in her new business.

Mary could never have coped without me despite all her assurances to me that she would. We have hired some very competent girls to work for her, I made sure that I picked the best. Our nephew James Middlewood, now a very capable fourteen year old, was running a team of the delivery boys, so we had no worries on that score. It all looks very promising and made me realise I should never have left that business. Manchester is a Town hungry for good quality, well-cooked food. I know that in time Mary will be glad she took the chance, even if she is yet all a-dither over having enough supplies and not having too much left at the end of the day.

I hope she will manage soon for I cannot spend every day at the shop, much as I would like to. I must work at my own business at the inn, although my heart is failing at the lack of profit at the moment. I must hope that our affairs will return to success, but I suspect that John has slipped from me again. His behaviour is once more erratic, one day he is all sweetness and cannot bear to be parted from me, the next he is abrupt, short-tempered and hard in his manner. I shall place my energies in support of Mary, for I know they will have more reward there than with John.

1776 Jul 9 G Washington

I have been so busy lately that I have scarce had time to look at my newspaper more than to check our notices are in correctly. The Mercury has been full of the American troubles, which is not as pressing as the day's work in front of me, but at last I have a moment or two to think about other issues.

The American General Washington gave me hope that he would be able to maintain some kind of civil solution to the fighting but the Rebels are by no means agreed on their course of action.

> The American Congress, says a Correspondent, is certainly broke up, and that in consequence of those Divisions, which had long shaken it (and of which we apprized our Readers). The last violent Commotion therein, was on account of a judicious Remonstrance from General Washington, who with a proper Spirit , though at the same Time with great Temper, informed them, "If their Aim was total Independency, he had much mistaken them, and therefore must beg Leave to resign the chief Command of their Forces, which he always thought were embodied for different Purposes, and which he headed, not with a View of separating the two Countries for ever, but to effect, if possible, a more lasting Union between them."
>
> The Congress, upon the Receipt of this Remonstrance, entered into all the fury of a republican Debate, and (after many Hours spent in this wild Tumult) several Attempts were made to divide upon it, but in vain, as the Party of Hancock and Adams refused to listen to any Terms of Accommodation; in consequence of which they broke up in the utmost Disorder, without coming to any Resolution.

It seems to be the people of Boston who are agitating most strongly to divide completely from England, claiming our Parliament seeks to oppose them. They do nothing but brew a spirit of revolt in their people. They would do better to get on with their work and then they would find no time for trouble-makers who do nothing but complain.

I may have been blessed with more sense than most, for which I give thanks to God, but I have worked all my life and know no other way to be. I have learned the skill of making good meals out of anything and that skill is available to any who may take the trouble to learn it and apply themselves to work. There will always be lawmakers above us and we can do no more than trust they will remember their charitable duties to the people.

1776 Aug 6 US Declaration of Rights, 5th The Experienced English Housekeeper Derby/10th aug Ipswich/Oxford/Derby

The American people are determined, it seems, to believe they are better without Great Britain. The Mercury carried more news of that but we must be grateful the reports are of talk and not fighting.

> "112 persons met in Convention at Williamsburgh in Virginia and resolved unanimously that the Delegates appointed to represent this Colony in General Congress be instructed to propose to that respectable Body to declare the United Colonies free and Independent States, absolutely free from all allegiance to, or dependence upon, the Crown or Parliament of Great Britain; and that they give the Assent of this Colony to such Declaration, and to whatever Measures may be thought proper and necessary by the Congress for forming Foreign Alliances, and a Confederation of the Colonies, at such a Time, and in the Manner, as to them shall seem best; Provided that the Power of forming Government for, and the Regulation of the internal Concerns of each Colony be left to the respective Colonial legislatures.
>
> "Resolved unanimously, that a Committee be appointed to prepare a Declaration of Rights, and such a Plan of Government as will be most likely to maintain Peace and Order in this Colony, and secure substantial and equal Liberty to the People."

It seems ever more likely that they will get their way, whether that is for their good or loss, only time will tell. As long as business is allowed to continue without threats of destruction we all may prosper, for without business there is no money, no food, no clothes. All depends on trade whichever way it is looked at.

Thanks to my eye for business, my nephew has a solid income from his shop, my sister now likewise, and I have been able to make enough to educate my girls to give them some pride in themselves. My dearest hope is that they can find a good husband in this growing Town, one who will provide a better life for them than their Mama has had. My hope for them is that they have their own houses, not to be a servant in someone else's, to give up the chance of caring for their own children because their work is to care for their Master's. I can see it is possible here in Manchester and I pray every night that it will be so, and work every day to make it so. It is the only wish I have left.

I was pleased to receive a letter from Mr. Baldwin that he has now published a fifth edition of my book, The Experienced English Housekeeper such is the demand still. He has placed notices for it in the newspapers in Oxford, Derby and Ipswich and once again asks if he may include physical remedies as an appendix, with an engraving of me as a frontispiece. I will write back to him to tell him once again that I will have none of it and am absolutely against the idea. I will not subject my trusting readers to remedies which may or may not work. I have never trained for it, it is not my domain, and as for an engraving of me, well what has that to do with cooking? He would do better to include an engraving of the parts of an animal, such as a pig or a cow. That would be of more use to the trusting young ladies who use my book.

1776 Sep 10 Mary's shop, father's story, Birmingham

Mary's shop is thriving better than my most eager expectations and the demand is keeping me busier than ever to keep up the supply of made dishes for her. My kitchen maids are working all the time to satisfy the demands of the customers but my poor feet do not like me for standing so long to supervise all their cooking.

I am a little disappointed that Mary is taking a while to settle into her role of proprietor, but she was always happiest working diligently in the background. She is not at all like me, but takes after grandfather Whitaker, such a gentle man who was the despair of his wife.

I believe I take more after grandmother Whitaker. I was told many tales of her incredible grit and determination when I was a child. Papa would tell us of her ability to create a meal from nothing when times were hard, for they had nothing but love to give and only the toil of their bodies to earn with, scratching a living on a Yorkshire hillside.

Papa was the lucky child, he was taken in by the local priest to be his house boy and because he was apt to listen carefully to his master, he was favoured and taught his letters. He was such a keen pupil he later became a scribe for the old man when his sight was failing. It turned the fortune of our family when he was able to make a living teaching others, enough to provide for his mother but for her being too proud to take it from him. She would walk five miles in the snow rather than accept what she called charity.

I wonder sometimes what she would have made of Manchester, this great town with great wealth, and great poverty. She would have spent her time feeding all the waifs and strays that gather here, of that I am sure, though I doubt she could have left her beloved hillside to cross to the 'wrong' side of the Pennine mountains. She would never have crossed to 't'other side' as she called Lancashire. I never thought that I would either, proud Yorkshire woman that I still am.

John was a very persuasive man back in '60 and his promises were enough to tempt me across. When he recommended me to be housekeeper at Arley Hall I was certain his intentions were sincere and so I made the journey. It has not all been to my choice but now, even with the problems I have, I would rather be here in Manchester than living as the wife of a hemp farmer as my sister Jane does in Yorkshire. How I would hate that life! Toiling on the land, each day the same as before, no culture, no business, no excitement of any kind. When I consider that I must believe I made the right choices along the way.

Manchester is growing all the time and we are not the only Town to do so. In today's Mercury Mr. Harrop includes a report on the town of Birmingham.

> "little more than a small obscure village at the beginning of the century but by the Industry and Ingenuity of its inhabitants has become richer and more extensive than many Cities in Europe. From only two Hackney coaches in '74 there are now twenty-six, besides six Diligences which constantly go from thence to London. All this despite the almost universal belief that our Breach with America would be the ruin of our Manufacturers, the contrary has been experienced in Birmingham."

I dare say Manchester can surpass their claims to progress. When I last looked at my pages on coaching for the new Directory we had at least that number. I am now got too busy to do any more work on a new edition. I must give my attention to the new shop until I can be sure that Mary is fully ready to take it on. I know she cannot do without me yet.

1776 Oct 1 shop, US issues, Card Assembly, 5th The Experienced English Housekeeper

I was incensed by a comment reported to me today, a casual remark that had been made by some person unknown to me, who had been in Mary's shop. Some person, unknown to me, was overheard outside Mary's shop talking to her neighbour, making the accusation that everyone knew it was really Mrs. Raffald's shop and Mary was just a puppet.

I straightaway took Mary aside and told her what I had heard and that she must pull herself together and start being more prominent in the shop. I can not allow it to be put about Town or John will get ideas of taking a share of the money. Of course he knows I am helping Mary but thinks it is only in a small way.

I do not mind Mary benefiting from my reputation but it must never be thought I have any financial interest in it or I am sunk. We agreed she will keep all the profit, on the understanding that she will leave money to my girls, which of course she was keen to do, having been a big part of their lives and loving them as much as I do. It means I can rest certain that whatever happens to me and John the girls have an assured future.

Mary is steady and is not in need of a man to run her life. She is sworn off them after she has witnessed what has happened with John. No-one needs such trouble. Men seem such vain creatures, desiring power and acclaim. Even the American General Washington, who I believed to be a steady, sensible man, is quoted in the Mercury as refusing an offer of a truce from our General Howe because the letter did not give him his full title. It was addressed to General Washington but did not style him as "General of the Army of the Free and Independent States of America". He even went so far as to claim it was a Mark of Hostility by General Burgoyne.

I declare, some men can start a fight in an empty room. Why can they not accept the spirit of negotiation and search for a compromise? I fear the reason is that they like strutting around like Peacocks, displaying their self-important tittles just as the peacock spreads his tail feathers to look bigger than he is.

I fear the belligerence suggests a truce is not truly what they want, and I fear there will be more expense and lost lives before the matter is settled That only means more taxation on us poor businesses, and more mothers and wives to lose their sons and husbands. Shame on them.

John put his usual notice in the Mercury for our Card assembly which we have begun again for the Winter season. I had need of a word with Mr. Harrop to make certain that my notice was positioned next to John's to advertise my fifth edition of my

Experienced English Housekeeper, which can be bought from his shop or from me.

Such gossip has reached me that I felt it prudent to insert a line into the notice to refute the rumour that my book is a copy of another. I added "the author avoids invidious Comparisons with similar Publications: all that she chuses to say in its Favour is that Oeconomy with Elegance are its great Recommendations."

Those who have promoted the rumour will know who they are and I hope that this public notice will silence their wagging tongues. Invidious Comparisons indeed! How dare they suggest that my book is the same as another's, as though I had copied them! Of course there will be similarities. There are, after all, only so many ways to cook Veal, or Mutton, but I know that my way of giving instruction avoids the high style of some and is more practical than that of others, who might presume too much prior knowledge on the part of the housekeeper or cook. All readers are not as experienced as I am.

I also took care to point out that such a large number of impressions must recommend my book. I took a further seven lines to tell how we have fitted up the King's Head with every Genteel Accommodation for Travellers, etc, with the Best of Wines and good Ordinaries every Day, with post Chaises and able Horses available on the shortest Notice, finally adding that we strive to provide the highest standards at the King's Head, sparing no expence.

1776 Nov 5 speech, lottery,

Such an affecting notice was in today's Mercury that I determined to save it and attach it entire here. It was a momentous announcement from his Majesty King George that the colonies of America have renounced all allegiance to the Crown.

> My Lords and Gentlemen,
> NOTHING could have afforded me so much Satisfaction as to have been able to inform you, at the Opening of this Session, that the Troubles, which have so long distracted my Colonies in North America, were at an End; and that my unhappy People, recovered from their Delusion, had delivered themselves from the Oppression of their Leaders, and returned to their Duty: But so daring and desperate is the Spirit of their Leaders, whose Object has always been Dominion and Power, that

they have now openly renounced all Allegiance to the Crown, and all political Connection with this Country: They have rejected, with Circumstances of Indignity and Insult, the Means of Conciliation held out to them under the Authority of our Commission; and have presumed to set up their rebellious Confederacies for Independent States. If their Treason be suffered to take Root, much Mischief must grow from it, to the Safety of my loyal Colonies, to the Commerce of my Kingdoms, and indeed to the present System of all Europe. One great Advantage, however, will be derived from the object of the Rebels being openly avowed, and clearly understood; we shall have Unanimity at Home, founded in the general Conviction of the Justice and Necessity of our Measures.

I am happy to inform you, that, by the Blessing of Divine Providence on the good Conduct and Valour of my Officers and Forces by Sea and Land, and on the Zeal and Bravery of the Auxiliary Troops in my Service, Canada is recovered; and although, from unavoidable Delays, the Operation at New York could not begin before the Month of August, the Success in that Province has been so important as to give the strongest Hopes of the most decisive good Consequences: But, notwithstanding this fair Prospect, we must, at all Events, prepare for another Campaign.

I continue to receive Assurances of Amity from the several Courts of Europe; and am using my utmost Endeavours to conciliate unhappy Differences between neighbouring Powers; and I still hope, that all Misunderstandings may be removed, and Europe continue to enjoy the inestimable Blessings of Peace.

It truly is a blessing that Canada has seen the advantage in staying connected with us, I am certain that must mean a reduction in the lives to be lost. His Majesty sees clearly that the people are being used to satisfy the Leaders in their Objects of Dominion and Power. They have rejected offers of Conciliation with insults and Indignity. We should never have presumed to travel to a land of savages and instead put the work into making peace in our own land.

1776 Dec 14 Oxford Journal, row with John

Oh I have had such a month of trouble with John. His drinking has got out of hand again and I fear he is beyond any control. No amount of threats or promises is having any effect on his state of drunkenness. Our Card Assembly is not receiving the same attention that we had last season and John is blaming it on Mr. Alsop who has begun his own Card Assembly at the Bull's Head.

John says we are on the wrong side of the river Irwell and too far from the Exchange. He believes all our customers are going to the Bull's Head, even though their Assembly is on a different night to ours. John will not listen to a word I say, or accept that his surly manner when drunk has any effect on our business.

When he is sober, which is now rare, he is as quiet as a mouse, not a word to say to anyone and cannot face company until he has supped two or three drinks, sometimes beer, but more often gin for speed. Then he is unable to stop and soon becomes quick tempered, easily lashing out at anyone who doesn't suit him. He ends up falling asleep in a stupor, often in the stables, until he wends his way to our bedroom, falling into it as I am rising to begin work.

It pleases me that I do not have to see him until later in the day for he is always full of self pity, asking me to help him. Once he has had his nip or two then he believes himself cured and is more pleasant for a little while.

I have not the time, nor the wish to help him any more, it is all I can do to hold back the answer I would give, for I know it will serve no purpose but to anger him and make him drink all the more.

1777

1777 Jan 7 Swain, Lady Betty's sisters die, debt begins

Such a sad letter I received today from my dear Lady Betty. I am touched that she still regards me so highly to keep me in her thoughts, but I am deeply sorrowful for her loss. She writes that both her sisters are now deceased, poor lady.

No matter a person's station in life, the loss of one sister is a sad event, the loss of two so close together is a tragedy. She is alone now, living in her sister's house in Knutsford. If I could visit her to give her some comfort I would be glad to, but she is still a Lady and I am only an Innkeeper's wife. It would not do for me to presume she would welcome the association, however well she regards me.

I will write to her with my sympathies and hint at my willingness to visit if she so wishes. In many practical ways I hope she will refuse for I can ill afford the time or expense to make a trip. I would need to take Mr. Swain's new London coach as far as Stockport or Congleton then change there for another carrier for the journey on to Knutsford. I could perhaps persuade John's brother George to collect me at the Stockport stage and transport me from thence to Knutsford, but I do not favour that choice. It would save me a shilling, but I would need to travel on his cart, and no doubt would arrive with more mud on my clothes that if I walked the whole way, and that would never do.

For Lady Betty I would spare no expense and pay the full cost of a coach. It would be more economical than hiring a chaise and driver, even with my discount as part owner for Mr. Swain would still want his full share. He has spent a lot of money on fast horses for his new five day service to London.

He has joined with a Mr. Jones of London, and with a Thomas Sharples of Blackburn to link Manchester with Blackburn, stopping at Bury, Blackburn, Clitheroe and Whalley in between. This last enterprise also has coaches to Worcester, Bristol, Wolverhampton, Shrewsbury, all parts of Wales, Bewdley, Derby, Sheffield, Rotherham, Cambridge, etc.

I declare, the world is becoming a small place, everywhere is now easily connected with regular services, so unlike my own journey from Doncaster to Cheshire, in the December of '60, sitting on the outside of the coach, in wicked cold rain, I was chilled to the bone before I reached Lancashire, and so shook up over the ruts and ridges of the roads that I was ashamed to present myself to John's family at Stockport, kind though they were.

I had not known that John had written to them to tell them of my arrival but I will forever be in debt to George's wife, Mary, for the kindness of a dry shawl and a hot drink with a nip of brandy in it to fortify me on my onward journey to Arley Hall. The rough pie she passed me was welcome too, though it was not to my preferred taste. I was happy to send her some of my recipes to try, for which she wrote her thanks for a kindness returned.

There has been good and bad since I made that journey but sometimes I wonder if I would have done better staying in Yorkshire. I will never know and must make the best of the life I have chosen.

1777 Feb 11 hatters

Mary has quite surprised me this last week with a new confidence about her in the shop and I was glad to see it at last, although she still would not manage without me. I overheard her admitting as much to a customer this week.

She was serving Mrs. Beswick, a woman with far too much to say on every subject, and was telling her what a lot of my dishes she had to sell, for which she was very grateful. She mentioned a few of her own dishes, which she hoped might one day rival mine, and was very complimentary about my knowledge in both in business and cookery. She said she held mine to be superior to hers for without me she would never have begun her own little business.

I doubt she was aware that I could hear her comments. She is a dear sister and has been a faithful helper to me these last dozen years, I am glad to have put her in the way of a little independence, there being so many opportunities now for a single woman in these changing times. With ten years between us I have always felt responsible for her care, standing in place of our dear mother, especially since she joined me in Manchester.

It has been very useful that Mary followed me into developing her skill in the kitchen and was not tempted into manufacturing work. The wages are regular but the risks of harm from the machinery are too real. With her own business, which it will be in entirety once I am no more, she will not be held ransom by the laws and disputes that are daily multiplying around the textile trades in this busy town. Laws for this, laws for that and taxes on everything, it leaves businesses in the grip of anyone except the poor owner who must work twice as hard and take what's left after paying everyone out.

The Mercury announced that a new law has been passed regarding Journeymen in the hatting trade. Thankfully, I have not much need of hats but the workers here have been combining together in associations and dictating to the owners who they can and cannot employ, insisting that any Finishers who are not part of their Agreement must be dismissed.

That would be the same as my scullery maids telling me I could not employ whichever kitchen maids I choose, forcing me to take ones of their choice. I would never countenance that. Who is the servant, I ask? Certainly not me in my own kitchen. Well, it seems the Law is against them and the Manchester Justices are ready to prosecute wrongdoers with hard labour in the House of Correction at Hunt's-bank, or sending them to the common Gaol for up to three months.

Manchester has an eye to the growth of business here. If business makes wealth, the owners buy goods from other businesses, which can employ more people, and so it goes on. Without business we are all back to living on the land, and that will not feed all the people who live here now. I have come to realise I was born for business, I have always had an eye for profit and I bless the day my path in life led me to Manchester.

1777 Mar 4 pew, linens

Well I am so beside myself with temper I can hardly compose myself to write tonight. Mary's confidence has taken her too far, I think, and she was unnecessarily sharp with me in the shop, criticising the basin of Jumballs that I brought for her to sell.

She bade me put them in the back room until she had time to tidy them over with a dusting of triple refined sugar. Then she added the comment that they were too misshapen to go in the window. I was too shocked to answer her. I simply gave them to her and left. It was fortunate for her that the Rev. Mr. Waincliffe was in the shop buying his usual lemon drops or I would have had some words of my own to say in return. We will see how she likes a day or two without my baking to help her out.

I will not have time tomorrow in any case as I plan on attending the auction at the Windmill Tavern on Dean's-gate where Mr. Chippindall will sell Pew No. 58 in St. Mary's church. It is a very good position, situated between the North and Middle Isles, and has a good view of the pulpit. I could not presume to afford it but if I do not attend the auction I will never know whether I may not have secured it for me and my girls.

John has very little interest in attending church any more, making the excuse that it is his time for cleaning the cellar which is more important than cleaning his soul. I see through his argument though. What he means is that he needs to have a drink before anyone sees him shaking like a leaf in a gale. No matter, I cannot change him now, but my duty to my girls and our eternal future is clear. It rests on my shoulders, yet another burden for me to carry.

I have never feared hard work but sometimes I wonder how I became such a beast of burden, so laden with troubles that small children will run away in fear when they see me coming towards them. I am nothing if not fair and only expect from others what I expect from myself. Some days it feels just too much and I wonder when it will be easier, though I seem destined to work hard all my life.

Tomorrow I will also call to see Mr. Cotes, the linen draper on Smithy Door. Poor man is terribly ill, worn down by the hard work of carrying on his business with no family to support him. He has my sympathy and I pray my fate will not be the same. His advertisement in the Mercury says that he is forced to sell his stock of cloth for ready money at prime cost. He has such a stock of Linens, printed Cottons of the newest patterns; striped, plain and flowered muslins; Hollands, Long Lawns, Table linen, Silk, Cotton and Worsted stocks and several other articles in the Linen drapery and Millinery business. I hope to make a few good deals with him while still paying him a fair price.

1777 Apr 1 US news

I am satisfied that I got some beautiful new table linens from Mr. Cotes last month, even though Mrs. Berry did her best to bid more for some of the Muslins. I declare, that Mary Berry is following everything I do, even copying my best recipes. Well, mine are published in a book and it will be clear to everyone that all her best ideas are courtesy of Mrs. Raffald.

I purchased a length of the pretty new floral muslin for a dress for my dear little Anna. She is growing so fast, I fear she will be tall like her father, but as long as she stays healthy I will not complain. I am thankful she is not a son and will not feel tempted to join the ever present call up for volunteers to fight the American rebels.

The Mercury weekly proclaims yet more terrible fighting in the American Colonies. The Rebels are ranging thousands of men, 1500 at Morris Town where they have George Washington to lead them; 1000 at Boundbrook, 1000 at Quibble Town, 1000 at Elizabeth Town, 500 at Prince Town, 500 at Trenton and more in the region of the Passaic River. Yet in Philadelphia it is a different picture. The Rebels there are poorly provisioned, are sickly and are dying in great numbers. It is a terrible war that is killing innocent people who, I'm certain, only want to get on with their simple lives in peace.

George Washington has made a statement that he refuses to inlist Deserters from our army. His statement says that men who have not been true to one side ought not to be trusted on the other. Those men should have more faith in their leaders, like our own Colonel Rogers, who has gained 400 recruits from the Rebels, choosing to fight the noble fight for their rightful King and Country rather than remain among the miserable Wretches.

1777 May 13 French, school

All is well again between myself and Mary. She has once more become the gentle sister I know. Her brusque manner subsided once I discovered the reason behind her temper. The gossip had become too much for her and she thought the way to cure it would be to keep me out of the shop as much as possible, and that if she was seen to be giving me orders it would quench the fires of rumour. I wished she had taken me into her confidence but she said she did not wish to add to my burden.

I must confess I am beside myself with worry over the inn. John has no control, and is more often drunk than sober every day of the week, even on a Sunday, may God forgive him. I am powerless to stop him, and it is taking all my wiles to keep my money from his hands. Not that I do not have other places to spend it, that is far too easy with so many people to pay.

My nephew William would like to add more liquor to his stock but the outlay is more than he can afford. He believes he can make more profit from that than he can from garden produce but I disagree, and not merely because I have come to perceive strong drink as a mocker of honest men. It is also because I have experience of how easily it can spoil. It becomes less than worthless if not kept well and is only fit for pouring into the River Irwell.

No, if I have money to invest in anything it will be a worthwhile venture, something that will improve or inform a person, such as education. I bitterly mourn the loss of my school venture. I see in the Mercury that a Monsieur Meuron is holding his new French school in the evenings at William Clayton's house on Hanging-ditch.

He is charging ten shillings and sixpence just for imparting his native language. I could halve that rate and give instruction that would be of similar value, but it is more fashionable to be taught by a native speaker now. It must be a good way of making some money, all profit and no outlay on goods or work to produce something to sell, being paid for talking, how pleasing that would be. I must encourage Mary to make room for a school in her shop for until I am free of a drunken husband I must keep to what I have to do here at the inn, as long as we are allowed to stay here. I already fear the bailiffs are not far away now.

My mind craves higher things such as intelligent conversation and good company, which is in short supply here, though my officers have not yet deserted me. I am sure there must be other women like me in this town, women of rank, women of business or educated women who also want to meet and converse. A ladies' Philosophical Association could be something that this town is ripe for. I will ask Mr. Harrop his opinion. A man of excellent taste, he has never failed me yet.

1777 Jun 3 US defeat, 10 George III's birthday

Today was a very gay day, and the town was alight with revellers celebrating his Majesty's birthday. The morning was ushered in with the Ringing of the Bells of several churches in Town. At five in the afternoon our Militia assembled in St, Ann's Square (attended by the Magistrates, a great number of Gentlemen and a numerous Populace) with Drums beating and Colours flying, where they fired three excellent Vollies, that would have done honour to any Regiment in his Majesty's Service. Between each Volley the Band played God save the King, and at the Conclusion the whole Company gave three hearty Cheers. Tonight is a brilliant Assembly for the Nobility, Gentlemen and Ladies of the Town and carriages were coming from far and wide.

There were so many that our stables have been busier than the inn. Mr. Swain at the Spread Eagle has also done a brisk trade with the visitors, I heard. It has been such a good day for trade that I gave all my kitchen maids an extra sixpence and bade them go join the revellers for an hour when their work was done.

I took my Anna with her nursemaid for a walk to St. Ann's Square to see the Officers' salute to the King. Young Captain Wilkins noticed us and tipped his hat to little Anna, which quite delighted her. The soldiers made such a brave sight, so gallant in their uniforms that it was quite reassuring to think they will defend us against any attack. At least these are home and not rotting in the colonies as the Rebels are. Mr. Harrop firmly believes that we will soon put an end to that fighting, having sight of letters from that country. He printed a copy of one from New York, dated April fifth saying the Rebels are laying down their Arms by thousands.

> In the fortnight prior no less than three thousand came into New York to take the Oath of Allegiance of his Britannic Majesty. General Lee was prisoner,

> George Washington delirious, Hancock fled the country. No-one would take the paper money of the Congress, and in a word, their credit was broke; they were on the Brink of Ruin. Their Troops are starved, naked and wrought out by hard labour. British Troops there were thought to number sixty thousand; twenty-six thousand under General Howe, thirteen thousand Canadians, seven thousand New Yorkers, and fourteen thousand on board ships.

Surely right must now prevail and the other places will come back to declare allegiance to their home country. There are still dark deeds afoot, however. One of the Rebels, a Doctor Franklin, had tried to broker a deal with France, offering to assist them in conquering all the British islands in the West Indies, and guaranteeing possession of them. I do not understand how he could make such a declaration when they are in such disarray.

Our continual disputes with France will never be settled when there is such intrigue being planned across the world. The French are a cultivated people, with many fine foods but they have an instinctive dislike of the British, who by nature seem destined to always be opposed to the French. They do not like us, our food, or what we do, and our King must constantly increase taxes to raise funds to fight them. And then who is it who bears the brunt, why, the British working people, poor business people who try to prosper by producing food or goods to sell. We are the ones who constantly suffer, paying tax on everything.

1777 Jul J Harrop presented with silver urn

Mr. Harrop is such a dear friend, I was greatly pleased to see that he has been honoured by his fellow businessmen for his contribution to our knowledge here in Manchester, of events around the country and from across the globe.

He was presented today with a large two-handled silver cup as acknowledgment of the service he has done by his early and useful intelligence. It was a valuable token of appreciation for his endeavours, in sending a man each Monday to Derby to meet the London night mail coach, so that he may have the news on his desk by Tuesday to give it fresh to us that day.

I am pleased for my friend that he has been quite rightly praised for his Mercury newspaper, together with his excellent printed publications for many businesses in the Town, not least of all my own. He is such a good man, supporting many local institutions and charitable or patriotic concerns including the Lying-In hospital, Manchester Infirmary and my own special choice, the distribution of soup and relief for widows and children of the Lancashire Volunteers.

I need to visit him this week in order to check the delivery of yet another edition of my cookbook, the sixth one, from Mr. Baldwin of London. I am astounded that there is anyone left who does not possess a copy, but Mr. Harrop assures me there are still customers asking for it. He says it has a usefulness for people's lives that will endure for centuries, which is very kind of him to say, but I am certain that cleverer minds than mine will find ways to improve what I have written.

Already men are inventing machines to harness power in many different ways, making machines do the work in less time, turning people into mere machine minders rather than workers with a skill. They say it makes work easier but I do not see so much ease about me. There are only weary looking faces trudging home to their poor houses with very little on the table to eat. I admire the inventions but not the oppression of so many people, making them a mere part of the machines.

When I worked in service we had many people doing dirty jobs but they were fed and housed and we knew our Gentlemen and Ladies were our betters. It is all so different now, so many opportunities but so confusing and for some poor souls it is merely the opportunity to starve with no-one to care for them, with no recourse to succour from any direction. Some days when I walk about town it breaks my heart to see so many wretches, but I can only do a little with a few clothes or cast off food. The way John is behaving I have a fear that one day I may be one of them.

Everyday is a struggle to make the money stretch out and often I hear the sound of voices raised in anger in the bar room, followed by the sound of footsteps to my little snug where I sit to work. It is John, or more usually, one of the cellar boys, come to ask if it please Mistress Raffald to spare five shillings (or more often a whole Guinea) for the spirits merchant, or some such similar), till the Master gets back from the market. I, knowing full well that John has not gone to market but is hiding in the stable loft, will have to give the boy his five shillings or a guinea for the sake of looking respectable, but not before I make the boy put his mark on a chitty and tell me the exact use it is being put to.

Later, when I show John what I have paid on his behalf he will berate me for being simple, and declare I need not have paid it, that he did not owe the money at all, or worse, that he will beat the poor boy for coming to me. I am in despair for our future and unless my book can sell many copies I fear we are heading for disgrace. I can see no way to avoid it.

1777 Aug 5 Mercury predicted end of war, ad for 6th Experienced English Housekeeper

Praise be, Mr. Harrop says the fighting in America will soon be over and he expects to hear by Christmas that our soldiers will have triumphed over the Rebels. He tells me he has seen letters from so many sources telling how dispirited many of the Patriots are. The ordinary man there must be sorry he ever listened to the rabble rousers for what would he gain but a change of master, and have to endure years of suffering poverty and starvation for the privilege.

Those who were born into the ruling classes have a different view of life and are taught from the cradle to have the care of others within their power. I remember dear Sir Peter Warburton, walking through the library in Arley Hall with Master Peter, explaining to him the duty that would fall on him when he became Baronet in his turn. Poor little boy was only eight years old and he stood solemnly listening to his father. I doubt he fully understood what his father meant but it was a rare honour to be with his father so he knew it must be important. His life was determined from the day of his birth, as was mine, but thanks to these times we live in, everything is changing, any many things are possible even for the humble classes.

Mr. Harrop gave my advertisement for the new edition of The Experienced English Housekeeper a good position at the top of a column in his newspaper. For, although he may promise me that it will sell well, it cannot harm to have a little judicious placing of the notice where it may easily be seen.

I saved a little money this time by omitting that it is available in London, etc, for there is no need to say that in a provincial paper. In this town, customers will either go to Mr. Harrop or call to buy it from me where it can be signed in person, a little touch that many appreciate. As long as there are plenty to buy, that is all that matters to me. Any profit coming to me from the book will help keep us going and that is what we need more than ever. It has come to the point where I may have to take Sarah from her school to save the costs, unless I can devise a way to bring in more money.

1777 Sep 14 Sarah's school, earthquake

Some days I wonder why I even bother to try, and today was such a day. I work every day trying to make enough money to keep our respectability and every day it seems that John tries to do the opposite. Now, our daughter Sarah has shown the worst ingratitude to her mother's efforts to give her a decent future. When I told her that I may have to take her from school she shewed in no uncertain terms how little she appreciated the opportunity she had been given, and made me wonder what kind of manners she was being taught at Barton School. Sarah, at only twelve years old mind you, was quite the little minx.

She called it 'that dreadful school' and said she would be glad to leave it. She complained of Miss Forsyth, the school mistress, being an old witch who showed her dislike of her at every opportunity. She pleaded with me to put her to some useful occupation, wanting to make her own money with a skill in making things.

She had no wish to be someone's wife and have her future dictated by a man, for which I could not fault her. She had seen what her Aunt Whitaker and Cousin William had done and she wanted to have her own business. She declared herself not suitable to make a rich man's wife, knowing herself to have too much temper, but she had a fire to be a rich woman for her own self.

All my hopes for her to be a fine lady and not have to struggle as I have done were all gone for naught. To punish her for her outspokenness I said she would need to finish the week, though I could not truly fault her. Despite my best efforts to refine her she always was a most untidy child, with her Uncle George's temper and I could see she was not best suited to being mistress of a fine household. She may make a good shopkeeper, a good business which I should never have left. She will not have the problem of a husband turned to drink, a terrible fate.

I shall certainly be calling on Miss Forsyth in the next week, not only to make certain she repays me the fees paid in advance only last month but also to make sure she is not giving Emma and Anna the same treatment. Sarah may have been rude but she would not lie, especially to her mother. No, I have that woman's measure and she will hear my displeasure and be glad to return my payment or she will lose two more of her scholars.

I am glad that the loss of school does not distress Sarah. It will certainly help me to have her earning an income. I have heard of a scheme which may provide an opportunity for her, though I will need to check out terms. Mr. Meredith, of Salford-bridge is offering proposals for boys and girls to learn a business whereby a decent livelihood may be got when grown up. He is offering three pounds per year, with four pounds for the second year and five pounds for the fifth year. It may be a good chance for Sarah to find employment and it will take the burden off the family purse.

I must record a dreadful earthquake that took place here in town on Sunday last. There was a dreadful shaking and a rattling of everything while we were at church. The whole town was affected and no-one knew if we would survive. Some screamed that we were being thrown into the pit of hell, saints and sinners together. Of course I knew it was a natural occurrence, but some people were blaming it on the canals, saying it was unnatural to divert rivers from their God-given course. Others said it was the rattle of the weaving machinery that had caused it and God was punishing the devilish machines that made cotton spin and weave at an unhygienic speed.

It was certainly frightening and I wondered if we would be entombed in the stone of the Church, or trampled by the crowd trying to leave the building. Thanks be to God, we escaped unhurt, though Anna was crying fit to burst. She buried her face in her nursemaid's apron and would not look up till the shaking had ceased. Mr. Harrop's notice quite described it accurately and made dreadful reading

> On Sunday last, about eleven o'clock in the Forenoon, the Town was greatly alarmed with two or three Shocks of an Earthquake, which came in such quick Succession as to throw the Congregations of the several Churches (St Paul's excepted) and Meeting Houses, into the greatest Confusions; at the first Shock the People were much startled, but the last being attended with a Noise and shaking of the Walls, etc, almost every one gave way to his Fears, and climbing over the Seats and Benches, made towards the Doors, which were so crowded that many were thrown down by the Press, and lost various Parts of their

Apparel: which, by the Vigilance of the Officers of the Church, were collected together and secured in the Vestry; the People of the Town was informed by the Bell-man of their Safety, and that they would be delivered to the Owners at 9 o'Clock the next Morning, which was done in as equitable a Manner as possible; happily no Lives were lost, nor any Damage done. Those Inhabitants who were at Home, felt the Shock as severely, and were as much affrighted as those in the Churches, whilst those abroad were but little affected. We have received Intelligence from the Country round about, and find that the Villages in this Neighbourhood were affected in much the same Manner; and that at Preston, Warrington, Wigan, Chapel-le-frith, Macclesfield, Stockport, Chawesworth, Mottram, Staley-bridge, Knutsford, Middleton and Ashton-under-line, the Shocks were as violent, and attended with nearly the same Effects as here. At the last mentioned Place, the Rev. Mr. Wrigley preached in the Afternoon an affecting Sermon upon the Necessity of Repentance and Amendment of Life, from the following Words of the Prophet Isaiah, chap. 16th, verse 9th, "When thy Judgements are in the Earth, the Inhabitants of the World will learn Righteousness."

1777 Oct school refund, US letters from Hancock & Washington, card assembly

It took me all of three weeks to persuade Miss Forsyth to repay my fee money. She was determined at first not to return any payment and I was equally set that I would have it. I have run a school myself in years past so I understand how she is set up. Be that as it may, I must claim every penny that is ours if we are not to end in debtors' prison. I dare not dwell on it, I must turn my mind to higher things, such as the state of the country across the sea.

Every week the Mercury carries more news of our triumphs there. A letter by George Washington published in the New York Gazette, says their losses in a recent battle were serious and he acknowledges that he is beat. He gave up Philadelphia, chased out by our General Howe, so it would seem Mr. Harrop is correct in his surmise and the war is all but over.

Once all that terrible business is settled it may be a place we can turn to for a fresh start, if ruin is all that is facing us here. On days when John is truly bad with the drink I believe he would not miss me for weeks. By the time he does I may have started again somewhere that I am not known, for a good cook can always find a place. I once braved a journey across the Pennine Moors to be with him. Now I wonder if I would have the courage to take a perilous journey across a wild ocean to get away from him.

I am just being foolish. It will take many years before those Colonies are settled back safely under the King's rule, before it is worth planning a business there. It is altogether too wild for my tastes and I will never come to that. I am not a coward. I will pray for relief from my present anxieties and try to find my fight to withstand the woes I believe may soon be here. We have begun our Card Assemblies once again and that is bringing us some fortune. We had a gay evening this last week with many compliments for my food, which has given me hope to carry on.

1777 Nov new building

Such a lot of building is constantly going on around us, I am astonished at the pace of new buildings going up, or old buildings being renewed. Close by St. Mary's church the Manchester Free Grammar School is having a new building on the site of its old one on Millgate. It looks to be a very fine building, much bigger than the last. There are going to be some lucky children in this town to be educated at such a fine school.

When I went into St. Ann's-square I saw scaffolding all around the church there, and at first I thought them to be taking down the building, which I thought was a shame, but on meeting the Rev. Mr. Waverley he explained that they were replacing the cupola on the top of the tower with a spire. The cupola was thought to be unsafe and a spire was the chosen replacement.

I returned home to look at our own inn, looking quite shabby and worn, in a street that is also shabby and worn, and I was quite ashamed of it. As soon as I got in I sent all the maids and stable lads out to the street to clean up the street and the front of the building. We cannot afford to spend money on a new building but we can at least look clean to passers-by. After they had done the outside I set them all to cleaning and tidying the inside. Certainly a little effort on my part made me feel better and hopeful for a better future.

1777 Dec Reports recd of General Burgoyne's surrender at Saratoga. In 1 wk Mcr offered 1000 men and new regiment formed, Mcr Volrs/72nd Foot

All the town is talking of poor General Burgoyne this month, forced to surrender at his battle at Saratoga. I feel sorry for the poor General's wife Charlotte, my own dear Lady Betty's sister. I know the General will have fought bravely, he has an excellent reputation as a fine soldier and the reports say he made the sacrifice to save his men rather than himself. He had only a small but gallant handful of men, only two thousand five hundred, and they were surrounded at a place called Ticonderoga by the whole of the New England forces of thirty thousand.

Anxious to spare lives General Burgoyne proposed terms of an honourable surrender which the Rebels thought it prudent not to reject. His men were given the promise of transport to the nearest seaport until they could find vessels to bring them home, after they were put under the most solemn promise not to serve in America during the remaining part of the war. Last week's Mercury carried full details of the terms of his surrender. It sounded most honourable and gentlemanly.

Now we have had this setback I do wonder if the war will truly be over this year, for a great surrender like this will surely have given the rebels fresh heart for the fight. Already there has been a regular beating up for recruits, every day there is a sergeant with drummer and fife along Chapel-street calling for more volunteers.

The news is that Manchester has offered the King a Regiment of one thousand men, to be called the seventy-second Regiment of Foot, known as the Manchester Volunteers, with a handsome blue silk flag. Major Horsfall, Captain Aytoun and several other Gentlemen are approved of as Officers.

On Wednesday last a regiment of Dragoons were drawn up in St. Ann's square to receive the recruiting party, and after paying compliments to the flag, discharged several Vollies in honour of the loyal toasts which were then drank. It drew in several lads, all in high spirits, who enlisted without delay. They were not local men but must have flocked into town for the promise of glory.

We benefited from the raised spirits for the men of the Town were so buoyed up and full of fighting fervour that our inn was well attended and our Card Assembly was thronged with bright young men with a wish to win. Everyone was in the best of spirits and, more importantly, it kept John too busy to spend any time drinking. I could wish every week would be as good.

1778 Jan 6 inn history, recruiting play

Everyday more lads throng to the recruiters, who use ever more elaborate ways to entice volunteers. The latest ruse is a play that the recruiting officers are performing at the Theatre Royal, called the Recruiting Sarjeant. All volunteers are to be given free tickets and the event will be followed by a dance for the recruits and their wives.

It is pleasing to see that Manchester has a great loyalty to their King but I fear that for many lads it is just a means to escape the poverty that falls around us. Pushed from their villages by need for employment and the promise of riches in the towns they find that machines are now taking their jobs. The rich take all the profits while the poor workers scrabble to raise the price of a loaf of bread. I see them around me everyday, in rags, hiding in alleyways, hands out begging for scraps. I do what I can but we can barely feed ourselves so have very little to spare.

I had a most interesting conversation this week with a dear old gentleman who had visited our inn on purpose to look at the building. He was a learned man and knew a number of facts about buildings in Manchester. He told me that King Henry VII had stayed here in the King's Head sometime in the year 1495. He had been on a visit to his mother Margaret who was then residing at Lathom. We truly are named the King's Head for a King's head has lain on a bed within these walls!

The old gentleman Mr. Pickridge, also knew of another notable character from this area, Ralph Byrom, a Salford man of some wealth. He came here in 1485 from Lowton and was a prosperous wool merchant. His descendant John Byrom, author of the great hymn 'Christians Awake!', lived in Manchester but had passed away the same year that we arrived in Town. Some said he had been born in the Old Wellington Inn, near where he used to live but the historic family seat was still at Kersal Cell, a house that had been in the Byrom family since 1660.

I was happy to listen to the old man's tales, for he was very courteous, but I began to fear he would talk all day so was grateful when Sarah came to fetch me as I was needed in the kitchen.

1778 Feb 3 public fast,

For one day this month I did not feel at odds with our customers when all his Majesty's citizens were under royal command to observe a fast, to humble themselves before God Almighty, in order to vouchsafe a special Blessing on our Armies in the Colonies and Provinces of America. Directions were given to the Most Reverend Archbishops and Right Reverend Bishops to compose a form of Prayer suitable to the Occasion, to be used in all Churches, Chapels and Places of Worship. I could have done without the excessive prayers but I hope the Almighty was not opposed to the one I added for blessings on our own future. John is back to drinking heavily and is in debt to some dreadful men from his reckless gambling at the Cock pit.

1778 Mar 3 bridge widening, John threat

After years of risking life and limb to cross the river to the Manchester side it is so much better now that the authorities have finally had taken away the dungeons that were on the northern side. The way the carriages rattled across the bridge whether or not anyone was walking on the bridge. There was never enough room for both carriages and people to pass safely, and of course the person always got the worst of it. Now we have a wide thoroughfare which carriages and people can cross in safety. Those dungeons were terribly unhygienic places. They flooded every time the river rose and so could not be used very much. Hunt's Bank House of Correction must be sufficient for the number of wrongdoers we have.

John is now in a dreadful state on most days. I discovered today that he has been trying to persuade our nephew William that he needed John's knowledge to taste the liquors in his shop to test them. Poor William, although he is a man now, he could not help himself but take pity on his uncle, but it helps neither John nor William and in the end William was forced to refuse him.

He finally told me that he has pleaded with his Uncle Raffald to leave him alone. His business is suffering from the attentions and he can give him no more. He has his own creditors chasing him for payments and does not know how much longer he will be able to continue. He has told John not to set foot in his shop unless he was able to do so without touching the liquor. Had John been a younger man he may have tried to fight William but I know he wouldn't truly wish to harm William. I think he had believed his own falsehoods that he was helping.

He was not a pleasant man to be around after that and he began to start each day later and later until he was not rousing himself until noontime. How much good that did him can be judged by his frequent threats to do away with himself. These alarmed me in the beginning but after several weeks of hearing them I began to lose patience with him. Yesterday he caught me at just the wrong time. The kitchen was in pandemonium and everyone wanted my attention at once, so when John joined in with his pitiful plea that he would jump in the river I could take it no more. I told him I wished he would for then he would be free of his anxieties and I of the harassing nature of his complaints. I hadn't meant to be so harsh but it seemed to be the tonic he needed, and he never threatened suicide again from that day on.

1778 April drapery widow

My reaction to John's threats worked nicely and he has stopped threatening to do away with himself, for which mercy I am glad. There have been times, may I be forgiven, when I wished he had done it and I could live as a respectable widow rather than a debtor's wife, but it may have left me in poverty so I must be glad it did not happen.

Poor Mrs. Cotes has been left a widow in the meanest way. She and Mr. Cotes had a thriving Linen Drapery business 'till six months ago when he began to suffer with sore teeth. He would not pay for a decent barber surgeon to attend to him but sought out a cheap backstreet man to pull his teeth. He died soon after from a dreadful wasting sickness. Now his widow, too sickly herself to carry on, is forced to sell up with a loss of everything, even their pews in St Mary's church and St. John's.

I had not realised they had done so well, but her husband had already taken the decision to sell the house and shop before he died, thinking that they would go to live quietly, maybe with their daughter. With their only son lost to the fighting in America and their daughter married to a wealthy cotton merchant in Liverpool, there was no-one to take on the business so it had to be sold. Mrs. Cotes has taken losing Mr. Cotes very badly, and she has all the stock to be rid of before the latter end of July next, which is no time at all to sell so much stock.

If only I had some little purse of money to spare I could find me some good deals, but money is scarce here too and it is not a good time for me. If only I was nearly finished with my next Directory for

Manchester and Salford, but I struggle to keep pace with the names of the new people coming into Town. I fear it may now be too much of a job for me to take on again, but I must keep trying. It is the only way I can see to bring in some profit.

1778 May 12 William Middlewood deed of assignment, miniature woman

I have determined to put my energy into a new Directory. That at least may bring in some more money. My nephew William is now being forced to give up his business, poor boy, but it is giving me new determination to prevent our fortunes going the same way.

Poor William had taken on a bad loan after I refused to advance him funds for the new liquor. As I warned him, if not kept well it can easily spoil, which it has. Now he has no stock and owes the total sum of the money he borrowed. Our whole family is in a sorry way and I cannot bear to think what will become of us. It will take a miracle to save us. The only good to come of this is that there is no spare liquor for John to drink.

William has now been put into bankruptcy by Teasdale, a nasty man who will give no quarter when it comes to reclaiming what is owed to him. John Teasdale is the kinder brother but Isaac counts every penny. I cannot believe that after all the business we have put the way of their corn supply business since I first started in business here that they have not the heart to extend some leeway to William. His shame will be known far and wide after the notice appears in the Mercury next week, and everyone will know of his debt and failure.

I have asked him if he will come back to us to work at the inn but he is so despondent he is more likely to be found drifting down the Irwell. He has spoken of returning to Yorkshire to care for his mother and sisters, sickened as he is by life in Town. It is not the exciting adventure it once was. More and more desperate, bedraggled creatures line the streets, begging for food. To my mind they would do better getting on their feet and walking back to the villages they left. They would eat better from the hedgerows than the gutters.

If they were as small as the Miniature Woman who is in Town this week, they would not take much feeding. Less than a yard tall, thirty years of age and supposedly weighing eighteen pounds, though I think that cannot be right. I will not be among those paying the sixpence that Rhodes Tavern is asking for the price of seeing her. I do not begrudge anyone a good income but it cannot be got from me, I need all that I can get.

1778 Jun William's attorney

William reported a worrying conversation to me yesterday. He had been at his Attorney's office and as he waited to see Mr. Stonehewer a gentleman entered the office and was shown straight through. William was most put out at being pushed down the line. He wanted to hand over his papers and get back to his shop, so he stood up and went to put his hand on the door handle to Mr. Stonehewer's room, thinking to march straight in, but he stopped as he overheard the men inside talking about the name Raffald.

Thinking he may gain some useful information he waited as near the door as he dared. He was sorry afterwards that he had, for what he heard left him downcast and in doubt as to whether telling me was the right thing to do. My heart ran cold but I insisted I had a right to know for nothing could be worse than my own imaginings.

He heard the new gentleman, who was called Mr. Milne, another attorney, advise Mr. Stonehewer that if he was approached by Mr. Raffald of the King's Head or by Mr. Hatfield, a Manchester Cornfactor, to effect a Deed of Assignment on the man Raffald,, that he should refuse for there was no money in it. Mr. Milne then said that he had been approached by Mr. Hatfield in the Bull's Head with such a sorry tale that he thought it wise to call and warn his good friend.

William heard Mr. Stonehewer reply, though not clearly, and caught the words Middlewood, and nephew. He heard sounds of the men approaching the door where he waited, so he thought it best to move away lest they saw him eavesdropping. He pretended to look out of the window when Mr. Milne left, though he said he could feel himself stared at.

Such black tidings can only mean that our affairs are truly getting out of hand. If Mr. Hatfield has not been paid I wonder to who else we are in debt. I knew times were becoming desperate but now I must look for more ways to bring in extra income. I need supplies in order to make things to sell, however. What is a cook if she has nothing to cook? There must be people who we have helped who could now do us a good turn. Not William of course, but Mary may have enough to help, and John's brothers, surely they will not see us fail? It hurts to beg them but we, or rather John, will need to do it.

1778 Jul 14 friend's death

Tonight I have not the heart for anything. Of all the problems we have, I am grief stricken by the loss of a wonderful lady. My friend was such a gentle soul, and now she truly is a soul only, for today her bodily remains were interred in the ground.

Poor lady, she had been so poorly, with no doctors able to find a remedy, she had slowly dwindled to a shadow of herself. Yet never did she complain. Her concerns were always for others. Whenever we met she knew more about me than I ever knew of her troubles. Only after she has died did I find out she loved to sing hymns, and she knew all the scriptures by heart.

I am proud to say my friend was attended by as many people as the church could hold. When it came time to pay respects her niece gave a pretty speech, full of love for a gentle, kind, compassionate person, fondly recalled. There was an audible gasp from the congregation when she described a vision she had received just before her aunt passed away. She had seen her aunt's face, lit up with an inner ecstasy, delighted that her faith had been true and she was in the heaven of her beliefs. It brought tears to my eyes to think my friend's goodness was rewarded.

I vowed to be more like her but I was barely outside the door before my temper was raised. Who did I see but my own husband, asleep or drunk, sitting on the church steps. He had no doubt come looking for me and fell asleep. Heaven only knows who he had left in charge at the inn, but it must be said that no one could be worse than the man himself. I am shamed by the disgrace of him. How can I find a compassion and kindness like my friend? I tried to think what she would have done but I knew that such a person would never have had such a husband.

1778 Aug coach from KH, Wm back to Yorkshire

We have a fine new venture this month, thanks to a little persuasion with John Swain. He has begun a new Diligence to run from the King's Head every morning at 6 o'clock, Sundays excepted, to Mr. Wood's King's Arms in Leeds, returning the same from there the following day. It will call at Rochdale, Halifax, Bradford, then Leeds. It cost three shillings to Rochdale, seven shillings to Halifax, nine shillings sixpence to Bradford and twelve shillings all the way to Bradford.

Each traveller is allowed ten pounds weight of luggage, only one pence per pound above that. Mr. Swain truly has a nose for business. Since running his Liverpool and Warrrington coach from our inn he has been copied by others, but none are as fine as ours. I made certain that the notice of our new coach carried a line to say 'Our friends are earnestly requested to take Notice that no other Diligence has any connection with the Liverpool and Warrington coach, which sets out from Mr. Raffald's, the King's-Head, in Salford, every Day.' One day soon we may be able to boast that we can carry a man from one shore of England to the other, I am certain it will be most popular.

My joy at the news of the new journey was quite spoilt at learning that my nephew William will be one of the first passengers. His affairs are now closed and all that remains is for the final sum owed to be calculated. He says he cannot bear to remain in Town to hear it. He has given Mr. Stonehewer his mother's address in Yorkshire, and his brother James will stand in his place as surety that the debts will be honoured. The poor boy is only sixteen and introduced to the world of debt so early in his life.

He is staying close to his Aunt Raffald for now, but I fear that it has quite unsettled him and as soon as he is able he will also choose to return to his home county. At least he will return with some useful experience of work and a letter of character from his Aunt. If he is as able as his brothers to learn bookkeeping it may help him procure a good position.

1778 Sep financial difficulties

This month has been so very difficult. As I come to make out my accounts for the month I cannot make my figures reconcile. Whilst I have been diligently attending to business it seems that someone else has been either recording amounts wrongly or, what is more likely, taking out some small amounts which they thought would not be missed. I am out on amounts of loaf sugar, of rice and of corn, all ingredients which may be conveniently stowed into a cloth in small quantities and hidden about a person so as to be unnoticed. In these days of sharply rising prices, corn is as valuable as wages and I shall have to keep a lock on my supplies.

In the meantime I will need to approach that dreadful man Mr. Hatfield, the cornfactor, to advance us some more credit. I have the Card Assembly beginning next month and the Officers' Mess annual dinner and I must have sufficient for those. The Officers will be bringing their ladies so it is my opportunity to impress them to gain some good commissions for dinner parties. It would do me no good at all if their husband were to suggest me for their wives to refuse for fear I would disappoint their guests. They would say I am spent, my pastries quite tasteless and not at all the best. They would no doubt prefer to choose Mrs. Berry, who is becoming quite the rival.

It is more important than ever that I keep to my standards, I will not have shoddy work and woe betide the person I find to have stolen from me. They will soon find themselves under lock and key by the Boroughreeve and either in the stocks on the market place or even on the next transportation ship. The justices are taking very seriously the theft of any foodstuffs in this time of shortages.

1778 Oct problems

And so it came about as I foretold. Mrs. Thompson cancelled my commission for her dinner on Saturday week. She sent word by her under footman, just a short note that Mr. Thompson and his associates had been called away to London and so the dinner was cancelled, with apologies, &c. Well, one of those associates came into our inn yesterday and my nephew James heard him let slip to a friend that he was looking forward to Mr. Thompson's dinner for which he had engaged Mrs. Berry.

Times are getting desperate and I feel I am losing my place in this Town. My Officers are still as yet loyal to me but they will not stay if I cannot find the means to feed them. Captain Haydock, bless him, came into the kitchen one morning with a veal carcass he had won in a card game. He presented it to me, as one who would make the best meals from it. Dear man, he has always appreciated my cooking. By the time my maids had set to it and Mary had sent some of her confectionery we had enough dishes to give the annual dinner the most respectable show.

If I had not been able to make that dinner I don't know what I would do. I find it difficult enough to step outside the inn, shamed as I am by the low state we are in, unable to help ourselves, and I have no wish to converse with those who might gloat over our current struggles. For certain it will be a long time before I have a new dress. It will soon be remarked upon that Mrs. Raffald is constantly seen in the same dress all the time. I will just have to do what I can with ribbons and embroidery to make it last. The shame of no money is worse than the embarrassment of an old dress though I would wish neither had to be the case. I am glad now that I bought that pretty muslin for Anna when I did, for it comforts me that my child will not know what her mama is suffering.

This month we should have announced our Card Assembly for the winter season but for the first time we are unable even to do that. Without the funds to supply customers we are unable to chase customers to bring in some business. I truly fear for our future now.

1778 Nov John's debts, creditors

And so we are brought to shame, to disgrace. I am glad my dear papa does not know his daughter is brought so low. We are harangued daily in our business by creditors shouting at us, presenting their bills like accusations of a crime, telling me I must pay whatever funds I have for John's debts, for in law it is all his money. There are four of them who are now taking us to law for their money, but I do not know how they expect us to pay what we do not have.

I've never ordered goods that I couldn't make into a dish worth twice or three times more, but it has been a hard lesson to find out that John Raffald has no such skill. I am so ashamed of him. I do not recognise the proud gardener I once married. I work all hours and all he has done is drink away and gamble any profit that he was making. I am glad he does not know how much money I gave to my sister Mary as protection for our girls' future.

Her shop is a replica of the business I began in the marketplace which was such a success for me. Hers is now providing her with a good income, with my help of course for she has not the business mind that I have. I was a fool to ever leave my shop in the market place. I was busy, successful, and had a chance to become a person of some importance in this town.

John was a persuasive devil then, talking me into this gamble, and it surely was a gamble to go from seedsman and confectioner, trades we knew better than any, to taking on a coaching inn. It was not right, I felt that at the time but a little devil of greed misled me so that I willingly believed John's conceits. He flattered me and promised me we would have an inn to rival the Bull's Head, the centre of commerce and progress. That has not changed, it is still the place for people of business and power to discuss changes for the good of Manchester and Salford.

For a short while we did gather them to us. My gentlemen officers of the cavalry stayed loyal to me, they were good friends, true gentlemen and appreciative customers. I looked after them well. I wish now that I had listened to Captain Stockwell when he hinted that I should cast an eye over my books. He had heard rumours about town and though he was certain they were idle gossip he had wanted me to know. I believed it likely to be from Mrs. Blomely, out to get revenge on me, although I have not been in competition with her since '72. Sadly it was not her and I have learnt to my cost that the rumours had a strong foundation.

How low am I brung. I am shamed and I will do all I can to hide every penny of my money from the attorney, Mr. Milne. Any money I make from now on I will say is owed to Mary and between us we will arrange the care of my daughters. While I am John's wife I must go through better and worse with him. He is forever promising me that he has learnt his lesson and is certain he can put it right with just a little financial help, but I have learnt that however much I give, it is but a drop in an ocean. His own brothers want no more to do with him, he has taken money from them too and they will not support him either. George is having his own troubles and James is hardly able to keep himself. His business has run down badly and he is barely managing.

John has been a fool to himself and he has made a fool out of me. I will not allow him to make a fool of me again. I thought him bright enough to encourage customers to drink and gamble while keeping his own wits about him, but it seems that it was the customers who kept their wits and used his friendship for their gain. Where are they now in his hour of need? What cost fair-weather friends? Not friends at all, that is plain but he is so addled that he does not see it. Well I will see it for him and make sure they do not get near him again. In future they must get past me and that will not happen, I am fixed on that.

Dec 1778 Deed of Assignment notice Dec 14

I am having such a black time now that I hardly like to put it down on paper but I cannot shy away from the facts which are in any case now public knowledge for all to see. The public notice in the Newspaper is out now, declaring John's creditors claiming rights to our Personal Estate and Effects, and calling for any other creditors to contact Mr. Milne, Attorney. He has already advised us we will have to leave the inn and expects us to advertise the lease at our earliest opportunity.

The action was brought by four men, Mr. Peter Wright, Agent on Old Quay, Manchester, Mr. Thomas Hatfield, Cornfactor of Manchester, Mr. Robert Hesketh of Liverpool and Mr. William Porter of Haigh. These are the biggest debts but now every little debt will soon be registered. In law my personal estate and effects are included as John's so I am not allowed to keep anything of my own if could be sold to pay a bill.

I imagine Mrs. Blomeley is quite exultant over my downfall. She has never forgiven me for being a better cook than her. I have no doubt Miss Forsyth will think of sending my girls home from her school once this term has gone but Mary has vowed that she will pay te fees for them until I can restore our fortunes.

I have found out who has been waiting for me to fail, having had so many people calling to cancel their commissions for dinners. I do not know what I can do to carry on, but I must try. Some people have been kind and assured me they will wait and trust me to pay my debts to them. Those friends are top of my list to repay as soon as I am able.

Daily meeting people who know about our debt and trying to keep my head up is a most severe test of endurance. We have no funds of our own with which to do business and I am shamed to be always asking Mary for help. Although she has had plenty of mine it is not easy to have the tables turned.

Mr. Hesketh, who is our biggest creditor, has made it his business to install one of his men with us and he watches every glass as it goes across the bar, ticking off the quantity from his list to make sure none is being undersold or wasted.

Having no drink is making John face his troubles sober which leaves him in such a temper. The only day he is set loose is Sunday when the man does not come but now I dread Mondays when he is at his most unpleasant. For the last week John would not look at me and each day was worse than the last. Finally he came to me and told me he was thoroughly ashamed of what he had done but would make me a solemn promise. He vowed to work diligently for the rest of his life to recover from our troubles. I was touched by his sincerity but felt I had seen it all before.

I began to upbrade him for bringing about our downfall but he cut me off and took my breath away when he accused me of wasting money. He said my high standards cost more money than they were worth, suited to a big country house but not to a city inn. I have always practiced economy with elegance so that was one accusation

I could not take. I drew myself up in temper and fired right back at him, all my fury at the suffering he has inflicted on me and his daring to criticize my work when he knows nothing about the art of cookery.

We parted bitter enemies that night. For days we did not speak and I checked every dish I made, to consider if I might use less, or cheaper meats. I found that extra spice would cover many faults in taste and so made a few savings.

I could never have imagined my life would come to this, all hard work and no reward after all my great endeavours. The best I can hope is that with a little hard work and diligence we can satisfy the creditors and leave here without debts, though where we would go is uncertain. Mary has not room for us. George perhaps could find us something in Stockport, though it would be a disappointment to live in a small country town after the life here. I will press my case on all the contacts I have in this town and one of them surely must find me a new opportunity, even if it is one that needs must includes John,

1779

1779 Jan 23 Prescotts ad/26th Mercury ad for KH to let

Since the advertisements for the inn to be let have been in the Mercury and in Prescott's Journal this month we have been visited by any number of people. Men of money were the first to pounce and they ask the worst questions. What we are leaving, whether we will leave it in good order, and if will I work for them for small wages are the most frequent.

Everyone wishes to prosper from our misfortune but they were nowhere to be seen when their help could have saved us from our present indignity. I refuse to do business with them now, when all they seek is to make profit from us. They all want me to work for them but they will not countenance John. He is too much of a risk, they say, no use to them. They do not want to see their profits getting washed down the street.

I could never work for someone else in a place where I am accustomed to being mistress. I am hoping I may yet save our business, and impress Mr. Milne with a new diligence to our affairs. We have until the tenth of next month to make a difference. It is now plain that we must leave this inn and let someone else have the worry of it.

I should never have given up the shop I had, or taken John away from his garden produce. When this is all settled I must look once more for another shop where I may make a successful business once more. Law or no law it will be mine and John will have no share of it, although I am concerned by what little strength I have. I find myself more easily wearied, due no doubt to all the worry I have suffered these last years with John, and I have little heart to start again at the beginning. However, I am too old to return to service now so I must find another business or die trying.

1779 Feb 9 recruiting,

We have not yet reached starving point but Mr. Hesketh's man would not pity us if we did. He begrudges any spare mouthful not accounted for in profit. He and I will come to severe words if he does not confine himself to the liquor and beers. He may watch john every minute of the day and have my thanks for doing so, but he will not dictate to me what I may or may not have in my dishes, or for spite I will serve him a dish made with his meagre rations and see how he endures that. I could wish he might fall prey to the recruiters here who are constantly in search of more men to add to their Regiments for America. Certainly he has a sour enough face that would scare an enemy without need to raise a weapon.

In this week's Mercury both the Earl of Pembroke's Regiment and the Royal Manchester Volunteers were beating up for recruits. The Manchester Regiment promised generous rations of seven pounds of bread, five pounds of beef or pork, five pints of Pease, five pints of Oatmeal, six ounces of butter and the same of cheese for every week they serve. John was talking wildly about joining up to get away from his troubles, but he is too old now, they do not want old men like him, only young bloods with fire in their eyes, until they reach a battlefield and see it is all just mud, and smoke, and injuries festering for lack of skill to tend them. I have heard too many stories from the men who survived. Many of their comrades did not return.

I am feeling very anxious for tomorrow, the day that all our creditors must have registered with Mr. Milne's office. Then we will find out the full extent of our debts. Mr. Milne will need to get us a good price for the Inn so that we can settle matters cleanly, even though it will cost a significant amount in his fees on top of any debt. I just hope he makes Mr. Hesketh wait the longest for his money. Whatever enterprise I take next I hope never to do business that with man again.

I cannot wait to leave here now; everything is tainted with the taste of failure, not an experience I enjoy. We had such high hopes and for a while we were the premier inn of Salford and Manchester. We were beloved by some important men, celebrated by many of the best people, and I could be proud of our endeavours. Now though, I am beat, and could be sorry we ever had such heights that make these troughs all the worse.

Everything done on my part is lost in the foolishness of John's carelessness. How did I come to be so mistreated and ill-used? I do not know how I will continue to go about my daily duties, but I must. Until we can obtain the best possible price for the Inn it is the only way to lessen our debts. Every day is like a knife in my heart.

1779 Mar 9 school rates

Last week we were called into the office of the Attorney to speak about how we proposed to settle our debts. I will say I thought Mr. Milne dealt fairly with us. He praised us for our efforts, although I like to think that he was referring to my efforts rather than John's. He then said plainly that we were fools to try to stay on at the inn, and told us that it was sucking money out of our pockets however hard we worked. I know John was holding out hopes of continuing but we are too old to work so hard so I was glad he stated it clearly.

Mr. Milne said he will make every effort to sell on the lease on our behalf but the debts must be settled in the next six months. At the end of this time he is obliged to take the best offer he has. Of course, any profit would first pay his considerable fees, whether it clears the debts or not. It will take some kind of miracle to overcome this problem and most likely I will be working until I am eighty years old to clear the debt.

I returned to the inn with a heavy heart and retired to my snug to enjoy a little peace away from prying eyes. It took me some time to regain my composure and I needed no witnesses to my misery. Later, as I sorted through the few orders I had, my nephew James came through with the Mercury for me to read. One advertisement caught my eye and set me to thinking. A Miss Richardson was advertising her new School for Needle Work and she stated her prices quite boldly in the Notice.

It struck me as a most vulgar way to proceed, but the modern woman can act quite differently now. They are not brought up in the old ways or understand genteel ways but I think they can be a little too brash for my tastes. Such prices she stated too, I was quite taken aback. She was asking sixteen guineas for Board and Needle Work, or five shillings per quarter for plain work or twenty-one pounds for Parlour Boarders. It put me in mind of the school I once ran and it occurred to me that I could do that once more with just a simple establishment. Mary could help me with such a venture. She has the premises but not the time. I could not begin a school for young ladies here at the inn, it is not the right place, but I can see that it would be possible at her shop.

I must do something in the next six months or I will go mad and end up in the Lunatic Asylum round the corner here. Our society may be advanced but it will not tolerate hysterical women. I must guard against sinking into melancholy or black moods. I have risen once. I must believe I can do so again. This time I will put my trust in a beloved sister, and never again be tempted by a man into great folly, such as this inn has been. My undoing was to trust and not to check. I was flattered by compliments and forgot the golden rule that made me a successful housekeeper for fifteen years. Make every penny do the work of two and check everything. Such foolishness will not happen again.

1779 Apr new school

Mary was most receptive to my idea of starting up the school and we have made great progress. She had been thinking of just such a thing herself so my suggestion was opportune. She had known my situation with John was wretched but knew it was of no use for her to advance us what little money she could spare. So many people had spoken to her of John's state and of the problems with the inn but she had not liked to tell me for fear of adding to my woes.

This time she is happy to move away from Chapel-street. There is a good house on Exchange Alley, close to the church and the Market-place, which will be much better for business. We can start afresh in the centre of town and not have to witness daily the problems of the King's Head.

My Sarah is now fourteen years old, quite fully grown, and she has learnt to make herself very useful to her Aunt Mary. She will make an excellent teacher for our little school, versed as she is in fine confectionery and with a good head for numbers. Mr. Turnbull is selling the lease of the new house and Mary should be able to do a good deal with him. I' think he hopes for more than a business deal with Mary but I am certain he will be disappointed.

I have written to Mr. Fichar, in Mary's name, to invite him to be our Master of Music once more, and to ask him who he would recommend for Drawing and French. I have already spoken to Miss Timmins, a most excellent Needlewoman. My Emma is fulsome in her praise for teaching her delicate skills with lace, of which I have an excellent cap as evidence, something I will treasure forever.

I of course will teach the kitchen skills as I did before and I have a plan to include a competition where each student produces their most excellent dish, to test if they have learnt the skills of economy and elegance most necessary to the management of a good household.

I need to be circumspect with my enquiries, however, for until we are free of the inn not a whisper must reach any prospective buyers. I say only that I am making enquiries on my sister's behalf. Slowly I begin to have hope again.

1779 May 4 prospective buyers

We were very close to securing a good deal for the inn this week, although not from our first visitor. A Mr. Johnson, recently of Bolton, had seen the notice of the King's Head to let and had come into town expressly to check it out.

Mr. Wright, the Agent, brought him in to see me in my snug bar although I was not best pleased by the manner of their approach. He had scarce knocked on the door before the two men barged straight in. I made no show that they had rattled me but continued to work tallying the column of figures I was working on. Once I had finished I put down my pen, blotted the ink and looked at them both as severely as I felt.

I told Mr. Wright, in my severest tone, that even though he had the authority of the lease in his hands I would have respect shown to my right to perform my offices in privacy. For the inn to realise its best price I would look to keep it at its best and he would do me the courtesy, in future, of sending a message to arrange an agreeable time and not interrupting my necessary work. Then I allowed him to introduce his companion.

The man had the decency to flinch and made a poor introduction, mumbling that his guest was a Mr. Johnson of Bolton.

He looked a rough, ill-mannered man, better suited to a country inn than one in a sophisticated town such as ours, but we cannot afford to choose. We need to be free of the lease at the earliest opportunity in order to satisfy the debts.

One of our neighbours, young William Joule, has shown an interest but I fear he cannot afford it. He has a small brewery on New Bailey-street and wants the inn for the space to develop his ales. Poor man, all his money is tied up in stock so he does not have the capital needed.

Mrs. Fairbrother, whose husband John lately ran the Ship inn here in Salford, paid me a call with a more hopeful applicant. When her husband died the family had moved to Liverpool but her son Robert never settled. He had a desire to move back to Salford which he considered his home. Robert has not long married a sensible young woman, very handy in the kitchen, and they are keen to make a start for themselves.

I remember John was a very capable landlord, and if his son is like him he will do very well at the King's Head. I advised Mrs. Fairbrother to send the young couple to see us and I would give them all the help I could. Of the enquiries we've had so far I am inclined to favour them as suitable successors to give good service to the customers. John and I have had our troubles, but that is no reason for the King's Head to lose its reputation for excellence and gentility.

Mary has had better luck with her shop and as I expected made a favorable deal. Next month she moves into Mr. Turnbull's old house at the corner of Exchange Alley, a wonderful spot for passing trade. Its thatched roof can create a lot of work for the cook trying to keep the mice out of her stores but it is too good a spot to miss.

1779 Jun Almost selling the lease

We had the rug cruelly pulled from under us this month, although it saved from being swindled. A deal was made, not a good deal but one which gave us grace to leave with a little dignity if not much of anything else. It was offered by that rude Mr. Johnson of Bolton, a man who needed his manners polishing before he came to town.

He had shook hands with Mr. Wright over the purchase of the lease, promising him sufficient to cover payment of his costs but leaving us with nothing. However, within a week of the paperwork being presented to the Attorney, Mr. Milne, he had been found to be in debt to so many creditors that his offer was worthless. Mr. Wright had been so sure of the deal that he had ordered us to pack up our few belongings and get ready to leave at a day's notice, making sure we left the inn in good order. I was not at all pleased to be ordered out of my home, however unhappy it had become. He is another man I shall do my utmost to avoid in future.

I gave Mr. Wright the benefit of my opinion of his valued friend. I was surprised he could possibly have considered Mr. Johnson suitable for such a prestigious inn. Of course Mr. Wright did not care about the inn, simply wanting to make enough to pay back his costs. I, however, believed it wasteful not to recognise the reputation I had built, and that a payment for goodwill was due. Mr. Wright would have none of it, saying that any reputation would leave with me.

I challenged him with all the nice touches we had introduced, making the inn of higher value than when we had taken it on, including the standard of cookery I had introduced but he was not abashed at all. I am only thankful his customer had let him down. He is a horrible man to deal with.

I am still hoping that Robert Fairbrother and Betty, his wife, may return with a good offer. I have written to his mother to encourage them. When they called to visit me they showed their kindness in bringing me a gift of some sugar, recently arrived from St. Kitt's in a large shipment, just the kind of thing I might have done. Betty seems a very competent hostess and was very able when I showed her how I run the kitchen here. She has studied my cookbook and already knew many of the recipes, appreciating the wisdom and skill built into them. She was very keen to keep things the same and would be a worthy successor.

1779 Jul 8 moving out

At last something good has happened and Robert and Betty Fairbrother are to take over at the King's Head. I could not have wished for better, other than not to leave at all. I think now that it might be for the best, however, as I am always tired, weary of all the troubles and wondering how I will face whatever comes next.

Tonight will be our last night spent under the roof of the King's Head. Seven years of hopes and dreams dashed to the ground, but I am glad to say I tried. I faced the challenge and might have conquered it, had I been married to a different man. I do not feel the failure of the business so much as I feel the failure of the marriage.

Seven years ago John was a man I was proud of, a little flawed as we all are, but nothing unreasonable. How that has changed, all due to the demon drink. I have little to say to him anymore. The man of good sense I once thought him has gone, but I must find a way to live with him. He is mine and I his until death parts us.

When I was a housekeeper and he the head gardener we had authority, respect, and positions of security and power. When I look back those times seem so simple, so easy. Day followed day with no greater challenge than cleaning rooms or preparing meals and I knew my place. Since then I have written books, contributed to the progress of a town, brought forth new life and created a place of high repute, however ignominiously it has ended. When I was a young woman entering service I never would have expected such things in my life. Then my only wish was to do a good job and avoid any disgrace.

Now I am a broken woman. I do not think I can raise the will to start again. I do not have much to begin with. I am old and now poor with a drunken sot for a husband. Tomorrow we must move in with Mary at her new shop and I must find something I can do. She has said I can help her but I have seen how she manages now and she is not in need of my help.

I feel so sad, sad to be leaving my domain where I ruled. I ordered, dictated with no-one to gainsay me. Tonight I have no heart to try to think of anything. Tomorrow I must wake early and set to cleaning before we leave. I will not have it said that Elizabeth Raffald ran a dirty place. I will have it sparkling and I will walk out with my head held high when Robert and Betty take over.

1779 Aug new opportunity

At last my prayers have been rewarded. God is good and I expect that giving the best payment to the Attorney did not do any harm either. This is a town that thrives on money. It can move almost anything you want. Today we were given the news that John has the licence to be Master of the Exchange Coffee House from October. It was not the best opportunity I could have wanted, but I would not take on another inn, I was firm on that.

He must break this cycle of destruction for his girls' sake, and mine, if not his own. He can't return to his trade as a seedsman with hands so knotted and stiff that he has lost his finesse of touch and most of his knowledge has been wiped from his senses by the strong drink over the years. A lifetime of knowledge, of value, wiped out by the abuse of alcohol. It is a tragedy that makes me weep when I see what he has wasted.

How well we could do if only we both worked at what we know. My success has come from doing what I know best. My cookbook is still selling well and my directories are much in demand. I will put out a third one, much improved and enlarged, for there are so many more people and businesses here since my last one. Now that the worry of the inn is behind us I am more inclined to get to work on it.

Six years have seen a lot of changes everywhere and Manchester grows at the speed of a lightning bolt. Where yesterday was fields, now is an elegant new building. Crowded, dirty streets have become clean wide thoroughfares fit for the many elegant carriages which fill the streets. The feel of the money is palpable, as it changes hands everywhere, especially in the Exchange. Rich men become richer and inventors find the money to back them. I see it happening all around me yet here am I, shackled to a man whose brain is in the gutter and whose idea of a good time is to lose money to the shysters and pickpockets around the cock pit.

Now we have an opportunity to be in the centre of all this enterprise and we must make sure we attract the men of money into our establishment. John may be Master but it will run to my standards. The cream of Manchester will flock to Raffald's in the 'Change. I will begin by drafting my usual style of notice for Mr. Harrop's Mercury. People will know from it that my hand is firmly on the tiller and they will know to expect high standards. To impress on those who may not yet have heard of it I will append notice of my cookbook being in its sixth edition. New customers must have no doubt of the quality they will find.

It must be in John's name, of course, but the rest of the notice will have my touch. We will have only the best wines and other liquors and spare no expense (which I will make sure is fully answered for in profit) to render the house agreeable to all who shall honour us with their favours. We will need to take subscriptions to the News-papers, which I can canvass for in advance. I am certain I can count on Captain Stockwell and Mr. Beswick, they have already assured me they will be attending once we are in there.

I will be limited to what my cooking can provide but I am sure that soup of all kinds may help bring in some trade, especially my famous Vermicelly soup. I can have that ready from ten in the morning. Likewise Families may be supplied with tureens of Vermicelly, brown, white, Sago, Pease, Celery and Transparent soups on the shortest notice. There's no reason to turn away trade of any kind. This new venture will be a success, it must be a success.

Mary has been very good to us but I cannot endure many more nights cramped into such small quarters. The noise from the creatures in the thatch is very disturbing at night and I can feel them scurrying over me at night. The news of the licence has meant I can make plans to move once again into my own home. We can take possession by the end of the month and then we can make the place our own.

I am in no doubt of the work in front of me. The place has been neglected by its former master and the Exchange itself is not a pleasant building. I have heard it described as a den of iniquity, filled with dark, unhygienic places, fit only for the listless and lacklustre to loiter, but that will not apply in our coffee house. If my name is to be associated with it I will make it of the highest standard.

1779 Sep The Coffee House

We have been in our new home only one week, having been forced to wait a further two weeks after our given date. The previous Master was refusing to leave without payment for chairs he claimed he owned outright. Such a troublesome man, but he finally saw the error of his ways when I called on him. I told him his chairs were a disgrace that we had no need of and that he should take them with him. With only a little more grumbling he gave up his fight and left, taking them with him.

A week's work has shown a vast improvement in standards. Everywhere was so dirty that my hands are raw and my back is breaking. There is hardly any linen to speak of and the seats in the Coffee House are old, some badly broken. One or two were not good enough to repair and these I took to Mr. Bury to make use of as he could in his carpentry yard, in return for one or two little repairs. He is a kind man who has done a lot of work for us at the inn and is always content to wait for payment if it comes with the promise of a pie or two from Mrs. Raffald.

Supplying my old customers is much the only cooking I can do for now. All that is wanted in the Coffee House is a little warming soup, of which I have a suitable variety to please any palate. I would like to return to more but I cannot take advantage of Mary's shop. She has everything under her management now and it is important that she does well, for I never know where I will end with John. I rely on him to keep the licence of the Coffee House. The gentlemen of the Exchange would not give it to me even if I am widow, which may happen soon enough as he seems determined to drink himself to death.

I will do what I can to give our Coffee House the highest standards, then turn my attention to completing the next Directory for the Towns of Manchester and Salford. I have found a cosy room that I can make into my snug and I can work from there, close enough to keep watch on John but not part of the house itself. With a little restraint on John's part this could be a good living for us.

1779 Oct 12 Exchange coffee house notice, cotton riot militia

At last we could place the notice for our coffee house in the Mercury. The coffee house is an entirely different affair from the inn, nowhere near as exciting, but more suitable for serious discussion. I am determined it will be a house of high repute, regardless of the state of the Exchange. Our coffee house is to be a genteel place, suited to the more discerning gentlemen, and I hope I have spelled this out in the notice. I would not want to leave anyone in the slightest doubt. The Raffalds might be down on their luck but while I am alive we will keep high standards.

Manchester, Oct. 12, 1779
JOHN RAFFALD
Begs Leave to acquaint the Gentlemen of Manchester, and the Public in general

That he has Entered on the Exchange coffee house, in the *Market-place*, and laid in a Stock of the best WINES, and other LIQUORS, and will spare no Pains or Expence to render the House agreeable to all who shall Honor him with their Favours, which shall be ever acknowledged. He also returns his most sincere Thanks to the Gentlemen who have already subscribed to the Newspapers, and assures them, that every Paper that may be thought useful, shall be duly taken in. – Soups of all Kinds shall be ready from Ten in the Morning till Two o'Clock in the Afternoon, for Town and Country Gentlemen --- Likewise Families may be supplied with Tureens of Vermicelly, brown, white,

> Sagoe Peas, Cellery, and Transparent Soups, on the shortest Notice.

John is on his best behaviour I am pleased to note, for I do not know what I would do if he disappoints me in this. I hope we have both learnt from the shame of losing the inn. It is a relief not to have the worry of how to procure sufficient food for a large assembly with insufficient funds, but I am left without a good source of income. I cannot make much money on a few bowls of soup. For now, I am reliant on John to make this business work, a prospect which truly fills me with dread at the present.

The Town is full of people, more and more each week. I must be able to find some way of earning money from them. Thanks to the debt of the inn leaving us with little money I cannot afford to rest on my laurels, weary though I am many days. I must press on with the Directory.

1779 Nov riot report

The Mercury reported the outcome of a court that dealt with cotton workers' riots in Wigan. I can thank my fortunes at least that I am not living there, the riots against the cotton engines sound terrible. Our magistrates acted quickly to arm numerous soldiers and other proper persons to defend the people against riotous assaults, so they may sleep easy in their beds.

I have a little sympathy with the plight of the rioters. I would not like to lose my trade to a machine that could do it faster and in greater quantities than I ever could. Fortunately there is no substitute for a good cook and with enough servants to perform the tasks I could provide any amount of meals.

I cannot foresee a machine that would replace me, for it is the cook's skills that turn a bad dish into a good one. I can imagine that there may come a machine to replace the manual labour, however, but that would mean less work for the lower servants and could never replace the skill of a cook. One to replace whisking would be welcome for that can become most tedious. I am not mechanically minded, however, and I would prefer to teach a willing girl what to do than wait until a machine is repaired when it breaks down.

I am generally in favour of progress. I believe that many inventions now are improving our knowledge, but I feel sorry for the workers. Many are now wondering how they will feed their family with no work for them and no money coming in. I have been too close to that, thanks to John's drunkenness, but they should not cause trouble.

The court resolved unanimously that "the invention and introduction of the machines are of the utmost utility to this country". This is from learned men who lead us, so we must be guided by them. They also said that there was plenty of labour and subsistence afforded to industrious persons so there was no justification for riots from want of work. This is correct, of course, but the learned men do not understand that it is having the say over your work that is lost. The rioters are men who have learned a trade and who know that being a slave to a machine is not the same as being a skilled tradesman.

In the court report they said further that "the destroying of machines in one country only serves to establish them in another, and that if the Legislature in this Kingdom was to prevent the use of them, it would tend to send the inventors to foreign countries which would be highly detrimental to the Trade of this Country". That makes a sense that is chilling and more to be feared than having to find work nearby or having to fight foreigners for work in their own land.

1779 Dec Coffee house, shoes, new opportunities

Our coffee house is now quite established. I notice that more of the Gentlemen are attending our house in preference to Mrs. Crompton's, which has long been known in Town as the centre of discourse. If I can just keep John sober we may win as good place in the society of Manchester.

We are ideally placed, in the Exchange itself and close to the Bull's Head, where most decisions of significance are made. Ours is the ideal place to continue discussions more privately, or to find a cosy corner to read the newspaper. Mr. Beswick is quite a fixture, here everyday for a bowl of Vermicelly followed with a few hours by the fire in the big wingback chair. He is a gentle old man, though fierce when challenged on his politics. He will hold his corner against all challengers.

I feel we have found our niche in this coffee shop. It is simple to run, so much less worry than the King's Head or even than my shop, which suffered from too many imitations. My ideas were taken up and copied, and too much of anything soon spreads the money too thinly, though I see now that taking on the inn was our worst decision. It was a leap for the stars which took us tumbling into the crevasse of debt and drunkenness.

The profit from this business has enabled me to keep my girls in school at Barton-upon-Irwell, and in a month or two I may have saved enough to buy myself a new pair of shoes. Rushton's Warehouse on Hanging Ditch has advertised good leather shoes for women at three shillings and tuppence, and men's for five shillings and thruppence. John's shoes are full of holes underneath so the chance of a new pair might just make him take care of his money and not be tempted to drink it away again.

I have a few new ideas of ways to make a little more money too. My soup is selling well to families wanting a nourishing broth without the expence of cooking it. There are other opportunities too that may yet allow me to return to the high reputation I managed to achieve since first setting up in business here. Free at last from the worry of the inn I begin to feel again the optimism I first had when I arrived here.

1780

1780 Jan ideas, midwifery

A new year and I feel I have truly been given a new lease on life. My girls are doing well in school again, John is remarkably capable in our new endeavour and, although not yet as sober as I would like, he is giving a good presentation of it. I am doing enough business to keep me in a little profit and I have time to spare for bringing together the entries for another Town Directory.

I am a little surprised that none of the businessmen in town have thought to make one to rival mine, but perhaps they think it is a kind of women's work, or that they cannot make it as thorough as mine. Mr. Harrop tells me there is sufficient demand to make it worth his while to publish another directory but he has not the time or the diligence that I have for the work. I am certain also that he would not wish to compete with a business partner, which I am, although he has almost repaid my investment in his newspaper.

I wish I still had some of my copyright payment left, but I doubt I shall ever see sums as large as that again in my lifetime. I do have ideas for other publications which I may soon have the time to write. I feel suitably qualified to compose a lexicon of words of French, together with their English counterparts. With so many more people moving between countries with the need to conduct business, knowledge of a foreign language is essential to avoid being cheated.

Perhaps I could compose a book on the role and duties of a good housekeeper. The demand for good servants grows with every big house that is constructed and there are not enough girls properly trained. Mary is so overwhelmed with requests at the Register Office that I think I should start a school to train servants in the essential skills.

First I must return to my discourse on midwifery practice which I began while still in my shop. Dr. White, who is the undisputed expert on midwifery in these parts, was very gracious to me at the time and offered to advise me, but our move to the inn quite put it from my mind and it was all forgotten. I heard last week that he is preparing a Treatise on Lying-in and particularly wishes to hear from women who have suffered serious difficulties in childbirth. I am squarely in that category, having nearly died from one of mine.

I would not wish to think about it in the normal course of things but he has entreated me most particularly to write to him. He has persuaded me that it will be of enormous value to future generations. To think that I may be immortalised in a learned study is very gratifying, even if my other endeavours are forgotten. Certainly the study of midwifery deserves to be advanced. Too many women suffer terrible fates from a thing they cannot avoid, not in this world of men. Doctor White has not mentioned if he will be paying for this information so I will discreetly mention that my time can be more usefully spent and that some of us have to earn our living. It must be worth saying and it can do no harm to ask.

Feb 8 Heaton Hall, Shudehill mill, nude race

This month began with the annual naked males race on the Manchester race course in Kersal. As usual there were many foolhardy young men chancing their luck, but many of the widows watching were mindful of the cautionary tale set by Mrs. Aytoun, Mrs. Mynshull as was. Her ill-advised marriage to Captain Aytoun, after just such a race in '69, has left her alone and in poverty after he managed to gamble away her first husband's wealth in less than five years. Poor Mrs. Mynshull, for I can never think of her as Mrs.. Aytoun, she was never a true wife to the captain, more like an indulgent mother. She is only occasionally seen in Town, preferring to live quietly at her son's house. Thankfully, now that we have left the inn, we no longer see much of her husband either. He is only seen when he comes with his fellow Officers to the Market-place to beat for recruits to fight the Rebels in America. He is very clever at drawing them in with a jovial challenge to a gamble or a fight. The bet is that they will join up if they lose, and of course they always lose, poor fools.

I spent a very pleasant day at the races in the excellent company of my friends, Mr. and Mrs. Harrop. He was in good spirits and told us of the many new houses being built all around us, a good sign of the growing prosperity.

Sir Thomas Egerton is having a new house built, called Heaton Hall, which is providing work for many local craftsmen. Mr. Harrop also had information about Mr. Arkwright's ambitious plans for his new mill at Shudehill. It is to be truly enormous, bigger than anything we have yet seen, and it will have in it all the most recent inventions in cotton engines to produce most efficiently, the best quality and the most quantities ever produced. Now there was a man who could always spot the way to make money off the slimmest opportunity. He was just a working man like us, but what a mind he has for business.

If only I could have married such a man, there would be no limit to our endeavours. We could have been as rich as Croesus, although I daresay his wife will never need to work. It serves no purpose to dwell on what might have been and so I must make what I can of what I have been given.

I have not the means to build a mill but I did find a possible opportunity while at the races. My companions were bemoaning the lack of a genteel refreshment stand at the races, and petitioned me to put my expertise to work there. I had not given much thought to this idea since I left the shop. There was never the opening for anyone to take a stand and then I was always fully occupied with my work at the inn.

The racecourse has quite changed since that time and with a little influence brought to bear by Mr. Harrop I will be excellently positioned to take advantage of an opportunity. I have more experience, and Mr. Harrop quite convinced me that my kind of genteel touch was just what was needed to raise the tone for genteel race goers, who would also be the ones with the most money to spend. The thought of all that money going to waste was enough to tempt me. Mr. Harrop has promised to speak on my behalf to the race organisers when he next calls to obtain the details for their programme which he prints. He is convinced it will be easy to arrange so I will apply myself to making the arrangements. It is exciting at last to have a new endeavour.

Mar 21 budget, midwifery, directory progress

This month has been a very quiet month, many people are suffering from excess humours of the chest. The cold weather has hung about us, leaving most people loath to leave their homes. The beginning of the month was better for the coffee house than the latter part as gentlemen came to make the most of the brandy with their coffees before the price rose in the budget, as was strongly rumoured beforehand. Their suspicions were proved to be well founded and Parliament did indeed put heavy increases on most drinks.

The duty on Malt went up a whole sixpence per bushel, making it ninepence in total, and on top of that a further penny per gallon on low wines made from malt, thruppence on spirits the same. Portuguese and French wines were also loaded with charges, but that doesn't affect us too much, but they saved the highest charges for foreign Wines and Spirits. Brandy, of which the best is of course French, and Rum from the West Indies, were increased by a whole shilling per gallon. The speech even went so far as to describe them as 'pernicious luxuries' but I do not agree for a good Brandy is more medicinal than any other spirit, if taken in small amounts, and cannot be beat for warming a body on a cold winter's day.

Mr. Harrop had to disappoint me about a refreshment stand at the races this month, but truth be told I was glad of it. I had not managed to make my arrangements and I was not in the frame of mind to be standing about in the cold. I would have to be there to greet people, and my back is giving me so much pain in this cold I can barely stand for an hour at a time. I am much happier in my warm snug writing my tale for Dr. White, even though he has not replied to my letter about payment. I am sure there will be recompense in some way. A little connection with such an influential person will not be wasted.

I am also close to finishing the entries for the next Directory, which I must soon finish. Mr. Harrop is constantly asking me to submit what pages I have. He says it does not matter that it is not fully comprehensive, as it can never be truly finished and must be updated each year. I fear that would cost me more money than I would make from it but I will continue placing my advertisement for entries until September, and then Mr. Harrop can have the commission to print.

1780 Apr 18 7th The Experienced English Housekeeper

Today Mr. Harrop delivered me a box of the latest issue of my cookbook, The Experienced English Housekeeper, sent to him from Mr. Baldwin in London. I cannot believe it is already on its seventh print, but Mr. H assures me it is still in such demand that he barely needs to advertise it.

He told me he had lost count of the number of young ladies who are grateful for the book. They tell him that without it they could not get up a good dinner, but with it as their guide they cannot fail to impress their guests.

That pleased me to know but I still placed my advertisement all the same. If I can reach the men who make the decisions in these families I may sell even more in places where they do not yet know my name. He was more than happy to await my wording for the notice. He knows how particular I am in how these things are said. It was still very pleasing to hear him say so and now I have more books to sell that will bring in a little pocket money for me. Such is the increase here in fine households from the wealth made in textiles that every year more young ladies find themselves in need of my essential guide.

1780 May Crompton's Mule

Such an interesting story I heard tell by one of the gentlemen in the Coffee House. Mr. Pilkington had just come from the floor of the Exchange where a new cotton engine had been displayed. Mr. Pilkington was most distressed at the poor reaction from the men of the Exchange. His friend, Samuel Crompton, had devised an engine which he called a Mule. It had been on Mr. P's persuading that it had been brought in to raise subscriptions for its development. This engine could produce better yarn than currently available. He claimed it was finer, stronger and could be produced in larger quantities.

I could not see the problem, for surely the men of business here would see the benefit if the machine was as good as he said. He bemoaned the lack of vision of his friends who had let him down by being too cautious. In the usual course of affairs anyone displaying their invention on the floor of the Exchange could be sure of raising at least two hundred pounds. For Mr. Crompton's invention they managed only a niggardly sixty pounds which was not enough. Mr C had left the Exchange in a rage, vowing to return to farming and keep his ideas for his own use only.

Mr. P went on to tell me the full story of how Mr. Crompton had developed his Mule last year, using rollers to squash and stretch the yarn, in a principle similar to Mr. Arkwright's Water Frame. To this he added spindles on a moving carriage to draw out and twist the thread as used in Mr. Hargreaves' Spinning Jenny.

After the machine-breaking riots of last year at Mr. Arkwright's factory in Chorley and Mr. Kay's carding mill in Bolton, Mr. C had been in fear for his machine. He had dismantled it and hid it in his loft at Hall 'i'th' Wood until the beginning of this year. Then he and his wife had begun working with it to make their own yarns at the Hall. They soon became known for this superior yarn, they were getting spies climbing ladder to peek in at his upstairs windows.

Mr. P had persuaded him to show his machine on the Exchange, confident he would raise two hundred pounds, but although no-one disputed the quality of the yarn, the machine was so humble looking that few were impressed. He was also burdened by the knowledge around town that Mr. Arkwright had a patent on his water frame, and that gentleman is known to defend his patents most vigorously. Many of the gentlemen had been reluctant to go against Mr. A. Until the patent expires in 1785 Mr. Crompton's Mule is looked at as a poor investment. I felt sorry for the poor man. In five years time who knows what other inventions might be put before us.

Mr. C was offered the chance to work for Sir Robert Peel of Bury or Mr. McAlpine but he declined, leaving, as told, in a rage, saying he refused to shackle his skills in order for another to profit. I felt sorry for him but such is business in these times. Cleverness alone is not enough. A level of cunning is also needed to undercut rivals. What I have seen is that men of ideas are too easily used by men of finance. They can persuade and beguile a man to sign away his rights for little reward.

Now I pride myself I am no fool when it comes to business but I have never needed to trick anyone. My business has been based on genuine offerings of good food for a fair price. I would never wish to be involved in such high business as the men of cotton undertake daily. John and I are simple folk and I am grateful to have stay within what I know. Next week I will have my first stand at the races and I am so hopeful it will do well. Mr. Harrop placed my advertisement in the Mercury this week and several of our gentlemen customers have complimented me on my endeavour.

1780 Jun 17 church bells rung all day at intervals, Mon 19 Dragoons & 48th Foot paraded to St Ann's Sq & fired vollies to 1000s spectators

All Town has been a joyous tumult this month, even Mr. Pilkington cheered up. He has been quite despondent since the disaster of his friend Mr. Crompton last month. We are in the month of the King's birthday and as usual we had the customary day of celebration, all the churches ringing their bells. I made a special celebration cake for our gentlemen at the coffee house to have with a small brandy each. My rich plumb cakes are well known now and a taste of it is almost guaranteed to gather me a few orders to take home to their families.

It seemed that no sooner had the bells stopped ringing for his Majesty than they began again to celebrate a great victory in America. Everyone says the war is sure to be won now that the Rebels have conceded a great defeat. The commander of our forces, Sir Henry Clinton, had a signed agreement from their Major General Benjamin Lincoln, who had tried and failed to hold a place called Charlestown.

The bells rang all day on Saturday the seventeenth, fair giving me a head pain that did not abate for almost a week. I was going out of my mind with the agony and no remedy would help any more than lying quietly in the dark. Only two days after that day of bell ringing four troops of Dragoons, from Colonel Holroyd's East Sussex Dragoons, paraded past our door on their way to St Ann's-square. Here they spent the whole afternoon firing off vollies to celebrate again, such a noise. There was a huge crowd in the square so I sent the maids out with some trays of sweet patties to sell. If the customer does not come to me there is no reason why I should not go to them.

It is all a far cry from my days at the inn but I have to put that behind me. I have been made to swallow my pride and must sell my wares to whoever will buy. In a week I will be at the racecourse with a stand. Finally Mr. Harrop was able to prevail upon the authorities to grant me a place. I have such great hopes of making a good name for myself once more, although I struggle to raise the enthusiasm. I have so many aches and pains all over my body that when my head joined in the clamour I felt only fit to lie down and not get up again. I know I must strive but it is becoming more difficult with every succeeding winter.

1780 July 4th Strawberry stand, riot

The heat of this summer is leaving me fair exhausted, though perhaps I am just dispirited. I can't seem to manage what I once could, my strength is deserting me. All my years of hard work have given me such weakness in my back and there are so many days when I struggle to get my breath even after the slightest effort. It might be that I am despondent at the poor results from my strawberry stand at the races. I had such high hopes of a regular place, something of my own, something genteel, but those hopes were soon dashed.

The day started well enough, even with the slight panic when a whole tray of strawberries were found spoiled. With a little careful application I turned it to my advantage, saving the worst to turn into jam. My friends were generous with their patronage and the day might have been a success were it not for a troublesome mob which came from Town, drunk and in a mood to give insolence.

It later became clear where they had come from, for the same day as the races there was a dreadful riot in Town over the punishment of a soldier stationed there. A Mob objected to the sentence passed by the officers and a magistrate was called on to quell their insolence and violence. The report of the incident was in the Mercury the following week and sounded most disturbing. It was bad enough to almost need force from the Military.

I do not understand today's Town dwellers. So many of them are quick to riot and complain. I too am unhappy with my lot but I always look for ways that I can improve or help others less fortunate. Those rioters who drifted into the races were a veritable menace. They were harassing people and causing mayhem, knocking over my stand and losing me a large quantity of tea and chocolate. The result was it cost me more than I made in profit to be there.

I have no wish to go there again. It was not the opportunity I believed it to be. I will be content with what little I can make from my soups together with sales of my remaining books. My best efforts will go to the completion of the new Directory and I will finish writing my thoughts on midwifery.

1780 Aug Lady B died age 64, work on the directory

What sad news I received last week in a letter from Arley. Hannah Bushell as was, Mrs. Parsonage these last eight years, took the time to write and tell me that dear Lady Betty had sadly passed away. It was a peaceful death, it seems. She had retired to bed early the previous evening complaining of fatigue and the next morning her maid had found her, quite cold, lying as though only asleep. She had lived to a good age, being sixty-four years old when she passed which must be a comfort to her children.

Hannah expressed her belief that Lady Betty had never recovered fully after losing first two of her daughters and then Sir Peter. I quite agree with that reckoning. Any letters I received from her after that last date had been full of sorrow. Such a good-hearted lady, she felt the losses most keenly.

Hannah writes that she was given a good funeral, her son Peter making all the appropriate appointments to give her due respect. It makes me sad to think that such a good lady is not in the world any more. She has gone to her blessed rest after a good life as a faithful wife. I made sure to say a prayer for her in church on Sunday last.

All I see recently is sadness and strife. Perhaps I am despondent about my lack of progress on the Directory. I feel my eyesight is not as good as it used to be when reading close writing. Several of the last drafts sent to Mr. Harrop for checking have been returned for mis-spelling and other faults. I must continue with it however, until it is done. It already runs to more than a hundred pages and still does not keep pace with the changes of people in town. I have already written my notice, to be placed next month in the Mercury, for people to come forward if they wish to be included. Whatever I have by the end of December is what will be published.

READY FOR THE PRESS

And shortly will be publish'd, The
Third edition of the

Manchester Directory

With Alterations and Great
Additions

The Author being desirous of making the Work correct, begs the Favor of the Country Gentlemen to send the Firms of their Houses, and where their Warehouses are to be found, and a Person will be appointed to take these down every *Tuesday* and

---

> *Saturday*, for three Weeks. Also begs the Favor of the Town in general, to send in any alterations in Partnerships, Removals, &c or any Thing that is expected to take Place very soon, as no Care or Expence will be spar'd to render the Book compleat. The Days for the Town sending in their Firms are *Mondays* and *Fridays*, when a proper Person will constantly attend for that Purpose, at the *Exchange* Coffee-House, in Manchester.
>
> All Letters, (post paid) will be duly attended to,
>
> *By the Publics obliged humble*
> *Servant*
> ## ELIZABETH RAFFALD

Perhaps what I do is not worth the work it needs, it may all be in vain. I have always tried to do my best in every endeavour, to help, to pass on what knowledge and skills I can, but it seems so difficult now. I feel that Manchester is moving swiftly onwards without reference to its dear Mrs. Raffald. It has benefitted from my efforts and now it forgets me.

1780 Sep 12, entries for the directory

This month is so different to the last. I am quite elated at the many responses to my advertisement. There are so many requests to be included in my publication which they proclaim as excellent, and thanks given to me for providing such an invaluable source of reference.

I received so many letters of the same ilk and to be so well thought of has quite raised my spirits. I have overcome the problem of the mistakes I was making by giving the work to little Anna, whose attention to detail is of the highest standards. Work is progressing tolerably well now.

September is being a mellow month. Its late summer warmth and sunshine have quite broken through my melancholy of last month. I am hopeful once more, determined to find a new purpose, an enterprise which is suitable for me.

I have received a reply from Dr. White, asking me to call on him in order to discuss the details of my childbirth experiences and suggestions for improvements in practices. He says I have much to contribute to the store of our public knowledge and the future of better, safer practices.

It is so good to feel valued again. My daily work is in partnership with a man who complains only that I am a nuisance and a nag just because I try to keep him sober, and it is very wearing. I see businesses all around us expand and develop. Manufacturers become gentlemen of wealth in a few short years and it had induced in me a feeling of failure, of having no influence in the world anymore. Working with Dr. White has restored my faith. We each have a role to play and to some is given the chance of wealth, to others the opportunity to contribute to the growth of knowledge. I can see that I have been part of the latter. On days like this, when the sun has shone and I am reminded of the value of my efforts, I can feel hopeful again.

1780 Oct 3 widow business, midwifery

Poor Mrs. Pinder has needed to advertise for a Proper Person to assist her to carry on her late husband's Tailoring business. She will no doubt have worked at her husband's side, performing most of the tasks, but without a properly qualified man to provide the Tailor's skills, the most work she can hope for is alterations and repairs. None of the gentlemen would pay for what is called unskilled work. I wish her good fortune in her venture and will call by her house on Red Lion-street to tell her so. It is only off St. Ann's-square and I will pass by it on my way to Dr. White's house in King-street.

Our collaboration is becoming very detailed and he is appreciative of my intelligent approach. He says I am unlike many of the women he interviews, which he finds a refreshing experience. I have assured him that I treat the matter most seriously. Women are suffering enough with the pain of giving birth. I do not see that they should suffer more because men of science have not yet applied themselves to the better practices that should be used. I do believe that many deaths can be prevented with more knowledge and I feel privileged to be able to play my part.

My present concern is that, as I have become more involved in this serious study, John has become more desperate. Not only is he seldom sober, his gambling losses have increased. I am quite distraught with the agony of worry. There are not many days pass without a resort to a remedy for the pain I have. I know I have value to people of consequence, and will have the prestige of taking part in a learned journal, but it does not remove the ever present threat to my livelihood.

I worry for my future. I do not know how I would bear the shame of debt once more and, if John were to die from his excesses, I would be left in poverty. Unlike Widow Pinder, I would not be able to employ a Proper Person and continue in the coffee house here. The coffee house must have a Master. The gentlemen of the Exchange would accept nothing less. I would be forced to move out, to throw myself once more on my sister Mary's mercy. Some days I think a genteel widowhood is preferable to a shaming marriage. Every day now I expect the bailiffs to chase us from the building but I can only keep working, it is all I know.

1780 Nov 14 newspaper business

I have hit upon a novel idea for a new business and I am certain I have only to talk a deal with Mr. Harrop to settle matters. It is in part thanks to him that I had the idea, for it was an advertisement in the Mercury that specified the details.

A woman no doubt similar to myself, one Mrs. Ann London, has offered a service to send on the London Newspapers to Country Persons for a fee. She has the advantage of living in the right place to obtain the papers clean from the Presses there, and has eight papers which are printed three times per week to offer.

She asks only thirty-nine shillings a year for each, or three pounds and five shillings per year for the Daily Advertiser which costs tuppence halfpenny per paper. She must have struck a good deal to be able to offer them at so reasonable a price.

I believe that although the London news might be of superior importance to the Country Gentlemen around London, our Manchester Mercury is of far greater value to the Country Gentlemen in the North of the country. It has the value of including the essential information from the London papers but also has far more useful information for Persons interested in business in the area. We have so many such persons now that at times it seems that everyone I meet is in one business or other. Certainly, the Gentlemen in the coffee house I have spoken to have agreed with me that it is an excellent idea. It now only needs Mr. Harrop to agree.

I needs must do something to improve our lot, as John seems ever more determined to destroy us. Last week I found him lying in the alley behind the Exchange, fallen dead drunk over a barrel. My first thought was that he had died, and may God forgive me, I know a part of me wished for the release from further shame. Once I saw that he was breathing still, I roused him with a pot of cold soup over his head.

I scolded him soundly, for my temper was truly roused. I told him to get himself out of the street and into his respectable bed and not disgrace me further. I was afraid that if he did not get himself inside the Constable would find him. I was absolutely at the end of my patience. I bade him clean himself up and we would have words later.

He gave me such a look at that moment that I feared I had gone too far and he might send me to the Constable for being a scold. They still have that barbaric Scold's Bridle as a punishment here though it is rarely used. I must have said enough to put him in possession of his wits. He shook his head and half-crawled and half-dragged himself into the coffee house. I was Master that day while he, pasty-faced and meek, worked in the shadows, not wishing to face me.

That evening we had words and I gave him my rules. Number one, that from now, I would be the one to control the purse. He would give me his figures for everything he paid and would tell any creditors that they were to deal only with me. This figure turned out to be far greater than I could believe. Our debts were already so severe that some creditors were already threatening to take us down as they had at the King's Head.

John confessed that the seriousness of the debt had made him afraid to face me. It was fear that had made him drown his sorrows. I would not allow of such a poor excuse, however, and told him plain that it was the drinking that had caused the debts, and that it must stop instantly, or he might as well go and throw himself in the Irwell and be done with it. It was his last chance.

He was utterly despondent but could take no more. He apologized to me and our children and vowed to make me proud of him once more. I said I would only ask that it would suffice if he no longer makes me ashamed to be his wife. He made me a solemn promise that he would change if I would promise to be his Elizabeth again and not always Mrs. Raffald the businesswoman.

I fair bristled at the injustice of his request. If I have worked hard it has always been for all our benefits. It is just as well that I turned my fears and worries into cakes, for if we had both turned to drink we would have no hope. I warned him to be careful what he wished for but I made him that promise and I will make sure he keeps to his word.

For a week he has been as good as his word and every time his control starts to slip I have been there to prevent it. I will be diligent and watch him with my eyes everywhere. He will not slip away while I am able to prevent it, I am determined.

1780 Dec 1 3rd directory issued

I am sad to say I was quite thwarted in my idea of a newspaper business. When I called on Mr. Harrop it appeared that he too had the same thought and already had the matter well in hand. To add insult to the injury he was using the names provided in my Directory to grow the numbers of his customers. I was disappointed but I was able to turn it to my advantage in securing a reduction in the cost of printing the Directory. I argued that the service it provided to him was worth a fee, and he reluctantly agreed. He is a good man and I am happy that our businesses are mutually beneficial. The latest Directory is finally finished and is now out to sell, so I hope I can put a little by and make some difference to the amounts we can pay on our outstanding debts. They are slowly reducing but and not growing even it they are still in frightening amounts.

John is now quite accepting of my instructions. As I have discovered, I can manage the coffee house very well without his efforts for most of the day. The coffee making is under my supervision and is a simple matter of pounding the beans to a fine grain and keeping them on the boil for a sufficient time. I have insisted on the best beans from a Dutch plantation in the West Indies. They are far superior to the French beans and our gentlemen seem to appreciate the extra flavour.

I sent John to work with his brother James in his nursery garden and with James's wife, Mary, on the market stall. He is happier for it, is busy most of the time and comes back with a few shillings to show for his efforts, a better situation for all of us. He thrives in the open air and I realise now he never was cut out for business.

Mary is grateful for his help, having found out only recently that their only son was lost at sea. It is such a sad affair. James is inconsolable, but Mary says she knew he had died long before they got the news. She told John the strange story of seeing her son standing on the other side of the market one day, his hand outstretched towards her. When she went towards where she had seen him, he had gone. She believes it was an apparition, for from the intelligence just received they found out it was on that very day and hour that he had drowned, having fallen over the side of the ship.

Who can truly say what she saw, or whether the sorrow of losing a child full grown is worse than losing them as a baby. There are so many things in our world that are known only to God. We all are subject to His wishes and can only do the best we can. I made sure to say an extra prayer for Mary, asking for His mercy to deliver her from her sorrow.

1781

1781 Jan 3rd directory, King's Head

Last week I set foot inside the King's Head for the first time since we had been forced to leave. It was very strange to see others running around what had once been my home. It looked different, of course. They had replaced some chairs and arranged them differently which I must say would not have been my choice. I felt so ill at ease, already so different to who I had been then. It was almost more than I could bear.

I had gone to give my condolences to young Betty Fairbrother who had taken over from us with her husband Robert when we were forced out. It is now only Betty, carrying on alone after poor Robert died last month, and I could see she was a little uncertain about being in charge. I commended her for her courage and wished her all success. We women of business must give an example for others to follow. She thanked me for my kindness and confessed that she always considered me her guide in matters of good taste.

All in all it was a more pleasant visit than I had expected it would be, prompted as it was by a sad occasion. I was glad to leave, however, and now I can think of the inn without too much sadness at what was lost. I am glad not to have the problems anymore.

A more uncomfortable experience was one in which I was asked to sit for an engraving of me, to be printed in the next edition of the cookbook. Mr. Baldwin has insisted that a drawing be made of me to be included in the eighth edition and as he sent the money to pay for it I had no reason not to oblige him. I attended the studio of Mr. Morton, a genteel man recommended by Mr. Harrop, who is also in favour of an engraving. He is sharing the cost with Mr. Baldwin so that he may use it in my books that he is printing.

Mr. Morton obliged me with the loan of a very nice gown and I wore over it my best kerchief which had been embroidered by my own dear Sarah. My hair was nicely dressed with my beautiful, elaborate lace cap sewn by Emma. It had taken her nearly two years to work it under Miss Forsythe's close supervision. I felt very elegant but I did not appreciate being studied so closely. Mr. Morton asked me several times to smile but I felt so displaced that I fear I frowned most of the time. It is not in my nature to be so forward about my image. I have never been vain and this was all vanity. I cannot imagine what it will add to my book for ladies to see me but if it will sell more then so be it.

1781 Feb 6 debts

What an unpleasant month February has been. As I sit to compose my monthly account I am hesitating to write down the facts. Hunted is how I feel, hounded by grasping hands unable to show the slightest kindness. Although we have been making higher payments than required, still that is not enough for some. My extra money from the sales of the new Directory has all gone to satisfying more of John's debts. I swear, the man's head cannot hang any lower, but his shame is not helping. It only means I cannot be angry with him, he is already like a whipped dog.

Mr. Shawbrook is particularly persistent in his demands. He says he needs our payment to satisfy his own creditors in turn, but I saw his wife in a new hat last week so I know he cannot be as poor as we are. I cannot remember when I last afforded a new bonnet. He just has a grasping temperament. He will get his payments as promised and not a penny over but I do wish he would cease to harass me. It is causing me so much worry that I have a surfeit where there is already enough. I feel pity for his wife who has to live with him. No amount of new bonnets would be reward for living with a bad-tempered husband.

My dear sister Mary has been a great support to me, bringing me sweetmeats from her kitchen for me to sell, and offering to give me whatever she had. I was loath to take them but she would not listen. She insisted that help must go both ways, from one to the other, as both are situated. When one is in the happy circumstance of being able to offer, the other should be mindful to receive as the circle of life turns. We are sisters and she would take my troubles from me if she could. I must be strong for her, and in turn for John, whose weakness is plain but I was so touched by her kindness I could not speak. I feel truly blessed to have such a sister.

1781 Mar making plans

The weather has been such a pleasure this month, with a surprising few weeks of warmth and sunshine and I remarked on it to John, though he did not see the joy. He was gloomy for the plants which would bloom early and surely be ruined by a late frost. He was thinking of the plants in James's garden, convinced that they will lose all the plants that had been fooled to bud too soon.

It was good to hear him speak as a gardener once more. For a long time he has been out of touch with the seasons but since I have made him return to his true work he is a changed man. He almost never takes any drink now, believing that even one would be a road to ruin. If we can only continue as we are I believe we may again have a good life together. We still have some debts to satisfy but I am hopeful that all will be resolved with another six-month of steady progress.

The Directory is selling exceeding well and Mr. Harrop has arranged to print more which is good news for both of us. He has suggested that I write another book to guide young women setting up home, to cover all the duties that do not feature in a book of recipes. He says that many ladies would appreciate my plain speaking instruction to keeping a house with elegance and economy, and a new publication may improve my reputation and financial situation.

I promised to think about it and have already devised the sections I believe are important. I hope to have an outline to present him when next we meet. I would want it to be a complete guide, for I will not do anything by half measures. I have seen such guides written by men who I'm sure have never had to practically apply their advice as I have. They also do not allow for changing times such as the ones in which we now live. It is all very well to instruct on traditional rules but as new products make new ways of working then methods of housekeeping must change.

I do feel able to write such a guide, and think the time is right, I pride myself that I have the qualifications and experience together with an eye for progress. It will be a work to interest me and may help to restore my reputation in Town. 'Guide to Household

Management for the Use and Ease of Ladies by Elizabeth Raffald'. Yes, that will give me hope as I fight to restore our fortunes. It will bring light to my darkness.

Postscript
23rd April 1781
By Mary Whitaker, sister to Elizabeth Raffald

Today we have put my poor dear sister Elizabeth in the ground and on looking through her possessions have found this record of her married life. After reading parts of it I thank god for sparing me dear Elizabeth's suffering of living with such a man.

For what man would allow of his wife's interment without a record? It is only thanks to the kindness of his brother George that she is not thrown into a pauper's grave here in Manchester. Dreadful man that John has become, he could not, or would not pay for his wife's name to be added to the family gravestone, nor would he allow any of us to authorise it either. If that is not wicked I know not what is. I never will forgive him.

To give a fuller picture of my poor, poor sister and her unfortunate family, let me record here that she went to her maker four days since, on April the nineteenth in the year of our Lord seventeen hundred and eighty-one. After suffering with her health these last few years she was gone in an instant. I tried my utmost to provide her some relief but she worked like a woman possessed. Nothing I could say would prevent it, she would not listen to my advice, a more determined woman I have never met. When once she had set her mind to something she would give it everything to bring about its success.

Although the speed of her decease astonished me, I cannot be surprised, for it is well known that overwork can kill. A human body can only take so much and my feeling is that it was sheer unhappiness that overwhelmed her. Like Sisyphus with his rock she toiled without end to give her daughters the best.

We were together in the end and I knew she was failing fast. It was shortly after nine in the morning, we were in her kitchen and she fell to the floor, her arms and legs limp, her mouth drooping. I and James, my nephew, carried her to her chair but she could not speak, one arm flailed wildly in my direction. Quickly I ordered James to run for Doctor Brown and sent Samuel to Barton-upon-Irwell to get the girls from school and insist that they came home directly, no haste to be spared as their mamma was dying. Elizabeth and I had seen this before in others and we both knew it would not end well. I tried to hold back my tears as I held her hands in mine. Her eyes stared into mine and I stayed there, repeating over and over my promise to keep the girls safe and put them beyond any harm from their father. Sarah and Emma are young women now and both very well suited to service but young Anna is only eleven and will stay with me. I must confess she has always been my favourite, such a pretty little girl, puts me so much in mind of our sister, Jane. She will be safe with me and I vowed to dear, dear Elizabeth that I would make sure she had an inheritance from me to make up for the lack of any from her father. As the end came I tried to soothe her by reciting our father's favourite Psalm, number twenty-three. I believe I saw her lips moving with mine and as I got to the last line I felt her hands go limp in mine. Then I knew she had gone to join our dear mother and father in heaven and I let my grief flow unabated.

When everyone came in to join us and I saw that reprobate John throw himself on her body and sob as though she meant anything to him I confess I wished him harm for being so late in his care of my dear sister.

Appendix I Index of names mentioned

1 Elizabeth and John's family

Elizabeth Raffald nee Whitaker – born 1733 in Wadworth, Yorkshire, one of 5 daughters; her father a schoolmaster and her mother Elizabeth. She went into service at the age of 15, became housekeeper at Arley Hall in 1760.

John Raffald – Elizabeth's husband, eldest son of a Stockport family who owned land in Stockport town centre where the Arden Aems now sits.

Anna Raffald – Elizabeth and John's 5th child, born in 1770

Betty Raffald - Elizabeth and John's 4th child

Emma Raffald - Elizabeth and John's 2nd child born in 1766

Grace Raffald - Elizabeth and John's 3rd child, born in 1767 and died in 1770 before her third birthday.

Harriot Raffald - Elizabeth and John's 8th child

Mary Raffald (& Male)- Elizabeth and John's 6th & 7th children

Sarah Raffald - Elizabeth and John's 1st child

George Raffald – John's younger brother who lived on the family land at Stockport, with his wife Mary, and kept an inn there called Ye Blew Stoops. When John was appointed Head Gardener at Arley Hall in 1760 he signed over his title to the land to George as next in line.

James Raffald – John's youngest brother, who lived in Salford on Gravel Lane with extensive gardens for horticulture.

Mary Raffald –his wife

Elizabeth Whitaker- Elizabeth's mother

Joshua Whitaker – Elizabeth's father

Mary Whitaker – Elizabeth's sister

Sarah Whitaker –Elizabeth's sister

Ann Whitaker- Elizabeth's sister

Jane Middlewood nee Whitaker-Elizabeth's sister living at Howden, with her husband, a flaxgrower

William Middlewood– first son born approx 1752

Joshua Middlewood- second son born approx 1755

James Middlewood –third son born approx 1762

2 Arley Hall – information taken from arleyhallarchives.co.uk

Sir Peter Warburton – 4th Baronet and owner of Arley Hall
Lady Elizabeth (Betty) Warburton – wife of Sir Peter, daughter of Earl Stanley Arley Hall while Elizabeth was housekeeper. She worked very closely with her, developing new recipes.
Peter Warburton – 1754-1813
Elizabeth Warburton – 1746-1760
Ann Warburton – 1748-1769
Margaret – 1753-1817
Harriot – born 1758
Emma – born 1759

Servants
Peter Harper - house steward/estate manager, May 1757-75 £40pa
Ann Worsley – Lady Betty's maid at Arley Hall when Elizabeth was housekeeper, 1751-68 £8pa
Martha Taylor – Housekeeper on the skeleton staff at Arley Hall while building work was going on, paid £5 19s 6d for 239 days
Hannah Bushell - maid 1758-72 £3pa ('68 became Lady Betty's maid, '72 retired & married Thos Parsonage)
Mrs. Bromley – housekeeper from April 1763 to December 1764, paid £16pa, same as Elizabeth had received
Mrs. Hutchin – Martha Hutchin was a cook from April 1762 to December 1763, paid £10pa

Aston park – where the Warburton family lived during 1758-1761 while Arley Hall had extensive building work.
William Widders, one of the witnesses on Elizabeth and John's marriage certificate. A Mr. Widders leased a farm at Budworth for cows, and shipped salt from Norwich to the Potteries, then ceramics to London. Then he would return with goods to Loughborough then bring malt back to Arley. He would also ship goods for Arley and shop for them in London, including tea from Twinings.

Other names used in the story

1763
Rev Burroughs – not the local vicar but a curate based at Goostrey who conducted Elizabeth and John's marriage ceremony at Great Budworth church
Market-stead-lane – an early name for Market Street
Lady Assheton - lived on Marriott's-croft, Manchester
Sir Thomas Egerton – 7th baronet and MP, later Baron Grey de Wilton, married Eleanor Assheton, daughter of Sir Richard (d 1765)
Christ/ Collegiate church – now Manchester Cathedral
Warden Peploe – Samuel Peploe, a worthy, honest, pious and good man, much respected and known for great affability, politeness ease and dignity. (ref James Ogden, A Description of Manchester, 1783)
Sir Oswald Mosley – Lord of the Manor of Manchester
Manchester markets – information taken from contemporary references
Daub holes – early name for damp area, now Piccadilly gardens
Mrs. Withnall – a midwife noted in the 1772 directory
Mr. Briarly – gentleman living at Heaton Norris
Mrs. Blomeley – a fictional character based on James Blomeley who appears in the 1772 directory as a cook
Mrs. Clowes – featured in the book the Manchester Man and also in the 1772 directory living on Dean's-gate
Mr. Priestnall - fictional
Rev Eccleston - fictitional
Mr. Harrop – Newspaper printer and bookseller, Market-place, Manchester

1764
Wadworth – the Yorkshire village near Doncaster where Elizabeth was born
Mr. Sheepley & White Lion – noted in the directory as book keeper for the coaches
Bulls Head – built c1690, a gabled front on the Market Place, abutting the old Exchange building, and had a considerable open space at the rear. The top of the yard reached the Cockpit, rumoured to have underground vaults extending to the church (cathedral)
Thos Highs – inventor, reed-maker and manufacturer of cotton carding and spinning engines in the 1780s, during the Industrial

Revolution. He is known for claiming patents on a spinning jenny, a carding machine and the throstle (a machine for the continuous twisting and winding of wool).

Mr. John Kay (1) – of Bury, inventor of the flying shuttle, patented in 1733

Mr. John Kay (2) – a clockmaker from Leigh who collaborated with Thomas Highs in investigating machinery for the spinning of thread by means of rollers.

Mr. & Mrs. Taylor – housekeeper and butler at Arley Hall

Marjorie Moorpout – as advertised in the Mercury newspaper

1765

Dr Smellie - a Scottish obstetrician and medical instructor who was one of the first prominent male midwives in Britain and designed an improved version of the obstetrical forceps, established safer delivery practices, and through his teaching and writing helped make obstetrics more scientifically based

John Armstrong - fictional

Dr Charles White – one of the founders and first surgeon to Manchester Royal Infirmary, 1752, and founder of the Manchester Lying in hospital 1790

Stamp tax – in 1765 this was a direst tax imposed on all printed matter in the American colonies

Lunatic Asylum – the building next to the Infirmary began 1765 in the area now known as Piccadilly, first patients admitted 1766

Mr. Green - fictional

Hannah Glasse – wrote an early cookbook in 1747, The Art of Cookery made plain and simple, reprinted several times,

1766

US declaration – taken from the Mercury newspaper articles

Widow Dalton – fictional, though a widow Dalton appears in the directory as a victualler

Eliz Woodcock – as on Arley Hall archives lists

Mr. Thompson – fictional, though there is such a bookseller in 1772 on St Mary's-gate

1767

Mr. Fischar – taken from advertisements of the time

Cookbook stockists – taken from the advertisements

1768

J Hargreaves – generally credited with the invention of the spinning jenny

E Higgins – true story

Richard Arkwright – began as a peruke maker, became well known as the father of the factory system, held patents for numerous inventions

King Christian –visit as detailed in the Mercury newspaper

Mr. Mainwaring - attorney

Dr. Byrom – well known Manchester personality, wrote the hymn 'Christians Awake'

Mr. Hurst - fictional

1769

Roger Aytoun/ Mrs. Mynshull – true story

Mr. Wainwright - fictional

Perfect's of Pontefract – nursery gardeners

Artingstall/Thwaite/Moresby - fictional

York Courant – one of the papers the advertisement appeared in

Mr. Fletcher – as shown in the advert

Mr. Wagstaff – apothecary that appears in the 1772 directory

1770

Richard Alsop – as advertised in the Mercury

Mr. Syddall - fictional

Mrs. Walker - fictional

Dragoons and oak leaves – symbol used at the time

Mrs. Ridge/Mrs. Towler/Mr. Cleat/Mr. Moratel – from Mercury advert

Mr. Baldwin – future printer of Elizabeth's cookbook

Crompton's – well known coffee house of the time

Blakeley – as in the 1772 directory

1771

Mr. Prescott – printer based on the Market-place

1772

Perfumes – as advert

Races Fernyhough/Radcliffe – taken from newspaper

Mr. Moorfield -advert

Mr. Deaz - advert
R Parkinson - advert
Finney/Mayer/Harris – from newspaper adverts
Wm Coe – as in a newspaper article
Mr. Holbrook – from newspaper article

1773
Sisyphus – legend of man condemned to push a rock up a mountain for eternity
Rev Whitaker – taken from the 1773 directory
East India Co - an English company formed for the exploitation of trade with East and Southeast Asia and India
Rev Wakefield -fictional
Tea salon ladies – fictional
Rev Ainsworth - fictional
Ratcliffe/Wainwright - fictional
Mr. Swain – business partner and licensee as in the 1773 directory

1774
Margaret – Lady Betty's sister
Rev J Bayley 181

1775
Aytoun notice – from the Mercury
Dark entry – early alleyway
Ben Lincoln – American leader as reported in the Mercury
Mr. Cavendish - taken from recollections of Manchester
Dragoons – reported in the Mercury
Theatre/Theatre royal - factual
J Bostock – Mercury report
Ducking stool – historic fact
Mary Wollstonecroft – well known advocate of female rights 1759-97
Town changes – advertised in the Mercury
Rev Clayton - fictional
Bonnie Prince Charlie – son of the exiled King James, pretender to the British throne, led a failed rebellion in 1745
Mr. Munday – from the 1773 directory
Col Katterfelto –Mercury advert
John Wesley – cleric and writer who founded Methodism
Servant stealing – story told in Harland's Collectanea

1776
Woman sold in a halter – Mercury article
Earthquakes – frequent throughout the time
Mrs Radcliffe – fictional
Thomas Highs – Moved into 6 Deansgate about that year
Father's background – fictional

1777
Coach service – advert in Mercury
Mrs Beswick - fictional
Hatters setting rules – article
Jumballs – recipe
Rev Waincliffe – fictitonal
Auction at Windmill Tavern – advert
Mr Cotes selling up – advert
Mrs Berry – advert
Col Rogers – advert
M Meuron, William Clayton, - adverts
Ladies Phil – fictional
Capt Wilkins – fictional
Dr Franklin – advert
Silver urn – ref The printed book
Lying in Hospital – founded by Dr. Charles White
US war soon over – Mercury article
Miss Forsyth – advert
Mr. Meredith – advert
Manchester Free Grammar School – Manchester Boys
Rev Mr. Waverley - fictional
Gen Burgoyne – article in the Mercury
Charlotte Burgoyne – nee Stanley, Lady Betty's sister
Manchester Volunteers/Col. Horsfall - advert

1778
Reruiting Officer play – The Annals of Manchester
Henry 8th story – history of the Bull's Head
Ralph Byrom story - ?
Fast – advert
John's threat story
Mrs. Cotes – advert
William insolvent – notice

Olga S – based on a present day character
Coaches – advert
Hatfield – creditor as notice
Mrs. Thompson – fictional
Mrs Berry – advert
Capt. Haydock – fictional
Capt. Stockwell – fictional
Mr. Milne – as notice
Insolvency - advert

1779
Recruiting – advert
Miss Richardson – advert
Mr. Turnbull – fictitious
Mary on Exchange Alley – Harland's Collectanea
Miss Timmins – advert
Mr. Johnson – fictional
William Joule – contemporary brewer
Mr. Robert & Betty Fairbrother –Neil Richardson's Salford Pubs
Mr. Bury – carpenter who features in John's later story, see Harland's Collectanea
Riots – article
Mrs Crompton's – genuine coffee house
Mr. Ainscliffe – fictional
Rushton's - advert

1780
Budget – article
Pilkington/ Crompton/ Hargreaves/ Kay/ Robert Peel/ Arthur McAlpine – true story
US news – article
Strawberry stand/riots – advert/fictional link
Lady Betty/Hannah – from Atley Hall Archives staff lists
D Pelham – fictional
Mrs. Pinder – advert
Directory enquiry – advert
Ann London - advert

1781
Betty at the King's Head – advert
Jones – from Mercury insolvency notice

Appendix III Manchester Mercury report of the Boston Massacre
'The case of Capt. Thomas Preston, of the 29th Regiment

It is a matter of too great notoriety to need any Proofs, that the arrival of his Majesty's Troops in Boston, was extremely obnoxious to its Inhabitants. They have ever used all Means in their Power to weaken the Regiments, and to bring them into Contempt, by promoting and aiding desertions, and with Impunity, even where there has been the clearest Evidence of the Fact, and by grossly and falsely propagating Untruths concerning them. On the arrival of the 64th and 65th, their Ardour seemingly began to abate; it being too expensive to buy off so many; and Attempts of that kind rendered too dangerous from the Numbers. But the same Spirit revived immediately on its being known that those Regiments were ordered for Halifax, and hath since their departure been breaking out with great Violence. After their embarkation one of their Justices, not thoroughly acquainted with the People and their Intentions, on the trial of the 14th Regiment, openly and publicly, in the hearing great Numbers of People, and from the Seat of Justice, declared, 'that the Soldiers must now take care of themselves, was treat too much to their Arms, for they were but a Handful; that the Inhabitants carried Weapons concealed under their Cloaths, and would destroy them in a Moment if they pleased.'

This, considering the malicious Temper of the People, was an alarming Circumstance to the Soldiery. Since which several Disputes have happened between the Towns-People and Soldiers of both Regiments, the former being encouraged thereto by the Countenance od even some of the Magistrates, and by the Protection of all the Party against Government. In general such Disputes have been kept too secret from the Officers. On the 2nd Inst. Two of the 29th going through one Gray's Rope-Walk, the Rope-Makers insultingly asked them if they would empty a Vault. This unfortunately had the desired Effect, by provoking the Soldiers, and from Words they went to Blows. Both Parties suffered in this Affray, and finally, the Soldiers retired to their Quarters. The Officers, on the first Knowledge of this Transaction, took every Precaution in their Power to prevent any ill Consequences. Notwithstanding which, single Quarrels could not be prevented; the Inhabitants constantly provoking and abusing the Soldiery. The Insolence, as well as utter hatred of the Inhabitants to the Troops, increased Daily; insomuch, that Monday and Tuesday, the 5th and 6th Inst. Were privately agreed on for a general Engagement; in

Consequence of which several of the Militia came from the Country, armed, to join their Friends, menacing to destroy any who should oppose them. This Plan has since been discovered.

On Monday night about eight o'Clock, two Soldiers were attacked and beat. But the Party of the Towns-people, in order to carry Matters to the utmost length, broke into two Meeting-Houses, and rang the Alarm Bells, which I supposed was for Fire as usual, but was soon undeceived. About nine some of the Guard came to, and informed me, the Town-inhabitants were assembling to attack the Troops, and that the Bells were ringing as the Signal for that Purpose, and not for Fire, and the Beacon intended to be fired to bring in the distant People of the Country. This, as I was Captain of the Day, occasioned my repairing immediately to the Main-guard. In my Way there I saw the People in great Commotion, and heard them use the most cruel and horrid threats against the Troops. In a few Minutes after I reached the Guard, about 100 People passed it, and went towards the Custom-House, where the King's Money is lodged. They immediately surrounded the Centinel posted there, and with Clubs and other Weapons threatened to execue their Vengeance on him. I was soon informed by a Towns-man, their Intention was to carry off the Soldier from his Post, and probably murder him. On which I desired him to return for further Intelligence; and he soon came back and assured me he heard the Mob declare they would murder him. This I feared might be a Prelude to their opening the King's Chest. I immediately sent a non-commissioned Officer and twelve Men to protect both the Centinel and the King's Money, and very soon followed myself, to prevent (if possible) all Disorder; fearing lest the Officer and Soldiery, by the Insults and Provocations of the Rioters, should be thrown off their Guard, and commit some rash Act. They soon rushed thro' the People, and, by charging their Bayonets in half Circle, kept them at a little Distance. Nay, so far was I from intending the Death of any Person, that I suffered the Troops to go to the Spot where the unhappy Affair took Place, without any loading in their Pieces, nor did I ever give Orders for loading them. This remiss Conduct in me perhaps merits Censure; yet it is Evidence, resulting from the nature of Things, which is the best and surest that can be offered, that my Intention was not to act offensively, but the contrary Part, and that not without Compulsion. The Mob still increased, and were more outrageous, striking their Clubs or Bludgeons one against another, and calling out, 'Come on you Rascals, you bloody Backs, you

Lobster Scoundrels; fire if you dare, God damn you, fire and be damn'd; we know you dare not;' and much more such Language was used.

At this time I was between the Soldiers and the Mob, parleying with and endeavouring all my Power to persuade them to retire peaceably; but to no Purpose. They advanced to the Points of the Bayonets, struck some of them, and even the Muzzle of the Pieces, and seemed to be endeavouring to close with the Soldiers, on which some well-behaved Persons asked me if the Guns were charged; I replied, Yes. They then asked me if I intended to order the men to Fire; I answered no, by no Means; observing to them, that as I ws advanced before the Muzzles of the Men's Pieces, and must fall a Sacrifice if they fired; that the Soldiers were upon the Half-cock and charged Bayonets and my giving the Word Fire, under those Circumstances, would prove me no Officer. While I was thus speaking, on of the Soldiers, having received a severe blow with a Stick, stept a little to one Side, and instantly fired; on which, turning to and asking him why he fired without Orders, I was struck with a Club on my Arm which for some time deprived me of the Use of it; which Blow, had it been placed on my Head, most probably would have destroyed me. On this a general Attack was made on the Men, by a great Number of heavy Clubs and Snow-balls being thrown at them, by which all our Lives were in imminent danger; some Persons at the same Time from behind calling out, 'D−n your Bloods, why don't you Fire?' Instantly three or four of the Soldiers fired, one after another, and directly after, three more, in the same Confusion and Hurry.

The Mob then ran away, except three unhappy Men, who instantly expired, in which Number was Mr. Gray, at whose Rope-Walk the prior Quarrel took Place; one more is since dead; three others are dangerously, and four slightly wounded. The whole of this melancholy Affair was transacted in almost twenty Minutes. On my asking the Soldiers why they fired without Orders, they said they heard the word 'Fire' and supposed it came from me. This might be the Case, as many of the Mob called out 'Fire, Fire', but I assured the Men that I gave no such order, that my words were, 'don't Fire, stop your Firing:' In short, it was scarce possible for the Soldiers to know who said Fire, or don't Fire, or stop your Firing. On the People assembling again to take away the dead Bodies, the Soldiers, supposing them coming to arrack them, were making ready to Fire again, which I prevented by striking up their Firelocks with my Hand. Immediately after, a Townsman came and told me, that four or five thousand People were assembled in the next Street, and had sworn to take my Life, with every Man's with me; on which I judged it unsafe to remain there any longer, and therefore sent the Party and Sentry to the Main-guard, where the Street is narrow and short, there telling them off into Street-Firings, divided and planted them at each End of the Street to secure their Rear, momently expecting an Attack, as there was a constant cry of the Inhabitants, 'To Arms, to Arms, - turn out with your Guns,' and the Town Drums beating to Arms. I ordered my Drum to beat to Arms, and being soon after joined by the different Companies of the 29th Regiment I formed them as the Guard into Street-Firings. The 14th Regiment also got under Arms, but remained at their Barracks. I immediately sent a Sergeant, with a Party, to Col. Dalrymple, the Commanding Officer, to acquaint him with every particular. Several Officers, going to join their Regiment, were knocked down by the Mob, one very much wounded, and his Sword taken from him. The Lieutenant-Governor, and Col. Carr, soon after met at the Head of the 29th Regiment, and agreed that the Regiment should retire to their Barracks, and the People to their Houses; but I kept the Piquet to strengthen the Guard. It was with great difficulty that the Lieutenant-Governor prevailed on the People to be quiet and retire; at last they all went off excepting about an hundred.

A Council was immediately called, on the breaking up of which three Justices met and issued a warrant to apprehend me and eight Soldiers. On hearing of this Procedure, I instantly went to the Sherriff, and surrendered myself, though for the Space of four Hours I had it in my Power to have made my Escape, which I most undoubtedly should have attempted, and could have easily executed, had I been the least conscious of any Guilt.

On the Examinations before the Justices, two Witnesses swore that I gave the Men Orders to fire; the one testified he was within two feet of me; the other that I swore at the Men for not firing at the first Word. Others swore they heard me use the Word 'fire', but whether do or do not fire they could not say; Others, that they heard the Word 'fire' but could not say if it came from me. The next day they got five or six more to swear I gave the Word to fire. So bitter and inveterate are many of the Malcontents here, that they are industriously using every Method to fish out Evidence to prove it was a concerted scheme to Murder the Inhabitants. Others are infusing the utmost Malice and Revenge into the Minds of the

People who are to be my Jurors, by false Publications, Votes of Towns, and all the other Artifices, that so from a settled Rancour against the Officers and Troops in general, the Suddenness of my Trial after the Affair, while the People's Minds are all greatly inflamed, I am, though perfectly innocent, under most unhappy Circumstances, having nothing in Reason to expect but the Loss of Life, in a very ignominious Manner, but without the Interposition of his Majesty's Royal Goodness.'

Acknowledgements

My research began with the electronic data available but I found so many contradictions and false information that it was only by accessing source documents that I was able to piece together the facts about Elizabeth.

Not much evidence remains of Elizabeth's life apart from clues dotted around in various historical books about Manchester, written by many respected names, although the most complete version I found was written by a man I had never heard of until I began my research. Writing in a series of books produced by the Chetham's Society, John Harland has given us the best rendition of Mrs. Raffald that is available. It is in fact the source material for virtually everything else written about her. He was writing in the 1850's, 70 years after her death, and much of his information is gained from a conversation with Elizabeth's (then elderly) granddaughter. Some of the recollections seem faulty but most have been confirmed by factual data such as church records and newspaper adverts.

In doing my research I was following in the footsteps of a select few. Most notable for me was Roy Shipperbottom, a Stockport man who dedicated 20 years to the hunt for information, and whose widow, Olga, was kind enough to allow me access to his notes. His book, The Experienced English Housekeeper with an introduction, is still available though hard to find. His introduction notes are available as a slim pamphlet from the Portico in Manchester. Olga also introduced me to a direct descendant of Elizabeth and John, her three times great granddaughter, Connie Jackson, whose family helped me to fund a blue plaque to Elizabeth in 2017 at the Arden Arms in Stockport, a pub built by John's nephew.

I was privileged to meet and make friends with Connie, a lovely lady who was very proud of her ancestor and who provided me with some family pictures. There are no family mementoes due to the sad way the story ended. Connie's relative produced a handmade book which includes a family tree, showing all the descendants of Elizabeth and John Raffald. A copy is held in Special Collections at Manchester Central Library.

There are brief mentions of Elizabeth in various books about early industrial Manchester but it is a period that I found poorly documented. The majority of focus on Manchester seems to be on the industrial boom period and although it was beginning in

Elizabeth's time it had not yet taken over. Manchester was just beginning to shape itself before the building boom of the 19th century. There were still wide areas of open land under cultivation, the canal had only recently arrived and most transport was horse driven or by boat. It was Manchester before railways and big mills, but with earthquakes, bad streets and food riots; just post Pretender passions and at a time of revolutions in France and North America.

References

Elizabeth Raffald, The Manchester Directory 1772, Baldwin 1772
Ditto   1773, Harrop   1773
Ditto   1781, ditto   1781
Elizabeth Raffald, The Experienced English Housekeeper 1769
Charles Foster, Extracts from The Experienced English Housekeeper, Arley Hall Press 2013
Roy Shipperbottom, Introduction to The Experienced English Housekeeper, Southover Press 1997
www.arleyhallarchives.co.uk
http://twonerdyhistorygirls.blogspot.co.uk/2012/05/what-maidservant-wore-c-1770.html#sthash.uytPubko.dpuf
W H Thompson, History of Manchester to 1852, 1967
Cass & Garret, Printing and the Book in Manchester 1750-1800, Lancashire & Cheshire Antiquarian Society 2001
Neil Richardson, Elizabeth Raffald's Manchester & Salford Directory 1772, c1970
Neil Richardson, Salford Pubs
John Harland, Manchester Guardian, May 5th 1852
John Harland, Local Gleanings No XXXII, Manchester Guardian, 19th May 1852
Vincent La Chapelle, The Modern Cook, 1733
The Manchester Mercury, 1763-1781
www.larsdatter.com
James Ogden, A Description of Manchester by a Native of the Town 1783

Printed in Poland
by Amazon Fulfillment
Poland Sp. z o.o., Wrocław

58439007R00154